C0-DBP-182

Publishers' Note

This story is fictional. Any resemblance to real people is entirely coincidental. All trade-marks presented are owned by their respective owners.

Some of the company names in this book are real and some are not. When real companies are presented, their details have been fictionalized and any resemblance to real persons within those companies is entirely coincidental. All fictitious company's rights, including their common law trade-mark rights and domain names, are hereby owned exclusively by the author.

Brief passages of *Technicolor Ultra Mall* may be quoted for news, review and discussion. All other uses of content within *Technicolor Ultra Mall* must receive written approval of the publisher prior to any form of reproduction.

Videos and photographs are either owned by the publisher or used with permission.

Contact the publisher for any queries or comments you may have.

TECHNICOLOR ULTRA MALL

by

Ryan Oakley

EDGE SCIENCE FICTION AND FANTASY PUBLISHING
AN IMPRINT OF HADES PUBLICATIONS, INC.

CALGARY

Technicolor Ultra Mall
Copyright © 2011
by Ryan Oakley

This is a work of fiction. Names, characters, places, and incidents are the products of the author's imagination or are used fictitiously and are not to be construed as real. Any resemblance to actual events, locales, organizations, or persons, living or dead, is entirely coincidental.

EDGE

Edge Science Fiction and Fantasy Publishing
An Imprint of Hades Publications Inc.
P.O. Box 1714, Calgary, Alberta, T2P 2L7, Canada

Edited by Susan Forest
Interior design by Kelsey Stephenson
Cover Design by Erik Mohr
ISBN: 978-1-894063-54-8

All rights reserved. No part of this book may be reproduced, scanned, or distributed in any printed or electronic form without written permission. Please do not participate in or encourage piracy of copyrighted materials in violation of the author's rights. Purchase only authorized editions.

EDGE Science Fiction and Fantasy Publishing and Hades Publications, Inc. acknowledges the ongoing support of the Alberta Foundation for the Arts and the Canada Council for the Arts for our publishing programme.

Alberta Foundation for the Arts

Canada Council for the Arts   Conseil des Arts du Canada

Library and Archives Canada Cataloguing in Publication

Oakley, Ryan, 1978-
   Technicolor ultra mall / Ryan Oakley.

ISBN: 978-1-894063-54-8
e-Book ISBN: 978-1-894817-97-4

I. Title.

PS8629.A555T43 2011   C813'.6   C2011-901627-3

FIRST EDITION
(A-20110611)
Printed in Canada
www.edgewebsite.com

Dedication

FOR
Hughie Beauchamp
Not everyone can see the green line at dusk

TECHNICOLOR ULTRA MALL

THEME SONG

"You will see a procession of game shows, violence, audience-participation shows, formula comedies about totally unbelievable families, blood and thunder, mayhem, violence, sadism, murder, western bad men, western good men, private eyes, gangsters, more violence and cartoons. And, endlessly, commercials—many screaming, cajoling and offending. And most of all, boredom."
   —Federal Communications Commission chairman Newton Minow, speech to the National Association of Broadcasters on May 9, 1961

PRODUCT PLACEMENT (1)

The other night I went to this Barcode bar and I was the only Rascitt there. On my way out I bumped into some guy. He started making a big deal about it and I told him to go fuck himself. He took me into the street and beat me senseless. I went home to my room in the housing complex, still drunk, and staggered to the shared washroom to throw up. Not sure what happened next but some Chinese guy woke me up. I was laying on the floor covered in blood, shit and vomit. My pants were around my ankles and my wallet was gone. So was my watch. Guess I'm on the edge.
   —TheEdge.dump
   Today's Music

ROBOT FIGHT TONIGHT!! ALL RIGHT!!
Place your bets for tonight's brawl! New Battle Bots with uber violent upgrades. Model Ivanna Suckyou performs her ping-pong lottery ball spectacular between fights. Get your odds and place your bets at Fatman's Casino and Battle Dome. You can win! Try long enough and you WILL!!

SIGN UP NOW FOR INFO DUMP! Connecting malls all over the world. It's the place where minds meet. DON'T BE LEFT BEHIND! SUBSCRIBE NOW!

SHOE SALE OF THE CENTURY
50% off next week's fashions and 75% off all of this week's fashions.* Get them now! This is the deal that won't last forever. Be fitted by our friendly and courteous staff. We're the ones that please your feet.
   *offer subject to the discretion of individual franchises and anti-competition bylaws.

"Today, an Edge ReOrbs Store was robbed by a white breed male in a suit. The bandit escaped with blank reOrbs and severely wounded the clerk, Maxwell Silver. We have that story and more at 11 o'clock. Join us then and we will ask Mall Security Chief, Rock Cockett, what can be done about this latest crime wave."

GOT IT? NEED IT? Today's synapacide. Not just the same old buzz. **GET IT NOW!**

Total Conformity—It's the new black. Buy rude boy surplus uniforms. Sharp collared, silver buttoned, black or scarlet tunics.* Complete your ensemble with a purchase of decorative powerbars. Stand out by fitting in! **EDGE CLOTHING.**
   *not self cleaning.

"What the fuck?" Sputnik said.

Budgie squinted at a man pushing through the crowd, wearing a gray ushanka with the earflaps pulled down and a golden emblem pinned upon its front. Budgie sniffed for gang odor but only smelled sweat.

Something about that was wrong. Budgie looked at the sigil on the guy's hat. A jolly roger with dollar sign eyes and a gold tooth.

"Fuck," Budgie stepped back. "Wolfe."

"Huh?" Sputnik tilted his chin into the air. His nostrils flared as he tried to catch the scent. "I don—"

Wolfe ran at him, the metal in his hand aflame with reflected red light. His arm swooped up and the blade caught Sputnik just beneath the jawbone. Wolfe bounded past.

Budgie pulled his dagger and brass knuckles off his magnetic belt. Sputnik stumbled towards him, gripping his bleeding neck with one hand. His other arm flapped at his side. Looked like a wounded bird trying to take flight. Bubbles of blood popped out of his nostrils and poured red down his face. Budgie didn't have time to watch the gore.

He spun, expecting to see Wolfe running away. But the guy stood in front of him. Looked plenty distorted. He wasn't even wearing a uniform. Just that stupid hat, a faux fur vest, filthy blue pajama pants and big, untied boots. His lips pulled into a skeleton grin.

Budgie stuck his tooled fists into the air. Panted. He regretted taking those acid-dipped OxyContin caps. They pixilated his brain. Everything except Wolfe looked digital slush, shoppers melting into a Jackson Pollack blur. Wolfe stood out in stark 3D focus. Sputnik gurgled and spat blood onto the advert covered floor.

Wolfe mouthed something. No words came out. Just white noise. His eyes flickered a blizzard and he swung the knife in front of him— back and forth and forth and back—like some idiot zombie on the late night.

Budgie waited for the blade to reach the far end of the arc then charged. His metal sheathed fist left a scarlet tracer in the air and he heard the impact of steel against skull before he felt the shock-wave up his arm.

Wolfe stumbled backwards and Budgie came at him low and hard with his blade, stabbing it deep into his stomach and twisting while he hugged Wolfe with his other arm.

His face next to Wolfe's, Budgie inhaled the chemical stink of hot breath. Orbs of sweat glistened on Wolfe's pale forehead and for a moment, Budgie saw his own bent reflection in them.

His hand worked the gut. His knife gnawed. Beneath his blade, Wolfe's meat felt as insubstantial as a balloon.

Over Wolfe's shoulder Budgie saw a man in a bright blue suit advertising Colgate Whiskey, pushing a shopping cart full of speakers, barking jingles and deals. Smelling something dank and awful, Budgie slipped his knife free and shoved Wolfe towards the man, who swore once, loudly, before stepping back. He slipped on the gore.

Wolfe's stomach was a huge red mouth that vomited a rainbow of intestines. His knees buckled and he fell to the floor. Laid there. Twitched.

Budgie stood very still and looked at the gawking shoppers. Some were tourists from the greens, identifiable by their understated clothes and overstated faces. They'd got more than they bargained for tonight. None met his eyes.

Budgie's heart pounded in his skull. Behind him, he heard another gurgling spit. Another splat.

Sputnik lay on the floor, holding both hands to his throat and looking at Budgie with feral eyes.

Doctor, Budgie thought. "Where the fuck is the doctor?" He attached his weapons to his belt and pulled out his gizmo. His hand convulsed. The machine blundered out of his grip and onto the floor. He just stared at it.

A rude boy doesn't drop his gizmo at a moment like this. He's cool, calm and collected. Shit, even those tourists were probably judging him now. Embarrassed by his hands gone wild, he reached down to pick it up. Wanted to glare at the spectators, to say: WHAT? YOU NEVER FUCK UP?

His gizmo still worked. Not like that one in the commercial where the guy drops it, and breaks it then kills himself. Not like that at all.

Budgie knelt next to Sputnik, tapped SNORT DONKEY and hit a synced-all-channel-dial.

Beeping, ringing.

Alone, surrounded by this gawking crowd, shook deep. Watching his friend bleed. Making a call. Waiting for an answer. He gripped Sputnik's elbow with his free hand.

Finally, he heard: "Yeah, Budge?"

"I need a doctor, fast." That was gibberish. Snort Donkey would think Budgie needed a doctor when Budgie was fine and it was Sputnik who needed the doctor. This was not calm. This was not collected. His next words blurted worse than the first: "Spu-Spu-Sputnik got loved."

"Really?" The voice was maddeningly relaxed. "At this time of night? By who?"

"Wolfe, but I need a doctor now, right now. Sputnik's pretty fucked up." The gizmo slipped in Budgie's sweaty palm. He gripped it hard, his knuckles white. He would not drop it again. Not ever. Not. "Now!"

"Simmer Budgie. Just getting your latitude. Okay, this is what I want you to do, look at his powerbar on his tunic and tell me where it is."

"Move your hand so I can see your bar," Budgie yelled. Sputnik just moved his mouth like a fish.

Budgie grabbed his fingers and shifted them. Blood leaked onto his palm. "Gone into yellow. Still dropping."

"Okay, I'm sending you the co-ordinates of a doctor now. He'll be waiting for you. I'll come by too, just to—"

Budgie hung up and looked at the directions. Memorizing them, he pocketed the gizmo and grabbed Sputnik by the armpits. "We're going to a Doctor." He pulled him up and walked him forward. "Get you patched."

People parted in front of him. The excitement over, they returned to their shopping. Some kids checked Wolfe's body for anything of value, found nothing and moved on. The ghouls would be by later to pick up the flesh. Budgie knew he should stay with it. Given the choice, protecting the dead trophy and confirming the kill was more important than saving his friend. But Sputnik's body was becoming limp. Budgie dragged him. Some of the kids followed like rats behind a food cart. Budgie glared.

The kids hesitated but raised their eyebrows with the same expression of haughty shock. Right about now, Budgie should be negotiating a price for any pocket litter on Wolfe. Instead, he hardmugged them. Had the kids monocles, they would've shattered then dropped. Budgie didn't care.

He rubbed his friend's head. "Guess we should have taken those coagulants tonight."

Sputnik mumbled something. It took Budgie a moment to under-stand—

"I should've flinched."

Yeah, Budgie thought. He dug a pack of gum out of his pocket. Unwrapped a piece and chewed. If Sputnik got too bad, if his powerbar hit black Budgie could stick that in the wound. It'd do a fast and dirty job of knitting the flesh back together. Very fast. Very dirty. Last ditch.

A middle-aged man gawked, his face a crumbled bag of loose white skin. Budgie flashed his blade and the guy retreated back into the crowd.

Everyone else just kept moving, eyes busy looking anywhere else. No one would report this to security. Even if they did they wouldn't be able to give a description. What would they say? A couple of skinny white kids in scarlet tunics, short hair and blue lines running up the side of their black pants. Other than the color of the skin and the color of the pant-line, that described every rude boy in the reds. Besides, the only people who would even think about making a report would be from the greens and what would they say they were doing down here? Window shopping? Channel surfing through the whorehouses and drug dens?

Yeah, they might think. They might judge, but none of them would do anything.

Budgie's gizmo beeped. They were getting close to the doctor.

A grinning man in a white coat waited in a doorway and waved them inside. "You must be Budgie," he said. "And that must be Sputnik. Knife wound?"

"Yeah." Budgie followed the man into a shabby waiting room, and through into an operating theater.

"Put him on the table."

Budgie dragged Sputnik to the metal slab in the center of the room. A small but boisterous audience drank beer and ate snacks in the surrounding ring of seats.

A fetish nurse in a latex uniform and white stockings organized the doctor's tools, only pausing to squeeze her inflated cleavage together and wink at the hooting fans. Budgie flopped the body onto the table. Sputnik's eyes rolled back in his head. His swollen purple tongue jutted out between his teeth.

The doctor pushed past Budgie and, with a magician's flourish, unbuttoned Sputnik's tunic. "You can't stay." He smiled at the crowd, some of whom booed. "Unless you buy a ticket. Mid-week special."

"No, that's fine." Budgie took a step back. Without meaning to, he stared at the doctor's mouth. The smile was a fake. Some sort of realistic makeup job painted on his face. Budgie's knees went mushy. "Where can I wait?"

The doctor ninja-flicked his eyes. "Grab a seat in the back room. I'll work this one fast." He looked back at Sputnik and sighed. "I've seen worse. So have they."

⬛▌▐▌▌▐▌▐▌ ▐▌ ▐▌▐▌▌▐▌ ▐▌▐▌▌ ▐▌▐▌ ▐▌▐▌ ▌▐▌▌ ▐▌▌ ▌▐ ▌▐▌

"One, two, three, four,…"

Dim yellow light. A red pleather chair that squeaked every time Budgie moved. A waiting room. Budgie waited.

He stared at his hands, counted to ten and then started again. Then backwards. No good. His long, pale fingers stuck out of his sleeves and trembled. He picked dried blood off them then waved them back and forth, watching the tracers. He had to get his shit together.

In a few days, this would be just another battle story, told over a few strong drinks to a few dumb sluts from the mini-putt or a couple of gape-mouthed prospects. This sort of thing impressed them. He tapped through his pockets, searching for caps. No good. Sputnik carried all the dope. "Fuck," Budgie said.

He thrust his body back into his seat and closed his eyes. A blue pattern of squares and triangles shifted in darkness. Puzzle like, these shapes snapped together into Wolfe's face. Budgie flinched and crossed his arms against his stomach. Rocked his body back and forth, in time to that backwards ten count.

A layer of smoker's grime covered the walls. Sticky rings of coffee and soda marked the coffee tables like the ghosts of dead drinks. Would it kill them to have coasters? No surprise the lights were dim. The glass ashtray overflowed. A mass grave for cigarettes.

Budgie needed a smoke. They had been about to buy a pack when Wolfe came at them. The butts in the ashtray wiggled like maggots. Budgie looked away. A deflated cot sat in the corner.

Doc must live here. And if this was the best a doctor could do on the Reds how much future did a rude boy have? True, Budgie could get to the top of the food chain but that wasn't likely. You had to be sharp to make beta. Needed to get past age twenty-five without getting chipped or crashing your brain into the hard drugs, and what were the odds he'd do that? He wasn't clever enough. It was only a matter of time before mall security caught him stealing or making runs. Security would chip him and he wouldn't be able to go onto the greens without having alarms go off. Would have to stay on the reds where they didn't much care what you did. Then it was only a matter of time before the dope got on top on him.

He dumped the ashtray into the garbage. He wished he could clean this whole dingy room. Messes bothered him. Messes were living monsters, building their bodies out of trash and creeping into well-ordered lives, feasting on the useful and clean, staining and breaking them, just to shit out more mess. This room was beyond infected. It was a burrow from which messes would crawl out. There weren't even any adverts on the walls, just cleaner spots where posters hung before the mess ate them.

The door to the street opened.

"Wasabi?" It was Snort Donkey.

"Not much." Budgie wiped his palm on his pant-leg. If they shook hands, he didn't want Snort Donkey to feel the sweat. It'd look wrong. They tapped knuckles. "Waiting."

"He hurt bad?"

"Pretty bad. Stabbed up here." Budgie pointed to the soft spot behind his chin and in front of his throat. "Uppercut."

"Fecal." Snort Donkey pulled a pack of cigarettes out of his pocket. Budgie asked for and was given one. Snort Donkey stared at him. "You gonna make me say 'Ahem'?"

"I'll pay you later." He pinched the cigarette tube. "When I pick up some tokens." Too hard. He broke the smoke. His eyes wide, he looked back at Snort Donkey.

"Two for the price of three."

"Fine."

Snort Donkey passed him another.

Not trusting his hands to feel up the smoke, Budgie stuck it between his lips, trying real hard to be gentle. "Lacy?"

"No, got a pack that's wet but we'd have to go outside. Doc thinks formaldehyde is bad luck."

"Nah, this is fine," Budgie said. Just what we need, a superstitious doctor. "I'm nuff fucked."

"Where's Wolfe?"

"He well dead."

"So...Where the fuck is he?"

"Left him in the hall."

Snort Donkey blinked and lit both cigarettes. Smoke leaked from his face. His black, laser-shaved head was holo-tattooed with silver and gold fighting dogs. They interlocked like one of those M.C. Escher adverts, battling between ridges of exposed skull. Shifted with every change in angle. From this way, silver dog wins: from that, gold dog wins. Snort Donkey tilted his head this way and that, showing it off, fishing for a compliment.

"Nice mod," Budgie said. "When you'd get that?"

"Couple weeks back."

Had it been that long since they'd seen each other?

Budgie thought of the last few weeks. His memory didn't work so great anymore but, as he recalled it, he'd been on steady patrol with Sputnik, just mopping up the remains of Wolfe's chapter. Not much had happened. Every time those swishes saw Vidicons they ran back to their hovels. Sometimes got yanked out and stomped. Past few days, none of them had been around. Not until tonight and it looked like Wolfe had to get plenty distorted to pop up.

"So help me out here," Snort Donkey said. "I'm trying to get this straight. You loved Wolfe but you left him in the hall? Unattended?"

"Yeah."

"So you could bring Sputnik to a doctor? For a fucking face wound? That's why we're gonna have to deal with ghouls to get confirmation on the kill?"

"Look, I know it ain't strict cricket but—"

Snort Donkey spat. "You sure you loved him?"

"Yeah," Budgie said.

"I'll take your word for it." He sighed. "That ain't no small thing."

"I guess not." Budgie knew he should be proud of the kill but just couldn't feel it. Kept thinking of Sputnik in that next room. Hoping he'd be okay but knowing it was just moving capital. If a dead Wolfe cost a living Sputnik, it was a good deal.

Problem was, he did not want to make that deal.

It felt like a straight rip off. Probably don't matter anyway. Wolfe was dead. Sputnik was getting help. That was a bargain and you'd have to be an idiot to turn that down. Still, Budgie wanted more return. Something.

Snort Donkey slapped him on the back.

Would that have to do?

It didn't.

"Guess that's it for the Dog Goblins," Budgie said. "Guy didn't even put up a fight. Just stood there, swinging his blade around." He wondered if that was really it for the Dog Goblins and if that'd make it all right. How highly did he value Sputnik? Puffed on the smoke. His hands finally stopped shaking. "Maybe I'm high but..."

"That your excuse for leaving him?"

"Nah, I mean maybe. But wasn't what I was gon say."

"Then what?"

"You ever see what a television looks like when it's not getting a signal?"

"Uh-huh."

"Wolfe's eyes looked like that. Snowy." Budgie remembered something else. "When he came at us he was running. He was out of uniform too. Looked like a mental." He pulled on the smoke. "That's why he ambushed us. Never seen anything like it. No gang with him or nothin'."

"I have." Snort Donkey shook his head. "Wolfe cranked some robo."

"Don know what that is." Snort Donkey was the Vidicon's chemist and Budgie got most of his chucking dope off him. But he stuck to basics. "Never heard of it."

"Yeah, well, you don't want to. Hardly anyone ever—ever—uses it. And I mean never." Snort Donkey smiled. His teeth were sharpened gold with a little green dragon slithering back and forth across them. Expensive work but he could afford it. "Gotta say, I'm kinda disappointed in him."

"Why's that?"

"Cause he gave up. Via Robo. You only click onto that shit once. It's suicidal. Cranks you up to thirteen and burns you out in one night. Turns your brain into fucking plasma. You pick up every free floating radio or microwave. And it all feeds into some central conceit, like he wants to kill Vidicons so every noise he hears is like a coded message telling him to do that. Pumping info through jungle telegraph. Kamikaze drug, you know. Not recreational. Just plain desperate shit." He shrugged. "Shit, I only cook and move it once a year when the betas up their supply. They don take it, just keep some on them. Just in case."

"Of what?"

"I dunno. If they ever have to start using robo, well, let's just say it'll be too late for it to do us any good. But I keep some on me too. Just like, if anyone fucks with me and there's no way out 'cept running, guess I can see cranking it. Sorta." He sat down beside Budgie. "Must be cause Harmony Kink notched his brothers."

"Harmony did that?"

"Truth: That little bitch is sick deadly. No one sees her coming. Sexism right?" He smiled. "Picked up Wolfe's brothers at some dimlight orgy and—

Harmony locked the door. "Take off your clothes." She turned to face Copland and Wax.

They glanced at each other and shrugged. Copland, on the left, ripped off his Velcro fastened pants and tripped out of them. Still wore his boots. No underwear. The younger bro, Wax, blushed and looked at the floor while he undressed. Funny he should be so shy at an orgy.

She knelt in front of them.

"Oh yeah, bitch," Copland said as she took his stiff cock into her mouth. It tasted like cheap orange soap. Her hands traveled up between both of their legs, while her head bobbed, chicken-like, in front of them. She played with Wax's balls. He was still limp.

"Close your eyes," she said.

"Uh-huh."

"Okay."

Each of her index fingers stroked their hard butts.

"I'm ticklish." Wax squirmed.

Then you're not going to like this. Harmony plunged her fingers into their rectums.

"Hey!" Wax's eyelids bounced open and he flinched forward.

Not far enough to dislodge her finger. Copland had a big juicy smile and she stuck her digit further up. She worked it around and pulled out. Left her rapid-dissolving fingernails inside. They weren't fatal but they wiped out motor functions. Copland swayed and stepped back, his cock slipping out of her mouth. Wax turned to face him then went lax.

Harmony wiped her mouth. The brothers stumbled to the bed and sat down like broken marionettes. Copland mumbled something. Harmony pulled a butterfly knife out of her back pocket. Flipped it open and strode towards him.

They weren't numb, just incapable of ordering their bodies. Good. Harmony wanted them to feel this. Wanted them to get the message. You don't fuck with the Vidicons. If the Vidicons want to throw the Friday night parties for mall rats from the greens they got to throw the parties. There was a lot of cash in that scheme and the Dog Goblins were not welcome a single global of it.

She grabbed Copland by the ball sack. Looking him in the eye, she sawed upwards. She plucked off his warm, bleeding genitals and held them in her hand. Shoved them into his brother's gaping mouth. Did the same to Wax.

Then she carved her tag, a musical note, into both their chests.

"Harmony did that?" asked Budgie. "That's fucked up."

"Yeah, man. Truth. Little bitch has these dead birds too. Hawk babies, like fetal hawk babies, that she nicks outta one of the bio-schools on the greens, so she put those on 'em too. Just so Wolfe would know who did it."

"Santa." Budgie cupped his nuts in his hand. "Don't seem cricket."

Snort Donkey laughed like a buzz-saw. Sent shivers right up Budgie's spine. "Nothing cricket bout that little psycho."

"Always been nice with me."

"Yeah, well, she has that candy dispo but it's mod. She's cold inside. Take my word for that." Snort Donkey frowned. "Few years back, saw her go to work on a tourist who tried to rent her. Some old gray yute who liked young pussy and mistook her for product." Snort Donkey didn't say anything else. When you talked as much as he did and something made you go quiet—well, that said it all.

The operating theater door creaked and Doc stepped into the waiting room, specks of blood freckling his white coat. He carried a small black box.

"Sorry," The doctor handed Budgie the little coffin. "Not much I could do."

Budgie looked behind the doctor, waiting for Sputnik to pop out of the operating theater. His friend had always been a joker and this must be one of his pranks.

I'm gonna beat his ass for this.

But the door didn't open. Snort Donkey's cigarette crackled.

"This for real?" Budgie asked.

"Afraid so," the doctor said. "He lost a lot of blood but that wasn't the main problem."

"Knife dressed?" Snort Donkey puffed on his cigarette.

Doc nodded and rubbed his chin.

Budgie's body shook. His head burned. Eyes went blurry. Rubbed them fast and hard. Couldn't cry. He had to get himself under control. This was business. That's all, just business. Money cost blood. Everyone knew that. Sputnik was worth forty globals. His death was profitable. No reason to grieve. Budgie knew all that.

"Motherfucker," said Snort Donkey. "So you left Wolfe for nothin'."

Budgie wobbled and his nose dripped watery snot. And he was afraid to speak because he knew his voice would sputter and sob. There was something swish about friendship. It made you look too emo to be trusted. Budgie pulled his face into a meat mask. Pulled it tight. Pulled until he thought it might snap over his skull. "Gimmee that," he said and grabbed the coffin from the doctor. "The blade was dressed?"

"Afraid so."

Poison. Not cricket. Went against the system. Wolfe had probably told himself it didn't matter, not after what happened to his brothers. And he was right. That's why people didn't fuck with the rules. It just escalated. Things had to be kept on a certain level.

That little bitch Harmony had killed Sputnik just as surely as if she'd poisoned the knife herself.

Budgie couldn't look at the doctor's pudgy face with that ridiculous makeup smile. It was an abomination. What did that guy care? He'd just farm the body for parts and sell the unusable bits as pet food or fishing bait. Obscene to think of some animal eating Sputnik. Budgie looked away; tried to think about something else.

He flipped the box open and looked at Sputnik's pocket litter. His wallet was there, some wadded up Kleenex, a credit card and the little rock from outside the mall that he kept for luck. No caps though. *Fuck. I need those.* "Where's his dope?"

"That's part of my fee."

"Don't worry bout it," Snort Donkey said and put his hand on Budgie's shoulder. "I'll hook you up. You can pay me tomorrow. Won't even charge you interest."

Budgie knocked his hand away and stood.

Snort Donkey and the doctor stepped back. Doc found something on the ceiling to look at but Snort Donkey held Budgie's glare. He stepped forward. Very slow, like a dare, he leaned in close to Budgie's face. Their noses almost touched. He spoke soft. "You gonna make another bitch noise?"

Budgie suddenly heard Sputnik's last words: *I should've flinched.*

Budgie blinked. Averted. He looked away and shrank down. "No, man, sorry, just fucked up, ya know. Sorry. Thanks. No interest on the dope?"

"I don't remember saying that."

Budgie stared at his boots.

"You can pay me for those smokes when we get outta here."

"Yeah, thanks." Budgie looked back at Snort Donkey but did not dare to meet the eyes. He'd flirted with enough danger tonight. Anymore and he might get loved too.

That's not what he needed. What he needed was something hard and numb before he told Sputnik's mom that her only remaining son was dead.

⬛⬛ ⬛⬛⬛⬛⬛⬛⬛⬛ ⬛ ⬛⬛⬛⬛⬛ ⬛⬛⬛ ⬛⬛⬛⬛⬛ ⬛⬛⬛⬛⬛ ⬛⬛⬛⬛⬛ ⬛⬛⬛ ⬛ ⬛⬛ ⬛ ⬛⬛ ⬛ ⬛ ⬛⬛

"Why'd they call him TeeVee?"

Sitcom's hand hesitated above the door. "Pull your fists out of your shirt." Slug was big and dumb, but smart enough to let other people think for him. His sleeves hung over his hands. "Don't want him thinking you're tooled."

"Oh yeah, sorry." Slug rolled his sleeves halfway up his forearm, a shaggy smile on his clean-shaven face. The skin above his wrists shimmered with holographic tattoos.

Stupid move. Tattoos made it too easy to be eye-deed. Not that it mattered to Slug. The lout was chipped anyway so he had to stay on the red levels. "They call him that cause he went television a while back."

"What'd you mean?"

"A sickness in the memes. Got it from watching too much." Sitcom knocked, memories of those bad days surfacing. TeeVee had gone weird, you couldn't talk to him without him spouting one liners from comedies, couldn't tell him anything without him describing a similar scenario in a soap opera. No advice or wisdom. Just analogy after analogy. Total brain infection.

After a while, Sitcom and a few of TeeVee's betas, came by and kicked in his television screen. They could've just taken it but the situation called for high drama. TeeVee hadn't even cried or yelled or fought or nothing. Just sat there. It was spooky. The way he looked all zombified, blue electric light still throbbing in his eyes.

They'd left him with a couple of whores, hoping the product would bring his head back to the basement and it seemed to work. Sort of. That television had wrecked some neural pathways and killed something in him. You still couldn't get him out of his apartment but at least you could talk to him now. Better than nothing.

The ENTER sign flashed red and bolts clanged. Sitcom pushed the door open and stepped into the dim apartment. Church quiet in here. Pumpkin orange light and oily shadow puddles. Although TeeVee was a notorious hoarder, the hutch was neat, organized and cramped. Everywhere you looked there was another pop culture artifact. Shelves from the floor to the ceiling where dolls stood silent watch in front of gadgets, papers, books, collectible bottles and other mall flotsam. It all washed up here like kitsch driftwood on a commercial tide.

"What's that smell?" Slug asked. His voice sounded loud and coarse here.

"Opium." Sitcom sniffed. "You never scented the real thing?"

"Guess not."

"Shame." Sitcom led the way. "He must be in his reOrb room. C'mon."

TeeVee, long, thin and louche, lounged on his red couch. A sleek mongoose curled on his chest and a big hookah sat on the floor next to him. TeeVee took a drag on a tube and blinked slowly, his eyes hesitant and blurry before they clicked into sudden focus. "I know you, Sitcom," he said. "But who is this fat comrade of yours?"

"This guy's all fucked up." Slug stood with his hands on his hips like he owned the place. Cocky bravado. Offensive in someone else's house. Shit, Sitcom thought. You couldn't dress Slug up and you couldn't bring him anywhere. "But look at all these reOrbs." He leaned against the wall and crossed his arms. "You record these or you some geeked out collector?"

TeeVee's hand slipped beneath the cushions of his couch. There was no way to stop it. Not that Sitcom would even think about trying. TeeVee was an alpha and you did not, hyperlinked DID NOT, fuck with those guys.

TeeVee's left hand came out of the couch in a smooth underarm arc, a dagger gripped between the fingers. With a wrist flick, he tossed it. The blade cartwheeled.

Too late and too slow, Slug realized the trouble. His eyes widened just as the dagger penetrated the wall next to his throat. It didn't even make a noise.

Damn that's sharp, Sitcom thought.

Blade a third buried.

Slug stood statue still and then looked at the ivory hilt. The blade touched his chin and cut him. Not bad, just like something you'd get shaving. Slug's face reddened. The blush pushed out more blood.

"Hey Sitcom." TeeVee's voice was more silence than sound. A space between every syllable and no expressive inflection to the words. "Tighten the leash around your poodle's neck before I fasten a noose to it. No one calls me fucked up in my own home. And I do not want that thing leaving eye trails on the reOrbs. Let alone its greasy prints." He smiled. Smooth metal teeth, crackling blue electricity. "Just the thought puts me in a murderous dispo."

"You know, you're fucked up." Sitcom pulled the dagger from the wall and wagged it at Slug's wide eyes. "Say you're sorry to the nice man."

"Sorry."

"Your aim is getting worse." Sitcom gave the dagger back to TeeVee. "Either that or you're getting soft."

"Neither," TeeVee said. "I just hired a girl last night to clean my floor and your poodle looks like it has a lot a blood in it..." He shrugged, the thought lost. "You would have been amused by her face when she came up. She believed I wanted sex and was removing her shirt when I gave her a mop. I don't think she had ever seen one before. Thought I wanted to shove it up her ass. And then tried to charge me extra to do so. This is, of course, the sort of thing you find amusing."

"I guess," Sitcom said. Visiting TeeVee never really put him in a chuckling sort of dispo. "Your delivery could use some fuckin' work."

"Communication is never easy." TeeVee looked over Sitcom's shoulder at Slug. "Don't get any blood on my fucking floor and if you so much as smear a reOrb with a foul-eyed look, I will choke you. To death. Right until you fucking die. You get me?"

"Yeah, okay. That's fine, man. Easy like," Slug held his sleeve to his chin. "I'll be careful."

"Was that better?" TeeVee asked Sitcom.

"Exactly perfect."

Slug was like a dog. You just had to show him who was boss and he'd take any shit, follow any order. It came in handy but it made Sitcom feel a little sick.

"Speaking of reOrbs," Sitcom dragged a red plastic chair out from the wall, "I need a mix. Something retro current but not too esoteric. Hosting a party of slummers down from the green. They want—"

"I can imagine," TeeVee said. "Something rude but not too rude. Just twisted enough so they can think they're in an authentic red level bash and can thus increase their social cache with one another."

"Well, I think they prolly wanna dance." Sitcom took a breath. "But speaking of social cache—"

"You're concerned about my marketing of you?"

"I appreciate it and all but you've flooded the green forum with bots. I don't see the point."

"When gathering information, the studios use simple tactics. They look for mentions of a name and its use in conjunction with certain key words. It's a counting game."

"Yeah but you get marked as spam and they stop counting. And what good is that?"

"It's safe." TeeVee pulled on his hookah and stared at the ceiling. The mongoose stretched, hopped off his lap and vanished beneath the couch. "I have their algorithm."

"All right if I smoke?" Sitcom asked, knowing that this conversation was over, not wanting to know how TeeVee came into that sort of information but never doubting that he had. "Tobacco."

"Yeah, that's fine." TeeVee's glass eyes blinked barcodes. "I'll be right back."

"No hurry." Sitcom sighed. TeeVee would never leave his seat but could be gone for a while. He'd trance out, travel through the info dump and then return with the right mix. Sitcom smoked and waited. Slug stayed quiet.

"They bored of KlashBan yet?" TeeVee asked.

"Everyone is bored of that shit."

"You never know. It takes a while for anything to percolate to the upstairs. And it's always some soft derivative nonsense. They put it through the production machines. Most of the time they just want to hear the wet version of the dried out corpse they get."

"Arid," Sitcom said. "Fucking mummified."

"Dry as outside," Slug agreed.

"Got some good PsychoTwist." TeeVee ignored Slug's comment, which was really too bad. That was about as witty as Slug got. Even considering that there might be a world outside of the mall took some work for the guy. Sitcom looked at Slug and smiled so he wouldn't feel like his sally had gone unnoticed.

"It's danceable but the visuals might be a bit ahead of them," TeeVee continued. "Bit too far, bit too fast."

"That shit's ahead of me," Sitcom said. "What is it?"

"I should lend you some. Not for the party. It'd be too intense for slummers but you'd like it. It's a real electric fucking current. Real fucking wet. Like a newborn. A yowling newborn."

"Sounds good. But what I need right now—"

"I know what you need and I have it." Sitcom blinked. "Now we discuss the price."

Budgie snorted a nose burning line off the table and vibrated back into his chair. He tried to ignore the blond mop of hair bobbing up and down in Snort Donkey's lap.

The chemist closed his eyes and grunted. Budgie looked away. It was impolite to watch an orgasm.

Nothing else to see though. The Fuck Palace was midweek quiet. All the slummers were sleeping with their wives. Budgie supposed everyone needed a change.

The product wiped her mouth. Her light bulb, lip-triggered teeth glowed florescent white but her eyes had gone out a long time ago. Now they were bloodshot embers.

"Your turn," she said to Budgie.

"Nah, I'm good."

"You gone queer?" Snort Donkey asked.

"Too high to get up," said Budgie. That might even be true. He didn't know. Fact was, he never liked hookers and tonight he just didn't feel like pretending anything more than he had to. "Can't even feel my fingers, don want someone fiddling round with my dick."

Snort Donkey took a long and funny look at Budgie and said to the product: "Go get us another drink."

She stretched like a cat and walked off.

"Sorry." Budgie watched her go. "Don mean rudeness."

"We are fucking rude boys after all," Snort Donkey said. "Besides, can't blame you. Worst head I've had this week."

The girl came back with the drinks.

"Thanks," Budgie said.

She shrugged and left. Snort Donkey hissed and glared. He leaned across the table. "How you holding up?"

"What's that supposed to mean?"

"Just seem shook."

"I got two bodies on me tonight. Not allowed to shake?"

"Not like that, you're not. That's not a good shake."

"What's that mean?"

"Just seems like you're touched." He leered. "You guys were friends, eh? A bit sweet on each other?"

Budgie heard the sour note in Snort Donkey's voice and clenched his fists. He wanted to tell Snort Donkey that yeah, he and Sputnik were friends but knew what that confession would set off. So he shrugged and looked at his whiskey. "Worked with him for a long time."

"Too long." Snort Donkey cut another line. "You think I'm snitch or some shit? That I'm gonna go up the ladder on you here singing,'Budgie had a friend. Let a little light into his heart and got all soft'?"

"Trap like that? How am I supposed to answer?"

"Fucking pathological." Snort Donkey inhaled the line. "That glowing heart of yours leads to mistakes. Like leaving Wolfe in the hall for one. Wonder what the second will be? A good friend is a bad comrade."

"Yeah, I read the rule book too."

"I bet you do a lot of reading. Clever, sensitive sort like you." Snort Donkey decked his drink and wiped his nose. "At least Wolfe is done. That's it for the Dog Goblins. Or so you say. Without the trophy, it's a bit hard to have the triumph."

"What the fuck you want from me? Made my choice. Stick by it. Wolfe is dead. Some parta him will turn up to confirm it."

"You sure?"

"Yeah." Budgie said.

"And what the fuck does that matter anyhow? Gonna cost money to deal with the ghouls. That cuts into the profit margin on this. Heavily. You know a dead Wolfe is worth more than a living gamma? You know that, right?"

"I know that."

"Then?"

"Fucking leave it the fuck alone." Budgie spilled whiskey down his chin. Knew what that meant. He was drunk. "Shit happens."

"Truth."

"Sputnik was still trying to scent him when he got loved. It was a fuck up. Top to bottom. You think I feel good bout all that? That I wanna hear bout it all night?"

"I'm just sayin'—"

"I don wanna hear, know or think bout what you just sayin'. Don care. Fuck it. Cut another line."

"You're not the first to freeze up." Snort Donkey leaned back and lit a spine of synapacide. "Not by far. A lot of people go statue. Especially when some robo-cranked idiot comes at them. It's cause they burst right into your routine, right out of the nothing. Just BAM!" He clapped his hand against the table. "They're there. Violence."

Budgie could make that excuse and maybe he could even believe it, but he didn't want to. His friend was dead and he was to blame. The guilt felt worse than the excuse but it also felt real. That had to count for something. "How'd you know the knife was dressed?"

"Sputnik died. Doc might drag out the operation for the popcorn eaters but he don't lose many people." Snort Donkey rested his forearms on the table and held his glass with both hands. "You gonna tell his Mom?"

"Not looking forward to that." Budgie looked at the little black box on the table. "What should I buy her?"

"You kidding? She gets a twenty percent cut from the wake. I think that'll do."

"Okay. Fuck, do I have to set that up too?" Weight piled on top of Budgie. He'd never had anyone close to him get notched; never really had anyone close to him. And he wasn't sure what the standard reaction was supposed to be. All he knew was that he felt awful and wanted out. But there was nowhere to go. He hadn't felt like this since he was a kid with a heavy nervous stutter. He'd wanted to talk right but just couldn't make his tongue work. The words were weights piled up atop him.

The more words he tried to carry, the worse it got. What might've sounded like something at some point just became gasping gibberish. When he'd given up on it, his concentration maybe broken by a joke, his mouth would finally co-operate and the words would pour forth. He'd speak. Just like a normal person.

Maybe he should give up on remembering Sputnik. *No. Won't do that. Not even if I can.* After all, Sputnik had never cared how Budgie talked. Usually, it was Sputnik who made the joke that rescued him from his own tongue. Budgie didn't need that anymore. But he still needed his friend.

"Partner setting the wake up is strict kosher," said Snort Donkey. "But who's that strict? I'll do it for your cut and you get paid a flat fee."

"How much?"

"Seven globals."

"Fuck that." Budgie was sad, confused and drunk but he wasn't stupid. "Ten. Not negotiating."

"Aight," Snort Donkey said too quickly.

Budgie assessed him for a long moment. Maybe he was getting ripped off but who cared. His only friend was dead and that's all that mattered. He looked away from Snort Donkey's weasel eyes and glanced around the bordello, the room moving out of focus. "I'm fucking fogged," he said. The booze clogged his senses and motor functions. The acid played a harpsichord on his mind. He felt like a psychotic ghost trapped in a meat cage. He needed out, to be anywhere but here. "We gon do this all night?"

"Can you think of anything else?"

Budgie thought and came up with nothing. It was funny. There was option piled on top of option but you just ended up bored. It came too easy. Fucking, drugs, whatever. It all had its price and it could all be had. Thing was, he didn't want any of it. *There must be something wrong with me,* he thought and downloaded the last of his whiskey. "I gotta go tell Sputnik's ma."

"You're going drunk?"

"Sure as Santa ain't going sober," Budgie said.

CHANNEL SURFING (1)
GONE FISHING

"That's the sort of rod that'll catch the Widow Maker."

"Yup," Dino Mondo clicked the last section into place. The salesman was right. Good balance, nice weight. This device was excellent. "How much is it?"

"Eight globals but, for a good customer like you, I could see my way to seven and a half."

"Can you see your way to seven?"

"I don't know, it's pretty dark in here." The salesman closed his eyes and stuck his arms out to grope the air. Opened his eyes and winked. "Okay, I see the light. Seven! Done."

"You're a real character, Sam." Dino paid with his card. "My boat available today?"

"Waiting for you on the lake."

"Good, good," Dino rented a fine boat here and occasionally sublet it through the store to help pay his costs. Unless it was too busy or they got a bribe, they always kept his boat available for him. He took his card back, pocketed it and walked out of the store to the fish stocked lake. Breathed deep.

It was a nice day. The fog machines had put a layer of mist over the water and the speakers played nature sounds. Long extinct birds welcomed a dawn that Dino had never actually seen. Never having witnessed a real sunrise, he was always surprised by his longing for them. He supposed that history was full of people like him, attracted to a glamorized vision of the past. Some people liked the plastic age and some people liked the Victorians.

Dino wasn't nearly that fussy.

He just liked the idea of being outside.

But it was hard to criticize the mall when the lake was like this: When you couldn't see the adverts or shoppers milling around. Sometimes, if the fog was thick enough, you could even smoke a pipe out in the center, far away from the electronic noses of robotic birds. That always completed the fantasy.

He strode to the dock, breathing in the scent of water and weeds. Just lovely. Sat down in his boat and opened his tackle box. Its familiar, worm and rubber stink smelled like good days. He attached his old reel to the new rod, threaded a hook and then untied his boat. The small electric motor carried him into open water, trolling as he went. Not because he ever caught anything doing that but because he might. You can't win it if you're not in it.

He steered towards the secret spot he fished on mornings like this, when no one could see him there. It was a quiet corner away from the well-traveled alleys and noisy adverts. Most people avoided this area, said that there was nothing in those lilly pads except snags and sunfish. And they were right except for one thing.

The Widow Maker lived here.

It was a huge, mythical beast and the source of much controversy. The old guys at the dock believed in the Widow Maker but said she was uncatchable. "If she ain't caught yet, she ain't never gonna be caught." The young guys were a bunch of cynics. "It's just a marketing scam set up by the sports store to sucker old men into snagging up and losing tackle in the worst part of the lake." But the young and old had something in common: They were both wrong. The Widow Maker was real and she could be caught.

Dino had glimpsed her.

Once upon a time on a morning just like this. (Well, every morning was just like this. They were standardized.) He'd been reeling in his line when something shook his boat. He looked into the water to see a massive bass staring up at him through the murky water. It must have been forty pounds of genetically modified fury. It passed beneath his boat, rocking it with its wake, and vanished. Dino cast in but nothing had hit. Not even a perch.

Certainly not the Widow Maker.

Really, the fish should be called the Divorce Causer. It had driven men to obsession and their wives to desperate boredom. What was the point of having a husband if you never saw him? Just ask Dino's wife. Another woman might have suspected a mistress but she knew him too well. He was in love with a fish and wanted it with every aching ounce of his being.

He didn't even know if he could afford to keep it—he'd have to pay the sports store for poundage. But it wasn't about keeping the fish. It was about the glory of catching it. About holding the Widow Maker over your head, about becoming a legend, an awed whisper spoken by the old guys when there was a special occasion or just a quiet moment. About proving the young guys wrong. If you caught something like that, the store would put your picture up in their window. You might even be in their adverts.

Besides how much time did his wife want him to spend at home anyway? He was retired. A man needed something in his life. Couldn't just sit on the couch watching television and playing on the gizmo. A man needed his mammoth hunt. She should understand that. He supposed she did. For that, he counted himself lucky.

Dino closed his front door, swinging his tackle box at his side, still excited about seeing The Widow Maker. The television made a racket in the next room and, after getting out of his shoes and into his slippers, Dino joined Jill on the couch.

"Catch anything?" she asked.

"Nothing good."

She smiled at him as he put his feet up on the coffee table and relaxed into the tempurpedic couch with a grunt.

"Few sunfish. But I…"

"You what?"

"I saw The Widow Maker again."

She laughed, her light purple curls bouncing around her head. "You and your Window Maker."

"*Widow* Maker," he corrected. This was an old game. She didn't mean any harm by it. Wasn't mocking him, just asserting her authority over his home life. Leave it at the lake, she said. It was sound advice. "Anything good on?"

"Just the usual garbage. Seems like there's more advertising every day. I was trying to watch Coronation Street, and I swear, they're interrupting it every two minutes. Disgusting. I have a mind to send an email to the Mall Trade Organization."

"For all the good it would do."

"The CEO listens." His wife patted his thigh. "As much as any man. More than some I could name."

"I like ads," Dino said. He used to work in an advertising firm though he hadn't been promoted as fast or as far as he'd like. "Good for the economy."

"They just get on my nerves. All that sex."

"This from a woman who likes Coronation Street?"

"That's different," she said. "And you know it."

"I'm going to fix myself a sandwich, you want anything, maybe a cup of tea?"

"That would be nice."

"It's in the cupboard." Another old joke.

As the water boiled, Dino made a cheese and mustard sandwich. He thought of the Widow Maker breaking water next to his boat today. Looking him right in the eye before it crashed back into the lake. The kettle clicked.

Dino poured the water into a cup with a lot of milk and carried it all back to the living room where he handed his wife the mug before sitting. The food tasted good. He always brought a meal and thermos of coffee out on the lake but fishing worked up a healthy appetite. His wife sniffed him.

"Have you been smoking again?"

"No," he said. "Some of the boys in the tackle store must have been. Didn't really notice."

"You know you can't smoke in open air until after teen curfew," she said. "I want you to quit. And quit lying about it too. You look so stupid when you lie."

"Yes Dear," Dino said. He was never much of a liar. The boys in the ad firm used to call him Honest Dino behind his back. But he'd heard. "Did the kids call today?"

"No."

"Maybe tomorrow then."

"Yes Dear," Jill sipped her tea and squeezed Dino's thigh. "Maybe." She flipped the channels on the remote, looking for a show instead of advertising and finally settled on "You're a Crazy Lying Bastard" with Bob Anger.

Dino shuddered. He couldn't stand that blowhard.

Dino's bladder kicked him awake at one thirty in the morning. While his wife snored, he snuck out of bed and navigated through the dark living room. He switched on the washroom light and urinated. Some pee sprinkled onto the seat and Dino bent over to wipe it off with a piece of synth-cashmere toilet paper. He couldn't afford the real stuff. Dino flushed the toilet and flicked the light off.

As he stepped into the living room the television turned on, painting the walls electric blue.

But—he'd disabled the motion detector. So what was this?

"Don't be broken," he whispered and crouched in front of the snowy screen. The warranty had just expired on this television and he didn't want to fork out good money on a new one. But used was worse. The ones they gave away at the charity shops had awful pictures and lacked a decent memory. Besides, that was charity.

He stared at the static. Something hypnotic about it. Pictures moved in the flickering white and black. After a moment he tapped the screen. It left a mark. He drew a crude face in the snow.

"Is that you?" the face said in a soft, fuzzy voice. "That *is* you. Dino Mondo. Hello."

Dino stumbled backwards and fell on his ass. His mouth dropped open. Alzheimer's. Senility. An old man's nightmare.

"You aren't mad," the television said. "You worked in advertising. You must know about biometric cameras."

Dino nodded.

"I'm in the red levels. You can call me TeeVee."

"Is this a robbery? Extortion?" Dino looked over his shoulder at the door. Any second now criminals would burst in just like Bob Anger had warned. "A home invasion?"

The television made choppy bursts of white noise. Laughter? "You have nothing to extort. And robbery is a bit crude. I want to make a deal with you."

"I don't make deals with—"

"I can get you the Widow Maker."

"What?" Dino's voice was too loud. He turned down the volume on the television. "What?" he whispered.

"I control that fish by remote. It's a real fish but I infested its brain when it was a fingerling. That's why it's never been caught. I've seen you out there every day, trying to bring her in. I recognize your lure and boat. Today I had her jump up to get a look at your face, put it through the biometric files and got your info."

"What do you want?"

"I need some help financing a project I'm working on. A hundred globals should do the trick."

"What sort of project..." Dino let the words fade. There were some questions you were better off not asking. "I don't have that kind of money. Not to spend on a fish. Not without guarantees."

"I'll tell you what," the face said. "You go fishing tomorrow and I'll make the Widow Maker circle your boat three times. If I do that, we should have a deal, yes?"

"I have to think about it."

"You have until tomorrow night. Then we'll talk again. And Dino, please don't make the error of thinking you can report this."

"I won't." Dino could imagine what they'd say about an old man with a talking television. They'd ship him off to a Granola Village with no lakes to fish. Just golf simulators and stores selling bedazzled Depends undergarments. Was this even a crime? It felt like one but he doubted it was on the books. Of course, the books changed depending on your finances. "I won't."

"I believe you. But believe me when I say that you aren't the only fisherman who wants the Widow Maker. You are the first I've contacted, because frankly, I respect obsession. And you should know, if I let that fish think for herself you would have caught her long ago."

The television switched off. Dino sat in the dark for a few long moments before he got up and returned to his bed. He could not sleep but he dreamed of the Widow Maker anyway.

⸻

"So you believe me now?" the television asked.

"I'd be a fool not to," Dino whispered. The fish had circled his boat just like this face had promised. "But I still don't know. It doesn't seem right."

"You feel like it's fixed?"

That was exactly it. He wanted to catch the Widow Maker but this felt like cheating. The last thing he wanted was a hollow victory.

"It *is* fixed," the face said. "It always has been. The Widow Maker only exists because I fixed it. As things stand now it is truly an uncatchable fish. And I could always have someone else catch it. I could even turn its brain off and have it sink to the bottom of the lake to be eaten by the craw-daddies and catfish. What a waste that'd be."

"It's not about that," Dino said.

"Explain."

"I mean the status of catching it would be nice, and Santa knows, I wouldn't be the first man to get ahead through a lie, but—" Dino struggled to find the words. He wasn't a philosophical man, preferring quiet hours to deep thoughts. This was the first time he had ordered his thinking about the Widow Maker.

"It's just that I've never been terribly successful. I didn't really want to get into advertising, it was just a job. When I had my kids…" He contemplated the screen. "I don't know how old you are but life has a way of getting behind you and—"

"I fail to see—"

"You have to understand the Widow Maker." Dino held up his hand and took a deep breath. He wished his wife let him smoke inside. A pipe would lubricate his thoughts. "It's the beast I've put myself up against. Some people run marathons. This is something I do for myself. You can't—you can't *buy* the Widow Maker." He sighed. "At least I thought you couldn't. I guess you can buy anything if you have the money. I should have known that. But catching it was, well…"

"Your way of proving you have some worth?"

"Yeah." Dino wiped sweat from his forehead. "Not to the guys at the dock but to me."

The face held still for a long moment. "Yes," it said. "I understand. Better than you might think."

"So, I can't just *catch* the Widow Maker."

"I see the solution. When you hook into the fish, I'll let her fight. And I'll help her. You'll have to beat the both of us. Is that sporting enough for you?"

"That sounds fair." Dino smiled. "I can pay for the game but not the victory."

"The price remains the same."

Dino nodded. "How do we set up the pay?"

"You'll never catch her." The old man cast off the dock as Dino eased into his boat. "That fish is a monster now, more monster than animal, and it would take a legend to bring her in. A real hero." The man looked Dino up and down. "And you, if you don't mind me saying, don't look like the heroic type."

Dino did mind. What did this guy know anyway? "You talk a lot for a man who's never caught anything bigger than a three pound bass."

"Nothing wrong with a three pound bass," the man said. "And I've never seen you catch anything bigger than a perch, even with all your fancy lures."

Dino squeezed his hands into fists. If he was a bit younger he'd get out of the boat and teach this old fool some manners. As it was he just said: "Would you like to put your money where your mouth is?"

"Sure," the man said. "Five globals say you never catch that fish."

"Five globals?" Dino said. "You think as small as the fish you catch. Let's make it interesting."

"Five globals isn't interesting?"

"Let's say 150 globals."

The man's face dropped.

"150 globals says that I catch her today. Before they close the lake tonight."

"150? You're on." The man laughed. "You're crazier than I thought. Or richer." He stepped towards the boat and they shook on it. "Happy fishing," he called as Dino took his boat out. "I'm gonna start running a tab at the bar."

Dino ignored the comment. Once out of sight of the shore he lit his pipe and shook his head. It was a stupid bet to make but it was too late to do anything about it. If he lost the Widow Maker he'd have to dip into his savings to pay and that'd be hard to hide from his wife. But his pride was worth something. Maybe not 150 globals but something. He anchored his boat and checked his equipment. Spider-web line, a three pronged hook and his best rod.

He impaled a writhing leech on the hook—wondering if he even needed bait—and took a few meditative pulls on his pipe before casting in. It was important to be focused. His landing net at his side. Dino did something he had never done before but often fantasized about. He fastened his safety belts. This fish was not going to drag him in. He slipped the pipe into his pocket and cast. The lure plopped into the water and Dino let it sink before clicking his line into place. Drew in his slack and waited.

A moment later the rod buckled.

The rod bent and Dino's arms burned.

The diving fish tried to tangle the line. He resisted its massive pull. Dino felt like he was trying to yank a car up from the bottom. He could not budge the Widow Maker. He only hoped to weaken it. He had to make the fish tire before he did.

The line slackened and the tip of the rod sprang up. The fish planned to clear the water again. Dino yanked his rod down just in time. The creature flipped through the air, tossing its head back and forth, and crashed into the lake, soaking Dino and rocking his boat. The fish's strategy was clear. Dive and jump, jump and dive. After twenty minutes its dives became less deep, its jumps less high. There was some give in it.

Dino found a rhythm and danced it through the water, gaining an inch here and an inch there. Losing line then getting it back. He muttered to the old beast and predicted its next move time and time again.

He felt like he was in the creature's head and that was dangerous. This fish was partly controlled by a man and that man could be bluffing, pretending to tire and establishing a routine, only to suddenly break out of it. Dino had to be prepared for anything. His nerves were on edge and exhaustion set in. His arms and back ached, occasionally exploding into bright sparks of pain. No matter the result, he would feel this tomorrow.

He felt it now.

Dino worked the fish closer. It still resisted hard and heavy but its vigor was gone. Dino inched his line towards the starboard side of the boat.

A huge shadow darkened the murky water. It stared up at him, tried to dive and failed. Dino grabbed his landing net with one hand and poked its tip through the water. He pressed the button and sent an electric charge into the fish's body, stunning it. Then he flipped the net around its huge head, got as much of its body as he could in and released his rod. He rested the net against the side of the boat and used all the leverage he had to hoist the monster in.

It stared at him, gills working hard, exhausted and stunned. Alive. Not for long, Dino thought. Not for long.

He pulled his knife from his sheath. He saw himself in the silver blade. Tired and old but smiling. His teeth the shape of the knife. The knife, reflection and all, bit into the thick throat. And chewed.

The manhole opened like a camera lens. Budgie climbed down the ladder and into the unit where Sputnik lived with his mom. *Had lived.* The place smelled like burned toast and sweat. He leaped off the last few rungs. Hitting ground, his boot caught in a broken chunk of floor. He caught his balance.

Sputnik's mom sat in a frayed orange chair balancing a plate upon her lap and watching television. Everything so normal, so ready to be shattered. Budgie felt guilty. What right did he have to intrude?

"Sputnik isn't with you?" Mrs. Dobject said without even glancing at him. She sniffed the air. "Damn Budgie, I can smell the booze on you from here."

Budgie's breath came fast and shallow through his dry mouth. The dope and booze should've buzzed the edge off but if these nerves were blunted he'd hate to see them sharp. This was the first time he had ever done this. Hopefully, it'd be the last. Losing your partner was bad enough but losing a friend? Who had one of those?

Snort Donkey was right. Everyone was right. Better to not make friends.

"I'm sorry—" He didn't know else to begin. Tears blurred his eyes. Thank Santa there was no one here to see this. He'd never live it down. "I'm sorry."

"Don't," Mrs. Dobject said and went quiet.

Budgie wiped at his face with a sleeve, looked at his steel capped boots. A little chunk of floor stuck out of the sole. He tried to tap it off. It refused to move. He pulled the little black box out of his pocket. "I gotta."

She finally looked away from the television to stare at the box, her eyes fat, plastic beads.

Budgie gave it to her and backed away. A sudden, sharp pain in his chest startled him. The box bounced off his tunic and spilled onto the floor.

Mrs. Dobject stood. The plate fell off her lap and bounced. Something about upended food reminded Budgie of Wolfe's body. His stomach twisted out an urking noise.

She threw something wet and soft at Budgie, hitting him square in the face. Half of a sandwich. Soaked in stew. She clenched her fists and stared at him. "You even feel that you little psycho?"

She strode toward him. Stepping though her spilled food. Stomping on Sputnik's pocket litter. Budgie backed up. He bumped the wall.

"It wasn't me," he said. "It was—"

"It's never you." Her face was close to his, her breath hot and stinking. "Sputnik looked up to you, you should have protected him, you should have—"

She kept yelling but Budgie's brain stopped making sense of it. It was just shrill noise in his face. Did she think he wanted Sputnik to die? He'd been closer to him than she ever was. What were they supposed to do?

True, they could've tried to get jobs on the green levels—not being chipped exiles but just native-born reds. But how did you come home and face these corridors when you did that?

The gangs hunted sellouts. Budgie had done the same and so had Sputnik. It was better to be dead.

Mrs. Dobject knew that. Did she seriously want that life for her kid? It wasn't their fault. If anything, it was hers. And now she wanted to complain?

"Back the fuck off me," Budgie whispered. He put his hand square on her chest, feeling how soft and fragile she really was behind all that fury.

He shoved her and something something clicked in his head: An old, evil switch that only got thrown when he was angry. His whole body went cold. "I'm not gon get shit hit by you." His voice got real quiet and slow. Some people freaked out and got high pitched when they got angry but not Budgie. He was a machine that worked better at high speed. Anger calmed him. Made things clear.

I could do anything right now.

He stepped towards her.

She's weak.

"Where was I?" He jabbed a finger into one of her big fake tits. "Where the fuck were you?"

"Those are expensive!"

"I don care." Budgie poked her again. Hoped to pop the breast and send it flying around the room like a deflating balloon. It just mushed up beneath his finger. "Sputnik ain't the one who got fired from his job, got chipped and got exiled. Didn't ask to be born, did he? You're the one that got sent down here and you're the fucking one who was never there. Too busy fucking Slummers for a bit of pocket money that went up your nose faster than it went into his gut."

Tremble faced, she backed up against the wall. Budgie had the horrible feeling that she'd been cut before. Maybe by a pimp and maybe by a john. There was something terrified and knowing in those eyes. She'd seen men act like this before, seen methodical, drugged violence and felt it slicing into her.

She's weak.

His hand slithered to his belt. It caressed the hilt of a knife.

Behind Mrs. Dobject, a cockroach crawled over the wall. On the television soaps, this'd be a heavy scene with Budgie cast as the sneering villain. There'd be no bugs. It should be melodrama but just felt pathetic. His ice insides cracked. "I've gotta get outta here."

Mrs. Dobject stood shaking. She looked so vulnerable and old. The cockroach crept onto her shoulder.

Budgie scooped up Sputnik's litter and dropped it into the black box. He couldn't believe he'd lost his temper like that. Should he do something? What? "If you need anything, like money or whatever." He remembered. "You'll get twenty percent of the wake."

She didn't say anything and didn't move.

Guilt wrung Budgie out. Drug shook and cold, bile rose in his throat. He clambered up the ladder. The space between the rungs played like a the worst flip-book in the world: Wall, wall, more wall, and a crack.

The manhole opened in front of him and he crawled back onto the street. He scuttled towards a dark corner. Bent over and vomited. Blue fluid sprayed his boot-tops.

He wiped his mouth with his sleeve and straightened, knowing his face was red and his eyes were wet. All he wanted to do was walk and keep walking, right into the wrong section, hoping someone would notch him. He couldn't take another fucking day.

He leaned against an advert and closed his eyes. In eye shut darkness, patterns formed spiderweb faces.

Time to call it a night.

Time to go home.

After a long and hard day, Vivian Shuckhart came home to a man who was short and soft.

"It would be nice," said Olin before she'd even taken her boots off, "for you to take some responsibility."

Hearing that warbling nag, Vivian wished she was back at the office. She didn't *hate* coming home—that was too strong a word—but she certainly dreaded it. Every day she spent managing the shoe shops —dealing with the buyers, sellers and, Santa forbid, the designers— decreased her authority here, even as it increased it there. Just another trade in a life full of them. Now Vivian felt like a ghost who appeared every evening in front of the dining room television to rattle phantom chains of authority.

"What do you want me to do?"

"Take an interest in your daughter for beginners."

"Lexus is fine."

"She's hanging out with the wrong crowd. They're like little mall rats, the way they cruise around after school. Be lucky if she can keep a job."

"She's fifteen," Vivian said. "I used to be the same and so did you. We turned out all right."

"If she does, it'll be no help from you."

Yeah, of course. No help from Vivian. She'd paid for this nice condo, put food on the table and paid for her husband's home decorating courses. Vivian sat down, undid the top button on her blouse and stared hard at the television. If she got into a fight she'd just lose. Better to hold her tongue. Men were too emotional.

"She started smoking. Did you know that?"

"Smoking what?"

"Tobacco, of course. Good Santa, what did you think I meant? It's not that bad. Yet."

"You smoke tobacco."

"I quit." Her husband thrust his chin up. That used to turn it her on. It used to look proud. Now it just looked smug. He was still the basic physical type she liked, short and stout, but his muscles had softened into fat. His clothes had changed from the security guard uniforms and jock gear into the plain and comfortable, nothing to look at, uniform of the perfect middle management house-spouse. Topped with a tasteful haircut and tasteful accessories that spanned from neutral on weekdays to less neutral on weekends.

In other words, boring.

Making love to him was on par with cleaning the garbage bags before reusing them. For starters, there were the starters. The vials and oils and pills, all saying MAXMIZE THIS and INCREASE THAT. Then, when Vivian had the energy to run that medical marathon, he'd top it off with a psychiatric session. She usually ended up holding his hand for twenty minutes while he whined about getting fat. It ended with her just laying there, legs spread, wishing he'd shut up.

When she'd told Burt about all that, he laughed and said she needed a new husband. She'd grunted and said she just needed a man.

"Don't we all," Burt had replied. "A hard man is good to find." Not that he had problems. Burt was a free agent and just kept getting better looking as he aged.

That might be why Olin disliked Vivian hanging out with Burt. The idiot even briefly suspected they were having an affair. When she told Olin that Burt was as gay as a Christmas line is long, Olin yammered about an 'emotional affair.' She'd listened or at least done a decent job of looking like it. Then she stopped using her old friend as an excuse to avoid coming home. Now she said she was working overtime. Sometimes it was even true.

The door opened, and Vivian wondered what excuse her daughter would use. Figured she was about to find out.

"Here's the little princess now," Olin said. "Will you say something to her?"

"About what?"

Lexus shuffled into the room smelling of cigarettes.

The scent reminded Vivian of better times. "Hi-ya, Lexus."

"Hi Mom."

"New haircut?" She was determined to never be offended by her daughter's style. Working in fashion, she often hired girls that looked crazier than Lexus.

Olin's problem was ignorance. He only ever went out to the food court. His reality was mediated through his loudmouthed know-it-all friends or his even more loud mouthed magazines and television hosts. Lexus's partially shaved head conjured up images of dark, forbidden debauchery, but it was just the current style. Nothing to sweat about.

"Yeah." Lexus fingered the plaid pigtails that hung at the sides of her head. She glanced at her Dad. "Got it last week."

"Your mother has something to say to you." Olin crossed his arms with a childish 'now you're going to get it' expression.

Was Olin was jealous of Lexus? It was ridiculous but she wouldn't put anything past him. He was becoming a ridiculous little man, smaller and sillier by the day.

Olin tilted his head. "Vivian?"

She wondered what she was supposed to say. "Umm, don't smoke."

Lexus looked at her for a moment. "Okay?"

"I'm serious!" Olin said.

Why didn't he say we? Was Vivian supposed to be a puppet that he spoke through?

"You smell like a red level whore house."

Vivian laughed. Only a man who had never been to a red level would say something that stupid. Only a man who had no understanding of teenagers would think that the red levels weren't cool or dry or whatever they said these days.

Olin glared at Vivian then threw his hands into the air and stormed from the room.

Vivian winked at her daughter, hoping for her to return the gesture. But Lexus just scoffed and went to her room.

"Teenagers," Vivian muttered.

INFO DUMP

"Welcome back to 'You're a Crazy Lying Bastard with your host, your voice, Bob Anger. By now you should know where to buy my book so we'll just get right back into the fray with our guest, the red-level Madam—*Madam*: sounds so respectable, let's just call her what she is: A notorious pimp—Jane Jane."

"Hi Bob."

"So this smut you've written—you don't mind me calling it smut do you?"

"Not at all."

"This smut—"Fucking Like a Pro—How to Keep Your Man," by Jane Jane, available for download soon—is what? A manual? Some sort of perverse how-to?"

"That's right Bob. I wrote it after seeing people complain about my bordellos on the reds. Mainly women, of course—"

"I don't know about that. I think those sleaze pits should be burned down and the whores run straight out of the mall."

"You're kidding, right?"

"You break up families, you destroy happy homes, you contribute to—"

"And that's what this book will stop. The problem is that women don't know how to satisfy their man. So their men turn to my girls."

"Who have nicotine coated vaginas."

"That's an outrageous lie and just the sort of nonsense that this book will dispel."

"Are you calling me a liar, Jane?"

"No, I'm just saying that there are a lot of things that a woman can do to keep her man happy. Since I'm an expert, I'm in a unique position to—"

"The only thing you're expert in is in being a crazy lying bastard. Sorry. Bitch. You're a crazy lying bitch and I'll tell you why after this commercial break when we return with more Hot Talk on "You're a Crazy Lying Bastard' with me, your host, your voice, Bob Anger."

Budgie woke and saw his mom climbing up the ladder. She slipped through the manhole and was gone. Off to work.

The television, which she always left on, played adverts with the occasional show spliced in. Just enough to keep you watching.

He lit a spine of synapacide from the pack on his bedside table. Tried not to think. It was too early and his gut ached. Hangover spiked with guilt. Seeing his mom made it worse.

He pulled his blanket up to his neck, leaned against the wall and twitched his feet, which hung over the edge of the cot. The synapacide eased the sick and aches. When confident he could hold down water, he swigged from the plastic container beside his bed.

The whole thing reminded him of those music ads in the green levels. Aimed at mall rat kids who flirted with being chipped, the ads read *Guess I'm on the edge.* "Guess I'm right fucking over it," Budgie said and pulled smoke. "Right into the chasm."

Some abyss had cracked open in his life. Something big and important was gone.

He'd known Sputnik forever. They met in the Ronald McDonald Daycare playground. During their first recess, under a monkey bar ceiling, they beat each other. Nothing fancy, no ducking and dodging, just two kids punching each other in the head. Each one dishing it out and taking it, neither one falling or flinching. The battle lasted the whole lunch hour and over the years it became an epic in their minds. After it was done they shook hands.

Friends forever.

And all that shit.

Things hadn't worked out quite like that, but it'd been close. They were inseparable for a long time. Running schemes on the other kids, pulling pigtails, stealing lunches, lying to teachers, sneak thieving food and flicking bras. But, when they were ten, their moms put them in different schools, Pepsi and Coke, and they ran with different crews.

At thirteen they met again in the Vidicons. Their friendship hadn't missed a beat. Sputnik completed something in Budgie. The guy was a joker and, maybe because they had been so close when they were young, maybe, because just speaking with that stutter had been so hard, Budgie never developed a sense of humor. He relied on Sputnik's jokes just as Sputnik relied on Budgie's seriousness. Between them they had a third mind. Better than either of theirs alone.

Their moms worked in the same place, which taught them to be careful. A lesson Budgie forgot last night. He knew his mom would hear about his fight with Mrs. Dobject and he hated to think of what she'd say when she got home. This might be the final straw. He was almost sixteen and would have to get his own place soon anyway. He should start planning. Get his money up.

He could always move into a Vidicon squat but was shivered by the thought of the shared washrooms and what happened in them. He wanted space. Not to be crammed in with a bunch of dead end kids, fighting for any scheme they could get a piece of. None of the Vidicons in a squat would ever move up. Budgie had enough weight on top of him without a bunch of anchors pulling him down.

Budgie needed to be alone. To be away.

He grabbed a reOrb out of his dresser drawer and dropped it in a bowl of liquid, where it spun and grew music. His sad soundtrack. Owned an orb for every emotion. He listened for a while but these store-bought feelings, packaged into droning songs, sounded phony. The cheap black and white visuals refused to take. It just made him feel trite. He pulled the orb out.

He should sleep. Maybe take the day off. Wondering how that'd look, he ground out the spine of synapacide and lit another. The electronic doorbell rang.

Budgie groaned and rubbed his forehead. Probably Vidicons who wanted to see where he was, what he was doing tonight, if he had any schemes or wanted in on theirs.

He didn't want any part of it. They were persistent though, just kept ringing away until, irritated, Budgie told the television to switch to surveillance.

It took him a moment to recognize the face. Harmony Kink? She stared up at the screen, smiled and waved. Budgie wanted to be angry but he was too worn down, too hungover and too stoned. "Open door."

Harmony climbed down the ladder. She wore the standard rude boy uniform, which was a change for her. Usually she liked to blend with the mall rats and tourists. Made it easier to pocket-lift their cards. But now she had that stiff necked, sharp collared, scarlet tunic, cut a size too loose around her petite body. Her black pants tucked into big steel capped boots. Budgie glimpsed the shape of her ass through her baggy pants and then remembered the story Snort Donkey told him. He looked away. Made his balls ache just to think about it.

"Hey," she said, hopping to the floor and looking around the room, her hands on her hips. Her face looked elfin but her green eyes were serious and assessing. Maybe even scared. If she put some work into it, she might be pretty. Budgie's anger softened. Good looks can do that.

She scratched the back of her shaved head. That haircut was a change too. Usually she wore a neon bobbed wig. Budgie figured she kept a blade under it. Why else would you wear one? Fashion? No one thought that shit was wet. No one was going to.

"What'd you want?" Her two powerbars glowed green so she was healthy and dead sober. There goes one explanation, he thought.

Without asking, she sat on his mom's chair.

"Just make yourself comfortable."

"Sarcasm." She turned towards the television and stretched her legs out, but she watched him out of the corner of her eye. Reminded Budgie of a cat. He didn't like cats. "Just wanted to see how you were doing. Heard about Sputnik."

"Doing fine." There was a long silence, and he wondered if his tone gave the lie to his voice. "Just tired. Heard about what you did to Wolfe's bros."

She nodded, her eyes fixed to the flickering television and her body tensing. Budgie tried to read her face. It was as blank and sad as he felt.

"The hawks in the pockets were a nice touch."

"More sarcasm." She pulled a pack of chewing gum out of her pocket. Popped a piece into her mouth. "Anyway, that was Snort Donkey's touch, not mine. Story gets crazier every time he tells it."

Budgie ground out the spine of synapacide in the ashtray on his lap. Set it on the floor. He'd have to clean that later. "Guess the thing about the cock and balls in the mouth ain't true either?"

"No," she said. "I did that."

"Santa. Why?"

She shrugged and blew a bubble. Pop.

"So what is this anyway? Courtesy call?"

"No." She looked directly at him. "I want to say sorry."

"What?"

"Didn't think Wolfe would come back like that."

"They always come back." Budgie avoided her gaze. Anger twitched his fingers. This conversation balanced on the pointy surface of things. If it stumbled into the depths, blades would be drawn. At times like this, manners counted for a lot. "Where they gon go?"

"Nowhere."

"Nowhere is right. That's why everything is kept cricket. You know Wolfe dressed his blade?"

She nodded. Of course she knew. If she didn't she wouldn't be here apologizing. The gum smacked in her mouth. "Cricket don't work for me," she said. "Works for you and the rest of the boys but not for me."

"Didn't work for Sputnik."

"Yeah," she nodded. "He was a good guy. Funny."

"*Was.*"

"You understand that I didn't mean for this to happen?"

"What you think would happen?" He ground his molars together. "What do I care what you meant? What the fuck *meaning* got to do with anything?"

"You don't get it, Budgie, and I don't expect you to care. I'm just asking for you to look at it from my angle."

"And what's that?"

"If I played shit straight, what'd you think I'd be doing?"

Budgie didn't need to think for long. She'd be a renting a room in some bordello and renting her body to pay for it. She'd probably be good product. Maybe she was good looking, smart and ruthless enough to start her own stable. But that took a lot of time. Right now, she'd just be working, dreaming and trying to stay off the hard drugs while keeping her good looks from getting sliced up.

It made him angry to think of it. Every day he saw his mom leave to work. He thought he'd grown used to the idea of sweating, green level businessmen crawling over her. Yet every time he thought about it something near his heart turned cold.

His dad was one of those fucks. Not that he'd ever met him. Not that he even wanted to. "You're right, I don care." Budgie kept his tone polite. He kept a knife sheathed below his pillow. He wondered if he could get it in time to cut her throat. "I don care but I get it. But shit, caring don make it right anyhow."

"This is mine." Harmony gestured at her body. Budgie noticed again that, beneath the baggy clothes, it was fine product. She popped another bubble. "And I'm not for rent. That's my fucking right."

"Why you here anyway?" Budgie snaked his hand towards the pillow. He wanted that steel close.

"I wanted to say sorry. Serious." She glanced at his hand then looked him straight in the face. "I'm sorry. I'm not trying to make things better. It's broke and it can't be fixed. But I wanted you to know."

"Why'd you care? I mean, shit, Harmony, it's just the cost of doing business." The words tasted sour in Budgie's mouth and he spat them out. Fuck money, he thought. It is not worth it. "The Vidicons will make back their forty globals. Maybe already have."

"I care cause you two were friends. That's fucking rare. I wish Wolfe had of hit anyone but one of you two. Anyone. I mean that." She took her hands away from her belt and held them up, palms outward, beside her head.

She'd sussed the knife and still gave him advantage. Even though she didn't owe him anything, that gesture lent him a couple of seconds to cut her with.

He wanted to say something smart-ass and devastating, the sort of thing that Sputnik would've said, but his mind was blank. "Put your hands down." Budgie put his palms on his lap. "It's not really your fault. I wanna blame you but, fuck, I can't. It's just the situation."

"Yeah," she said. "The situation is very bad." She lowered her hands and relaxed. Glanced around the room. "You keep a neat hutch. It's very... Severe."

"Can't stand a mess." Everything had its place and stayed in it. Budgie took some comfort from that. "This whole fucking thing is mess enough."

"I'll say."

"How come Wolfe's bros didn't scent you?"

"I took a couple of pills to kill the odor. Didn't want them to smell Vidicon on me. Don't really want anyone to. Don't even like smelling it on myself."

"Damn." Maybe that's why he didn't scent Wolfe. The guy probably killed his stink. It had never occurred to Budgie that someone would do that. But it explained a lot—even why he had frozen up. The smells were built into your reflexes. An enemy's sweat-cologne cued violence. If Wolfe wasn't odored then, of course, Budgie's reactions were thrown. The excuse didn't make him feel any better.

"So are we clear?" Harmony asked

"Yeah, we're clear. Peaceful like."

"That's a weight off my brain," she said. "I was worried you'd make trouble for me. Santa knows, I made some for you. You'd have the right."

"These fucking rights always turn into wrongs," Budgie said. "And I don politic. If I had trouble with you I'd let you know straight. It'd be me visiting you. I don like going behind people's backs. It's not..."

"Cricket?"

"Gon to say efficient, but sure."

"I'm bored," she said abruptly. "You layabouting all day?"

"Figured."

"Glum cunt." She looked around the room and Budgie sneaked another look at her body. Her tits must be real, he thought, considering how small they were. She caught him staring. "You want to fuck?"

"Was thinking about it." He'd bought a few orgasms last week but hadn't gotten around to using them. Maybe he needed to pop. It'd take his mind off things for a bit and help him sleep. "I guess, yeah," he said. "As long as you keep your fingers out of my ass."

"Okay," she said and undid her boots, stepped out of her pants, left them in a messy heap and crawled into bed with him. "But be quick, I have stuff to do today." She rubbed his crotch with medical hands.

He unbuttoned her tunic and then let her remove it. She wasn't wearing a bra.

"I have latex if you don't," she said.

"I have some." He got out of bed, fumbled through his jacket pockets and pulled out a spray can. Told his television to go internal and it showed an image of the room on its huge screen. When he got back to the cot Harmony lay naked on the bed, her hand between her spread legs. She stared at the ceiling and smacked gum. Budgie glanced back at the television where she did the same thing. "You want an orgasm?" He reached under his mattress for the vial.

"Sure," she said. "I left mine at home."

"No problem." He popped one into her mouth.

"Better make it two."

She swallowed, reached out a hand and lackadaisically played with his balls. Budgie ate his pill, started to get hard. His penis bobbed in front of him like a dowsing rod.

"Turn around," he said, thinking it was best to keep her dangerous end pointed away. She got up on all fours and faced the television screen. Looking at that nice ass Budgie wondered just what one was her dangerous end.

He knelt behind her and spritzed his cock before setting the spray can down. He rubbed her cunt with two fingers, making sure the pill had got it slick, and then entered.

He didn't look down at her but watched the image of them fucking on the television. She did the same. Made it better that way, somehow more real. After a few minutes she squealed and Budgie groaned. His body shuddered. He was done but he kept humping at her until she finished up and told him to stop. He pulled out and grabbed a Kleenex, which he passed it to Harmony. Used another one to dab at his cock. He didn't want to stain his bed. They were both quiet. Not much to say really.

"That wasn't completely awful." Harmony got dressed.

Budgie flipped through television channels.

"At least you're quick."

Budgie laughed. It felt better than the fucking.

░▒▓ ▓▒░▒▓ ▒▒ ▓▒▓▒▓▒ ▒▓ ▓▒▓▒▓ ▓▒▓ ▒▓ ▓ ▒▓▒▓ ▓▓▒ ▓▒ ▓ ▓▒ ▒▓

Sitcom stepped out of the elevator, crisp in his bousgie clothes, like a commercial's idea of a hip yet responsible twenty something. Blended right into the green levels. Holding a black attaché case in his gloved hand, he strode through the crowds. Security guards meandered past without a second look.

That was to be expected. He was twenty-seven now. Never been chipped. That put him in a high class in the red levels, put him right near the top, in the betas. An aged rude boy who'd never been caught. Guys like him were rare and they were organized. They knew what they were about. On the reds they were feared and on the greens they were invisible.

An insolent mall rat with a shaved head and a barcode tattooed over his skull slowly bladed past, staring at him. Sitcom met the kid's eyes and held them. He smiled. *Little shit, try to intimidate me? I will fucking kill you. I should, just for wearing that ink. Your type has cost me money.* Before they caught on, those barcode tattoos were wet. They disrupted and crashed any cameras that scanned them.

Now Sitcom had to pay to avoid the biometric lenses. He rented a virus that turned his measurements into a hopeless blur. Sometimes, he paid extra to have another face put over his. Might just be for style points—like when you use a celeb—but usually it was a scheme. He'd use a business type, his face stolen from the files in a whorehouse. When the hapless bousgie got arrested and shipped to the reds, rude boys broke into his apartment and stole his stuff. Maybe they'd even grab him and turn him out. Beyond the joke, it was a decent way to pay the whore house for his face. An old scheme but a good one.

Just like those barcode tattoos. Sitcom remembered when those worked. Now they were just some dry style worn by idiot kids like this. The mall rat looked away and disappeared into the crowd. Stupid little bastard.

Sitcom sniffed and kept walking. Things were easier on the reds. He could just slice someone for glaring at him like that. But who would dare? He saw his target up ahead.

An Edge ReOrb shop.

This was the price. TeeVee said he'd have his mix ready but Sitcom had to pay. No money or any of that crap. TeeVee wanted some top quality, blank reOrbs that he could record onto, erase and record onto again without losing any quality. He'd come up himself but it meant he'd have to leave his apartment. And that wasn't gonna happen anytime soon. It was a good deal but TeeVee always cut a good deal. No greed there. Just wanted his music and drugs and paid in both for either.

Not like Sitcom's old comrade Jar. That guy was getting too lustful for the spoils and too cautious in their taking. Was coming up on twenty four and thought he could make beta by playing it safe. Wanted a cut in everything and a part in nothing. He'd even asked Sitcom why he should help get these reOrbs if he wasn't getting paid. Sitcom kept his disgust to himself. Just said: "Look Jar, when you scheme to get

something I don't ask what's in it for me, I just help you get your loot.
I do that cause I know when I scheme you help me. And if it's your
idea it's your loot. My idea, my loot."

Those might not be the rules but they were the manners. Jar knew
that. But he wasn't the first guy to get the greed and lose his manners.

Pained Sitcom to think about it. He'd been running with Jar for
over six years. Didn't matter though. If Jar didn't get his act together,
he'd break the rules. Then Sitcom would enforce the law. Someone
who'd caught greed was a fucking liability. You could twist it into
betrayal. That old child song meme popped into Sitcom's head: "Rudies
can't trust rudies with the lust. Been a comrade to you, it's true, but
now its ashes to ashes and dust to dust."

But, for now, Sitcom depended on Jar.

Sitcom came to the reOrb shop. Jar was up here somewhere, spread
out with the rest of the crew, ready to cause a diversion if something
went wrong. Start a riot if they had to. It was easy enough. You just
took down the calming muzak and started screaming 'sale' and 'fire.'
But that was strictly last resort. Sitcom glanced around and walked
into the store. One clerk, no customers. Perfect.

Hoped it stayed that way; was ready if it didn't.

He plucked something off a shelf and walked towards the cashier
to pay. Some stupid teenie album. The clerk looked at Sitcom with
a raised eyebrow.

"For my daughter," Sitcom said and shrugged.

"You know, I have something here that she might like better. Something, actually, kinda good."

Sitcom ran his tongue over the back of his teeth. *This green knob
trying to tell me about music now? About teenie pop of all things? Who cared
what a kid listened to? Dumb fucker thinks he's current with that lame shag
cut. Guy's just a Different Son. As in bousgie party conversation gambit
#16—'Well Janet, our boy Bob, he sure is different. He's a real original that
one.' Fuck him. Gotta stay in character though. Don't want to tip off.*

"This will be fine." Sitcom extracted a card from his wallet with
gloved hands and passed it to the man. The shag took it. Sitcom waited.
The card was brushed with enough roof to knock out a barbiturate
addicted cow. Should absorb right through the fingers. That's why
Sitcom wore two pairs of surgical gloves beneath the bousgie styled
ones. Just in case.

The clerk brushed the card through the machine and paused.
Swayed. His eyes rolled back in his slacken face and he fell straight
down. Knocked his chin off the counter. Bit of blood but he'd be all
right. Maybe a couple cracked teeth. Sitcom hopped the counter and
grabbed the blank reOrbs off the wall. He put stack after stack of
clear balls into his black attaché case.

He lugged the bag onto the counter and demagnetized the product. Didn't need alarms going off. Bent down and took the card away from the guy. Stuck a pin in his hand. They'd think he'd been injected. Maybe by himself. And that knock on the chin was good too. Might make security think he'd been punched out. Probably by an irate customer. Someone who didn't like the Different Son attitude. They'd relate to that and might not even check the cameras. That is, if they were even real and not just those cheesy props.

Sitcom kicked the guy in the ribs.

Just for being such a knob.

"You'll feel that in the morning." Sitcom grabbed the bag and walked out of the store. He matched his pace to the shuffling crowd. His arm ached. These reOrbs were heavy but the denser the better, and TeeVee demanded the best. No one looked at him askew.

He got to the elevator, hit the red button and a few numbers. He waited. It arrived and he stepped inside. *Mind the closing doors.* This was the worst time. You never wanted to be caught this close to escape. And being alone and trapped like this? They could just stop the transport, pump in gas and collect him at their leisure. He was running on faith right now, faith that he hadn't been caught. Sometimes you didn't know until you woke up with a chip in your head. That was a cheap way to go out.

The floors passed slow, numbers changing on the read out, the news playing on a small screen. For all Sitcom knew, the red level he was getting to was three feet away. Might be up, might be sideways. The MTO kept the maps wrapped up to prevent crime.

"Wonder how that's working out," Sitcom muttered.

If they paused the elevator he'd hit the emergency button. When the technicians saw that they might override the stop order and let him down. He smiled. You could always rely on incompetence. Didn't matter how many techs you threw at them, bureaucrats didn't communicate. And when they did they just got more confused and had meetings to try to figure out what they were saying.

The doors slid open.

He stepped into the dim lights and crowded shops of his red level. Home-free, he thought. He needed no map down here. This was his territory.

⁕⁕⁕

"Here's the man of the hour." Farticus stood up, managing to make the gesture look sarcastic.

Budgie tapped Farticus's knuckles. They both sat down. Budgie looked at the animated map on the wall.

The Vidicon territory was highlighted bright green. There were a couple of extra blocks now. Blocks that, just last week, had been colored orange to signify war.

So that's why Sputnik's dead, Budgie thought. *So we can have some more green on a fucking map.* He clenched his fist, wanting to shove someone's head through the screen. Maybe his own. He couldn't be sure. "Where's Sitcom?"

"He's got business. I'm filling in."

"Great."

"Try not to look so chuffed."

"I need a new partner."

"Yeah. I heard. Condolences."

"Accepted."

"We got confirmation on Wolfe." Farticus pulled a long thin knife with an ivory handle from his pocket. An antique. He tapped it on his desk. "This was his. You should have taken from his body but you were, what? Preoccupied?"

"Something like that."

"Sitcom thought you should have first bid on it."

Budgie stared at it. "Is that the one that..."

"Sent Sputnik northward? It's the same."

Budgie picked it up and turned it over in his hands. Too small and cheap to take a life. He pushed it back to Farticus, not wanting anything to do with it. But his hand paused. That'd look bad. This was his trophy and, when he thought about it, just about the only thing he had to remember Sputnik by.

"It's a girl blade," said Farticus. "Ornate. But the old ones are like that."

"What you asking?"

"A globe and it's yours, otherwise it hits the open market."

"Aight." Budgie paid and stuck the knife to his belt. He'd have to find a better place for it later.

"Against my better judgment, I've also been told to give you this." Farticus opened a drawer, fumbling around, metal clattering. He pulled out a small black star and passed it to Budgie.

"Shit," Budgie said. There was a gold '100' in the star's center, signifying his worth. "My first medal."

"Yeah," Farticus said. "Killing Wolfe—Wolfe on Robo no less—drove up your value."

"Drove it up a lot."

"Too much if you ask me but no one did. Anyway, Sitcom is very big on controlling the parties these days." He shrugged. "You're a century fucker now. In old days, they would have called you a centurion."

"Great." This bought Budgie a bit of safety. It meant that he wouldn't be killed for anything less than 100.01 globals. Life was cheap but his just got a bit more expensive. "How much are betas going for these days?"

"They keep it metric. Lowest beta is 500, highest is 999. Lowest alpha is 1000 and after that no one counts except for other alphas. If they even bother. Who knows?"

"Ain't there supposed to be a ceremony or something?" Budgie pinned the medal to his chest.

"Yeah but like I said, Sitcom got business so you just gonna have to make do with that."

"It gon make any diff in my life?"

"Other than looking pretty?" Farticus ran his tongue over his top lip.

"Yeah, other than that," Budgie said. Farticus went gay when it was the fashion and didn't get the memo when the fad was over. He played it to his sexism. Always said women were just dirty bags of disease. One time he had said to Budgie: 'Their pussies fart. Did ya know that? If I'm gonna fuck something that farts it's gonna be an ass. A nice ass too, not those fat woman things.' Then he had leered just like right now. He'd told that story so many times and the one about how in the ancient world Spartans became warriors by having sex with men, that he'd been given the nickname Farticus. His real one was Trevor or something. Thing was, most of his history was wrong and no one had ever even heard of Farticus actually having sex with a man. So he was a poser to boot.

"Pause," Budgie said. "Stay on the point."

"Well, other than looking prettier, everything is the same. Same duties, slightly bigger cut. Not enough to notice. You wanna meet your new partner?"

"Don suppose I could put that off? Just to, you know, take a rest, get my head together."

"What?"

"Just, I dunno."

"Not a chance," Farticus said. "You know how it is. New area. Keep a high profile. Make sure everyone knows who they're dealing with. Otherwise you just get a bunch of random crime and shit. Maybe another gang creeps in." He scrutinized Budgie. "What'd you need to get your head together for anyway? Were you and Sputnik *close?*"

Budgie didn't like how Farticus accented 'close.' Like it meant something low and dirty. Pretty odd that this guy who went around posing as gay suddenly got strange when he thought other people might be. Maybe he thought they were biting his style. Budgie couldn't explain himself to this mental. Didn't even want to. What was the point? Budgie stroked that ivory hilt. "Who am I working with?" he asked.

"A prospect," Farticus said. "Wants to be everywhere and down for everything. But I should warn you, he's a stickler. Complete rulebook freak, you know."

"Great." Some rude boys were like that. They had a fetish for the rules, for what they thought being rude was all about. They called it hardcore. If you bent the rules you were soft, if you broke them you were just some poser fuck, surfing their scene and they'd get ya. Laugh while they did it too. Budgie hated those guys. The rulebook was important but it was just a book. At the end of the day, staying alive meant more than a bunch of text. "Not a fucking fanatic is he?"

"Is that a problem?"

"Might be."

"Then you have a problem. He's your new partner. On Sitcom's direct order."

Farticus relaxed into his chair and tapped the table a couple of times. Looked ready to say something. Budgie's back went up. If this guy even mentioned Sputnik's name again they'd have armshouse. But Farticus seemed to realize that. He looked away and said: "His name is Griff."

<hr />

"So what was it like killing Wolfe?" Griff asked. "Super wet?"

Ignoring the question, Budgie accepted the card from the barkeep and swiped it beneath his tunic's collar. The globals were uploaded into the Vidicon account and distributed into the commonwealth.

Griff growled behind him. The guy ached for action. Protection tax collection obviously bored him. Like most things, it went well when it went routine. Budgie passed the card back to the bartender and ordered a couple of drinks.

He looked at Griff. "You fucking stupid?"

"What?" Griff stood with his arms crossed and his chin jutting out. Scars marked his vicious pale face. The old cigarette burn over his left eye made Budgie think Griff had the misfortune of knowing his dad.

"You heard me."

"Guess I did. You called me fucking stupid."

"I asked." Budgie collected the drinks and grabbed a table. Griff slumped into a chair across from him. Budgie crushed a couple of pills and dropped them into his. They fizzed and he swigged.

"I'm not stupid."

"Then don act like it. Don ask shit like that in public houses about the old boss in new territory."

"What? Why? War is over."

"You just don't."

"That ain't a rule."

"It's fuckin' manners."

"Don't give a fuck bout those." Griff fingered his glass. "So?"

"So what?"

"So what was it like killing Wolfe?"

Budgie couldn't be honest with this little shit. The guy would just parrot a bunch of platitudes about how Sputnik died for the gang and he should be proud and blah blah blah. A lot of the prospects were like this.

Shit, Budgie had been like that. Hungry, wanting to kill, to climb the ladder and make beta. After a while you just gave up on that. Better to keep your life quiet. But try explaining that to a hormone crazed fourteen year old with a drug lit brain and a second-hand tunic.

"You do what you have to do," Budgie said.

Griff's eyes registered disappointment then frustration. There was an animal quality there. Not stupidity exactly but a sort of obstinacy. He had the rulebook. He didn't need to think.

Budgie finished his drink and gestured for another. "You want details?"

"Yeah. How'd that fuck look? You kill him slow?"

The bartender arrived, put a bottle down and walked off. He didn't want trouble. Just like Budgie.

"You ever kill anyone, Griff?"

"Not yet. But I am primed and ready to go. Believe that."

"Then just do both of us a favor and shut the fuck up."

The prospect met Budgie's eyes and blinked before looking down at the table. That was enough.

Budgie swirled his drink and swigged. He didn't care if he was this guy's idea of a good Vidicon. Budgie had gone over the murder in his head again and again, trying to see what he could have done diff to save Sputnik. He didn't want to sit here and discuss it with someone who'd just revel in the gore, imaging himself doing it and seeing himself as some sort of hero. Fuck that. Budgie wasn't in the mood. He never would be.

This prick just made Budgie miss Sputnik even more. If he was here they'd be joking with the barkeep and having fun, not staring each other down. He wished he'd been partnered up with Harmony and wondered if he could ask. Probably—no, definitely—not. "Griff." He had another drink. "How'd you get that handle?"

"It's a long story..."

"Then fuck it." He stood up. "We've got about twenty more places to collect from before we're done."

"Would you look at this?" Griff dropped his sleeves and elbowed Budgie in the ribs. "Toppy boy right there."

A young man shuffled down the side of the corridor with a pack slung over his shoulder. His head hung, he peeked up at the world from beneath a furrowed brow.

"Pull your sleeves up," Budgie said.

"What?"

"You heard me."

"Yeah okay." Griff popped his hands back out. "Gonna bare-knuckle him?"

Budgie said nothing. He willed the floater to turn down some other street but he just kept walking towards them. "You *know* he floats?"

"Yeah," said Griff. "That was Wiles. He was with the posse that jumped me in." Griff spat. "Look at him now."

Budgie checked the time. "We got a lot of places to get to."

"Won't take but a minute," Griff said. He looked down, found a loose chunk of cement. "Watch this."

He wound up and threw it on a straight line into the floater's chest. Wiles yelped and jumped. Head up now, he looked around. Spotted Budgie and Griff. Rubbing his chest, he stepped back.

"Hey Wiles," shouted Griff. "Wasabi?"

Shit, thought Budgie. He kept pace with Griff who strode down the corridor. Budgie knew what came next and wanted no part of it. By the rules, they should jump this guy. He'd left the gang to work on the greens. That sort of shit had to be punished. There was only one way out of Vidicons. The same route Sputnik took.

"Nice fucking costume." Griff stroked the guy's shirt. "Say, what you need bousgie clothes like this for anyway? Haven't seen you around? Where you been?"

"I've been..." The guy looked at Budgie.

"Been what?" Griff leaned in and sniffed. "Now that's fuckin' funny. Ain't that funny, Budgie?"

"What's that?" Budgie asked.

"He don't smell like nothin' but soap." Griff waved a hand in front of his face. "And not much of that."

"I don feel much like laughin'," Budgie said. The floater refused to look him in the eye. Budgie wondered how brave the guy had been when he stunk Vidicon. Bet he never looked away then. "You floatin'?"

"I, uh..."

He wanted to shake Wiles. The guy was older than Budgie and Griff. Bit bigger too. There was no reason he couldn't put up a decent fight.

"Why the fuck you so scared?" Budgie asked.

The guy stood there and cowered.

"Those tears?" Griff shoved the floater into the wall. "You crying?"

Budgie felt sick.

"Just leave me alone," the floater said. "I don't want trouble."

Griff laughed. The prospect wanted to use his newfound power. Budgie remembered feeling like that. That burst of adrenaline, knowing you could do almost everything and get away with it because you had back up. You put on the uniform and you weren't just one man but an army.

And if Griff was just one man, would he be so brave? Or would he be cowering and crying against this wall too?

"Ease up." Budgie put his hand on Griff's shoulder. The prospect stared at him. "Let's think bout this."

"Think?" Griff said.

"Yeah." Budgie wondered why he paused Griff. They were supposed to beat this floater. To make his life long and hard. Maybe even kill him. Set an example. But Budgie had seen enough blood. "Think."

"What the fuck is there to think about?"

Sputnik. If he'd left the Vidicons, he might still be alive. Instead he gave his life to the gang and got what from it? Nothing. Budgie was going to give the same and get the same. They all were.

Even Griff. Though he was too young or too stupid to see it and, even if he did, would just say he'd be proud to die for the gang. Maybe he would be. But that's easy to say before you spent years living for it.

Prospect probably thought he was going to make beta then alpha. Really, he was gonna wind up chipped and stuck down here. Then, cut out of good schemes and strung out on hard drugs, he'd get killed. Probably by Vidicons. Young ones. Just like him. And for what?

So they could stroll the halls, beating up pathetic assholes like this? Beating up guys doing what anyone with any sense wanted to do? Get out.

Budgie bit down on his brain.

He looked long and hard at that floater.

"All I'm thinkin' bout," Griff said and yanked a knife off his belt. "Is getting' wet. Right here. Right now."

"Put that vorpal fucking blade away," Budgie said.

"What?"

"You heard me, prospect." Budgie had rank but Griff had the history, the rulebook and the traditions. Powerful allies. "He done us no wrong."

"What the fuck?" Griff stomped his foot like a frustrated child. "You outta your mind?"

"Maybe," said Budgie.

"Tell you what I think," Griff said, still holding his blade. "I think you gone as soft as this fuck right here."

"That so?"

"I think I gonna chop him up and you ain't gon do shit about it." Griff turned his back on the floater and grinned at Budgie. "I think, fuck you."

Budgie hit Griff with a left jab. A thick crunch. Broke his nose. The blade dropped from Griff's hand. Griff covered his face and stumbled into the floater.

"You wet now," Budgie said.

Looking at the blood squeezing from between Griff's fingers, he thought of Sputnik. He and Griff had the same sorta eyes. Griff broke the spell by speaking, his voice loud and pain stricken. "What'd ya do that for?"

"You don tell me 'fuck you' you little bitch." Budgie kicked Griff's shin then knocked his feet out. He rested his boot on Griff's throat. Looked at the floater.

"Thank you," the guy said.

"You just better fuckin' run," said Budgie. He wondered if he should do the same. The guy stared at him and Budgie touched his knife. Raised his eyebrows.

The floater bolted.

Budgie looked down at Griff and thought of excuses. He might need them. "You gon behave?"

Griff jerked his head.

Budgie stepped off his throat and bent over to offer his hand.

Griff scoffed and stood on his own.

"You need to learn some fuckin' discipline," Budgie said. "Don ever tell a superior 'fuck you.'"

Griff just glared.

WE'VE COMBINED MAN'S TWO GREATEST INVENTIONS, FIRE AND THE WHEEL. RING OF FIRE SPICY FOODS.

Method #6 for Bailey's Irish Cream Uber Enjoyment. Spray it on your bitch's face. It's bukkake in a bottle. **Let Your Senses Guide You.**

conversation is sexy; conversation in spitfire procession is sexier convo brand Speed.
Is sexiest.

Consumer Reports Guide to Consumer Reports. What ones can you trust?

EDGE is sleeping on SITCOM. SITCOM throws the best bashes. EDGE needs to wake up.

WHITE NOISE. Increases Productivity. WHITE NOISE. Discourages Eavesdropping. **WHITE NOISE**. Calms you down and keeps you sane. **WHITE NOISE GENERATORS** from **MUZAK-TECH**. Now on Sale.

FEATURE PROGRAM (4)

"Yes Dear," Vivian said into her telephone. "It *has* been a lot of overtime lately." She waited patiently for her husband to finish talking. He sounded angry but he always sounded like that when he got some wine into him. She looked around the empty, closed up shop. Burt waited outside, shifting his weight from one foot to another. "Friday is our busy night though." Paused. "Yes dear. See you later." Clicked off.

She stuck the gizmo in her pocket and set the store alarm. Used her card to open the door and looked back once before stepping outside. Rows upon rows of shoes. All built for women like her. She closed the door and metal shutters slammed down. Gel oozed from their surface. If someone was dumb enough to touch them they'd be stuck there until first bright light. Burt smiled like a cat.

"Gonna get some woot tonight." Burt lit a cigarette. After eight, smoking was tolerated outside the official sections. After the ten o'clock teen curfew it was allowed.

"Can I get one of those?" Vivian had quit and started again more times than she could remember.

"Sure." Burt was in a rush. His dick a dowsing rod, pulling him forward.

Vivian lit the smoke and coughed. *You'd think something so addictive would taste better.* "Why do I bother with this crap?"

"Because Olin hates it."

"Oh shut up, you."

Burt just smiled.

They walked to the elevator in giggling silence. Vivian glanced around, ready to abort the whole thing if a neighbor saw her. But she didn't recognize anyone and felt reasonably certain none in the crowd knew her.

They stepped into the elevator and Burt hit the big red button. At least there were no cameras in these things. The Citizen's Privacy Council had fought to have them removed. Vivian suspected that they were men and women like her. People who resented their images being captured when they could be used for blackmail. It'd happened before.

The door swished open and Burt slapped her on the back. Another cough erupted from her protesting lungs. Vivian dropped her cigarette and stepped into the red level.

It was always dim down here. The mall didn't waste hydro on the low rent sections. Although the illumination was constantly tuned to 2:13 AM, private fuel-cells fired a mishmash of garish bordello and bar windows. Those screens and signs made the place look like a perverted cartoon. A group of rude boys stood drinking in a store's entrance and communicating in sign language. Vivian avoided their challenging eyes and ignored their catcalls.

Jostling through the crowded streets, Vivian wished she'd brought earplugs. Music from the bars competed in an ever-escalating volume war. Sentimental sounds mixed with Irish jigs and African drums. Discordant noise battled with electric thumping and sleazy algorithms. If you closed your eyes, that mishmash induced hallucinations. She sighed. Just another Friday night.

"What are you in the mood for?" Burt shouted in her ear.

"I heard that Jane has a new franchise. Called John's. You wanna go there, have a drink and see who's on the menu?"

"Yeah!"

They walked slowly, their passage obstructed by natives, exiles and tourists like them. What did they call them? Slummers? Something like that. A cocaine stench polluted the air and gave Vivian a lift. Burt paused and pulled out his gizmo. "Let me double check the map."

He tapped away. The mall maps were notoriously unreliable. Within a few blocks, they were always right but there were so many maps that, at long distances you got a general idea at best. The MTO designed it like that, saying that complete maps of the mall posed a security threat. They were probably right. "Got it."

They wove through street after street, into the bowels of the mall, until they saw a huge flashing sign: "JUST OPENED: JOHN'S FUCK PALACE!!!" All red and pink light. Bright enough to drown out the other signs and soak the corridor in a gaudy haze. Like the bulk of Jane's franchises this place was a bedazzled, soundproofed bunker that catered to tourists like Vivian.

They lined up outside, ignoring the street hookers who flashed them, hoping they were too horny to wait, too drunk to see. These whores were low rent, their faces chewed by disease and drugs then covered up with makeup. Vivian masked her revulsion lest one took it personally and made a scene. It had happened before. They were either too old or too ugly to get a job in bordello. Usually both. Couldn't even find employment in one of the fetish places.

All they could hope for was to get some impatient, drunken slob and rob him blind.

You saw those guys wandering around here late at night. Naked and bleeding, weeping about what their wife would say and trying to beg your clothes and elevator tokens so they could go topside again.

Vivian never spared a token or a second glance, afraid their misfortunes were contagious, but she often wondered what happened to them.

A big doorman searched her and Burt then let them in. Told them to behave and leered. Vivian forced a smile. A sudden change from the streets, it was quiet and civilized. The music, exotica. Men and women sat at tables, having drinks and examining the menu. A pretty young boy, no older than fifteen, his body painted with white latex, took them to their seats, smiled sweetly, and walked off to help the next customer. The place was huge and only about half full. Doors rimmed this massive central lounge, leading to private suites and the loud but soundproofed sex parties.

"I'll order." Burt tapped at the table. "Couple of Viagra whiskeys. Shame to come down here and come in twenty seconds, be all spent and go home. I like to last." He smiled at Vivian. "These minnows can fuck your dick right off."

His crudity made Vivian uncomfortable even as it thrilled her. She smiled back.

A saran wrapped boy with big brown eyes brought them their drinks and winked. Burt returned the gesture and had a sip of his whiskey before looking back at Vivian. "So when are you going to lose the old boar anyway?"

Vivian sipped her whiskey. "Can't afford the divorce."

"You can't afford to keep living like this."

"I know." Burt knew she had been dipping into the till and either covering it up with paperwork or framing the employees. If she got caught, if the boys upstairs in the blue levels ever found out, she'd be exiled. Better to get a divorce and have her own money after alimony and support. She knew that but—"It's not that simple."

"You're scared of Olin." Burt laughed. "That's okay. So am I. Is that sort of boring contagious?"

"I'm scared of everything." The truth slipped out before Vivian could censor it. Burt did that to her. His casual crudity put Vivian at ease. She wondered what Burt would think if he knew their whole friendship was based on accidents of the tongue. "Scared of getting fired, scared of coming home, scared of coming down here."

"Everyone feels like that. It's cause we're all cornered." Burt lit another cigarette and offered another to Vivian. "If we could get out of the mall, it'd be different."

"True, that," Vivian said. Right now, she'd just be happy to get out of her marriage.

"Outside's still too polluted and it's not getting any better. Not now that the mall is polluting it too."

"So they got us by the balls."

"You either move up or move down and out," Burt said. "Most people are just like you, Vivian. Me too. Treading water, trying to keep their head above the waves so they don't end up down here." He exhaled a cloud of smoke and had another drink. "And, every so often, we come down to depths and look at the weird sharks and fishies to remind ourselves why we're treading water so damn hard."

"For the good life."

"To avoid the bad one." Burt shook his head. "At the end of a long day it's still better to be selling shoes than it is to be chipped."

"You're right, of course," Vivian said. "I know that but—"

"But nothing! Everyone has issues. Get a tissue."

"But don't they *seem* happier down here? I mean, they have less than us, but they're happier than we are."

"Honey, that's crazy talk," Burt said. "You need to get a divorce, stop stealing from the till and do what you want. While you still can. Before you get caught. Cause sooner or later you will." He reached across the table and squeezed her hand. "I don't want to be coming down here to visit my girl."

Like you would, thought Vivian. She pulled out of his grip and tapped at the table menu. Leafed through the pictures and profiles of available boys. She needed one who didn't mind taking a few knocks. She sure felt like parceling them out.

• • •

"Budgie, you asshole!"

Here it comes, thought Budgie. He leaned against the club wall with his eyes closed. Music vibrated his chest and set his little medal bouncing. The toaster played the same old songs with the same new twists. Budgie crawled out of the alley-mouth where he'd been sleeping to come to this party. And for what? To get called an asshole.

Fine. Let it all come down to this. Better sooner than later. He'd divided the route, giving half to Griff, just to avoid seeing him. Working alone was dangerous, but maybe not as dangerous as working with a partner who hated you. Budgie's excuse—Griff needed discipline for telling him to fuck off—had worked pretty well with everyone— no one liked a prospect—but Griff knew different. Sooner or later, everyone would.

Sooner or later.

Shit if Budgie was going to go home and deal with his Mom. Better to crash in the streets and grab what shut-eye he could. Not much. When he wasn't having nightmares, he slept with one eye open. Nights, he went from one party to another. Took drugs then more drugs. Tried to stay awake a bit longer. Just got paler and sicker. Frayed.

Just let it end.

Too tired to go on.

He just wanted out. Just wanted to be over.

Sooner. Better than later.

He pictured himself out of the Vidicons, living a nice, quiet life. Fantasy. The dangerous kind. The kind you can't afford. What was wrong with him? He'd always been this way but the more alone he was, the wronger he got. Sputnik had given him a reason to stay. But he was gone. What did Budgie have? Fuck all.

"Budgie! You asshole!"

He waited for the knife or the bludgeon. Waited for whatever it would be. Instead of a fresh wound, he felt fingers on his face. He opened his eyes. A ridiculous wig bounced around below him.

"Budgie! You asshole!" Harmony stood on tiptoes to yell in his ear. "Why aren't you dancing?"

"Not in a dancing mood."

She leaned back in. "I heard about you smacking Griff."

He shrugged.

"Not exactly cricket old boy." She laughed. And laughed. She bent over and held her stomach. Still laughing. She was off her head. What was she was on? He smiled. She straightened and got back in his ear. "Bet I know why you did that too, I bet I do!"

Budgie stopped smiling. He shrugged and tried to look casual. She made him nervous. He was terrified that he'd start stuttering again. And she'd laugh. But at him. "What? You've met Griff?"

"I have!"

"So ya know, someone shoulda done it sooner," Budgie yelled, relieved that the words came out right. "Little shit needs to learn some manners. Told me to fuck myself."

"Fuck yourself!" She crossed her arms. Mock challenge. When he did nothing she shouted into his ear: "You're a fucking liar. I'm not stupid."

"What'd you mean?"

She looked at him for a minute then wrapped her arms around him, hugging him close. Budgie stiffened. Her affection wiggled his guts. He tried to pull away and she didn't let go. After a moment, he hugged back. Hard. Rested his face on her wig.

"I also hear you're out in corridors."

"You hear a lot."

"When I want to," she shouted into his ear. "Tonight you're gonna crash at my place—Okay!"

Budgie looked up and saw a couple of rude boys staring. Always staring. Everyone always looking at everything and never seeing nothing. Budgie gave them the finger. They glanced at each other and smiled. Returned the gesture.

"Thanks but—"

"But what?"

"I can't pay ya anything."

"You can pay." She grabbed his crotch. When he smiled, she frowned. "What's so funny?"

"Just thinking," he yelled into the top of her head. "That wouldn't be completely awful."

"Yeah. Won't last long either."

▆▊▎▊▋▊▊▌▏▏ ▍▊▌▊▊▏▋▊ ▊▋▏▊▊ ▊▋▊▊▊ ▏▊▊▏▏ ▊▊▋ ▏▊▏ ▊▋▏▏ ▊▊▏ ▋▏ ▏ ▊▊

Sitcom slipped another clear reOrb into the machine. This was lame music but TeeVee's mix made it sound good. Definitely worth the trouble. The guy's brain might exist in electric limbo but he knew how to bounce slummers around like rubber balls in a shaking box. Sitcom checked TeeVee's list, what drug should go with what song, to enhance the visuals. He pulled a lever and spouts of fog poured gaseous MDMA from the ceiling. Quick acting shit, almost instant, and it faded just as fast. Everyone fell in love.

Slug stood at Sitcom's right hand, nodding his head and keeping his muscular arms crossed. He was the deterrent to rowdy slummers, but even he seemed to be enjoying himself. The music clacked and throbbed. Fast chattering then slow drones. Screaming, chants, television samples and string sections of old national anthems, rousing the crowd.

Slummers always started the party playing the wall, looking around, drink in hand, pills ingested. Then the beats got at them. Slow at first. A few people took the floor, writhing, punching, twisting and jumping. Contagious. Click-boom, horny loas flung their bodies round the room.

Faster, louder, more gas, wetter, more current, until they hyperlinked to NOW. Time broke down. Flesh bent in still space. That clicking sound was everywhere. This rhythm, that repeating loop. Tribes formed, dissolved, formed again, a body collective made of sweaty human cells. Interchangeable people in one dancing monster. Sweating shadows of a meme riot.

Sitcom snorted a fat bump of sobriety. Couldn't afford to feel the gas. That'd wreck the party. He'd get confused and the music would stutter. Song switched. He yanked another lever down. LSD in the air. Sitars shrieked like strange insects. Feedback like a space blastoff.

He was the calm center of the sweltering chaos. This was his element. He even felt some empathy for these green slummers. Bit of jealousy too. He wished he was still like them, could get all whacked out on music and just go crazy. But he'd been riding the current so long he'd tripped into the future, listening to music that no one knew, in private

mental parties. Him and TeeVee were birds of a feather that way. Thing
was, Sitcom was next week and TeeVee was next century.

And Slug. Well, Slug was a mountain. He was here today and he
would be here tomorrow. Just a big immobile mass of hard muscle
and face cracking knuckles. Look at him over there. Music left him
untouched. Didn't even get visuals off it. That bobbing head was just
a tree shook by wind.

"Hey Slug," Sitcom signed. Too loud to talk. "Having fun?"

"Fucking loud."

Sitcom laughed. That's Slug for you. Cranked up on acid and all
he could think was that it was loud. "Party will go all night," Sitcom
said. They had to keep it up until the slummers went broke or back
upstairs and tonight'd go until the greens grew light. "How about
you grab us some action? Long night like this, I need company."

"Sure."

"That one." He pointed.

A pretty young thing with a shaved head and bright, plaid pigtails
growing just above her ears.

"Fake birds?" Slug said,

"Yeah." The birds hovered above her shoulders. One was all mangled,
bashed by a swinging lock of hair. "Pick her up for me."

"Okay."

Slug wandered into the crowd. Slummers parted in front of him
like meat under a knife. They might be high, stupid and crazy but they
weren't suicidal. Slug towered over the lot, his face a concrete mask.

He shouted into the girl's ear. She looked at the stage. Sitcom waved
and gestured for her to come up. She smiled and followed in the quickly
closing wake behind Slug. She looked smug, and so she should. After
all, she'd been chosen.

She climbed onto onto the stage and rested her hand on Sitcom's
back. He passed her a headset so they could hear each other.

"Hi," she said.

"Hey, what's your name?"

"Lexus."

"I'm Sitcom." Shook hands.

"I know. Seen you before. Great party. Music is so good." She wriggled.
Some sort of semi-dance thing. Maybe erotic, hard to say. Her blue
irises were just tiny rims around massive black pupils. "I love this
stuff. Try to come to all your parties."

Doubt that, Sitcom thought and smiled. She prolly figured he felt
the same way about this music—after all he was playing it—but to him
this was all two weeks and ten meters ago. It called up some pleasant
memories but that was about it. Now if you went back fifteen years,

back to when he was twelve, he still loved that music. He'd lost his virginity to it in a bordello that served people under thirteen.

Sitcom ignored the urge to lecture her. It'd just make him look geek. "What're you doing after the show?"

"Going home," she said. "But I could put it off for a few hours." She shrugged. "I'll be in trouble anyway."

"Home?" Trouble? Sitcom disliked the sound of that. A couple of hours, he thought. What is this? A fucking romance? She suddenly looked very young. He felt very old. "Where's home at?"

She paused for a heartbeat but it was enough for Sitcom to hear 'with my parents.' Not that he was adverse to slummers in theory (they paid his bills better than any scheme) and not that he was even adverse to parents, (someone had to raise ya) but Sitcom was adverse to risky gambles. He'd known she was green but this was too green.

If anything was bad news, it was a rookie. With parents. Who thought she'd get a couple of hours of his time. No doubt about it, he was getting old.

"I live around," she said. "Upstairs, ya know. It's so limp up there."

Slug smiled like a big happy dog. Was he funny or just stupid? Probably neither. Just didn't care. Slug'd fuck her without a second thought of notch artists hired by angry parents.

Sitcom shook his head. *I don't need this*, he thought. *I don't even want it.*

PRODUCT PLACEMENT

Let the Honeymoon begin. Chunky chicken and tuna. Newlyweds.

Just the idea of it intrigued her. "This is going to be fun," she whispered to herself. REVLON lipglide and lipglide sheer. Full color and shine, Sheer color and shine, One quick glide. Twist. Glide. Smile. **REVLON**

Millions of pictures are being taken. Is your smile ready? Or are you ugly? Crest, 60 watt tooth implants.

Ever wonder what it feels like to be with someone else? Someone bigger? Buy it for your husband and find out. Braun Penis Sheath.

SET YOURSELF FREE Sierra Mist Free Diet Lemon-Lime. **SUGAR FREE. CALORIE FREE. CARB FREE. CAFFEINE FREE. FLAVOR FULL. DRINK FREELY** (trademarked)

Swanson Broth. Replace water with flavor.

It's my skin not my 2 carats that's SPARKLING tonight. (Moving picture of naked, large breasted woman straddling and humping bongo.) Caress. Skin to be seen in.

HIP: The Updated History. Hip is not just a marketing tool but a way of life. Demonstrates the surprising links between Edge reOrbs and Edge Movies. The rules you need to follow and things you need to buy to be hip. But not too hip J

EDGE SITCOM loved it LAST NIGHT!!!

Vivian looked at the clock.

I've done it now.

It was 6:30 am. She'd crossed the threshold. Her lies had now lost the support of reality. When she went home there was nothing she could say to Olin. No explanation would work. He'd know.

The boy crawled out of bed, a handcuff dangling from his wrist. Makeup smeared just the way Vivian liked it and blood trickling out of his nose.

"The first day of the rest of my life," Vivian said.

"What's that supposed to mean?" the boy asked over his shoulder.

"Nothing. Just when I get home my husband will know. I'm looking square at a divorce."

"Your husband?" The boy looked down at the handcuffs. Touched his fat lip. "Is that who I was supposed to be?"

"Nice hutch," Budgie said. Harmony's apartment was bigger than what he and his Mom could afford. Didn't know how she paid for it but that was her business. He sat on the cot and lit a cigarette.

All of her coaxing had not convinced him to take anything stronger than some synapacide but she'd forced him to dance anyway. For hours. His legs ached and his head weighed heavy on a twinging neck. Must be tired. The light drugs had worn off. Now all he wanted to do was sleep.

"It works." Harmony's pupils dilated within shifty eyes, still a bit keyed up. She locked the door and flipped on the television. The laughter channel. Old shows, dramas mined out of the info dump and remixed with laugh tracks. Budgie had heard that you could buy a joy buzzer on the greens that stimulated your humor centers while you watched it. That old black and white, Psycho, was playing.

"No!" Norman's Mom said. "I will not hide in the fruit cellar. Ha! You think I'm fruity, huh?" Hysterical laughter from the audience. "This is my room and no one will drag me out of it—least of all my big bold son!" Fake audience coos taken over by a loud *Awwwwww*.

"Now, come now, Mother," Norman Bates said. "He came after the girl and now someone will come after him." Cheers, hoots and hollers.

"Love this one," Harmony said and sat beside Budgie. The couch creaked beneath her weight.

"I used to," Budgie said. "But I saw it one night at a party Sitcom had. He had this version without the live audience—don't know where he got it. It's completely diff. Like fucked up. Still funny but fucked. Just the music in that shower part"—shook his head— "Messed up. Hitchcock must have been on some crazy shit."

"You know Sitcom?" Harmony asked.

Her fawning voice irritated Budgie. A defensive dispo even though no one was attacking him. The guy was about as close as this area got to a celebrity but you shouldn't act like you cared. Then again, he'd dropped the name. On some level he must have known what he was doing.

"To say hi to," he said, not wanting to think about the rest of it. "Used to throw more movie bashes. Got into straight music bout, don't know, two years ago. When he went beta." He puffed on his smoke, dipped it in the ashtray that sat at his feet. "Wrecked this movie for me though. This version, leastly."

Harmony pulled off her wig and leaned against him. Didn't grab for his nuts or anything. Budgie sniffed her scalp, liking her smell. He wrapped an arm around her. It was funny. He didn't want to grab her tits or flop over onto her. Just hold her close for a bit, all intimate, like she was a teddy bear, except without those cunt boxes they put in them now. Budgie tilted his head and rested his cheek on her fontanel.

"I know why you hit Griff," she said.

"Newbie told me to fuck myself."

"Save the shit for someone who might believe it." She unwrapped her body from him and Budgie felt amputated. From what, he couldn't say, just knew he wanted to bring her close again. But he wouldn't do that, wouldn't force her. "You know I have an older brother?"

"No. Do I know him?"

"No one does. Not even me. He turned floater bout five years backwards. Was a rude boy before that; vintage Vidicons back when they were Dog Gobins and ran this whole area. Pre-Schism. I was just, like eleven or so when he turned toppy. But I remember." She smiled. "He got a look like you have. This sorta heavy, despond dispo. Saw it on you the other day. He hit his partner over the same thing. Right before he left. That's the way it always happens." She stared at Budgie. "Most of these guys are so full of shit that they don't recognize a line of shit when they see it. But you're not fooling me."

Budgie's face heated. What was this? A trap? "I'd never turn toppy," he said. "This don float."

"I think he doth protest too much." She smiled. "Didn't they teach you that poem in school? 'He who fucks nuns will later join the church?'"

"Taught everyone that," Budgie said, refusing to look at her. Felt like he had a bunch of words in him that he couldn't get out, words sparking together like live wires. His tongue wanted to get crazy and disobedient. He didn't trust it.

"You never thought about it?"

"Bout what?" Budgie said slow, remembering his exercises, trying to relax. "The po-po-poem?"

"Bout what it means. About Rudie Goes Topside." Her voice stiffened. "I want to do that. Just don't have the nerve."

"You wanna go topside?"

"You wanna stay down here?"

"Does anyone?" Budgie loosened with relief. He could talk to her. If this was a set up he'd just tell them that he'd say anything to get laid. Call them prim if they doubted. "It's been playing on me, yeah, be lying if I said it didn't."

"Cause of Sputnik?"

"I don know. Think so." Budgie put out his smoke and lit another. He suddenly felt some confidence in his voice. "Like this—all these guys, Snort Donkey, whoever—they don't give a half global fuck about me. I'm a tool. They need someone who can do this, that or the other, they get me and I do whatev. Perform my function. I know cause that's how I see them. Don't give a beggar's shit bout their lives. If I have a scheme, I just get who can help me and get my product. Don give a fuck bout them and they don give a fuck bout me. We just trade."

"The situation."

"Sputnik and me were diff. We were friends. Truth. We had each other's backs. Bring on the blades, who cared? If I could've taken that knife for him I would've. But he took it for me instead and…"

She nodded.

Maybe she was just being polite, but it felt good to get all this off his chest. "Now he's gone, I don have nothing. No one. My mom don care, all she cares bout is what the other whores think and they're not gonna think much of me after…"

"After what?"

"I got into a fight with Sputnik's ma when I told her. She was in my face just screaming and—fu-fu-fuck—I was in a murder dispo. Pure cyanide. My mood as dressed up as Wolfe's love. I was ready to kill her before I realized what I was about."

Harmony stayed quiet but Sam and Norman Bates talked on the television: "I'm not saying you shouldn't be contented here," Sam said. "I'm just doubting that you are. I think if you saw a chance to get out from under, you would unload this place."

Norman responded, indignant and creepy. Always sounded creepy after that Sitcom screening. "This place? This place happens to be

my only world. I grew up in that house up there. I happened to have
a very happy childhood. My mother and I were more than happy."

So strange, Budgie thought, that someone could be trapped with all
that outside around him. Just air and fields and other places. Norman
could go anywhere, do anything. Not like he had a whole mall above
him, crushing down. A commerce bubble in a sick world. What did
that spooky old shit know about being crushed?

"Do you think people will be any different up there?" Harmony asked.

"Doubt it." Budgie shrugged. "Maybe I'll be. Dunno."

░▒█ █�▐▐ ▐am█▐mm ▐▐▐▐ ▐▐▐m▐▐ ▐▐▐▐▐ ▐▐m ▐▐▐ ▐m▐▐ ▐▐▐ m▐▐ ▐▐m

"You're in the shit now," Burt said when Vivian met him in the lounge.
His clothes were rumpled, his eyes bagged. Vivian figured she looked
the same. The place was all but empty. A gaggle of tired prostitutes
sat at the bar drinking but their bedazzled asses and glowing cocks
prompted no leers.

"I am, indeed," Vivian said.

They walked towards the EXIT in silence. The streets were quiet,
the music gone. Storefronts shuttered like sleeping eyes, their lights
extinguished and only the soft, moon glow from the overheads pouring
down. If you were going to get robbed, Vivian thought, this was
the time for it.

But even the rude boys had vanished. Probably in bed or at private
parties grinding into forever. Upstairs the world would be coming
to life. Early morning deliverymen and workers dutifully shuffling
towards work. Down here it was dead time. At least she had the day
off. Could spend it in bed while her husband got lawyered up.

They turned a corner towards an elevator. A few people stood in
front of it and Burt kept walking.

Plaid pigtails.

Vivian stopped. It was too late.

Her daughter stared at her.

░▒█ █amm▐▐ ▐am█▐mm ▐▐▐▐ ▐▐▐m▐▐ ▐▐▐▐▐ ▐▐m ▐▐▐ ▐m▐▐ ▐▐▐ m▐▐ ▐▐m

The girl, what's her name, Lexus, waited by the door.

"I think she's in love," said Slug.

"Shut up." Sitcom looked over his console at Slug who carefully,
very carefully, put reOrbs into their cases. Other than the three of
them and some people laying on the floor—passed out or overdosed—
the club was empty. It was a mess too. Crushed cups and cigarette
butts carpeted the floor. But all that was the next host's problem. This
place was a rental. You cleaned it up before your show, not after. If
you could be bothered.

"You want a smoke or something," Sitcom shouted at the girl. "Before you walk to the elevator?"

"Sure," she said, her face lighting. She bounded towards him.

He handed her half a lit cigarette.

"Good show," she said.

"Not bad." He felt thoughtful, in a calm, quiet sort of dispo. He wanted to get high but it'd take half a day for all that snorted sobriety to wear off. This didn't bother him too much. Truth be told he had been pulling back on the drugs for a couple of months. Getting bored. He supposed he should make some conversation. "So you come down to the reds a lot?"

"Past while, yeah. Every week."

Sitcom sniffed and wiped his nose. "Like it down here?"

"It's fun."

"Yeah?"

"Do you like it?" she asked. "Living down here, I mean."

"Does it matter? Don't have much of a choice." That wasn't really true. He could leave. Wasn't chipped so all he needed was forged documents and he could be working upstairs. But he was a born and bred red native. Wouldn't know what to do with himself up there. "Yeah, I like it fine."

"Isn't it dangerous?"

"Nah," he said and then corrected himself. "Well, yeah, if you're dumb." Or unlucky, he thought. Could get some random shit happen to you. Best not to worry her about that though. He made a lot of money off these slummers and didn't want to spook the clientèle. He looked at Slug. "Ready?"

"Yeah, I'm ready."

Sitcom dropped his cigarette to the floor and ground it beneath his leather boot. "We gotta get going," he said to the girl. "It's like seven, you should be topside by now. So, uh, yeah. It's been a piece."

"I guess." She lit one of her own cigarettes. A long thin thing, looked light as fuck. Like smoking air. "Going to get in shit when I go home."

You probably should, Sitcom thought. *If I had a sister that acted like you, I'd kick her ass. And mine too, come to think of it.* But he didn't have a sister—thank Santa—and his brother was dead or something. Didn't know. The crazy bastard had vanished about eight years ago. Just took off in the night. No one knew where he got to and Sitcom had stopped caring. Prolly run into him one day. The mall was big, bout twenty million people, but it wasn't infinite. Wondered if he'd recognize him.

He walked Lexus to the door. Kicked a shoe out of his path. Someone always lost their shoes. It was like a rule. You could build a wardrobe out of abandoned clothes and some people did just that

—gave them a fresh, eclectic look. Made their poverty seem like a fashion statement.

Sitcom used to keep trophies from every show he did or went to but there got to be too many of them. Now he just kept souvenirs from the best, stuff with actual sentimental value. He wondered if he should get something from Lexus and decided against it. The show had been average.

He glanced over his shoulder at Slug who carried a case full of reOrbs and miscellaneous equipment. "Okay," Sitcom said to Lexus. "You get back to mini-putt and maybe I see you out at the next party."

She stared at him. Like she was waiting for a kiss or something. Sitcom shut the door.

"She was cute," called Slug.

"She was a problem waiting to happen," replied Sitcom. "Girl like that has family. Family like that has money. Money like that can buy a pro to come down here and find whoever upset their daughter and take care of him. I don't fuck outta my class with rooks. Good way to get loved."

He watched Slug fumbling with the equipment. "How you doin' there anyway?" he asked and opened the door.

"Good," Slug grunted.

Sitcom felt bad for him. The bird Slug had picked up flew the coop. They usually did. Slug just looked too big, ugly and mean. Couldn't help it. Just built that way. He decided to get Slug a hooker tonight. It paid to keep the gammas happy and afraid. Slug might not be the brightest bulb but he could be trusted.

That went a long way in Sitcom's estimation.

<hr/>

"Hey, hey," Griff leaned against the wall and leered at the girl with the pigtails standing outside the elevator. He'd been cruising the parties, hoping to catch Budgie sleeping in corridors. The girl ignored him. Griff hated that. Strode right up to her and took her soft by the arm. "I said, hey hey."

She yanked her arm away.

Griff smiled. "Feisty."

The girl looked at him, then glanced over his shoulder. Her face dropped. "Shit."

"What?" Griff said and looked behind him. Two bousgies were coming this way. Looked right shagged out.

"That's my Mom."

Vivian couldn't turn around. She had to bluff. "Lexus!" She strode
to her daughter, trying her best to ignore the thug beside her. "I've
been looking for you all night!"

"Like fuck you have." The rude boy sniffed her like an animal. "You
been fucking."

"This doesn't concern you," Vivian straightened and glanced at
Burt. Sweat soaked his forehead. His huge eyes fixed on the rude boy.
"We'll talk about this upstairs, young lady."

"That true?" Lexus grimaced. "You've been at a whorehouse? With him?"

"We'll talk about this upstairs." Vivian reached out to grab her daughter
by the arm.

The rude boy slapped her hand away. He stepped between them
and fingered the knife on his belt. "Do I not fucking exist?" he asked.
"Am I invisible?"

"Now come on—" Burt said.

The rude boy pulled the knife off his belt. Didn't say anything.
Just stood there.

Burt stepped back, palms up. "I don't want any trouble."

The thug lunged. Burt stumbled back and fell on his ass. Laughing,
the rude boy turned his attention to Vivian. "Wonder what you're
into," he said. "From the look of that bruise on your knuckle I'd say
you like the rough stuff."

Vivian flushed.

"That true, ma'am?" The rude boy stepped forward. "You like the
rough stuff?"

"I don't want any trouble with you," Vivian turned her shoulder
to him and pressed the elevator button. "This isn't your business, it's
between my daughter and I."

"Your daughter, you say? No shit? This lil' Lolita, your daughter?
Red runs in the family."

Vivian looked at Lexus. She wanted to protect her but didn't know
how. "I don't want any trouble."

⣿⣿ ⣿⣿⣿⣿⣿⣿ ⣿⣿⣿⣿⣿⣿ ⣿⣿⣿⣿ ⣿⣿⣿⣿ ⣿⣿⣿⣿ ⣿⣿⣿⣿ ⣿⣿⣿ ⣿⣿⣿ ⣿⣿

"I don't want any trouble," Griff mocked.

The lady flinched. If there was one thing Griff couldn't stand, it
was scared bousgies. Contemptible. Said they didn't want trouble
and that's exactly what they came down here looking for. Bunch of
weasels. They wanted trouble they could control. But they didn't
control him. Far from it. Griff wanted to set some things straight in
this bitch's head. Let her know who was boss. "What you do upstairs
anyway?"

The woman blinked.

"Ah, a manager type." Griff pretended a thoughtful dispo but all
he really felt was poison. "Let me ask you something there, then:
You ever fire anyone?"

"Do you want money? Just let us go."

"I don't want money," Griff said and backed up. "I've got money.
You don't think I've got money?"

"I didn't—"

"Money ain't what I'm after." Griff wrapped his arm around the
girl's trembling shoulders. Let his hand wander down to her breast
and gave it a little squeeze. Fear froze the little bitch. Good. Griff's
other hand traveled lower. Rested on her cunt. She shook. Better.
Griff flicked his tongue at the old lady. He liked the look in her eyes.
Things were getting real crystal there. "Matter of fact, I got money
to spend. How much does she cost anyway? You know, if I want to
smack her round a bit."

The woman was pale silent. The elevator door opened behind them.
After a long moment it closed and left.

Tears wet the woman's eyes. Begging would be next. All that, 'do
what you want to me but leave my daughter alone.' Heard it before.
Like he'd want to do anything to an old woman. Griff figured he was
doing a public service. Be the last time she came down to party here
and the last time her Mom came to bang a whore.

That gave him pause.

He'd been warned about this sort of thing. The betas didn't like
business getting scared off. Not behind some macho crap like this.

Proud of his restraint he shoved the girl forward. He was about
to tell them fuck off back upstairs when that lady's buddy made
a mistake.

IIII III II III II I I IIII III II III III III IIII IIII IIII III III II III II I IIII

Vivian saw Burt take his swing. So did the kid. Skinny and agile, he
dodged the bulk of Burt's shy fist. It grazed his jaw. The rude boy
smiled, blood on his lips, and spat. Very quick, he grabbed the side
of Burt's head and brought the butt of his knife down on his nose.
Exploded it. Burt stumbled to the ground.

Wiping his mouth, the rude boy looked at Vivian and said, "That
was a mistake. You wanna make one too?"

Vivian shook her head, holding Lexus close.

"That's good." He hit the elevator button. Stepped out of the way.
"You two get the fuck out of here."

The doors opened. Keeping herself between the rude boy and Lexus,
Vivian shuffled into the elevator. Her daughter's body felt stiff and

cold. It was like moving a doll. Once inside she looked at Burt, who had come to all fours and stared in at her with wide eyes.

She closed the door.

"Wallet's gone," Sitcom said. A bousgie lay unconscious and bloody next to the elevator. Red stains on the wall where he'd tried to reach the button. "Been mugged. Hard too."

"What're we gonna do with him?" Slug asked.

"Pick him up for starters," said Sitcom.

"I don't like this." Slug threw the groaning bousgie over his shoulder. "Ghoul work."

"Oh, I'm fucking sorry. Is this beneath your dignity, Slug? You gonna put in your monocle and step?"

"No, I just..."

"Look, this isn't straight ghoul work though..." He thought for a moment. Jane had just franchised into Johns and were on the lookout for queens. They'd only pull about ten for him, depending on the market and considering he wasn't chipped yet. Guy like this came with overhead. They had to get a lot of drugs into him. Hire rape breakers. And all that was expensive. Nah, ghouling him wasn't worth it. Not like that at least.

He picked up the cases. Heavy. "We're taking him to TeeVee."

"TeeVee? What'd he want with him?"

"There's some questions I don't want the answer to," Sitcom said. "I got my orders and that's good nuff for me. Should be for you too."

"If not?"

"If not, how about the twenty we'll pull?"

"Twenty?"

"Half that good nuff for you."

Slug smiled.

INFO DUMP

"Young. Impressionable. Deadly? Are your kids at risk? Join us at eleven when we talk to an expert about what music and fashions you should watch out for."

"Mall Security reports that they have chipped and deported Edge reOrbs Clerk, Maxwell Silver to the red levels. They say that there was no corroborating evidence of his claim that the store was robbed by a mixed breed male. Silver fell into suspicion when it was revealed that the store cameras were off, something the young man claimed to know nothing about. His family could not be reached for comment."

"No doubt SITCOM is the wettest DJ working in the reds right now. EDGE needs to stop sleeping on SITCOM!"

CHANNEL SURFING
CALL HER LUCK

Just a couple of weeks ago, Lexus would've barely noticed the pair of security guards strutting past. Now she did her best to look casual.

The upper levels messed with her nerves. Too much fake sunlight. Too much oxygen in the air. If you were a straight it kept you shopping or working but if you were bent it just made you edgy. She'd been able to fake normal for a few days. But it hadn't taken long to get used to the dim red levels, where it was always two in the morning.

She'd only lost her job last week. The week before that, she'd slept on the couches, stealing her rest in short naps, until security had identified her as a vagrant. A mall rat. Not knowing where to go or what to do, refusing to live with Dad, who just kept crying, or Mom, who didn't want her anyway, she'd moved downstairs.

She tried to find Sitcom and what had that prick told her? Go home before I turn you out myself?

Well, fuck him. Fuck all of them.

She moved into a different section of the reds and only came back up here to nick the essentials.

And to mess with the straights. You had to do that. It was part of being bent.

Right now she carried some stolen tampons and panties in her purse. Lifted right out her old employer's shop. They didn't even recognize her. Just another sketchy mall rat. She might even have bought them if she had money. But she had none, and none coming in.

For now, she'd just surf the commerce, take what she needed and get out. No one paid any attention. The employees relied on the techs to catch shoplifters and those machines could be fooled. Everything was insured anyway. Lexus knew. She used to live and work up here. Before her idiot parents had screwed everything up.

Before everyone had heard about what happened.

Before it happened.

Her stomach clenched as she walked past the huge fishing pond. This was stupid. She shouldn't do it.

But fuck them.

She yanked the shock bomb out of her coat. It was a mess of wires with a huge battery in its center. Looked sorta like a mangled baseball. She flipped it on and tossed it into the pond. A matrix of blue lightning streaked across the water, forming into tight shapes and then briefly spelling 'FUCK YOU," in capital letters. A buzzing noise like a giant fly was followed by a gunshot pop. Then silence.

She looked to where the noise had come from and saw a machine coughing smoke. Stunned fish floated to the surface of the pond. Hollering men dropped their rods and jumped in to grab them.

Wet.

Lexus spun on one foot, straight into a rent-a-cop's barrel chest. He grabbed her by the shoulder, turned her round and kicked her feet out. A rough hand grabbed her by her belt then smacked her, face first, into the ground.

"DON'T TOUCH ME!" she shrieked.

He pressed her cheek flat against cold tile and pinned her arms behind her back. Big hands searched her, the sweaty palms patting her fast then moving slow and heavy over her small breasts. She couldn't move.

"DON'T TOUCH ME!"

He hoisted her up and yanked her wallet out of her back pocket before turning her, trembling, towards him. He had a big stupid face with small dark eyes that flicked between the cards he had pulled out of her wallet and her face. "Lexus Shuckhart?"

She spat at him.

He wiped it off his cheek and nodded. A crowd had gathered. He pulled a gizmo out, typed something and then took her picture. He studied the screen. "You are Lexus Shuckhart and you are a vagrant. Looks like you can't afford to buy any rights." He grinned, revealing a mouth that was more gums than teeth. "So you don't have any."

Looting fishermen skulked off with armfuls of their ill begotten catches. Shoppers stared at her, whispered and pointed. Lexus avoided their disapproving eyes. Red flashes of shame heated her cheeks. The cop grabbed her by the back of the neck and marched her to his little vehicle. Tossing her into the back he said: "Watch your head."

Then he knocked it against the door.

<hr />

Lexus sat in a small, empty room for hours that felt like days. They took her bootlaces and belt so that her pants hung low. Boredom set in. Thirst burned. She'd given up begging for water some time ago. Gave up begging for a phone call long before that. She had no money to buy any rights. The cops had no kindness to lend her any.

She read the graffiti carved into the wall for the fiftieth time. It all said 'Fuck you.' It always said 'fuck you.' She understood why.

She was alone. No one knew she was here.

When the guard came back, swinging a thin television at his side, carrying a paper cup of water in the other, Lexus was almost happy to see him. Then he sipped the water and she saw his stupid expression.

He hung the screen on the wall, clicked the remote and an image of Lexus appeared. There she was, tossing the shock bomb into the pool. Busted.

"You have anything to say for yourself?" He finished the water and put the empty cup down in front of her.

Staring at that, Lexus shook her head and tried to look tough but her sneer felt childish. What was she going to say? Fuck you? Everyone said that. "I have parents. They have money."

He spat water in her face.

She wanted to drink it but bit her lip instead.

"This won't hurt a bit." He pulled the chip gun out of his holster. Held it to the back of her head. "But you ever try to pull it out and it'll turn your brain off." He snapped his fingers beside her ear, "Like that."

Metal punched the base of her skull.

She woke up outside an elevator on a red level.

██ █ █ ███ ██ █ ██ ██ ██ ██ ██ ██ ██ █ ███ █ ██ ██ ██ ██ ███ ██ █ ██ █ ██

Ken was about to leave the Joyce when the chip in his skull twinged. He saw the girl wobble through the front door and he sat back down. This one wasn't a hooker or a dealer.

She caught him looking and her eyes lit. She approached his table. Probably figured she'd hustle the horny old man for some drinks. That was fine. Ken was in the mood to be hustled. He could use the company.

"Come here often?" she asked.

"Sometimes. Have a seat."

She slipped into the chair. Her mouth twitched and she rubbed her temple. Short red hair sprouted from her head. Wincing, she put her cute face back on. Batted those green eyes.

"I'm Lexus." The waiter arrived with the whiskey. "And I never come here."

"What are you having Lexus?"

"I forgot my card at home and—"

"It's on me."

"In that case"—sweet smile—"a White Russian."

The waiter rolled his eyes and returned a few moments later with the drink. Ken leaned back and lit his hash-packed pipe. This girl was fresh. "You're new down here."

"It shows?"

"Like a light." He sipped his drink.

She had a long swig. The White Russian left a milk mustache that she wiped off. She frowned and rubbed her temple. Winced.

"Do you have a headache?"

"Yeah, well I should, seeing how I just got chipped." A smile tight-roped across her face. "Fucker said it wouldn't hurt."

"They lie." Ken tried to keep his voice calm. This girl was exactly what he was looking for. "I'm gonna call you Luck."

"Don't get ahead of yourself."

"No, sorry." Ken shook his head. "I didn't mean it like that."

"Good thing." Lexus made a disapproving clucking noise but her eyes were full of mischief. "A man your age…"

Ken forced a smile. He remembered when his advances weren't seen as comical. A time when he'd already have one hand on this girl's leg and the other in her purse. But that was years upon years ago. Although his mind was sharper than it had ever been, age had made him into a joke. The clarity of his thoughts just made it worse. "What I meant to say is that I have a job for you."

The girl looked into her drink. "I'm no whore," she said. Somehow she didn't sound convinced. Like she wanted to add 'yet'.

"A real job."

She looked up. "Doing what?"

Ken glanced around the room. Everyone was minding their business. He'd rehearsed this scenario often but still worried about botching his delivery. He leaned across the table and spoke conspirator low, so anyone who saw would think that the horny old bugger was playing for tail. They'd laugh. He didn't mind.

"I run a business. Shipping people in from the outside and out from the inside."

"The inside of what?"

"The mall." He expected the question. These youngsters didn't remember a time when the outside world mattered. They grew up here and died here. That was all. Outside was a rumor of pollution. Something their stoned friends philosophized about. "I'm getting old. I need someone to do the leg work for me."

"I'm listening."

"But the thing is, I gotta get that chip out of your head and replace it with one of mine, so we can communicate."

"The security guard told me—"

"You'd die if it was removed?"

She nodded.

"He also told you it wouldn't hurt. Like I said, they lie."

"But I heard about this guy—"

"I know," Ken said. "I've heard that story too. Mall myth. Parts of it are true. Probably. You can't yank chips out with pliers. They're not even really chips, they're a biotech. More like a tumor. Grows right into your brain. But a man with the right tools, a man like myself, can take them out." He smiled his most charming and harmless old geezer grin. "Do you really think they'd put something in that they couldn't take back out? Doesn't that sound a bit severe?"

"I guess."

He tapped at the menu to order another round. "There's only one thing you need to ask yourself. Do you want to be a whore? Because if you don't take me up on this job, that's what you'll be." He had to break her before she could think too much about it. Drown her before she could steal a breath. "Do you want to be selling your pretty little body to slimey old bastards like me until you get too old and too dry to do it anymore?"

Revulsion flooded her face. He tried not to take it personally.

The waiter set the drinks down in front of them, raised his eyebrows at Ken and left.

"I don't want to do that. Ever."

"Then you don't have many options. How old are you anyway?"

"Seventeen."

"Uh-huh." He smiled at the lie. "And you weren't born down here so how are you even going to get in with a good bordello? There's a lot of pretty girls out there, Lexus, and a lot of bad men."

"I know that, I just…"

"You just want to think about it."

She nodded. "Yeah."

"Don't think too long," Ken said. He downed his drink and swiped his card across the table. He wrote his name and number on a napkin and handed it to her. "Call me when you make up your mind. But the longer you wait the harder that chip gets to remove. If you wait over a week, just forget about it."

He stood to leave. When he walked past her, something tugged at his coat. Lexus looked up at him.

"What the hell?" she said. "I'll do it."

"Good girl," Ken said. "Forget about your drink. Come with me."

Lexus couldn't believe her luck. Literally.

Before they left the bar, she went to the ladies room and used the scrambled tokens in her pockets to buy a switchblade from a vending machine. If this guy got weird she'd cut first and ask questions later. She clicked the knife a few times to make sure it worked. Then she met Ken on the sidewalk.

He seemed trustworthy and she almost felt guilty about the blade. The guy was probably too old to even want to fuck. She could snap him in two if she felt like it. But somehow, when she looked into his old gray eyes, she didn't feel like it. "So where we goin'?"

"My office."

They paused once on the way, when a blind man bumped into them. Ken checked his wallet to make sure it was still there. Lexus waved at the girls dancing in the windows as the two of them continued up the street. Dumb cunts. She wouldn't be one of them. She felt high. Maybe from the drink, maybe from the unexpected opportunity. Perhaps it was just the idea that she might get to actually see the outside. Heard it was too polluted to live in but she'd still like to have a look-see at that big sky.

Ken led her up some stairs to an apartment door, which he opened with his card key, and she entered ahead of him. The walls were packed with machine parts. Wires and chips stacked on top of each other. At first glance it looked chaotic but an order revealed itself. She couldn't put her finger on it but these things were *arranged*.

A large desk with a bare surface stood in the center. There was no bed and no door that might lead to another room.

"You live here or just work here?" Whatever this guy did, it didn't pay well. She checked the exit. A small sign above it, which glowed tar-stained yellow light, read: 'Locked.'

"Both," Ken said. "Have a seat."

She had no options other than trust or the blade. Lexus sat on the only chair.

"Put your head down for a moment." Ken walked behind her.

She obeyed and felt his fingers prodding around the base of her skull.

"It's fresh," Ken said. "It'll work."

"Happy to hear it." She fingered the switchblade in her pocket. She didn't like how the old guy was acting. It was funny. Like when she looked at him everything was candy but when she looked away she was creeped. Lexus was about to turn her head, to try to suss his expression, but before she could move her face she felt a pinprick at the back of her neck and leaped to her feet. She spun around. "What the fuck?"

He held a hypodermic.

"You didn't tell me you were…" Her voice sounded distant. "That you were…"

She tried to pull the blade from her pocket but her arm was stuck. A beige veil dropped over her vision and a voice whispered in her head.

"It's fine," the voice said.

Ken's wrinkled face hovered in fog. His mouth was closed. "Just sit and relax."

Even as her mind rebelled her body obeyed.

░▒▓█ ░▒▓█ ▓▒░ █ ▓ ░▒▓ █ ░▒▓█ ░▒▓ █ ▓▒░

Ken injected the girl and stepped back. So, she'd bought and brought a blade. Not a surprise. Violent thoughts always came across nice and red, painted in lurid detail. He doubted she could use it in time but it was best to be careful.

"Double you tea eff?" she asked as her eyes misted. She kept talking but Ken ignored her words, observing her symptoms. The pupils dilated and then contracted to almost nothing.

He concentrated on sending her a message, ordering her body to sit. It was easy to do now that her personality was drugged down. All of the thoughts that formed her concept of herself, all those little lies a person told about their past and all those little promises they made about their future, just got in the way of their immediate truth.

He slipped his hands under her armpits and maneuvered her slack body onto the desk. He flipped her onto her side and pulled his toolbox from the drawer. He pulled out a long, thin piece of metal, sanitized it with a wetnap and eased it into the back of her head until he felt resistance. The chip. A computer stacked against the wall read its signal and translated it into quantum spins represented as a binary interface, and that into a series of charts and graphics. Each layer had less and less to do with the actual information. Manipulating the actual reality was more art than science.

Checking levels and turning knobs, he modified his chip's output frequency. He sweated.

The computer buzzed, saving all of his thoughts and memories to orb.

He wiped his forehead with his sleeve. He altered the machine's output to exactly match the girl's chip, complementing it so the transmission was a perfect ying-yang. His mind—rather a copy but who cared?—would be transmitted into the chip and stored within her brain.

"Loading," the computer said.

But that was just the start. His never tried, but theoretically viable virus—the cuckoo—would hijack her personality, altering neural-pathways and affecting the chemo-electric discharge of thoughts until they matched his. Her brain would run a functioning, exact simulation of his own. Whether or not it would remain stable was another question. Ken slowly turned a gray knob and watched as his mind infested this young shell.

Her body twitched.

"Loading complete," the machine said and a single bell being rang. Ding. Like a microwave.

Ken took another needle from his toolbox and slipped it into a vein in her neck.

The girl shuddered, turned on her back and sat up. She looked at Ken and smiled. "I'm looking at you looking at me looking at you looking at me—"

The body kept talking, caught in this loop. Ken had expected this. Non-localized consciousness was impossible. A quantum might be able to exist in two places at one time but a whole mind could not.

He had to manually turn his own brain off to boot up the other one. Ken pulled a handgun from his desk drawer. He looked at the barrel for a moment before pressing it to his left eye.

He should've been scared but wasn't. Aside from the faith he placed in his work, he'd always been a bit of a gambler, holding down a day job at Fatman's Casino that allowed him to pursue this research. So he knew the odds and knew that, on this bet, he had a lot to win and not much to lose. At most, he had a few more years left. But if this worked he might gain eternity.

The scientists kept saying they were close to mastering mortality but they'd been saying that for as long as he remembered. The Grim Collector was a tricky bastard. So was Ken. Difference was, Ken was getting older. Death was not.

When the scientists failed, yet again, to cure dying and Lexus's now young body got old and useless, he could always repeat this. He could even sell the idea. It was brutal but when had that ever stopped people?

He wouldn't even miss his flesh. This frail frame was not how he pictured himself. In another second, he'd be in that girl's body, with her youth fueled by his brains and money. It was a good gamble.

Ken pulled the trigger.

Budgie laid in eye-shut darkness, balancing on the verge of sleep. Wolfe waited for him there. The knife arced up at his face and Budgie jerked back to total wakefulness.

Harmony slept next to him, her arms wrapped around his naked body, her head on his chest.

Her hutch was almost completely black. Unlike him and everyone he had ever met she slept with the lights, television and radio off.

She fidgeted and snored. An ancient toad of feeling shifted within Budgie. The quiet, the dark and the fear. He squeezed her closer.

⁞⁞⁞⁞⁞⁞⁞⁞⁞⁞⁞⁞⁞⁞⁞⁞⁞⁞⁞⁞⁞⁞⁞⁞⁞⁞⁞⁞⁞⁞⁞⁞⁞

Sitcom dragged the warm body into TeeVee's reOrb room and dropped him on the floor. "Heavy."

"Where's your fat poodle?"

"Slug? Told him to wait downstairs." Sitcom looked at the slummer. He'd started groaning on the way up here and looked about ready to come round. Sitcom nudged him with his boot. "Feel like a cat bringing a mouse home."

TeeVee crouched next to the man and stroked his hair. He sniffed his fingers then tasted them. Looked up at Sitcom. "He's not exactly mint."

"Where the fuck am I gonna find a mint condition human?" Sitcom pulled his cigarettes out.

"No smoking."

Sitcom put them away. "Besides, he's just knocked out. Not like he has brain damage or anything. I don't think."

"How pleasant for you."

Better tread carefully. TeeVee was in one of his moods. Sitcom folded his arms behind his back. "Someone worked him over pretty good. Rude boy'd be my guess."

"So they left his gizmo."

"I disabled it."

"Get him out of his clothes." TeeVee stood up. "And put him over there."

"I know the routine." Sitcom hated undressing unconscious people.

As TeeVee left the room, the slummer mumbled nonsense. His face had swollen into a purple watermelon. Sitcom taped the bousgie's ankles together, hands behind his back and knees to his chest. He balanced the guy against the wall and stepped back to examine his handiwork.

"Where am I?" The man's eyes rubbered around the room.

Sitcom ignored him.

TeeVee returned with a black bag and crouched beside the man. "What's your name?"

"Huh?"

"Your name?"

"Burt."

TeeVee opened his bag and pulled out a piece of soft leather. On this, he laid out his tools. Blades, spoons, long pieces of metal and some reOrbs.

"Are you a doctor?" Burt asked.

Sitcom snorted.

TeeVee held one of the reOrbs to Burt's eye. Checking the size. "Something like that."

"He hurt me real bad." The man blinked and cringed. "Wait, where am I?"

"I need to be around for this?" Sitcom asked.

"Of course not," said TeeVee.

"You gonna give him some painkillers at least?"

"Your concern is touching."

Sitcom shrugged.

TeeVee pulled what looked like a half-reOrb from the bag. A long thin needle poked out of its flat side. He slapped this into the man's chest, above the heart.

Burt twitched like a fish then slumped.

"He doesn't need painkillers," TeeVee said. He left that device, whatever it was, in the man's chest for a few seconds, watching it change color. When it darkened to a deep burgundy he slowly pulled it out. The wound sealed behind it. TeeVee stroked the man's head. "He can't feel any of this." He stood up. "Twenty globals, correct?"

"Yeah."

TeeVee yanked out some bills from between the cushions of his couch. Without counting them, he gave them to Sitcom. "What's your name?"

"Huh?" asked Sitcom.

The man on the floor made a sound like static.

TeeVee cocked his head, as if listening intently. His eyes grew wide and turned to snow. "Oh," he said. "Oh."

Sitcom looked between them, realizing that TeeVee wasn't talking to him.

TeeVee blinked and came back. He smiled. "Very close," he said. "I see through."

"Uh-huh," said Sitcom. He jerked his thumb at the man. "You want me to get rid of him?"

"Not this one. Not yet."

Sitcom glanced at the guy, static and froth pouring from his mouth, his body shaking like he was being electrocuted and his eyes rolled back in his skull.

He wondered what was different about this one. Well, he was still alive for one thing.

Unlucky, Sitcom thought. He could've used the two global disposal fee.

Over a breakfast of smokes and coffee Harmony said: "Going to the recruiter today?"

Budgie stared into the oil slick surface of his coffee. "We look quite the couple," he said. "Breakfast before work."

She looked at him for a long silent moment.

"Yeah," he said. "I guess the recruiter's the thing to do."

She leaned across the little table and kissed him on the forehead. He blushed.

"Aw shucks, lil' lady" he said, taking on the Western voice from the movie that played after Psycho.

"Don't do that," she said. Stared hard. "Ever. I hate when people talk like televisions."

"I was just kidding round. Not infected."

"Yeah, well... Quote a movie at me again and see if I am."

"What's the issue? I was just fucking about."

"Every single time someone almost..." She looked away, her mouth tight, her eyes sour. "Sorry."

"Okay."

"Just bugs me. These fuckers wandering around, chopping up shit and repeating it back all the time, like broken robots. Think they got such clever dispos." She imitated a wheedling moron's voice: "How many adverts do you have memorized, maaaaan?"

"Okay," Budgie said. "Okay." Truth was, he'd never really thought about it. It was annoying, he supposed, in the same way that the noise got annoying. A bedrock that you just never thought too much about. "I won't do it. Just thought it was funny."

"Don't it bother you?"

"What?"

"Being programmed like this. 24-7. We're all so infected with this shit we don't even notice it. Like other day, I saw these two tourists talking in a bar. Whole convo was parts of movies, parts of commercials, parts of shows. Talkin' loud. Weren't saying nothing, just advertising at each other. It's like—" She paused and lit a cigarette. "It's like you are what you eat. You just consume and you become what you consume. So this guy likes one show and that's supposed to say something bout him. The other guy likes another show and that makes him diff. But the two shows are the same sorta thing so they can get along. Their clothes were same sorta fashion, straight outta Edge."

"Go to the monastery much, llama Harmony?" Budgie asked. "Never pegged you for Buddhist and shit."

"I'm not," she said, impatiently rapping her knucks against the table. "Just get a bad dispo in the morning. Just thinking about going out and having to deal with it for another day…" She looked at Budgie through a cloud of smoke. "Don't need it from you too."

"K. Dub-tee-eff? Just a joke."

"I know, sorry. You're fine. I'm just fucked up."

"Vice versa," Budgie said. He as about to put on another television voice, just by reflex, then stopped. He cleared his throat. "Wish I was more like you. Honest, like."

"Don't say that."

"Anyway," he said and grinned. "We're wearing the same clothes too. Straight outta the rule book. One, maybe two steps over the Edge." Sniffed the air. "Even scented the same. Vidicon stink."

"Yeah, I know. That's not what bugs me, being the same. It's being the same when you think you're diff. It's just stupid."

Budgie lit a cigarette and poured another coffee. Left the sweetener out this time. Too much made him feel ill. "All that shit don't bug me," he said. "Guess it should but just can't get horny bout it. Sputnik used to like all that anarcho mumbo. After his cousin got infected, he always tried to peak me on it but just never took." He thought for a long sad time. His hand trembled when he sipped at his coffee. "You'd get along with TeeVee. If he's healthy. Don know."

"Never heard of him."

"But you've heard him."

"What's that mean?"

"Well you know Sitcom right?"

She nodded.

"Sitcom is just a front. He don't make that music, don't even mix it. Watch him close sometime. He's reading off a list. It's all TeeVee and TeeVee ain't even beta anymore, he's gone fuckin' alpha. But he don't like going public so he let's Sitcom and a few other guys spin his shit."

"How'd you know all this?"

"Met him a few times. Spooky. TeeVee's Sputnik's cousin. Lot older though. Turned Sputnik onto the anarcho. After making him a Vidicon."

He thought about the man, how he had seemed like he wasn't really from this world and when he started moving you just knew nothing could stop him. Like hypnotic. "Spooky."

"Weird," she said.

Budgie heard the disappointment in her voice and it made him happy. She wouldn't be fawning over Sitcom now she knew the truth. "Yeah, TeeVee got meme fucked a while back, before I ever met him. Now he's totally fucked. Every time you talk to him you feel like you aren't talking to him. It's like he's putting on an act. Like he ain't human or some shit, just watching us and trying to act like us and not doing a good job either. Almost like he's making fun of us." Budgie shuddered. Watching TeeVee talk was like watching a slow boiling pot of explosives. Didn't like visiting him one bit. Alpha or not.

Wondered if anyone had the guts to tell him about Sputnik. Prolly not.

"This is a nice place." He wanted to click into another conversation before this one got old. He pulled out his gizmo and checked to see if he had TeeVee's number. He did.

"What you doin'?"

"Just thinkin'," he said, typing in a text. "Prolly no one told TeeVee bout his cousin so…"

"You're going to?"

Budgie nodded.

"That's his mom's job. Telling family."

"Yeah, well, usually."

"Just don't tell him by text."

"I look savage to you? Just telling him to call me." He hit send. "There. done. Did my bit. It's on him now."

"Feel better?"

"Not really." He felt scared. Just contacting an alpha was running a risk. Best to stay off their radar. But if he didn't at least try to tell TeeVee, there was no telling how he'd react. Damned if you do, damned if you don't. Better to be damned if you do. "But it's the right thing. Prolly won even get back to me anyway."

Harmony kissed him on the cheek.

PRODUCT PLACEMENT

Back shot of a handsome man. Waiting. A woman approaches with an expression of recognition. Her expression suddenly changes into horror and revulsion. She veers away, pretending to not know the man. **Show his face**. He has a filthy beard. Maggots crawl and writhe in the bristly hair, eating old bits of food. **"MACH RAZORS—don't look like a bum!"**
Ad replays, with an even more attractive woman approaching. She hugs the man and gives him a kiss. They walk off holding hands. He looks at the camera, clean-shaven and quite handsome. Winks.
"MACH RAZORS—get you laid."
Product shot.

A knock on man's apartment door. He's making Jiffy popcorn and leaves the kitchen to answer. Three beautiful girls are out there waiting, sniffing the air.
"You making Jiffy pop?" one asks.
"Yes. It's the best."
They enter the apartment, still sniffing the air. "Can we have some?"
"I don't know girls, what will you do for me?"
Cue the funk. They undress, make out with each other, have sex with the man. Porn sequence lasts about fifteen minutes with numerous subliminal flashes of Jiffy Pop logo. The girls moan and scream—jiffy, jiffy, jiffy. Oh Jiffy! Product is always in foreground or background. Sequence ends with money shot.
When they're done he grabs a handful of Jiffy pop and throws it into the hall. The girls chase after it and he locks the door behind them, sits down with a bag of Jiffy pop in front of the television. Product shot, sounds of girls begging to be let back in.
"JIFFY POP—get your own!"

INFO DUMP

"Not that you'd know Bob, but it is an academic principle and it's called lack of synthesis."

"Oh, aren't you the smart one."

"I'm just saying that we are basically the same as plastic age people and that—"

"Ridiculous."

"—we suffer from the same mental problems. Our ancestors could watch the evening news full of—"

"Here we go."

"—full of reports of robbery, rape, murder, assault, climate change, wars, prisoner torture, genocide, concentration camps, extinctions—"

"And on and on but I don't see what—"

"—riots, executions, pedophilia, school shootings, carjackings, car crashes, protests, suicide bombings, vandalism, random violence—"

"We get the point, Lenny. It was—"

"—extortion, air quality alerts, water quality alerts, drug pushers, gang warfare, shrinking civil liberties, tyrants, eating disorders, new diseases, dog attacks, bankruptcies, corruption—"

"You done?"

"Not quite. Then they'd watch the commercials that played during these newscasts without drawing a correlation."

"So you're saying we should just go live in a cave?"

"Not at all. I'm saying—"

"We'll hear what Lenny Niedenberger, author of best-selling book *Superstition: Then and Now* has to say, when we come back from commercials. Stick with me, your host, your voice, Bob Anger, on "You're a Crazy Lying Bastard.""

Budgie burst into the recruiter's office and straight into the sights of a shotgun.

He'd slammed the door behind him, panting. It'd been a cold sweat scramble through border territory to get here. Bout twenty feet from the door, gagging on the swirling stinks of rival gangs, terrified he'd get notched *this* close to his destination, he panicked straight inside.

That's when he heard the click.

He waited for the boom.

Nothing.

"Easy." Budgie stared into double barreled eyes.

A short skinny man in a tweedy brown suit two sizes too big sweated behind the stock.

"Just take it easy."

"Slowly!" the man shouted.

"You got it." Hands held high, Budgie looked away from the gun. The man had lank hair, frizzy in some places, disappearing in others, and freckles. The shotgun wobbled.

Nothing made Budgie more nervous than nerves. "Take it easy. Take a breath."

"Don't move!" The man jabbed the gun forward like he wanted to stab Budgie with it and Budgie flinched back. He'd never dealt with guns before. You'd have to be crazy to use them in a corridor. By the time you pulled out, a knife would already be in you. Besides, ricochets killed the shooter as often as the target. Bullets often hit a stray chem bucket and blew a whole hallway. People got smart and stopped using firearms. Rulebook outlawed them. No upside in such close quarters.

"Easy," Budgie said.

"There's no money here."

"I'm not here to rob you." Budgie cleared his throat, watching the antique weapon. This was a border territory, not controlled by anyone. Robbery was not formalized into tax collection. No wonder this guy was scared. Someone could get hurt. "I want a job."

The man tilted his head and his face relaxed. He wiped his forehead with his sleeve. "You don't have an appointment."

"Didn't know I needed one."

"Thought you could just show up, 'cause what? Cause we're just looking to hire rude boys these days? Cause they're so trustworthy? Always work out so well?"

"I dunno."

"Dunno," the man mocked. "Dunno much."

Budgie ground his jaw. Wondered what this guy would look like with a knife through his neck. His fingers weren't on the trigger and that'd give Budgie the jump. He could chop that pale throat before he could fire.

"Why did you come running in here like that? Trying to give me a heart attack?" In spite of his thinning hair and stress lined face, the guy didn't look too much older than Budgie. Too young to be having a heart attack. Why would he say something like that? No wonder he had a gun. Needed one if you were gonna be acting that way.

Budgie wanted to say: "Look, I didn't know I needed an appointment. Scented rival rudies. Didn't want them to see me." Instead, he shrugged. Pictured what that gun butt would do to a skull. Wondered what the rules were about using one as a bludgeon.

The guy eyed him suspiciously but Budgie had the feeling that he always looked that way. Scared and wary and ready to pop. A paro dispo. Maybe it was the freckles. Either way, he had to be careful.

"Speak up!" the man shouted.

Budgie jumped.

"And take off your weapons. Slow."

Budgie unclipped his brass knuckles and the two knives that hung from his belt. The one that had killed Wolfe and the one that had killed Sputnik.

"Put them on the table."

Budgie did as he was told. Felt naked without his tools. "You gonna keep that pointed at me?"

"Huh?" The man looked down at the gun. "Oh." He lowered the barrel. "It's not loaded anyway. They won't pay for bullets and it's not like I can afford them. Not on this salary."

Budgie tried to process this. The guy had—in a short period— admitted to being afraid, unarmed and poor. He's gotta be bluff, thought Budgie. Or crazy. I don't even know what's worse.

"I need an appointment?" Budgie lowered his hands but kept them visible. He did not want to spook this man any more than he already had.

"We look busy to you?"

Budgie glanced around the empty office. A few chairs sat against a wall. The dust on them indicated that they weren't often used or cleaned, though one had an ass mark on it. He looked back at the guy and shrugged.

"Just take a seat," the recruiter said. "My name is Tory Commisong. You may refer to me as Mr. Commisong."

"I'm Budgie."

"And that is your real name?"

"Kinda." Budgie brushed off the chair in front of the desk before sitting down. "My full name is Budgerigar Saltmarsh. You can call me Budgie."

"I will call you what I please, Saltmarsh."

Budgie thought it odd that this guy seemed a lot more confident without a weapon. Mr. Commisong pulled a tablet and small camera out of his desk. He sniffed and wiped at his nose with a yellowed, previously used Kleenex he kept in his pocket. "Dust," he complained. "Have you ever been through this process before?"

"No."

"Do you have representation?"

"I represent the Vidicons."

"What?"

"I said I—"

"A lawyer. Do you have a lawyer?"

"No. Do I need one?"

"It's better that you don't have one." Mr. Commisong smiled at Budgie. "This'll go easier if it's between us."

"I bet," said Budgie. He saw that Mr. Commisong still hadn't turned the camera on. "It okay if I smoke?"

"Certainly not." Mr. Commisong flipped through his tablet with his fingers, scrawled with his stylus and, without looking up, asked: "Are you an exile?"

"No."

"Have you been chipped?"

"No." Budgie glanced at Mr. Commisong's white hands. They were damp and shaky. His fingernails were filthy and chewed down. "I was born down here."

"Are you wanted for anything?"

"No," Budgie said. "Wait, do you mean—"

"That's fine. I can't take your word for that anyway." Mr. Commisong tucked some of his hair behind an ear. "I'm going to take your picture and cross reference with our biometric files. Look straight at the lens."

Budgie stared into the glass eye and Mr. Commisong hit a button on the camera.

The man watched the slate then nodded. "Okay, fine. You're not wanted. Good for you." He put the slate down and leaned back in his chair. "So what happened, Saltmarsh? You piss off your friends and want out?"

"No," Budgie said. "Nothin' like that."

"Maybe a friend was murdered and you started thinking it could be you next?"

"Is this important?"

"What do you think?"

"I dunno."

"That's right. You dunno."

"A comrade was..." Budgie trailed off. He'd wanted to say friend but couldn't. Not to this guy. "He was stabbed up pretty guh-guh-guh—" Budgie stopped talking.

"Pretty what?"

Deep breath. "Good."

"And that scared you?"

"Something like that."

"Something exactly like that?"

I dunno, Budgie almost said but stopped. He wished he could smoke. There was a dirty half full ashtray sitting right there. Why wouldn't this guy let him smoke? He nodded. "Something exactly like that."

"I figured." Mr. Commisong leaned back in his seat. It creaked behind him and Budgie imagined it breaking, the man's head cracking off the wall and the blood smearing it. He'd lay there all twitchy and quiet. Not sitting there all smug and talking. "In my experience, your average rude boy is a fundamentally cowardly sort. Every few months or so a new one comes in here and it's always the same old story. Someone is either after them or something scared them. Always running away. Never ambitious. Just afraid."

He sighed, as if deeply disappointed by the despicable portion of humanity it was his sad lot to deal with.

Budgie dug his fingernails into his knees. He couldn't look this man in the face. He felt like a balloon losing air. Every word this man said was another pin prick. He don't even need that gun, thought Budgie. He's got that tablet. He's got my future aimed at me. He's got my past aimed at me. He's got all that locked and loaded and pressed right to my fucking skull and there ain't a thing I can do about it. I just gotta nod. Just nod.

He nodded. And felt like that wasn't enough. "Yes, Mr. Commisong."

The man smirked at his tablet. "Have you even bothered to think about what sort of work you want to do on the greens? Have you sobered up long enough to do that much at least?"

"Yes, Mr. Commisong."

"Well, out with it then."

"Shopkeep, I suppose, maybe a clerk," Budgie said. It was the first thing that sprang to his mind. "I'd like something clean and something safe."

Mr. Commisong shook his head and fumbled over his messy desk for a pack of cigarettes. He lit one. Budgie did not bother to ask if he could smoke again. He had the drift of this and it did not smell like that. "Those would be entry level positions for people who are born on the greens," he said. "Educated people."

"Yes, Mr. Commisong."

"Decent people."

"Yes, Mr. Commisong."

"As I'm sure even you can imagine, most, if not all, stores don't want to hire people straight out of the reds. They certainly don't want them in positions of any fiscal responsibility. You care to guess why?"

"I'm not one for a lot of guessing."

"Humor me."

"They're afraid they'll get robbed." *Just like you?*

"And can you blame them?" Commisong dipped the cigarette and spilled ash on his desk. "We can get you a job with minimal opportunities for corruption. That way you build up trust in the community and make your own contacts. You do a job that basically no one up there wants, and you do it well for a few years, then maybe you can work on getting hired somewhere else. That's not what we do. After we get you the position you're on your own."

"Okay," Budgie said.

"It will not be clean."

"Yes, Mr. Commisong."

"And safety is a relative term."

"Yes, Mr. Commisong."

Mr. Commisong grabbed his slate and tapped at it, looking between its screen and Budgie's face. More ash dropped from his cigarette. This time it landed on his lap.

"You have a gizmo?"

Budgie pulled his out of his pocket.

"You all have gizmos."

Budgie wondered what that was supposed to mean.

"Right now, we're looking for people to perform small maintenance jobs on the robots." He slid the tablet across the table so Budgie could see the screen. "Are you handy? I've found that many of you so-called rude boys are quite clever with machines."

Budgie nodded and leaned forward to look at the screen.

"Not that this requires much cleverness. You travel outside with the robots when they mine the dumps. If one gets clogged you clean out the clog."

"Outside?" Budgie said. The slate had a picture of a big truck and some robots. A bunch of text that he didn't bother to read. "Like outside-outside?"

"You'll have equipment that protects you from the pollution and there's no opportunity for crime. And, even better, no one born green wants to do the job."

"Is it hard work?"

"Does that matter?"

"No, I guess not."

"It's boring work. Not exciting like this job. Not nearly as fulfilling as dealing with wayward rude boys. I mean you'll be dealing with trash and I, well, I get to deal with you." He smirked. "The pay is decent."

"How much are we talking about?"

"A half-global an hour, ten hours a day, five to six days a week."

Budgie did the math. It was like making a small score every week. Of course it took a lot more time than swinging a small scheme. More dangerous too. Coming home, that is. Being toppy was risky and he always figured it'd pay more than this. Like, he'd never take these chances for a caper this cheap, but this was a gamble. Double up or step away from the table, he told himself. And step away to where? Just a smaller table. And more doubling up.

"How much is rent up there?"

"Cheapest places are about 250 a month. You need first and last. References too. There are some work-camps you could live in but you need to qualify for those. They require a drug test. I doubt you'd pass." He cleared his throat. "And if you're thinking you could run a small scheme and pay for a place up there, you should know that we audit your cash. If you have a rent of 250 a month and we know you're only making 200, we get suspicious. And, unless you can buy some rights, that means you get fired and chipped. Maybe you could even end up here, doing this. You don't want that. Believe me."

"I guess not." Budgie pretended to think for a moment then said: "I'll take it." It wasn't much money but he knew he couldn't hack it down here anymore. If he could get his foot in the door upstairs he could kick it open. Just needed the chance.

"I'm sorry?" said Mr. Commisong.

"I said I'll take it."

"Oh, you're planning on hiring yourself."

"I don't... Huh?"

"It's not up to you to take it, Saltmarsh. It's up to me to give it."

"I thought you said—"

"Said what? That these positions are available? That's right. They are. And there's that form, on my tablet, not on your Gizmo. Seems I have something you want."

"Oh," said Budgie.

"I find this surprising. Usually you people are bit quicker on the uptake."

"Yes, Mr. Commisong."

Mr. Commisong raised his eyebrows.

"How much do you want?"

"How much do you have?"

Budgie emptied his pockets.

"That, my rude little friend, is not nearly enough." He looked at the weapons. After a moment he picked up the knife that had killed Sputnik. "Do you know what this is?"

"It's a knife."

"It's a Damascus knife."

"Ivory handle," Budgie offered, quickly reaching the end of his knowledge about the weapon.

"That's not ivory. That's human bone."

"Oh."

"This will do."

"I, uh…" Budgie wanted to tell him to take his filthy, chewed nail hands off that blade. This was the knife that had taken his friend from him. It was his trophy and by any rights he could think of, it belonged to him.

"You 'uh' what?"

Double up or step away from the table. Was there ever any end to the doubling? "I thought it was a lady blade."

"Shows what you know."

"I guess."

"Something like this," Mr. Commisong said, "is wasted on someone like you." He opened a desk drawer and dropped the knife in. "Completely wasted."

"We have a deal?"

"Sign here," Mr. Commisong said, pressing the slate with his thumb. Budgie wanted to break that thumb.

Instead he smiled. And said thank you.

Budgie stepped outside and sniffed the air for threat. Scented nothing but ambient danger. He lit a cigarette and walked. Felt filthy and cheap. He wanted to put some distance between him and the office. Fast. Not so easy in this terrain.

The streets in this old section were uneven. A few steps here, a staircase there, and a slope beside it. Potholes and half broke fences. The remains from a busted up barricade from some long forgotten fight. Most people walked in the flat, narrow bike lanes, which were crowded but basically clear. Budgie took the maze of steps beside. The roof was about fifteen feet above the street and covered in moving advertisements. "Buy Synapacide!" one said. Coke, Pepsi, cigarettes. A never-ending assault on the mind.

This ceiling was designed to increase a sense of space. It was supposed to show a moving picture of sky so people wouldn't feel like they were living inside. Over time, the companies had rented out a spot here and a spot there. Now they had it all. Was that old image of sky still behind all those ads or if it was gone to save on processing? He'd often stared at it. Never got a glimpse.

Having never seen any stars inside, he wondered if he'd see them outside. Just the idea of all that space above him made him feel strange. Bit queasy. He'd seen sky in the old movies but what would it be like to look up and not see a naked woman hawking a product? To stand under a bunch of nothing? Wtf was up there anyway? Anything?

A few hollering drunks stood under staircases passing bottles. Robotic litterbugs scoured the floors, grabbing rubbage in pincer jaws and eating it. Other than that, the corridors were quiet. Most people were resting up. Budgie should be doing the same. Didn't feel tired though. Just edgy and nerve sick.

He needed a drink. Somewhere not quite normal for him. Somewhere he wouldn't see anyone he knew. To think.

The hair on the back of his neck twitched and he stopped walking. Sniffed the air—

—scent.

Not Vidicon but gang. He flinched and threw up a hand. A bottle exploded against the wall. Shattered glass rioted into his face. A piece cut into his forehead and foamy beer blinded him. He spun on one foot and wiped his eyes. The smell clicked.

Air Pirates. Strong scent so there must be a few of them. Got the blur out of his vision. Three guys stood in front of him. Sleeved.

Shit, Budgie thought. Oh shit, oh shit, oh shit.

Could he run? No. Cornered.

Big guys. Muscles rippled beneath their tunics. Might just be padding but you could never be sure.

I'm a fucking idiot, thought Budgie. He'd been dreaming and scheming out of his zone. Rulebook: Know where you are. The guys didn't move on him and Budgie took his fighting pose. "Waiting on what, fuckers?"

One stepped forward and sniffed the air. "Vidicon," he said. "Flew a bit far from the nest?"

"We talking?"

They hadn't pulled their weapons. Maybe they wouldn't.

"We talking?" one of them mocked. The others spread out. "What we got to talk bout, Vidicon?"

"Nice day," said one.

"Local sports team not doing as well as expected," said another. "Local politico tells lie."

"Just let us know when we find the right topic."

"He's a fucking expert conversationalist, might be hard to find something that interests him."

"We boring you?"

"Want some excitement?"

Every step these guys took, secured their positions. They moved forward. Budgie's back touched the wall.

They were just cat and mousing him, counting on him being too afraid to start, counting on him hoping for the best. Planting that doubt in his head, that little thought that said: *Maybe they won't do anything.* A lot of things were dangerous. Nothing more so than optimism. Budgie tried to pick out the leader.

Fuck. All looked alike.

"You got some tax for us?"

Budgie thought of Mr. Commisong and the tax he'd levied. There was nothing left in his pockets.

They'd taken position. The boys on the edges looked twitchy. Kept checking behind them. Sniffing. Nerves.

Chances were, they felt more fear than they let on. Finding a solitary Vidicon wandering their turf had put them to thinking. Maybe there were more. Maybe this was a declaration or an ambush or both.

He pulled his knife and knucks. "I got no thing for you."

"Look at that piece of shit on his tit."

"Saw that."

"Hundred globals for this fucker."

"Fancy."

"Wonder what brings a boyo like that out."

"Poaching?"

"Maybe."

"Sniffing round for soft spots."

"Could be."

"Wonder if the Vidicons think Air Pirates get punked as easy as Dog Goblins."

"Wonder if they got that victory sickness."

"Wonder that indeed."

"Then again..."

"Then what?"

"Then again, maybe our boy here, maybe his boys don't know where he is. You know we got that office near by."

"You know we do."

"He look toppy to you?"

"Could be."

"Could be a lot of fucking things," said Budgie. "Could be this, could be that. Could be I just wandering."

"Lost like?"

"Like that."

"Want some directions?"

"You naught but a bunch of barking cats," Budgie said. He slapped his knife and knucks away. "I won be needing these."

"What's that?"

"Fucking talk. I'd heard you Air Pirates talk but you fucking talk and talk. Got me to thinkin': Why you talk so much? Why all the woof-woof?" Budgie grabbed his cigarettes and lit one. "Only one reason I can think. Cause you pussy. Cause you don wan no problem with the Vidicons." He blew smoke. "We been at peace how many years now? Huh? And you gon fuck that up now?" Let em think on that. "How about this? How about one of you hold my hand and lead me back to my land, all sweet like. Maybe I make you my girl when I get home."

They just grinned.

Enjoying the show, thought Budgie. They knew he bluffed. He knew he bluffed. They just wanted to hear it. See if he turned soft. They had a sample Vidicon here. They knew they'd get the best of him in a fight, but wanted to see how hard he stood his ground.

They wanted to see him beg. Wanted to talk to all their mates about how he begged. Wanted to hear him wheel and deal and negotiate. Maybe then Budgie'd get their mercy but maybe then he didn't. All the toppies he'd knocked down over the years. They all wheedled.

Mr. Commisong and all that "Yes Sir" must get to be a habit. Here, in the real red world, people'd hear that "Yes Sir" and "Please Mister" and beat you anyway. Beat you harder cause now they didn't even respect you. Beat you harder cause they wanted to beat that "Yes Sir" outta of themselves. Then they'd talk shit about you after they were done. So you couldn't even be proud of the beating you took. So you couldn't be proud of nothing.

He had another haul on his cigarette and dropped it. "You wanna know why I'm in your section, my sweet comrade?"

"?"

"Cause I heard your mom is charging half for pussy tonight." He smiled. "Still too much for that old—"

The first one came at him from the side and Budgie ducked most of the blow. He heard the crack of bone as the fist slammed into the wall behind him. The next came from the front. This guy landed a kick square in Budgie's shin. Budgie threw a hook that missed, and someone else knocked his feet out. He landed on his back.

Without even landing a blow.

He stared up at those signs, those ads for Synapacide and Coke and Pepsi. At the naked women hawking those wares. All this craziness going on down here and that ceiling just played the same old adverts. *Am I in the market for some coke right now?* wondered Budgie. *Should I follow my thirst?* One of the advertising ladies, did as she was programmed to when she caught his eye, and winked. A boot caught Budgie in the ribs. He winked back and laughed.

"My fucking hand," someone said. "Shit. It's broken."

Budgie pointed up at the ceiling, remembering something Sputnik used to say about these adverts. "I think she likes me."

"What?"

Budgie paid no attention to their moon faces looking down at him. He pointed back up. "That one, the blond, she just winked at me. I think she likes me."

They looked up.

"Damn, I feel like a coke," said Budgie.

"Shit, she just winked at me too." The guy looked back down at Budgie. Smiling. "You got some competition boyo. I think she likes me better."

"The fuck," said the one holding his hand. "My damn knucks are shattered here and you're bantering."

"Keep your panties on," said Budgie. "I got smashed ribs. Nothing a coke can't solve. You know where I can—"

That earned him another kick to his other ribs. He grabbed the leg and pulled himself up on it. He bit above the boot. Hard. Put all his jaw into it. The kid yowled like a cat and Budgie let go. He looked back at that ceiling. At least he'd got a blow in.

"Shit," said the one who'd bantered at him. "Stop kicking this motherfucker. Not his fault you punched the wall. We ain't killing him, dumb-fuck."

"But he—"

"Suck it up, cupcake." He put his boot on the center of Budgie's chest. "He nuff fucked up. His tax is paid." He snapped his fingers at Budgie who looked him square in the face. "You not coming back here anytime soon, are ya?"

"Depends."

"I'm gon warn you: You said nuff bout my mom."

"Fair nuff." He looked at the guy with the broken hand and bit leg. Budgie winked. The guy chewed his lip.

"Too rude," the one with his boot on Budgie's chest said. "Find your way back to friendly climes." He stepped off. "Fly straight too. We be watching."

"And you won't be needing these," said another snatching up Budgie's weapons. Trophies.

Budgie got to his feet. Slow and ginger. The Air Pirates backed off him. One cradled his broken fist. Guy's eyes were wet. Budgie should thank him. If he hadn't embarrassed himself so badly with his whine, they might still be beating on Budgie now. As it was, they felt shown up. Knew they couldn't beat that outta Budgie.

He'd won.

His prize was a busted up chest.

Budgie winked at the loser. Aside from the smashed hand, what was that guy's prize gonna be? Nothing good.

Budgie waited until he was back in deep borderland before he wiped at his forehead. Hand came away red. Rubbed it on his pants and held his sleeve to the cut. Even doing that much hurt his ribs. The adrenalin faded. Now every breath stung like a chest full of hornets.

A couple of litterbugs flashed lights at each other, engaged in some territorial dispute. Budgie was about to step on one, just outta frustration, when it looked up and hissed. Its pinching jaws opened and closed. That wasn't the threat though. You stepped on these things and they gave off a horrible stench. He and Sputnik used to explode them by remote when they were kids. Do it in a crowd of bousgies and watch them scatter.

"Fine, you little bastard." Budgie liked its attitude. "You can live."

It hissed by way of reply.

"Too rude," said Budgie.

He gave the bug a gentle kick. It scuttled into darkness. The other went back to hunting garbage.

There was a prole place up ahead. Least they'd think nothing bout a bit of blood.

Fiddle music, dim lights and empty tables. Some old guy slept face down at a corner table, a half empty bottle beside him. The bartender polished a glass and watched Budgie. Barkeeps in spots like this always kept one big glass for polishing. Tradition. Budgie knew they used that cup for a weapon when they didn't have time to get whatever they had hidden. That was tradition too.

"What?" the guy said as Budgie sat at the bar.

"Absinthe."

"Whiskey, then."

"I said—"

"I fucking heard you." He poured a whiskey

Budgie pulled his card from his collar. "You take these?"

"Yeah."

Budgie downloaded the drink.

The barkeep poured him another. "You gotta bit cut up there."

"Yeah," Budgie said.

"Suppose I should see the other guy?"

"Sure, just look for the big fuck with no cuts."

The barkeep laughed. "Had a few of those myself." He rolled up his sleeve. Scar tissue wrapped itself round his muscular forearm. "Bet you can't top that one, eh laddie?"

"No Sir," Budgie said and saluted. "Ungh."

"Broke ribs too?"

"I look like a fucking Doctor?" asked Budgie.

The barkeep poured another drink. And one for himself. Reached behind him and produced a sealed vial of pills. "Painkillers. On the house."

"To what do I owe this honor?" Budgie checked the vial to make sure it was sealed. He cracked it and dropped a pill into his drink where it fizzled.

"Got a promo going. Come in with broken bones, get some free painkillers." He gestured round the place. "As you can see, it's working. Business is booming."

"What we toast?" Budgie lifted his glass.

The barkeep decked his drink and poured himself another. Budgie sipped his. Hurt to swallow. He gestured at the man's arm. "What happened there anyway?"

"Machine did that to me. I was a clogger before I got myself chipped. The drunk fucker I was working with didn't turn the machine off. Read me as trash. Knew me better than my own mom." He laughed. "Thing tried to pick me up but all it got was flesh."

"Fecal," Budgie said. "A clogger?"

"Worked in a garbage mine, unclogging the machines." He shrugged. "Did it for a bout a year, then I got scheming, got caught and got sent back down." He put on a mock horror movie voice: "Never to return. Never to return. Got nuff money to open this borderland retreat."

Budgie glanced over his shoulder. The guy passed out on the table snored and farted. No one else here. Budgie leaned forward and spoke quiet. If the walls could talk, they'd tell you they have ears. "I'm gonna be doing that work," he said. "Start up Monday."

"You're shitting me?"

"I shit you not."

The barkeep poured Budgie another drink. He rolled his sleeve back down. "You want to get those bones knit then. You'll need em."

"Figures."

"What brought all that on?"

"What? The beat down?"

"Your uniform answers that, kid." The barkeep shook his head. "The move topside. What brought that on?"

Pill kicking in, Budgie relaxed. Didn't need to worry about this guy blabbing. Barkeeps had their own rulebook. Barkeeps don't gossip crime. Not if you tip. Budgie always tipped. He told the barkeep about Sputnik getting killed.

"You got spooked," the barkeep said. "Happened to me too. Death ain't the movies. Ain't glamorous."

"No, it ain't," Budgie said.

"Lemmee ask you something: Before all this, you ever kill anyone?"

Budgie shook his head. "Doled out a few shit kickings but never did anyone dead. Not till Wolfe."

"That's your problem. Better to meet death when you're giving it than when a buddy is getting it. First impressions you know." The barkeep swigged his drink. "Your crew should have got you wet. We used to call it making your bones. You met death and shook its hand. Work for the Grim Collector before he worked you. That way, you don't get so shocked when he comes knocking at your door."

"Maybe you feel like…"

"Like what?"

"Like he's collecting something owed," said Budgie.

"Maybe. Don't know." The barkeep lit a cigarette coated with hash oil. "Do know this, things were diff then. Rude boys were just one sorta gang. There were others and it was pretty much open war. But the locals got fed up with us and came down hard on the side of the rudies. You guys won, penned that rule book and there's not half as much fighting now."

"You guys?" Budgie said. "You weren't rude?"

"Nope. Skinhead." He smiled. "That's why I went tops. Get out or patch over or get killed. That's what spooked me. Saw all my crew, the Nation, getting offed. Hanged till they were dead, dead, dead. Like Christmas ornaments all along this street. Spooked me. Couldn't bring myself to join the gang that did it so I fucked off. Weak knees, I guess."

"Never met a skin before," Budgie said. "What else was there, like punks and emods and clockers. Eightboyz. Teddies. The Jox."

"Yeah there were those. They were all wiped out or made into chapters. There were others too. You know Hell's Angels? The Bloods? The Crypts?"

"Yeah, they're companies."

"Are now. Weren't always."

"Telling me they were gangs?"

The barkeep nodded. "Yeah but they were highly organized, supplied all of us pikers with weapons and shit. One foot in the reds and one in the greens. Now it's one foot in the greens and one in the blues. Shit, most of these companies got a pretty checkered past. Don't you have any anarcho friends?"

"Yeah, I got a few."

"Ask them about Baileys sometime and what they did to the cows. Shit, I can top that. Ask them about Lockheed Martin and the nation states or Phillip Morris. How about genetic weapons? We're talking xenocide, genocide, slavery, the whole bit. This mall is founded on crime. Runs on the same. The only real crime is being poor."

"Ask 'em?" Budgie said. "Try to get 'em to shut up about it."

"Yeah, they go on, don't they? But older I get the more sense I see in it. And the more worried I get. A couple of hundred years ain't that long if you think about it. You ever listen to the Bob Anger Show?"

"Never heard of it. Wait—maybe seen an advert."

"Yeah, well, he's this green level prat they got on the radio. He wants us all shipped outside to die." Pointed at Budgie. "You especially, Rude Boy."

"They'd never do that."

"You sure of that?" Barkeep took a swig of his drink. "Cause I sure as fucking on a Friday ain't. Look what they did to Africa."

"Thought you were a skin. Didn't you guys like that?"

"*Was* is the key word. Grew up a lot. Plus, when you get your ass kicked by a goulash gang like yours, it makes ya rethink your whole superiority angle." He shrugged. "Turns out race is shit poor way to arrange things. Money works better. Always has. Always will."

"Don't matter to me anyway," Budgie said. "Floating topside, remember?"

"Just don't forget your crew. If you're like me and get booted back down here you'll need 'em. You know, keep you shit secret and don't go telling any more barkeeps."

"What bout your code?"

"That code is like a lot of things."

"How so?"

"Ain't how it used to be and you can't afford it anyway."

"My crew won't have shit to do with me after I go up."

"You might be surprised. It's like a lot of things."

"Not how it used to be?"

"Yeah kid." he shrugged. "These be funny days. You don't know cause you haven't lived long enough to see, but trust an old bastard's word. These be funny bloody days. Just got a feeling like the world needs a bleeding. Wants one, even. Felt that before. Diff is, now I know the scent. Something coming down from above."

Budgie looked at the blood on his hand and wondered. Behind him the sleeping man snored. "I should get going." Budgie stood up. "Run the card."

"Yup," the barkeep said and looked at the clock. "That'll be a half global."

"A half global? Shit, thought you said those pills were free."

"They were." The barkeep grinned. "But the smiles aren't and convo never is." He grabbed that heavy glass and started polishing it. Tapped it once, lightly and with meaning, on the bar. "You gotta problem with that?"

PRODUCT PLACEMENT

"I want my kids to know the difference between right and wrong. That's why I choose Tooty Frootys in the morning instead of Frooty Tootys. **The right choice. Tooty Frootys.**"

GLOBAL HELL INCORPORATED. Network Security Systems that work. We will protect you. From us. Global Hell.

Brew Dog says: "Rude Ales are made with the finest hops and barley malt, free range water and Pacman top fermenting proprietary yeast. Preservative, additives, chemicals: Never! Rude does not pasteurize its products. Rude Ales are bottled using an oxygen absorbing cap, brown glass for better shelf life, and plenty of malted barley and hops to provide stability."

TERRORIST CHIC. We Sell Capes and Ringo Starr Masks. Buy your Yassar Arafat Headgear here! TERRORIST CHIC: The look that kills.

"Me and my friends were hanging out in the food court. We were all pretty stoned on acid and decided to head down to the red levels to par-tay. It was great. They played all the songs on The Edge and things got really crazy after curfew. We came back up that morning and bought all those reOrbs. After that I went home and boy did I get in trouble. Didn't matter. That night we were all back in the food court doing it again. After all it's the weekend. No work till Monday. Guess I'm on The Edge."

Drowning in debt? We have the solution. The best selection of ropes, razors and pills. Talk to one of our experts today. **SERENITY: YOUR ONE STOP SUICIDE SHOP.**

When does SITCOM host and toast again? Never seen him. Can't get his shit thru EDGE!!! :← HELP!

INFO DUMP

"Now Bob, the problem isn't the garbage mines. That's just a red herring that your type—"

"You crazy lying bastard! You know that's—"

"I'm not done, Bob. You had your turn, now let me speak."

"Okay. Give you enough rope..."

"Thanks Bob. Like I was saying, the garbage mines are not the problem. There is enough raw material in there—plastics, metals and what not—to keep us going for years. So their benefits actually outweigh their costs. And they've already done most of their polluting—"

"I have to—"

"The problem is that we're still spewing waste into the outside. That's why it's uninhabitable. We can't keep blaming our ancestors. When does it become our responsibility?"

"I'll agree that the genetic pollution—that our ancestors left, not us—is the main problem but if you really think that—"

"I do."

"—that those dumps, and I call them dumps because that's what they are, are clean now, then you're a crazy, lying bastard. You hear me, Jack Off? You and everyone like you should be forced—at gunpoint—to mine them yourself. That would teach you something about real life."

"I'm not saying that—"

"We'll be back after these messages with more hot talk, with me, your host, your voice, Bob Anger, on 'You're a Crazy Lying Bastard.' The topic tonight—Burning the dumps to clean up the outside. The guest, Lenny Niedenberger, author of "You're a Zombie Asshole!" More, more and more when we get back. Stay tuned."

Thank Santa. Budgie's key card still worked. His mom had left the encryption intact. He wasn't kicked out.

He slipped off the ladder and stumbled down the last few rungs. Thud-Thud-Thud. He grabbed its sides and stared at the wall. Grey. Flat. The pain in his ribs cut through the pills. His sweaty palms greased the ladder.

Behind him he heard false voices. His television had sensed his presence and flicked on. If he wanted some quiet, he'd have to turn it off manually. Best to just leave it. Thing did a decent job of drowning out his thinking. The flickering screen played some movie he'd seen a few times before. Never all the way through. Just five minutes here, five minutes there, tens of times.

At the bottom of the screen stood a line of text. Budgie sat on the edge of the cot and fumbled through his bedside table's drawer for a spine of synapacide. Some crap in there, needed a cleaning. Old candy wrappers and a couple of dead pill vials. There should've been more left. His mom must've got into them. He shut the drawer, lit the spine and looked at the television.

"One message for Budgie." He read the text aloud, giving the machine a voiceprint, and the screen changed.

Snow. Like Wolfe's eyes when he killed Sputnik. What was it Snort Donkey had said he was cranked on? Robo?

"Weird." Budgie stared harder, trying to see what was going on. Long time since he'd seen a dead channel. Budgie got off his cot and sat cross-legged in front of the screen, the burning spine dangling from his lip. The snow looked like electric, two tone, MC Escher geese. They flew from the bottom right corner to the top left but their progress was an illusion. When a white goose left a black one replaced it. Again and again.

He touched the screen with a single finger. Geese rippled outwards from the contact point. He dotted out two eyes then drew a mouth.

The face stayed there, watching, growing more detailed. "Everyone draws a face sooner or later," it said with a voice like compressed static. "Nature has programmed it into them."

"Nice graphics." Budgie returned to his cot. "Had me tweaked for a bit there. Who is this?"

"TeeVee."

Fecal. "I called you."

"I know."

"You know?" Knew what? Budgie shivered. Did TeeVee know how he'd treated his aunt? "I didn't know if you did or not. Thought I'd..."

"You're going topside. Is Sputnik going with you?"

How'd he know that, but not about Sputnik? "How did—"

"I've got a line. Saw your name on the list today. Is Sputnik going with you? I can't get a hold of him."

"So, you don't know?"

The screen hissed and flashed pink. The eyes turned to question marks. "Know what?"

"Hate to be the bearer of bad news..." Budgie took a drag of mouth-numbing smoke. He hoped the pause was long enough for TeeVee to figure it out himself. "Sputnik's dead," he said. "Wolfe loved him with a dressed blade."

"Oh." A long, hissing noise. "That explains something."

"What's that?"

"His mom keeps calling."

"You spoke to her?"

"I've been busy."

The muscle knot in the base of Budgie's neck loosened. "Sorry about this."

"About what?"

"Your cousin, going North. Bout me, going topside."

"These things happen and I would not deign to concern myself with your career plans," TeeVee said. "Aside from this: You have just become valuable to me."

Might've known, thought Budgie. Explains why he called back. "How so?"

"I'm a collector these days. Info mainly. Most of it is redundant. Got percepts everywhere on the reds, though apparently not everywhere enough..."

"Yeah, can't believe no one told—"

"Dishonesty is to be expected. Information turns to noise, lies or omissions as it travels upwards through a hierarchy. Do I make you comfortable? Do you want to tell me truths I may dislike?"

"Not sure what the right answer to that is."

"And you have it exact."

A long squirming pause.

"I have grown adept at reading these omissions through the years, at seeing what is not shown and hearing what is left unsaid. Shadows and silhouettes. Yet I did not see this."

"We all make mistakes."

"And we all die. We do not all commit suicide."

"Okay."

"I have information sources all through the reds but I need more on the lawn."

"Getting samples? For a new mix, like?"

"Something like that."

Budgie rubbed his eyes. Looking at the screen made them ache. Supposed he should just be happy TeeVee didn't take offense at his query. Asking why an alpha did something was out of bounds. The pills and pain had blurred his judgment. "Sorry," he said without being prodded. "That's none of my business anyway."

"This method of conversation often makes people feel more at ease than they otherwise would. Or should. I accept that as a cost and a benefit. But let's not turn mistakes into habits. Or dwell too deeply upon them when we do."

"Course not, sorry." Budgie rubbed his sides. "I don't have any info for your collection."

"Not yet."

"Just a guess, please don take offense, but sounds like you want me to gather some."

"I'm a bit more ambitious than that."

This reminded Budgie of his childhood games of pick-up dodgeball. One of the much bigger kids, a fat prick, notorious for his cruelty, always performed the same routine. He'd meet Budgie's eyes and, even before he hurled the ball, Budgie knew it was coming and knew it was going to hurt. There was nothing he could do. Dodging would just result in a beating. So he'd hold still and let the ball slap him square in the face. It'd knock him to the ground and blister his cheeks. Looking at this television screen, he looked back through time and into those mean, swine eyes. He should flinch.

"I want your eyes."

"You want my eyes?"

"You repeat plenty," said TeeVee. "That must be the origin of your name."

Budgie wondered how he could play for time. He couldn't. "But my eyes, though. Shit."

"Not literally. I wish to plug into your brain and use you as a passive information gathering creature."

"You can do that?"

"Well."

Was that a question or answer? "Permission to speak honestly?"

"Peculiar that you don't ask permission to lie."

"It's cause I figure you might like a lie but the truth, I don know that you're gonna like that."

"Permission granted."

"I don know that I can help you."

"?"

"It ain't easy going toppy. You know that, of course. Know I'm not relaying any fresh news there, but I'm sayin' I got a lot on my plate. Lotta gristle and bone and shit. They tell me, I get caught in a scheme, I get booted. They gon be auditing my cash, they gon be looking at me. And any shit go down that I look privy to, my..."

"I see your problem."

"Like it ain't easy to do this straight but I get the idea that doing it crooked ain't even possible. I'm just sayin' with all respect, and thinkin' there ain't no sense lying to you nohow, that you be asking me for a lot. A real lot. Maybe more than I got to give."

"Your problem is that you're scared."

"Could be, yeah." Usually, if someone said that, it was a challenge. Not now. It was just fact. "Likesay, I get caught. I get booted. My life is over. Done." He shrugged. "So yeah, scared."

"You should be."

"Yeah?"

"A life can end in a variety of ways."

"Guess it can."

"None of them are pleasant."

Budgie thought it best to keep quiet.

"I notice that you keep touching up those ribs of yours. You also grimace every time you twist. This made me curious. It occasioned a switch to X Ray."

"You see my ribs then?"

"I do. And I can guess how you got them."

"Like I said: Lot of bone and gristle on my plate."

"That's on everyone's plate," TeeVee said. "Life can end in a variety of ways. A rib bone can puncture the lungs. Throat gristle can be cut after a hard day's work on the greens. A man might be beat to death in his bed, die of cancer, break his neck with a fall or drown in his own vomit after being poisoned. Variety. The spice of life. Mrs. Dash. On the bone. On the gristle."

"Look, if you're gon threaten me into doing this, I ain't gon say you're bluff. But I need you to come out with that. I'm no gon to submit to my imagination. Just you being here is nuff implication. Just me listenin' is submission. We know that. So, what you wanna do?"

"When I threaten you," said TeeVee, "you will not require your imagination."

"Good."

"If anything, I wish to protect you."

Budgie snorted.

"Something funny?"

"Well, ya, kinda. Just that we tell that to every business we run collection on. 'We're gon to protect you.' 'From who?' 'From us.'"

"And from everyone else," TeeVee said.

"That's true too."

"You have value to me. And I wish to protect you from the threats you already face. Have you thought about these?"

"Almost nothing but."

"I'm sure that you're also aware of the cost of living on the greens and I'm sure you can perform enough rudimentary math to know that you will not be able to live upstairs for quite some time. If ever."

"That's the width."

"That also means that you will spend a lot of time toppy, every day multiplying the variety of ways that your life can end. Until, finally, what? You move upstairs?" The television hissed something like laughter.

"That funny to you?"

"You think you're welcome on the lawn, Rude Boy? You think entry level actually enters anywhere? You think it's possible to play it straight? And to succeed by doing so?"

"I get the impress that it's tough but there ain't no other way. Besides..." Budgie was going to mention Harmony's brother. She'd told him that he helped pay for that nice hutch of hers by working on the greens. But, before the words were out, Budgie checked himself. There was no sense involving her in this. "Some people do it."

"Anyone you know?"

"Not really."

"Friend of a friend?"

"Could be."

"Everyone has that friend. No one has ever met them."

"Okay."

"What I have seen from people I actually know, from those I have seen and those you will soon see, is that they don't want you on the greens. The only people who ever actually make it up there are the ones who are clever enough to scheme without getting caught. The others die. Or come home. And then die. Or, having at least made some money, serious money, and being semi-responsible with it, get semi-respectable."

Budgie thought of that bartender.

"This is all more test than route. If it was a route, they'd give you a place to stay. They don't. That should tell you something. That should tell you they don't care."

"I don need them to care," Budgie said. "I just need them to give me my shot."

"You don't need them for that. I'm giving you your shot. A good one. And you'd be wise to take it."

"And what is it? What's in it for me?"

"That depends on what you see."

Budgie lit another spine. Would need a few more hits if he was going to negotiate with an alpha. Trick was not looking greedy. Just try to get what he's willing to give and don't aim for anything more. Fact was, TeeVee had been more than reasonable. He coulda just said: Do what I want or I will have your throat cut. And Budgie would've hopped to. That TeeVee had spent time explaining was still not enough to convince Budgie that no was an option. It did convince him that TeeVee had some respect for his intelligence.

"Let's say I see nothing. What then?"

"Let's eliminate that as an option."

"Okay. I don know what you need. I can't gauge my value. Would have to rely on your word."

"You don't trust me?"

"I'm a long way from being guided by trust," Budgie said. "I fear you. I respect you. I also know alphas keep their word even though I know they don have to. I also think you're right. Bout all that, them not really wanting rude boys on the lawn and whatnot." He felt his ribs. "I spent the whole day getting rolled and getting shit-kicked. My knucks and knives have been nicked. I'm unmanned and unarmed and I ain't even turned toppy yet." He smiled. "I need a steady salary with bonuses."

"No," TeeVee said.

He's just letting that sink in, Budgie thought. *Wants me understanding that he has the upper hand. He doesn't need to haggle with me. But just wait, don't cave, and let him counter.* Long moments passed, each one deadlier than the last. Budgie wished he could read that static face.

"Salary or bonuses. It's your gamble. Bet one way or the other but not both. I won't be hedged."

"What sort of salary are we talking about?"

"Three globals a workday. And that's for doing nothing. I just want to get a flow."

"Make it six." Budgie saw the static face smile.

"I'll make it two."

So it *was* like that. Budgie took a deep breath and, although it hurt him to do so, thanked Santa that he was going to live. "We have a deal then."

"When is the soonest that you can come over?"

"Tonight?"

"Fine."

"And I need those globals cleaned and encrypted. They audit me."

"I am aware of the niceties." A pause. "Do not go to a doctor. I'll take care of those ribs for you."

The face sank beneath tides of static. Hard to say the exact moment it vanished and became a suggestion. Hard to say if it was ever there.

The television, reading nothing, auto-changed to one of Budgie's most watched channels. No show, just the mini-dramas of commercials. Budgie butted out his spine and laid back on the cot. Listened. This station played the best adverts, Nike and such, but Budgie had seen and heard them all before. Wondered when some new ones would be out. Wondered if they had different ones on the greens. He'd know soon enough.

He felt odd, maybe a reaction between the whiskey and the synapacide. Maybe because he'd be scheming on the greens. Wasn't what he wanted but since when had that mattered? It was what he had.

His mind spun like a reOrb and kept turning to Harmony. He imagined her beside him, just sitting there, his arm round her shoulders. He felt wrong without her, like he wasn't quite real. Faded.

The commercials turned into a show. He watched it for a while and then said: "Play Harmony and Budgie tape."

Screen shifted and played a movie preview before showing him having sex with Harmony. He had the thing loop on itself. Thought about dropping an orgasm and wacking off. Decided against it. He'd rather talk to her. Maybe go to her place and touch her in real time.

"Message Harmony." He gave her SSN and the screen changed to a still advert. Ringing. No answer. Budgie stared at the ceiling. Where was she? Why did he care? Felt like he was watching a show bout his life. Like someone else was playing him and mashing it up with emotions. Doin' things he wouldn't, thinkin' things he didn't, feelin' things he never knew were in him. Ticklish things.

He weighed his options for the night. He'd rather hang out alone or with Harmony than go the old party route. But she'd be going the old party route. If he wanted to keep that girl he couldn't bore her—she'd already called him a glum cunt—so he'd have to party even harder than usual.

Did some math, figuring out what globals he had and what he could afford to spend. Not much, but enough. Where was she anyway? Was she with anyone? Thought about calling her again and twisted his body just to hurt his way outta that.

Another man? Budgie's muscles bunched. It was the same gut feeling he got when someone, a stranger, touched up his property. Not just any old thing but something valuable. Like they were gonna take or break it. So what was going on here? Did he think he owned

Harmony or something? It wasn't like he was her pimp. Wasn't like she'd even have one.

The door buzzed open and Mom scrambled down the ladder. He could see up her short skirt and looked away. He cleared his throat so she'd know she wasn't alone.

She steadied herself against the ladder.

"Hi Mom," Budgie said.

"So you decided to come home?" She put her hands on her hips. "To what do I owe this great honor?"

Great. She's drunk. "I just thought I should drop in."

"I don't know why you'd bother. Not after what you did to poor Simzy." She coughed. "I wish you wouldn't smoke in here. You know what it does to my lungs. And I can't believe you acted like that. It's my fault I suppose. Spoiled you. That's the problem."

Spoiled him? Before he became a rude boy, Budgie'd been starving. After joining the gang he had paid for everything he owned and most of what she owned too. If that was spoiled he'd hate to see deprived. "Yeah, sorry bout that."

Her face softened and she flopped into her chair in front of the television. "You were gone so long, after what happened to Sputnik, I thought... I don't know what I thought. What happened to your head anyway?"

"Banged it on a low ladder." The cut still hurt. He knew she didn't believe him but she wouldn't ask about it.

She crossed her legs and lit a cigarette. "Simzy's not even angry at you. She knows you two always had each other's back. She knows that." Coughed smoke. "It's been real hard on her. You should go see her or something. She always liked you."

"She's not mad at me?"

"No."

He felt even guiltier. If Mrs. Dobject had been angry—like she had every right to be—he could, at least, be angry back. That was a feeling he could understand. Not like all these other things his gut kept playing with, guilt and affection and the rest of it. But Mrs. Dobject was being nice. He didn't deserve that. "Thought she'd be murderous."

His Mom stared at the wall over Budgie's shoulder. "Enough of that feeling going around." She coughed phlegm rattling noise into her hand.

Should he tell her he was going topside? Mom had a big mouth. She'd brag to all the girls at work. The word would filter into the street and he'd be fucked. It was bad enough that TeeVee knew but TeeVee was quiet as they came. Pure enigma. He wouldn't say anything to anyone until it was time.

Budgie's life was breaking fractal. One Budgie, two Budgie, three Budgie, four. Two Budgies more. There would be the one down here, doing rudie schemes and the one up there, living all upright and air tight.

Fooling Mom would be easy. She was hardly ever home. Fooling his crew would be tougher. He couldn't be seen in the street without his uniform. It was a lot of bone and gristle. A lot of stress. And if he mucked it and got chipped, life would get naught but a lot tougher. Didn't know what he'd do then. Needed a plan B.

"You okay?" Mom asked. "You seem a little off."

"Just a bit high."

"Yeah, I smelled that when I got home. That smoke bothers my lungs." She coughed again and stared at Budgie with her big drunk eyes. Budgie didn't trust that look. He'd seen it before. The bloodshot cracks coiled around her irises. "When I was pregnant with you," she said. "I saw a budgie."

"I know, Mom."

"Thought it was the prettiest thing I ever saw. Then I saw you. And look at you now." She shook her head. "You're trouble Budgie. You always have been. You always will be." She shrugged. "I'm sick of dealing with it. You're my kid but I give up. I really give up."

"I thought you said—"

"I know what I said. Simzy isn't angry. But I am. I know you better than she does and you don't make it very easy to like you." She sighed. "This was the last strike. You can't live here anymore. I won't be associated with whatever it is you get up to. You've gotta go."

Budgie glared at his boots. He figured this was coming but it still bothered him.

If he just told his mom he was going to work upstairs she'd let him stay. But—no. She'd fuck it up, just like she'd fucked up her job on the greens.

He wasn't even sure that he wanted to live with this woman anymore. It was always lies with her. Even now he wasn't sure that she wasn't running some con on him. Get the place to herself but leave on good terms so he'd keep paying her. She had another thing coming if she thought he was going to keep dumping money down this hole.

Maybe he'd buy her a fucking bird.

■■■ ■■ ■ ■■■ ■ ■ ■ ■■ ■ ■■■ ■ ■ ■ ■ ■■ ■ ■■ ■■ ■ ■ ■ ■ ■■ ■ ■■ ■ ■ ■ ■ ■ ■ ■ ■■

Sitcom swiped his skeleton key card through TeeVee's lock. He didn't usually use it here. It was mostly for when he visited gammas and wanted them to know that he was in charge, that they couldn't lock him out. The door swished open and Sitcom entered, carrying the blank orbs that were payment for the mix he'd used at the slummer party. Tonight he had something better going on. A wake.

TeeVee sat on the couch in the back room, zoned out. Against the wall, slumped the body of the man Sitcom had delivered. Metal balls stared from his eye sockets and a long antenna corkscrewed out of his right temple.

Sitcom put the case of reOrbs down and approached the body. He felt the neck for a pulse. Nothing. The gizmo on the table flickered and projected light onto the wall, forming a copy of TeeVee's face. "Hello Sitcom," it said.

Sitcom hated when TeeVee did this. He never knew if he was actually talking to the alpha or a chat-bot. He took his fingers off the corpse's neck and, for some reason, wiped them on his pants. "Wasabi?"

"You're spinning at my cousin's wake."

"Your cousin?"

"Don't be coy. I know what happened to him."

"Oh shit, that's right. You two were related."

"And don't play dumb."

"Shall I try contrite then? Sorry, didn't think it mattered and it kinda escaped my mind with you know..." He gestured towards the body. When TeeVee remained still, Sitcom shrugged. "Yeah, I'm spinning tonight, at Old Union."

"See the reOrb on the table? The blue one?"

"Yeah."

"That's your mix for tonight. All done. You just need to play it."

"What cost?"

"The usual."

This pissed Sitcom off, just a little, but he was careful to keep his face blank. He didn't know if TeeVee was watching or not. He'd been wanting to break out on his own, to start making his own music. TeeVee used him like a puppet.

Can't let it bother me. TeeVee made my rep and I owe everything to him. So what if I have to play his shit? I get the credit and I get a good chunk of the money. Just a soldier. TeeVee's the general and I'm just a solider.

"A good one too," the screen said and Sitcom's gut twitched before he realized that TeeVee hadn't been reading his thoughts. He was talking about the mix.

"Is it?" he asked.

"Yeah."

That mongoose poked its head out from beneath the couch and glared at Sitcom. Hustled towards the body and chewed at the shin. "Never understood why you couldn't just get a cat."

"What do you know about ants?" the static face asked.

"I said cat."

"I heard you. What do you know about ants?"

"Nuthin'. Why?"

"There's a type of ant called monomorium santschii. It doesn't build its own colonies, it invades other ones. Then it secretes a chemical that drives its hosts crazy and makes them kill their queen."

"Ants have queens?" Sitcom always felt stupid when TeeVee started up on the speeches.

"Yes. But that's not the point. We were talking about cats. Cats carry toxoplasma gondii. It's a parasite and it rips your brain apart. Induces insanity. It makes you get more cats. This increases the effect. You ever wonder why the Egyptians worshiped cats?"

"Shit, when did they do that?"

"A very long time ago. They were subverted by their cats and their cats took over their empire. A cat is a furry parasite. They are monomorium santschii. They should all be notched. Every time I see a commercial with a cat or one of those all cat channels or one of those channels that cats are supposed to watch, I just think it's happening again. The fucking cats will take over."

Sitcom nodded like he understood wtf TeeVee was talking about. He didn't like when his friend spoke like this. Reminded him of when TeeVee was sick. Sure, he wasn't parroting television shows, but something about the tone of voice echoed those bad days.

"Okay, you don't like cats." This room bothered him. It was too quiet. The corpse didn't help. "I've gotta head over to Old Union. You want me to dispose of..."

"Oh him. Yes. I forgot to water it."

<hr>

Budgie leaned against a wall. Across the corridor, on the ground, an old guy with a beard shook and wrapped his arms around his legs. He mumbled. Above his beard, two beady eyes darted back and forth at the pedestrians. They settled on Budgie. He pointed and smiled.

Budgie pulled his gizmo and flicked it open. "Do I have my job info yet?"

The gizmo buzzed and identified him. "Yes."

Budgie put it back into his pocket. They were good devices for the price. Not quite as intuitive as he'd like but it had more storage than he'd ever need. Most importantly, the voice recog was good enough to work in the corridors. It fucked up if he was at a party but—

"Budgie." A couple of Vidicons ambled towards him, each one gripping a bottle of cheap beer. Pillar and Nightcap. Pillar carried a black case.

Budgie tapped on of their fists as the guy swigged with his free hand.

"Wasabi?" Pillar asked.

"Not much," Budgie said. "Well, just got kicked outta home." He shrugged. "So there's that."

"Wonderin' why you had the pack," Pillar said.

Nightcap nodded. Though these guys, like Budgie, couldn't afford any good cosmetic upgrades, their porcelain skin was bedazzled with golden sparkles. It made them look like dolls. Nightcap wore a pair of small black goggles affixed to his head with a leather strap. "Thought you were muling."

"Nah." Budgie thumbed at the strap of his pack. He'd forgotten it was there. Funny, he was turtle-like right now, carrying all his possessions, and he'd forgotten all about it. Didn't know if that meant he didn't have much or that he had a good pack. "Just got my shit in there."

"So you need tools?"

"That's the width."

"Knives and knucks?" Pillar dropped to his knees and unfolded the case. "Here's the select."

Trying not to cringe with rib pain, Budgie bent over and looked through the case. He found a pair of knucks that fit him and a knife with good balance. A bit better than his last. "How much?"

"Couple of good choices, there. Give them to you both for a globe."

"Got it." Budgie paid and attached them to his belt. "Just gotta break them in."

Pillar glanced at Nightcap who stared at nothing. The guy covered up his eyes because they were damaged. He was blind. Could see moving shapes but not much beside. What he lacked in sight he made up for with smell. Like a hound.

"Say Budge," Pillar said. "You holdin' at least?"

"Nah."

"Fecal." Pillar folded his case back up. "Gotta keep digging for Snort Donkey. You see him round?"

"Nah."

"Guess he'll be at the wake tonight."

Budgie started. "Sputnik's?"

"Yeah. You didn't know?"

"Forgot," said Budgie.

"You gon break in those tools tonight?" asked Nightcap.

"Why would I? Just Vidicons."

"So you don't know bout Griff?" Pillar glanced back at Nightcap. "Shit, we thought you were lurking. Were wonderin' why you kept so mouse."

"What's there to know?" Budgie reached into his pocket for a spine of synapacide. When he saw Pillar gawking, he felt guilty. "Personal," he explained. Just how hard up were these guys? They prolly wanted to pick up something stronger from Snort Donkey and not squander their money on corporate dope with the strength regulations. "Not for sale."

Pillar shrugged. "Wouldn't waste globals on that shit anyway. But how bout barter? Our info for a spine. And believe me, that's a deal."

"Fine." Budgie gave them each a thin white stick. "So what's there to know bout Griff?"

Pillar lit his spine and it crackled electric blue light. He looked at the tube, twisted up his mouth and exhaled a cloud of smoke. "It'll give the beer a bit of a kick anyway," he said to Nightcap.

"Good for you," said Nightcap.

"Nightcap don smoke." Pillar tapped his nose. "Bad for the schnoze."

"Would you walk round blindfolded, motherfuck?"

"Don worry bout it," said Pillar. "We'll find you some pills and get nice and rabid later." Looking back at Budgie, he tilted his head and inhaled again. "Griff's been a busy boy in the forum."

"Says you've gone bitch." Nightcap had a funny look that Budgie couldn't quite read but he knew it wasn't happy. Contempt? Maybe, but directed at who?

"What?" Budgie said.

"Shut up, Cap," Pillar said. "It's supposed to be deaf and dumb not blind and stupid."

"Fuck you."

"Whatev." Pillar smiled at Budgie. "Yeah, Griff says that you hit him cause he wanted to do up a toppy. Been talking shit ever since."

"That true?" Nightcap asked.

"Fuck no." Budgie looked between the two of them, his mind racing. So Griff was politicking. "I hit Griff cause the little bitch told me to fuck myself."

"People been talking anyway," Pillar said.

"Like who?"

Pillar stuck his thumb out and pointed it at Nightcap. "Like this guy."

"Just think it's fucked up is all." Nightcap swigged his beer and stared at Budgie with those black lenses. "Why wouldn't you pound those guys? What the fuck a toppy ever do for you?"

"Nothing." Budgie touched the hilt of his knife. He expected to see Nightcap's eyes twitch towards the blade but, of course, that didn't happen. Nightcap smiled and his hand rested on his belt.

"You smell like Air Pirate," said Nightcap. "What put you in the market for tools anyhow?"

"Easy guys." Pillar stepped between them. "Easy." He swigged at his beer and turned towards his friend. "Cap, you're a dumb fuck. I've known Budgie for years. His loyalty is solid. How much you worth Cap? Forty globals. Budgie is a century global fucker. And fuckin' Griff—he's a fifteen value newbie prospect bitch. You seriously believing fifteen globals over a hundred and putting your forty up against Budgie's hundred? Shit. I know you can't be serious cause you'd just be too fuckin' stupid if you were serious. And Cap, I know you aren't *that* fucking stupid. No matter what anyone says." He looked at Budgie. "And you Budgie, I don't know what you're playing at and I don't give a fuck. But you gotta keep connected. Letting a bitch like Griff talk this shit bout you is not good. Not good at all. Makes you look guilty in the eyes of certain, stupid-ass comrades. And when we hear that you're off in other sections, talkin' to Air Pirates and when Air Pirates show up, in our forum, showing off Vidicon tools and you show up looking for replacements for said tools..."

Word sure got round fast and not even the right word. Budgie pulled his hand off his knife. When he saw Nightcap do the same he looked at Pillar and pointed at the cut on his forehead. "See this? I was poaching. Got caught. If I had a partner who was worth a shit, might not have to go hunting by myself and get jumped for my trouble."

"Course you were—but Budgie—you gonna let Griff status fuck you? I mean, serious, you gotta set an example." He dropped his spine and ground it out beneath his boot. "You gotta fuck him up. If he's all bluff and bluster you gotta show your cards."

It was true. Budgie's beef wasn't with Nightcap. It was with Griff.

Santa, he thought. He wanted to keep a low profile but that was impossible. All these people and it was impossible to disappear into the crowd. Whatever you did people talked. You were eye-deed everywhere you went and your rep was everything. "Griff gonna be at the wake?"

"Everyone is. Sitcom is spinning and it's a big bash. At Old Union. Guillotine and everything."

Snort Donkey really went all out. Usually the blade was reserved for the best loved rude boys. Unusual for a gamma to get that treatment but Snort Donkey wouldn't promote crap, especially when he was getting part of the door. Sputnik had been well liked but he couldn't have expected someone to kill himself for the sake of a party. At least his ghost wouldn't be as lonely as Budgie's flesh. "Then me and Griff got business tonight. By the rules."

Pillar nodded and Nightcap grinned.

Budgie wondered why he cared what these people thought and remembered: Because his life depended on it.

"You gonna patrol with us before the party?"

"No," Budgie said. TeeVee's static face briefly flickered at the back of his thoughts. "Business first."

INFO DUMP

"Of course there wasn't an alien invasion."

"But there was. Not a physical one but there definitely was one."

"You crazy lying bastard! What do you mean by that?"

"What happened was this: The aliens invaded our electronic media. They invaded the minds of some people and spread out as memes to test us. If there had been a mainstream belief in them, then they would have become physical. Witnesses saw them and there were crop circles, which now look like a warning about our agri-techs. So all that was required was faith."

"That just means that some crackpots thought they invaded."

"The rest of us failed the test. We refused to believe and they left us. But they're still out there. Who knows, maybe they're floating around the mall right now. Maybe they've set up colonies on Earth. If these MTO guys didn't have us all locked in here we'd know. Maybe that's why they have us all locked in here."

"You crack me up Old Bob. And we'll have more zany theories when we get back on 'You're a Crazy Lying Bastard,' with me, your host, your voice, Bob Anger."

PRODUCT PLACEMENT

Sick of memes you don't want? Infect yourself with Old Uncle Joe's Anti Meme Meme. WE have the antidote. Uncle Joe's. The Memetic Research Division you can trust. (Uncle's Joes is a division of Monsanto.)

"When me, Dino Mondo, goes fishing, I'm known to make a widow out of the wife of the Widow Maker. And I couldn't do it without the Widow Maker Killer." (shot of the 21 year old actor/model playing Dino catching fish, his ample crotch emphasized by camera angle.) "The Widow Maker Killer. It's the big one."

Just grabbed the new SITCOM mix! Been spinning nothing but!

Budgie walked through the little Bistro. A big-bellied, bald bartender sat at a table nursing a bottle of beer. A gizmo projected a video game onto the wall. The guy played by tapping the image and the smart light responded. Nice gadget. Budgie couldn't afford anything like that and wondered how this guy could. Must have money. But from where?

No one went to this place and he was the only guy who worked here. The Vidicons didn't even bother collecting protection from this bar. More hassle than what it was worth. Maybe they should start.

Budgie shrugged it off. Most likely a customer had left it behind and TeeVee had cracked the code for the guy. Budgie'd heard TeeVee was friendly with him in a distant sort of way.

Budgie headed through the back door, climbed the stairs and strode down the empty hall. Lights flickered and buzzed, jerking his shadow around the floor. On the wall, a cockroach kept pace with him, occasionally pausing to twitch its antennae and whistle through holes in its armored back. When Budgie reached TeeVee's door, the insect darted into a crack. Before Budgie touched the bell, the door hissed open.

"TeeVee?" Budgie stepped inside. The closing door clanged an exclamation point. "Anyone home?" Stupid question, he thought, sniffing the smoky air and looking around. Hutches don't open by themselves. At the end of the room another door, this one hinged, hung ajar. Orange light wheezed out of it. Budgie swallowed the gathering lump in his throat and entered.

TeeVee sat on the couch, one leg up on the cushions, the other hanging down. On the floor was big hookah, one of the tubes leading into the corner of TeeVee's mouth. Limp and broken as a dead snake. The man puffed slowly, staring at nothing. He stroked the mongoose on his lap while it glared at Budgie with intelligent, brown eyes.

Budgie cleared his throat and TeeVee shifted. Instead of the Vidicon uniform, the alpha wore fitted black fur. It looked like the short, down-turned hair of a cat. Budgie had the horrible feeling that TeeVee was actually naked, that he'd got a mod that let him grow cat fur over his chest arms and legs. Budgie didn't mind mods—he liked them—but something about this struck him as all wrong. Upgrades were just cosmetic shit. Growing hair over your whole body so you didn't have to wear clothes wasn't just excessive; It was fucking crazy.

TeeVee's pale skin shone in stark contrast. You couldn't even say the guy was white. He was past that. Translucent and baby bald. Purple veins glowed beneath his skin and his eyes were cataract blue orbs. Something about TeeVee reminded Budgie of a baby rat.

Hairless and fetal looking.

Budgie sat down on the chair across from the couch.

The gizmo on the coffee table projected a stream of blue light against the side of TeeVee's bald head and drew a face. "Give me a moment," the face mouthed, the sound coming from the gizmo. "You're earlier than I expected and I need to finish something up."

The face vanished, leaving orange light on saran wrap skin.

"No problem." Budgie rubbed his palms on his pantlegs. Having heard that TeeVee hated people looking at his reOrbs, Budgie stared at his zippered boots. The polished steel toes bent the orange light. It was almost hypnotic.

"Sorry." TeeVee stretched out of his strange rigidity. "I hate poor manners but I just couldn't leave. Things to do, always things to do."

"Hear that."

"You're the center of a small controversy," TeeVee said. "A well liked character though one that makes some people uneasy. Recently acting very weird and you..."

The words faded away and the room returned to its default silence. Budgie wished that he had some stronger drugs in him and asked TeeVee if he could smoke a cigarette.

"You may."

The mongoose hopped onto the floor and TeeVee stood up, his body creaking and popping.

When had he last moved? TeeVee dropped the hookah's tube onto the table and wandered to one of the walls stacked with reOrbs. His long fingers tapped through them, selected one and held it to the light. A smile teased his lips and he returned to his seat.

This place was like the nature shows Budgie watched; the ones about old school underwater life. The red levels were a coral reef. You had your big sharks, your schools of scared prey, your electric eels, your cleaners and your crabs. Vidicons were barracudas, dangerous singly and even more dangerous in a pack.

But TeeVee's hutch was no reef. This was the ocean floor. And TeeVee? He was that ugly, old fish in the solid darkness of the deep sea, dangling a light bulb above its huge mouth. Budgie was just the little prey fishy, fascinated by the light and hovering in the tooth-spiked trap. Fuck, he was dumb. How'd he end up here?

"So TeeVee." He cleared his throat and lit a cigarette. "I'm not sure about this."

"Jitters?" TeeVee's voice was casual, as if fear was natural and irrelevant. He clicked open the reOrb and split it into two parts that he set on the table. A thin spike poked out of one, and TeeVee spun it. It swirled in place, the needle wobbling. TeeVee leaned back into the couch. The mongoose crawled into his lap but he brushed it away. "Or maybe there's a deeper moral dilemma going on here. Perhaps you think it's not right to sell your body for your future?" He tilted his head. "Sudden attack of conscience on an unguarded flank?"

"No." Budgie's knees shook.

Pupils formed in the center of TeeVee's blue eyes.

"I'm just sca-sca-sca-sca—" He put his hands up and his head down. Took a deep breath. Counted to three. Tried again without looking at TeeVee. "Santa, I'm scared. I dunno what the fuck you're gonna do to me."

"I'm going to rent your percepts. You're going be a satellite of mine so I can gather some information that I'm finding rather tricky to get my hands on. There's so little quality in the dump. Opinions, yes. Feelings and thoughts and adverts yes. But it's all smog and I need some clean air. Some reality. I need you to provide that. Just a filter. A wee bit of the old quality control."

TeeVee smiled. Budgie had never seen his teeth before. He never wanted to again. Looked like butter knives.

"You see my pet here?" TeeVee asked.

"Yeah."

"You know what it is?"

"A mongoose." Budgie had watched them fight snakes in casinos. "Tough little beasts."

"You're close but not quite right." He tapped his thigh and the animal crawled onto him. TeeVee rubbed its head. "Her name is Riki-Tiki. And she's my familiar."

"No shit?" Budgie leaned forward to look at the animal. "You mean she's a—"

"DNA computer. Yes. Homemade. You bet." In TeeVee's mouth, orange light shone against silver metal. "You notice that she's healthy? Nice fur, bright eyes?"

"Yeah."

"You'll be the same. I'm going to convert you into a computer and you won't know the difference. I'll see things through your eyes and I'm going to dedicate you to extra processing. It'll be rough the first few days—you'll have some bad dreams while you brain adapts to all the extra info you'll be filtering—but the brain, particularly the human brain, is highly adaptable. In a few days you'll be back to normal. Maybe even a bit better. You'll certainly be less dependent on drugs."

"What if I say no?"

"Just say no."

"What?"

"Just say no."

"No?"

"No."

Something burned Budgie's fingers and looked down to see his cigarette was done. He butted it out in the ashtray with a trembling hand. "Likesay, I get second thoughts about going toppy and whatnot? What then?"

TeeVee wore the blank ghost of an expression. His lack of eyebrows, his translucent skin and his pupils, all agreed to show nothing. After a moment he rested his hands on his knees. "What makes a pile?"

"Huh?"

"If I take some pebbles and I take them one at a time and I stack them on top of each other. When do those little pebbles become a pile?"

"I dunno what you—"

"Is it after one? Is it two? Three, four, five. Fifteen, sixteen, seventeen. And let's say it's seventeen and I take one away so there's only sixteen. Is it still a pile then? I'd say yes. So what makes a pile?"

"I dunno."

"And you must be forgiven your ignorance. It is a difficult question. Men have been puzzling over it for thousands of years. I don't think we'll find an answer tonight. I don't think we should try."

"Are, we um, supposed to?" Was TeeVee was even talking to him? Maybe a line got crossed somewhere and someone else was now listening to TeeVee explain about how he could or could not change his mind about going toppy. Budgie had never felt so stupid. "Cause, like, I don't get it."

TeeVee sighed. "When you make a choice, even a little pebble of one, you are piling up little stones. One after another after another. When do they become a pile?"

"At, uh, seventeen."

"Let's say that is the case. And let's say your decision to come here is the seventeenth stone. And you take that away. Now you have sixteen stones. You still have the pile. You decide not to go toppy. You're down to fifteen stones. Still a pile. Having made a pile, it's difficult to get rid of one."

That's a pile of something, Budgie almost said but checked himself. Calling bullshit would not fly well here.

"You are going toppy. You already have. You can't come back here because you've already left. Your future is just waiting for you to catch up to it and meet it."

"I can't change my mind?"

"You can just say no. You just did. It makes no difference. It's too late for that. We have a deal. You have a pile. No matter what you say."

That much was true. He'd agreed to this and they'd even settled on a price. Whatever TeeVee had to say about stones and whatnot, you didn't break deals with alphas. If Budgie backed out now, he'd be dead or worse. Probably worse. Then dead. And it didn't matter. TeeVee owned him from the moment he became a Vidicon.

He supposed he should be grateful for the opportunity. This would just increase his value. "Not that I want to say no," he said and forced a smile. Just harmless old Budgie here. No reason to get excited. "Only asking, you know."

"You know. I know. We know."

"So how do we do this?"

"Take your tunic off. I want to see to those ribs."

Budgie hesitated then unbuttoned his coat and pulled it off. He looked down at his pale chest. The ribs were corduroy beneath muscles. Deep purple and nauseous yellow bruises up his sides. Looked as bad as it felt.

TeeVee knocked Riki-Tiki off his lap and, reaching under his couch, pulled out a black bag. "There was a time when one had to know doctoring to be a rude boy. Was a time when one had to be able to fix bones." TeeVee opened the bag. "But, these days, you don't even know enough to tape this up. No knowledge."

"No, well." Budgie jumped. Something cold and wet pressed into his side. "What the—"

"Be quiet. Try not to breathe. This will numb you and stop any bleeding."

Budgie's sides froze.

"You might not want to look at this," TeeVee said.

A scalpel flash in the corner of his vision. "Oh Santa." He gawked.

TeeVee cut down from Budgie's armpit to the bottom of his ribcage. The flesh split like a coat. There was no blood. Looked like everything was covered in some thin plastic. Budgie gasped and the layer cracked. Blood squirted.

"Do not breathe," repeated TeeVee.

The ribs looked like food. Budgie gagged as TeeVee poked and prodded at them. He looked into that blank face as TeeVee pulled out a paintbrush, dipped it in something and coated them. He closed his eyes. His head swam. "Done this side," TeeVee said after a few minutes.

Budgie opened his eyes, just a little, and looked down. A long, thin but tidy pink scar ran through the still-bruised flesh.

"You're done." TeeVee put his black bag back, beneath the couch. "They're knit."

The mongoose stared at him.

"You fixed em?" Budgie felt his sides. They were still numb.

"They'll be fragile and itchy for an hour or so, after that, back to normal. Don't scratch. You can tear that meat apart if you're not careful. It's still building bonds."

"Okay. Thanks."

"It's nothing," said TeeVee. "Three global surgery at best. You should know how to do that yourself. And you would if the doctors taught it." He picked up the half orb with the needle in it. "This is a bit more difficult."

"What is that anyway?"

"Just some processors and radio units. They bind to your strands and transmit so that Riki-Tiki can pick it up. You know anything about spin radio?"

"No." Budgie's pounding heart wanted to jump out of his chest. He folded his jacket and laid it across his lap. "It okay that I'm sweating? I don wanna mess up your work."

"It's fine." TeeVee held the half orb aloft and admired it. "I asked you about a pile and you knew nothing. What do you know about an avalanche?"

"Even less," said Budgie.

"You have a pile, a big one, and one of those pebbles falls. Sometimes that's all it takes to make them all fall. If it's the right pebble, in the right place, it creates a cascade. Your thinking is a bit like that. A neuron fires and then you have an avalanche and that's an idea. A cascade. It creates speech, action, movement. A life. Pebbles in a pond. Rippling."

He paused for a long moment.

"Idea here is entangled opposites. When one quantum processor spins one way in you, its match spins in its counterpart in Riki-Tiki. So you just say, spin left is one and spin right is zero and you have a binary system that operates instantly. I record the avalanche in your head, run it backwards and then straighten it back out."

Budgie thought he was supposed to say something but had no idea what. So he rolled his eyes and heard his idiot mouth blurt out: "Fascinating stuff, professor."

TeeVee pulled his empty hand back. Budgie was too afraid to flinch. The open palm swatted him hard and square across the face. His head whipped to the side and his eyes watered. He stared down at the jacket on his lap.

TeeVee's other hand, holding something glittery, pounded the center of his chest. Budgie gasped.

Knife, he thought. He's loved me. Budgie tried to stand. A riptide of nausea yanked him down. He looked at his chest.

No knife in him.

The half orb stuck to him like a metallic tumor. Something very soft and cold around his neck. TeeVee's hand. His face was close.

"Just relax." TeeVee's nostrils flared as he sniffed around Budgie's face. Stroked the side of his head. "Don't pull that out. Are you still sane?"

Wide eyed and terrified, Budgie nodded.

"What is your name?"

"Budgie."

"This is very good." TeeVee let go of his throat, straightened up and took a mincing step back. "It's telescopic and it's in your heart, pumping the processors in."

Budgie wanted to vomit. The ceiling seemed very far away.

"I'm actually surprised that you stayed conscious," TeeVee said. "Most people pass out right away but, then again, most people—"

That was the last thing Budgie heard.

CHANNEL SURFING
ROBOT FIGHT TONIGHT ALRIGHT!!!

"What's everything times two?" Fatman asked.

A rope-muscled thug in an ill-fitting suit wrapped a metal tracking collar around Rohl Consolver's sweaty neck.

Too afraid to move, he held very still. "I don't know." His bobbing Adam's apple pressed against chilled steel.

"It's still everything. You want double or nothing but you can't double what you already owe me. Look at this bill. I'm starting to wonder if you can even pay that."

"I have something," Rohl said. The collar clicked closed. "My body. If I lose you can have my flesh on top of everything else."

Fatman pulled a contract from his desk and nodded. The thug unlocked the gleaming band.

<hr />

Rohl ignored the elbow to the ribs. The hot jostling crowd cheered and cursed at the battling robots in the center of the ring. Rohl stood very still, occasionally glancing up at the balcony where Fatman sat, but the casino owner ignored him. The first round ended without a blow.

The girl carried the sign around the ring. Rohl had bet on Bach, an egg shaped machine on two feet with super spring loaded, titanium spears. Though wobbly and slow, this robot could do damage. It just needed one good hit. Just one.

But locating the other fighter, Poly, presented a problem. That little robot never held still. Man-shaped, its arms ended in two claws. Bach was a tough old girl, but Poly was all about speed and precision. To succeed, it needed to dodge and run, work on one spot with its weapons. When it broke metal skin, it'd dig into the wound, spraying water to short the circuits. All Bach needed was to land one blow. Just one.

Round two. The crowd cheered, waving betting tickets in the air. "C'mon Bach, kill that little bitch," Rohl shouted. "C'mon Bach!"

The bots started this round like the last. They circled and felt each other out. The crowd craved action. "We came to see a fucking fight, not a dance," a man shrieked.

"Do something!" shouted another.

They roared when a barbed spear exploded from Bach's front. Couldn't see it move. It wobbled there like an erect phallus. Poly's motion detectors had warned her.

She stabbed at Bach's side with a claw. Another spear shot out and grazed the side of her head. Poly retreated to the other side of the ring and Bach sucked the harpoons back into her body.

"Damn," Rohl whispered and then consoled himself by yelling. "It only takes one hit Bach, just one! C'mon!"

Last night had started off good. He could do no wrong. Surfed on a wave of cash until Lady Luck flipped a bitch. Just couldn't get it back together, couldn't get anything right. But instead of walking away from the table he'd ended up betting more, to break even. Lost his condo on a microbot race of all things. The casino stopped accepting his IOUs. Thugs materialized at his sides and walked him to Fatman's office. There, he cut a deal.

But what a deal.

Either he won this bet and broke even or he became property of the casino. Sweat busted out of his forehead.

Round two ended and the third began. Poly was a new fighter. She kept moving in, coaxing spears out of Bach and then dodging away without even trying to land a shot. Rohl hated the look of this. Poly appeared to be memorizing Bach's weapons, figuring her out, testing theories. As the round wore on, Bach missed her target by progressively larger degrees. The crowd became very quiet. They'd seen this sort of thing before. Poly was smarter. It made for a boring fight. A mismatch.

Rohl ignored the girl carrying the round card and looked at the EXITs. No escape there. Each one was manned by thugs, each wearing biometric lenses over their eyes. Rohl's face was registered.

Fatman stared down from the balcony, smiling. Chills ran all over Rohl's skin and heat behind his eyes. Ready to cry.

"Just one!" The bell rang and Rohl yelled at Bach, knowing his voice was getting high. Sounded hysterical and lonely in the bored crowd. Some people looked at him, raised their eyebrows and elbowed each other as if saying: *Get a look at this one.*

The bell rang.

Poly wove through the spears, punching at Bach's side. The fight became one-sided. The same move repeated again and again. Bach's metal weakened. You could hear it in the noise Poly's claws made.

"Please Santa," Rohl prayed. "Let Bach have something up her sleeve. Just something. Just one thing."

People shuffled to the concession and betting lines. It was a blow out. A matter of time. The rounds passed in mumbling silence as people talked amongst themselves, waiting to see what round would be Bach's last. Rohl sat in his plastic seat, his back soaked with sweat, his thinning hair lank and damp. He looked at the ticket in his right hand.

It was a simple bet, a fifty-fifty sort of thing. Bach to win. No round specified.

He heard a sizzling noise. Maybe just maybe, Bach had landed a blow, just the one she needed to impale that little fucker. After a long terrified moment, he looked. Bach was dead. Rohl should be so lucky.

Someone tapped his shoulder.

"I wasn't worried." Fatman leaned back in his plush chair. A small, woman-shaped robot danced across his desk, its nipples flashing pink lights. "Even if you won, you'd be back and you'd lose again. Just a matter of time. You realize I've never lost money at this casino. Never had a day when I didn't turn a profit?"

Rohl nodded, afraid to meet the man's swine eyes. That little silver woman seemed to be mocking him, its dance a victory jig. He wanted to smack it onto the floor.

"So, why do you guys all figure you'll be the one to change that? Never understood it. You think Santa is looking down on you, cheering you on?"

"I don't know." Rohl had already tried begging. It didn't work.

His guts churned grief. Felt like the first time he'd lost his subway pass and, as a result, his job at the sports store. His wife left him, taking the kids with her. His parents no longer talked to him because he only came to them to borrow money and always left stamping his foot like a five year old. A couple years ago, they'd all reappeared to hijack him with a reality show intervention, which failed, and then they all vanished again.

Now everything and everyone was gone. Including him. "What's next?"

"So you want to get right to it?" Fatman asked. "No sense putting off the inevitable?" He smiled. A sick looking expression full of gold, diamond studded teeth. "You know why Poly won tonight?"

"Because I bet on her?"

Fatman squealed like a pig. It took Rohl a moment to recognize the noise as laughter. He shuddered.

"You aren't that important," Fatman said. "You guys take everything personal. That's your problem, right there. You figure the whole mall revolves around you. You figure luck or money gives a damn. It doesn't. Odds don't care."

Rohl withered into his seat.

"Bach lost tonight because Bach is stupid," Fatman said. "And you're even dumber for betting on her. Probably figured she'd get in that one lucky shot."

"It'd only take one." Rohl nodded. "Just one."

"Robots don't get lucky. It's all programming and statistics. Only fools like you think they'll get lucky, and why do you think that? It's cause you think you're lucky. And luck? Is bullshit." He lit a cigar. "You know, Bach is one of my designs and I don't like seeing her lose. Even if it earns me a cretin like you. I don't like blaming luck and I don't like betting against my own bots. And I especially don't like seeing a prancing jack-off like Poly running an algorithm execution on it. Sickens me, actually. Bach is my baby. So I'm gonna upgrade her and you're providing the material."

"I don't understand."

"You don't need to."

A man in a white coat strapped Rohl to a table and put a mask over his face. The anesthetic tasted like licorice. He dreamed of a place outside the mall, a place he had never been to or thought about. The ground wasn't charred. It was a green meadow domed, not by a ceiling, but by blue sky. Birds sang.

He woke up. And screamed.

Goodbye, sight, touch, hearing, scent and taste. Hello, thought-flash code and knee-jerk animal reaction. Brain translated motion-detector signals into something resembling sight. Waves of moving force sketched patterns. Like being underwater. So deep that no light moved. Blind, Rohl felt the heat of huge beasts swimming around him. And he knew: DANGER. His side was hit.

Think, he had to think.

Words made psychic noise. Reassured him.

Start with basics. My name is Rohl. My brain is in the new Bach Bot, model number 666. I am supposed to fight.

Other sounds outside him, not heard but sensed. Shockwaves rode the air. Translate this into the alphabet code of words—

"I want that sight up and running. Santadamn brain can't think right if it can't see. Don't need a crazy fucking robot, Ken! If that thing starts shrieking again, you'll be shrieking too. Like the little girl you are."

Time vanished. So did he. He came back.

Black and white checkerboard pattern. The squares shrank and rearranged. A system emerged. A chunky thing. Rohl realized pixelated sight.

Okay. Relax. Just relax. Two shapes. The squares shrank. Greater detail. That was Fatman. Someone else, too. Face not recognized. Body language indicated a subordinate unit of Fatman. A teenage girl. Pigtails.

"Can you see?"

Vision reformed in greater, almost human detail. Black and white. His imagination filled in the blurry spots. Message was text at bottom of two-dimensional screen. Rohl watched the screen.

He tried to find himself. His mind floated backwards into a void. There was no 'behind him.' Just the surface. A labyrinth of thoughts that possessed no sense of place or body. He directed his thinking at the screen.

"I (?) can see," he said. The words printed at the bottom as he thought them. Instant.

"Couldn't understand that. Go slower."

"I... Can... See."

"It's working," Fatman said. "I want to see how it does against a Bach 1. See if it can beat itself."

All Rohl had to do, he realized, was nothing. The robot part fought.

It locked into a stalemate with the Bach 1. Could neither hit nor be hit. The machines struggled for position. They countered each gambit before trying the same one.

Why didn't his mechanical body use its lower spear to distract the opponent and then hit it with another? Just a one-two combo. Simple.

He ordered the metal body to do it. Bach 1 reacted to the first shot and Rohl fired the other spear through its center. Bach 1 stumbled back and then stopped. Dead.

Fiery blue joy bloomed in Rohl's mind. He had felt like this before. One night he'd put two grand on a forty-to-one pit bull in a dogfight. The thing was old and it was her last battle, but she'd come out of her corner like a snarling hellhound, grabbed the other dog by the throat and chewed. That bet paid crazy money but the happiness didn't come from the cash—he ended up losing it over the next few weeks anyway. It came from that moment before it paid, before he knew. When he just let it ride. He had the same feeling now.

Part of him knew that he must be wired to feel this but it didn't matter. He always had been. The feeling was all that counted. He wanted to fight again, to win again. When he and another Bach 1 entered the ring, he went straight after it. Took it down with one fast blow and, click-boom, same feeling. But, this time, maybe it wasn't quite as strong.

"Again!" he yelled. "Again!"

The pig-tailed girl looked at him and pulled out a gizmo. A few minutes later Fatman arrived to examine the robot corpses. Fatman read the folder the girl passed him and walked to Rohl-Bach's side. He patted it on the head.

"Real good," he said. "You figure you can do that in a real ring?"

"Again!" Rohl said. "Again, again!"

"Easy there, big gunner." Fatman returned the folder to the girl. "Ken. Have it ready to go for tonight. I'm gonna schedule a bout."

The girl picked up a remote control. "Lights out."

Dreams of a clear blue sky, birds flying. Rohl watched and made a bet with himself. "Bird on the left to win."

He woke to a ringing bell. A robot—a flat box with a spiked hammer head hanging off a pole in its center, mace design—advanced on him. The pole spun, and centrifugal force pulled the blunt clubs away from the center. A whirling dervish. The mace moved in fast then pulled back. Rohl-Bach avoided it and shot a warning spear to keep the enemy at distance until he learned its moves.

Rohl had seen a fight with one of these maces. The thing had a hidden tentacle, a lasso that pulled its opponent into its swirling weapon. It bluffed and dodged until the other bot went in for the kill. Then it grabbed and tilted the dervish forward to tear the challenger to pieces. It had a small but heavy body, hard to hit.

Rohl-Bach had a couple of spears that could kill it but not from this distance. Problem was, he couldn't get within range without getting his top knocked off.

So he danced. Until the mace figured out where the spears were, it would just run in and test. Rohl thought about it. Rohl needed to get lower and get the mace higher. Perhaps, if he tipped himself onto his side.

He ordered the feet to throw the Bach into the air and flung himself forward. Rohl-Bach landed hard, face first. What would the crowd think? Malfunction? Would they believe that the fight was all but over, cheering mace in for the kill? He wished he could hear them.

Mace bolted forward, tilting its hammerheads down so that it looked like a sideways helicopter. Rohl waited for it to come within range then shot a spear into the swinging ropes. They spun around the spear and tangled. He yanked the harpoon back in, pulling mace over so its flat body laid on its side, presenting a large target. Rohl fired every spear he could, each armor-piercing head smashing metal.

A single word came up on his inner screen. "VICTORY."

Rohl convulsed with joy. When they put him back on his feet, he did a celebratory lap, watching a crowd that went quietly crazy.

━━━ ━━ ━━━━ ━━ ━━━ ━━ ━━━ ━━━ ━━━ ━━━ ━━━ ━━━ ━━━ ━━━ ━━ ━━ ━━

With Rohl's brain locked safely within, The Bach 666 won fight after fight, each in the first round. Fans loved it because it added unpredictability to a tired sport. When Rohl-Bach finally reached the championship match, the odds were stacked heavily in his favor.

Rohl read this on the news reports Fatman uploaded into Bach so that he'd have something to occupy his thoughts. Rohl figured Fatman was concerned about the time he spent alone, worried that his cash cow might go nuts. Rohl spent more time turned on, sitting in the corner of Fatman's office, watching his boss snort coke off his desk.

He read the advert in the news: "ROBOT FIGHT TONIGHT ALL RIGHT!!! Watch the weathered and wily Poly take on the new unpredict-a-bot, the upstart with the wacky programs, heavy favorite, Bach 666! Place your bets at Fatman's casino. TONIGHT!! BE THERE!!"

Fatman brought his head up from his desk, a bit of white powder clinging to his sweaty upper lip. Through shifting pixels Rohl saw a smile. "Gonna make me money tonight?" he asked, sniffed, wiped his hand across his mouth and sneezed. "Big money?"

"Yes," Rohl said.

"I know you are." Fatman opened his desk drawer and pulled out a little chip. "Got something for you."

━━━ ━━ ━━━━ ━━ ━━━ ━━ ━━━ ━━━ ━━━ ━━━ ━━━ ━━━ ━━━ ━━━ ━━ ━━ ━━

The bell rang. Rohl's Bach body entered automatic fight mode. From across the ring, Poly ran at him then backed off. The two robots circled each other.

He'd wait for Poly to repeat the strategy from the first fight then use a well-timed harpoon to take her down. Winning in the first round was getting a bit boring. Had to think of the audience.

But Poly seemed to remember Bach. She immediately started testing his reflexes. Rohl's mechanical frame ran just as it had in the first fight. Robots were a lot of things but adaptable wasn't one of them. Poly played it cautious and waited until the second round to start hitting. Her movements were regular. Rohl watched, adapting to the rhythm of the thing. Duck, weave, run forward, pop with right hand claw, duck, run back, do it again. And again.

He waited for Poly to come in then ordered the body to spin. Nothing happened. Poly hit again, dodged back out and came in again. Rohl tried to fire a spear.

Nothing.

A memory. Fatman sticking a chip into him. "Big money."

His metal shell ruptured. Poly ducked and wove back in. She reached into the wound. Something pierced Rohl and for a moment he smelled burning. A deep disappointment seized him. He had lost. And it hurt.

〓〓 〓〓〓〓〓 〓〓 〓〓 〓〓 〓〓 〓〓 〓〓〓 〓〓〓 〓〓〓 〓〓 〓〓〓 〓〓 〓 〓〓

He flew over a field, his body disjointed. He was a flock of birds, watching wind currents through countless eyes. He made a bet with himself that the one on the left would be the first to the tree. That little sparrow pulled ahead.

〓〓 〓〓〓〓〓 〓〓 〓〓 〓〓 〓〓 〓〓 〓〓〓 〓〓〓 〓〓〓 〓〓 〓〓〓 〓〓 〓 〓〓

"I wasn't worried," Fatman said to the three men who sat in front of him. All of them had bet their bodies and brains on the Bach 666 and all of them had lost. He glanced at the female robot who danced across his desk, pink light flashing from its nipples. "You realize that I've never lost money at this casino? Never had a day when I didn't turn a profit?"

Like cheap stickers, dreams peeled from the surface of Budgie's mind. He was in TeeVee's hutch. It took him a moment to remember why.

The half orb was still stuck in his bare chest. "Can I pull this out now?"

"Yes," TeeVee said. "Do it slow so it can knit your meat. I do not want you bleeding over everything."

Budgie gripped the surface. It looked smooth but felt like sandpaper. He gave it an experimental tug. It didn't move. Cringing, he pulled harder. It came loose from something deep and solid within him. Not wanting to think about what that might be, Budgie clenched his jaw and worked it out. It didn't hurt but the pulling and screwing movements disgusted him. The long needle reminded him of a clown's handkerchief. It just kept coming and coming.

A teardrop of blood welled in the round bruise. He wiped at it, smearing red across his flesh. The skin was unbroken, but purple from the impact. Budgie prodded the wound with his finger. Sensitive.

"That it?" He put the reOrb on the table and rested his elbows on his knees. Dropping his head, he took a few sick breaths.

"Yes."

"How long was I out?" Budgie picked up his crumpled tunic from the ground. Felt a wet spot and sniffed it. Fucking mongoose. Pissed on his clothes. The shirt'd clean itself but the hydrophobic weave needed to suck up some of his body heat and kinetic energy to activate.

Before buttoning, he searched the pockets for his cigarettes. "Out a long time?"

"A couple of minutes. Your brain crashed but they usually reboot."

"Usually?"

"Well, no, not usually. *Usually,* the subject suffers a catatonic insanity then starves to death."

"Lucky fucking me then."

"Luck has nothing to do with it." TeeVee tilted his head. "The brain dreams the mod into itself."

TeeVee's fingers disappeared into the fur around his armpit and re-emerged with a blue card. He flicked it across the room. Budgie tried to catch it and missed. The card slapped the bruise on his chest with a brief plume of burgundy pain and bounced into his lap. "It's heavy."

"That's the cred card that your globals will appear on. It's matched to your retinas and biometrics so you won't have any problems using it."

"How encrypted is it?" Budgie flicked it this way and that in the orange light. So this is what he sold his perception for? So small and plastic. But people had sold a lot more for a lot less. "Just in case I get audited."

"It is not encrypted and you will be audited daily."

Budgie frowned. Was he being ripped off? Likesay, even more than the puny little card indicated.

"Relax," TeeVee said. "The money is buried in data smog. Encryption is a red flag. Nothing gets attention like something that's hidden. And codes can always be cracked." He sighed. "I find purely computer based solutions, well—short sighted. It's much better to find the gray area where the social systems and the electronic ones meet." TeeVee patted his lap for his mongoose. "I've just left it all out in the open but buried beneath porn pop-ups. To get to the data on that you have to go through almost every fuck-ad in the info dump. And the bureaucrats, should they try, will get a deluge of porn. Watching porn at work is a much bigger offense than a bit of money laundering. Their computers try to block it but it's a code race. So they just don't go near the stuff. They can't get into the room because using the door gets them fired. Trust me, the moment an ad for 'All-Anal Tweenie-Party' comes up they panic and start logging out as fast as they can. So don't worry, you're safe."

"Okay." Budgie had to take TeeVee's word for that. He had no idea how computers worked. Budgie was pure user, disinterested in the circuitry underneath his daily life until it broke. Then he called someone. The Vidicons had people who specialized. Their labor was cheap and for all Budgie could tell, fairly useless. A knife or drug solved most of his problems while computers just seemed to cause them. "As long as I get paid."

"You'll get paid," TeeVee said. "I want to keep you happy. Can't have you cutting out your eyes."

What? TeeVee expected him to blind himself if he didn't get paid for the rental. TeeVee just *assumed* that everyone would do that? Keeping your vision and providing an unpaid-for product was unimaginable.

That total fuck you/constant dogs of war attitude must've been how TeeVee had made alpha. Not something to toy with. Even knowing about it scared Budgie. Like glimpsing a monster in the dark. *And this is what I'm doing business with*, he thought. *This?*

A shaking panic took his hands. Whatever TeeVee had done to him, could not be undone.

Budgie's shirt forced the mongoose urine to the outside, where it dribbled down his belly and followed the curve of his pants to the floor. Disgusting. Looks like I pissed myself. Maybe I did.

He grinned. The expression surprised him. "I should get going." His fingers stumbled over the buttons on his tunic. He flexed his muscles. One at a time. Shifted his weight from foot to foot. His body ached but felt better for moving. Still woozy shaky and disgusted, but better. His body still belonged to him. It still worked. His tunic, however, was buttoned crooked. He chewed his tongue. "I gotta—"

"I'm sure you're late for something," TeeVee's pupils shrank to nothing. "Don't mind me if I don't see you out, inside, out-inside-out of the inside…"

Budgie walked towards the door, hoping it'd lead somewhere better, not at all sure it would.

Back in corridors, Budgie pulled out his gizmo. Compared to the equipment he'd just seen, it looked cheap. Maybe he'd use some of his new money to buy a better one. It'd be nice to get that intel-light feature. It'd save him cash cause it'd let him get rid of his television.

Wait. He didn't have a television. Not anymore. His Mom did but he sure didn't. Well, it'd save him the trouble of getting one.

He said Harmony's name and the voice recog picked it up over the music and ambient noise.

"Budgie?" Her face appeared.

Her voice was turned up too loud. Budgie fumbled with the volume while looking around to make sure no one was looking. "Yeah, it's me," he said and switched the audio to text so he could read her words without the whole world hearing them. For some reason he wanted a bit of privacy. It seemed more intimate. No reason for eavesdropping Vidicons to know who he was talking to.

"What'd you want?" she asked.

Good question. "Uhhhhhhh."

She raised her eyebrows. He blushed.

"That's cute," she said.

Truth was, after the beating he took and all that shit with TeeVee, he wanted to see her face. But how could he tell her that? "I just wanted to say hi." Then, embarrassed, said: "You know, see how you're doing."

Oh Budgie, he thought. You idiot. That sounded lame. He never should have called. This was stupid.

"I'm fine," she said. "Yourself?"

"You mocking me?"

"A bit." She shrugged. "Look, what do you want? I got things to do and as much as I want to sit here, watching you blush, I gotta do 'em."

"Ah, yeah," Budgie said. He wondered if she wanted company then suddenly feared that she had some. "Feel like a stranger to myself."

"What?"

Did he say that aloud? He decided to just let his mouth work. It'd always felt like a separate creature to his brain anyway; doing what it wanted, ignoring orders from above and wrecking things. Might as well let it take control. Not like his brain was doing such a bang up job here. "I'm kicked out of my hutch so—"

"You had a hutch?"

"No, well yeah. My mom's hutch."

"I thought you already were."

"No, well, yeah, but anyway, I'm kicked out." And his mouth just gave up. The words hung there like a noose. Budgie took a deep breath. *Just stick my head through and kick out the trapdoor, Harmony. Let's get this over with.* "And, I was like, wondering, cause you know, you let me, uhh…"

"Is this a fucking booty call?"

"No, it's not like that. I uh—"

"Wait, let me guess—you want to crash at my place?"

It was a good guess and Budgie wanted to say yes. But, scared of looking weak, he blurted out: "No!" He shook his head. Maybe to disagree with himself.

She squinted.

Budgie just wanted to click off, get some drugs into his head and some blood on his fists. He glanced around, hoping to catch some wayward prick's eye. Anything to get rid of this choking feeling. "I just wanted to say hi and whatnot. You know."

"What's the whatnot?"

"Huh?"

"Well, you already said hi so…"

"Oh yeah, was wonderin' if you're going to Sputnik's wake tonight?"

"For sure. Sitcom's playing."

Budgie felt a twinge of something in his chest and for a moment thought it was the bruise. But it wasn't. He recognized this emo prompt. She liked Sitcom and Budgie hated that. He wanted her all to himself. And Sitcom of all people? Just the mention of that guy always made Budgie cringe with a memorized beating.

⬛⬛ ⬛⬛⬛⬛⬛⬛ ⬛⬛ ⬛⬛⬛⬛⬛⬛ ⬛⬛⬛⬛⬛ ⬛⬛⬛⬛⬛ ⬛⬛⬛⬛⬛ ⬛⬛⬛⬛ ⬛⬛⬛ ⬛⬛⬛ ⬛⬛⬛ ⬛⬛⬛ ⬛⬛⬛

Standing in a ring of bare-knuckled violence, Budgie glanced from Vidicon to Vidicon. Sitcom in front of him, arms crossed and smiling. "Let's see what this fuck's got," he said. "Hope he fights better than he talks."

Budgie spat. So what if he couldn't talk pristine like these bastards? That didn't mean he shouldn't be in the gang. He turned red. Knowing he was supposed to wait for them to land the first blow, that he shouldn't even dare to fight back—but too angry to care—he kicked low and backwards. The Vidicon behind him yelped.

Budgie spun, fist flying at the first body he saw. Solar plexus. The guy grunted. Uppercut.

Someone grabbed his other arm and yanked. His body twisted and fists pummeled his ribs.

So what? He was used to his stomach hurting. His Mom always had money for candy but none for food. A hungry troll had lived in his gut for as long as he could remember. It gnawed the scent of food into bright colors and pains. He hated the smell of cooking.

That's why he had to do this, that's why he had to jump into the Vidicons. Budgie couldn't take another day of starvation, poking through dumpsters, the shame burning in his cheeks. He needed meat.

Or he'd fucking kill someone.

Budgie pushed the guy pulling him, throwing him off balance and twisting his body.

A face flashed into his vision and he snapped his head down, forehead smacking into nose. The grip on his arm released and he threw his elbow backwards. It hit something soft. He took a few fast steps forward, over the collapsed body, and bounced off the human ring.

Vidicons in front of him. Vidicons behind him. Side to side. Vidicons lifted their fists and closed in.

Shit.

They beat him until he was only a punch drunk chunk of meat. Their methodical violence kept him awake to feel every thing. Budgie gurgled and crawled and bit and clawed. But he did not beg.

"Stop!"

The group backed off. Sitcom stood over him. Budgie flung himself at Sitcom's shins. The guy stepped aside and Budgie fell short. He rolled onto his back and stared up. Blood bubbled from his nose.

"I've seen enough. You're in."

"I'm in?" The words were liquid.

"Fuck, you like to repeat shit. Repeat this—She sells sea shells by the sea shore."

Budgie heard his breath shrieking in his skull. Every inhalation stung. He tried to hold Sitcom's eyes but got scared. The guy was serious. Budgie gazed at the ceiling. Thought about his ragged, mismatched sneakers, his shitty third hand pants. "Sh-sh-sh-she-sh-sh-sh-sh."

"Speak up, fucker. And look at me."

Budgie pulled his head back and stared into Sitcom's eyes. That old, evil switch flipped and turned his insides to chilled liquor. He spoke slowly, trying to remember his exercises, pract iced in front of the mirror so he could see his tongue. He could do this. His stutter had faded since he was little, only returning when he spoke too fast or got too excited. Just needed to calm down and to speak slow.

"She sells sea shells... by the sea shore."

"That's better," Sitcom said. "I can hear all that sweet poison in you." Without taking his eyes off Budgie he yelled at the other Vidicons. "Get this fucker a uniform, a hot meal and something to drink." Lowering his voice and offering Budgie his hand, he said: "We'll give you a reason to talk with that drunk fucking tongue."

Budgie bumped into someone and looked up. Been paying too much attention to the screen of his gizmo to see where he was going. The man looked over his shoulder, a snarl on his lips. Then he saw the uniform.

"Sorry," the man said. The snarl collapsed. He moved faster, checking his pockets. "Very sorry."

Budgie stopped walking to read his gizmo. Harmony hadn't said anything but, for a moment, he could've sworn that he saw text saying, 'she sells she shells by the sea shore.' He shook the feeling off. "You wanna meet out front?"

"Yeah, call me when you get close."

"Sure." Budgie clicked off.

Budgie scented the Vidicons before he saw them. Some other chapters used colognes but, twice a month, the Vidicons took two little turquoise pills that gave them their gang odor. It leaked chemicals out of armpits and the sweat was designed to stick to their clothes. He turned a corner and saw a huge mass of tunics.

This was big. Snort Donkey had done a good job. The gang clogged the entrance. The doormen took info for the lottery that would be held at 7:06 in the morning.

Budgie stood on tiptoes to see over the heads of his comrades. No luck. Where was Harmony? It'd prolly be easier to find her inside than out here in the packed corridor. There'd be some space in Old Union, until later when the bulk of the party showed up. These were all just people who had no patrols to get to.

He pulled his gizmo out and called her.

"Hey," he said when she picked up. "I'm outside Old Union. It's taking a while to get past the door. Do you just want to meet indoors?"

He felt a tap on his shoulder. Harmony stood there with her own gizmo. "It'll prolly be easier to meet out here."

Should he shake her hand, tap her knucks or bow? How was he supposed to greet her? A hug and kiss? Harmony punched him affectionately in the gut. He flinched, expecting pain from his ribs, but felt none. Her hand lingered and Budgie grabbed her wrist. He looked into her eyes and she looked back. They both smiled.

"I'll break your fuckin' arm for ya," he said, grinning.

"I'd like to see you do that with your nuts in your throat." She slowly swung her knee up. It touched Budgie's crotch and Harmony left it there, balancing on one foot. Budgie's dick stiffened and he pulled her towards him. She let herself stumble into his chest and stood real close, rubbing her leg up and down the inside of his thigh.

Budgie smelled her. Something a touch different in the Vidicon stink. Something atop it. She whispered into his ear. "Did you go to the recruiter?"

"Yeah." Budgie wondered if his breath tickled her like hers tickled him. "I got a job. Start next week. Got kicked outta my house too."

She pulled away, looking hard at his eyes. Budgie let go of her wrist. Her finger tips tickled the back of his hand. "You already told me that."

"Yeah," Budgie said, remembering. "Guess I did. Did I tell you bout Griff?"

PRODUCT PLACEMENT

INDULGE YOURELF! Subscribe to The SunPost for just 3 credits a month and keep on top of all the latest in fashion, home decor, movie and book reviews. Celebrity sightings, society gossip, recipes, news for the Toronto Mall and from other malls worldwide, business and much, much more. TREAT YOURSELF BY SUBSCRIBING NOW!

SKIN IS IN
Top by Kitty Duck. Skin by Jergens.
(picture of naked model)
ROOTS spirit
Move to your own rhythm

The Sparkle in Your Eyes. ILLUMINATED.

Almay bright eyes, shimmer pearls. Nano color-enhancement. Pick and choose. Beautiful for life.

SALEM stir the senses
Rich. Intense. Black Label.
Smooth. Spirited. Green Label.

Feeling like your best self only if you've had a drink is not healthy. Unless it's CAROLANS. Set your senses free.

THE BIRTH OF A NEW YOU. JCPenneysalon.

You can't go to SITCOM's show tonight dummy. That's a red level wake. You wanna get killed?!

"CAREFUL!" Harmony shouted into Budgie's ear.

He glanced down. Her fist was below his nose, a little pile of neon green dust balanced beside the thumb.

"Not old is it?" Budgie shouted. "Not new?"

He jerked his head towards the Pfizer-Jansen booth beside them. The drug company had sponsored this event because a wake was a good place to move large quantities of expired drugs while testing out a few new ones. They actually paid you to take those but you had to be a bit crazy or a lot broke to do that. Some of those experimentals had pretty weird side effects.

Budgie had heard about this guy who thought his dick was conspiring against his brain. He sawed it off and bled to death. They found him on top of his fridge. Funny enough, that actually made more people try out the new ones—the logic being that the self-castrator must have been wrecked. Especially because he was on the fridge.

Harmony shook her head.

"Good cause I don fuck with that." Budgie plugged a nostril and inhaled the bump. Harmony tapped another verdant hill onto her hand and snorted it.

A huge guillotine dominated the stage. The Pfizer-Jansen colors and logo gleamed across the blade. That device guaranteed a good party. No one knew who was going to end up in it and they acted accordingly. 'Tonight we drink for tomorrow we die,' was never truer than at a rude boy wake.

Sitcom stood beside the apparatus, pulling levers and spinning orbs. Funny that he looked so bored cause this was good music. Heavy as lead but with melodies and rhythms that burrowed right into your brain, lighting up the parts that said "Shake your ass" until your spinal cord thrashed and writhed like a basket cobra.

"I gotta dance," Harmony yelled.

"I gotta take care of Griff first."

"You should've jumped that floater. Stupid risk to take. Looks bad."

"I know." Budgie's thoughts got tangled up with each other. He had no way of controlling what was coming out of his mouth. It was like a word lottery. He wondered if it was always like that—and he had never noticed—or if it was just the drugs. "I felt sorry for him."

Harmony rolled her eyes and leaned into Budgie's ear. "Felt sorry for him? Feel sorry for fuckin' everyone why don't ya? It's a whole world of shit. You gotta pick your battles and do what's good for you." She pulled away and poked her finger into her chest by way of explanation. "For you!"

She made sense but that could just be the... He looked up at the ceiling. Faces stared down, except they weren't really faces. Just random patterns of paint that suggested them when you were high. One of the faces, a coke lady, winked at him.

But that wasn't the thing he meant to look at.

He brought his line of sight down—not feeling his head, different images folding out in his vision—and scanned until he saw Griff worming towards him. Then he focused. Budgie lightly elbowed Harmony and directed her vision towards the guy.

Griff stopped and his face turned to porcelain. Big bruises ringed his eyes and the middle of his face was still swollen. Looked like a puffy raccoon. With rabies.

Budgie cracked his knuckles. "We got business," he signed. "And we do this now." He grabbed his knife and knucks from his belt and closed in, Harmony following.

Things were usually kept bare-knuckle between Vidicons but this was different. Calling someone a bitch—not to their face but behind their back—was serious shit. If you went after someone's rep, you best be prepared to back it up with everything. If you weren't ready to do that, you better keep your silence.

A couple of Vidicons spotted the trouble. Their hands burst into bird-like life as they signaled to others. A tight ring of bodies quickly formed around Budgie and Griff, leaving a corridor between them.

The Pfizer-Jansen reps backed into the booth, terrified. Green level boys. One grabbed his gizmo, prolly to call their security company, prolly thinking they were about to be swarmed and robbed, when a Vidicon reached into the booth and plucked it from his hands. He gestured for quiet with a finger over his lips and nodded at Budgie, who turned back towards Griff.

Budgie put his metal-knucked fist up and kept his knife low in front of his stomach. Turned sideways and kept his weight on his back leg. Scuttled forward. Griff had his own blade out. A big hacker that he held in front of him. His other hand was a fist held beside his head. As Budgie neared, Griff used that hand to talk: "Sucker punched me last time," he said. "Don get to do that again."

Stupid asshole. The time for talking was done. What's he doin'? Playin to the crowd??

Griff wound up to take a big slice across the air. Budgie dodged the blade, thrusting his weight forward. His knifed hand shot into Griff's gut while the whizzing hacker sliced air above his head.

Budgie's blade grabbed flesh. He straightened and came up behind Griff. Wrapped his arm around the kid's neck and squeezed. Griff dropped his machete. Fever heat radiated off Griff's scalp. His hands flailed until they grabbed Budgie's arm. He tried to pull it off his throat.

"Put your fucking hands down." Budgie yelled into his ear. "Or I'm gonna make your belly smile so wide it'll look like Ronald McDonald." Griff dropped his hands and Budgie loosened his grip—just a touch—so Griff could drag a breath into his lungs.

"I want to hear you say, 'I'm sorry Budgie, I'm a lying fuck,' and—since you like playing to the crowd you fucking loudmouth—sign that shit so everyone sees."

Griff took a moment too long to answer. Budgie twisted the blade. Griff screamed. "I'm sorry." His hands danced. "I'm sorry. I'm a lying fuck, I'm sorry, I'm sorry."

"Now say 'uncle.'"

"Uncle!"

Griff's powerbar dipped into yellow. He'd had enough. Careful to keep the wound small—Budgie didn't want to spill intestines—he slipped the knife out. Really, he should leave it in but he wasn't about to lose this blade too. Anyway, it took a long time to die from a stomach wound. He'd be fine. If not, who cared?

Budgie shoved Griff forward.

A Vidicon caught him by the shoulders and another held him up by the armpits. They dragged him away, to the medic, most likely, while another cleared a path.

Budgie looked at the Pfizer-Jansen guys. The Vidicon tossed their gizmo back and plucked a vial of drugs from the counter. They looked relived but still scared. Budgie didn't even want to look at the crowd.

Harmony grabbed his arm, kissed him on the cheek and offered him another bump. Budgie inhaled it and thought about taking Griff's machete as a trophy. Instead, he kicked it across the floor.

"Contempt?"

"Fuck that," said Budgie. "Let's dance."

Budgie's body bounced in the crush. His limbs drew tracers and his dance—if it could be called that—tore him free of the spider webs before tangling him back up in them. The blurry ghost of his forearm wrapped around his torso and he jumped forward, through its sticky grip and into someone's side. They shoved him back, smiling, and that face detached from the head. It hung blank and blurry in the air.

It hovered in front of Budgie, its mouth a black hole that screamed music. The eyes stared in opposite directions. One winked and Budgie slapped at it. His palms passed easily through the image.

Budgie twisted his body. The tracers turned bright pink and radiant. They grew thin and stretched out in a snared mess that covered the whole dance floor. Everyone tried to tear themselves free from the loopy web.

Someone held all the ends and gave them a giant, simultaneous yank. The thin streaks snapped into taut lines. They formed a criss-crossed grid, reaching out from the speakers, each person getting fish-hooked by one. But the line that reached Budgie paused above his head, not quite touching him.

The crowd stood at sudden zombie-faced attention. The music kept grinding, but there was no movement in here except for the heaving of Budgie's chest.

He wiped sweat from his face. What was happening? Did he miss something? The hot pink cables held solid.

Budgie rubbed his eyes. Opened them again. Still there.

Shit.

The lines throbbed. Orbs traveled through them like food through a snake. One of these wiggled towards him, and he watched it with blooming fear.

He stepped back and knocked into a hard, unflinching body. The orb reached the end of his disconnected rope and it exhaled a cloud of green smoke and noise. Scrambled inhuman voices. His brain decoded it: "STEP SOUTH."

A wall of bodies took a single step towards him. Unrelenting and indifferent, they banged into his chest, knocking him back, but not quite down.

Now his line stood above someone else's head. But he still made out the voices in the next plume of hallucinatory gas: "WEST."

The crowd lurched to the side, knocking him that way. "EAST." Same but opposite.

"NORTH." People shoved Budgie from behind, knocking his head down so that he looked at the floor. Boots moved, stomped and kicked. He looked up.

The pink lines were gone and the bodies were a chaos of dancing. The music pounded, the lights hammered at his head and Budgie stood still.

"What the fuck?" he finally asked.

No one answered.

Budgie pushed through the bodies. He had to get to the wall.

He was obviously too fucked up. Needed to chill. Get off this
floor, get a bit of space and think. Or not think. Let his brain rest.
Music spiraled around the room, working itself into faster and faster
circles. The beats went one way, the harmonies went another. It started
at the bottom of the floor and traveled up in smaller laps until it
formed a cone, topped by a ball above the center of Old Union's dance
floor. The orb shattered into sharp fragments that fell amongst the
dancers. The music shifted into underwater down-tempo, swollen
bass emanating from everywhere, even shaking out of Budgie's panting
chest. It was heavy, claustrophobic music. Smothering lungfuls of
liquid. Ghost fish flickered.

A microphone voice bubbled out of it, speaking one word that
hushed the crowd. "Lottery."

Budgie looked up at the stage. The guillotine.

He was supposed to meet up with Harmony before the lottery
but he'd been too fucked—still was too fucked. He'd never find her
in this. Frantic, he looked around.

Santa, his name was going to be called. He'd be chosen as
tonight's victim.

A lump of ice formed in the bottom of his throat, spread through
his chest and froze his whole body.

He didn't want to die. Not now. Not like this.

He should crave it. Should be proud; honored to be a ghost roaming
the corridors with Sputnik. There was even a sort of logic to that: Close
in life and close in death.

But now he couldn't bear the thought of dying for a party or a
corpse or anything. It must be something about Harmony. Something
about her had taught him contempt for doing things cricket. What
did cricket benefit him? Or her? Or anyone?

The music's volume ebbed. A fat heartbeat rattled the walls. Budgie
stared at the Pfizer-Jansen logo on the guillotine blade. Below the
stylized "P.J." was their motto: "The cutting edge of research."

The silence and stillness in the room congealed into concrete. Sitcom
walked to the Lottery Machine. His breath hissed through the speakers.
"Is everyone ready?"

No one responded.

They must have all been thinking the same thing as Budgie. Was
this it? Their last moment? Would they die proud, knowing they'd
lived a good life?

Budgie didn't like these questions. Cause he thought he knew
the answers.

Everything he'd ever done had been useless. He just jumped from
one appetite to the next, consuming everything that crossed his path.
He was horny and he fucked. He was dry and he drank. Sad? Go

shopping. Budgie never wondered what lay beneath these persistent hungers. There was nothing he could look at and say, "That makes it all worthwhile. I might die now but at least I <BLANK>"

Maybe if he'd saved Sputnik he could die proud. But all he'd done was kill Wolfe. Who'd care about that in a year, when this new territory was all taken for granted? Shit, who cared about that now? This was his third wake with the guillotine. He knew how these things worked. He couldn't even remember the names of the men who had their heads lopped off, let alone the men it'd been done for. They were a guild of nobodies.

Sitcom pulled the crank on the slot machine. Paranoid violins cut suspense music through the air like razorblades drawn over skin. A ticket emerged.

This is it, Budgie thought. He wished that Harmony was with him, that he had her hand to hold. *If I live through this—shit, if she lives through this—she'll be pissed at me.* He tried to smile at that but the grin faltered. *Maybe I should run.*

But where?

Sitcom looked between the ticket and the crowd for a long moment. Cleared his throat. It should have sounded like a machine roar but it was a pathetic little noise. "The winner is..." He stretched out the last word like a game show host. "Jingles the Rabbit!"

The crowd shrieked. Budgie joined in. The shouting helped shake off the fear.

Someone grabbed him by the shoulders and bounced up and down. Celebration. Budgie traded knucks with everyone nearby, seeing crazed relief on all their faces, knowing he wore the same expression. He'd made it. He'd live to consume another tomorrow. The Grim Collector was held off for another day, the bill dodged.

Shit, Budgie thought. *I don't even know Jingles.*

Another figure joined Sitcom on the stage, waving his arms above his head like a conquering champion. The man's long ears stretched up above his head and his two front teeth were white tombstones. It was a fucked up mod.

He stared at the face, trying to remember it from somewhere, but he couldn't see beyond the surgery. The guy had prolly done it to stand out, to look different and be memorable. But it looked so dime a dozen.

"You fucker," someone said behind Budgie.

He jumped at the sound.

"Where were you?"

Harmony. Her arms crossed over her chest.

"Hey," Budgie said.

"Don't hey me—you said we'd meet up. I had to track down your gizmo."

"I lost, uh—" Budgie's voice bothered him. He hated speaking when he was high. It just sounded like noise and he was too aware of his tongue darting around his mouth. All those years of teaching himself how to talk had fucked with his buzzes. "I lost time."

"You're wrecked." Harmony smiled. She gripped his hand.

Feeling the sweaty palm Budgie realized that she'd been scared too. He'd let her down. "Sorry."

She rested against him. Budgie wrapped his arm around her waist. The squeeze reminded him of the choke-hold he'd used on Griff. He held her tighter and softer. Like...

All those people with pink cables reaching out of their heads, moving this way and that. "Did you see all that shit earlier?"

"What?"

"Those lines?"

She looked at him for a moment, her brow furrowing. "You mean to get in?"

"No. The..." Must have been a hallucination. But that didn't seem right. Hallucinations didn't knock you around. And it'd been so detailed. Every time he closed his eyes he watched it again on eyelid cinema. "Never mind. We'll talk later."

She nodded and looked back at the stage. Jingles the Rabbit hopped, bunny style, towards the guillotine. Playing it up. The audience laughed.

Budgie stayed quiet, sneaking glances at Harmony. She frowned.

Jingles reached the guillotine and straightened. Sitcom put his hand on the guy's shoulder. The crowd got quiet.

"Any last words Jingles?"

"Yeah." His voice sounded shaky but good. His ears swayed about his head. Budgie strained to hear. What does a guy say when he's about to get chopped?

"I just want to say—Fuck all of y'all!" He held up his fists, giving the room the finger and grinning like a kid. Everyone cheered. The noise did not subside until Sitcom locked Jingle's head in.

"All right, I want everyone's attention," Sitcom said. The last of the cheers died.

A loud and inappropriate screech resounded in the heartbeat silence. Someone howled laughter.

Sitcom ignored it. "Everyone pull out your gizmos."

Budgie looked down at the screen. 7:05 AM.

"I'm gonna tell you the code to drop the blade," Sitcom continued. "You punch it in and when I say 'send,' you send. Not before—got it?"

"HOO-YAH," Budgie yelled with the crowd, his voice lost.

"Good. It's six, five, four, six, B."

Budgie punched in the numbers.

Harmony's hand was empty.

"Where's your gizmo?" His thumb shook over the send button.

"Not doin' this."

"What?" He looked back at the stage where Sitcom held his own device.

"On the count of five," he said. "Five, four, three two one, SEND!"

The clock clicked 7:06. Budgie's thumb clamped down. Electronic signals from the whole room hit the guillotine.

The blade dropped in a Pfizer-Jansen colored blur. Blood shot out in a huge arc, splattering the front rows. The audience recoiled and their movement rippled backwards, shoving Budgie against the people behind him.

He steadied himself. On the stage, Sitcom held Jingle's head by the ear. "Sputnik's ghost is not alone," he shouted.

The home crowd roared.

"He has a partner with him now." Sitcom grinned, carrying the head back to his console, where he propped it up. "Wolfe's ghost better watch his ass!"

Music, loud and hard and sudden, tore through the room, drowning out explosive cheers. Sitcom tossed the head to a ghoul who wandered onto the stage, and paid him.

Harmony grabbed Budgie's arm, her face pale, her lips trembling. A moment later, she was gone.

INFO DUMP

"Don't tell me that you're going in for this space mumbo-jumbo too, Lenny. For some reason I expected more from you."

"It's not mumbo-jumbo it's—"

"MUMBO-JUMBO! MUBO-JUMBO!"

"It just says a lot about us. We can't say that the space program died because of space litter."

"Sure we can. This whole planet is surrounded by nuts and bolts. Every idiot knows that, except maybe, you. And I don't think you're an idiot."

"No?"

"A crazy lying bastard, yes. An idiot, no."

"All I'm saying is that the space program was in deep trouble before shoddily made communications satellites locked us in a ring of litter. People simply lost their nerve."

"Sure, big brave Lenny is now tougher than those simple, simpering NASAnauts."

"In the span of two, maybe three generations, we had become an empire of spectators. Space was a dangerous adventure, something that everyone had to take part in. It was not just a question of technology but one of guts, determination and curiosity. These are qualities that died in people long ago. I would say, they were murdered."

"You know who should be murdered. Those rude boy scumbags. We should send them into space."

"And an important aspect of space and post-space era spectacle was the media tragedy. People became hysterical when celebrities they never met, died. Suicides often followed. It seems that the spectators developed a deep connection with these media figures—"

"Blah, blah, blah. MUMBO-JUMBO!"

"—even if they knew little or nothing about them. The space program was a victim of this. It only received major press when something went wrong, thus creating the expectation of failure. People even seemed to crave failure, just to have something to mourn. Disasters made for better television."

"Santa, would someone take away his gizmo before he reads his whole book?"

"The clarion call of the early twenty first century was SAFTEY SAFETY SAFETY. It was also its death knell. There was no safe way of going into space, just as there was no safe way of crossing the ocean in the 1400s. Yet people expected it. This expectation turned into a demand. These people simply did not have the guts they needed. They lived in fear, crouched in their houses, terrified of the unknown like the savages they looked down upon. Like I said, they were an empire of spectators who believed that reality was someone else's business (usually a deity or priest king of some kind) and their only duty was to consume it."

"Are you done yet you crazy lying bastard? We have to—"

"Not at all. We're not very different."

"Sure Lenny. We'll be right back after these messages with more ranting from that crazy lying bastard, Lenny Niedenberger, author of 'Superstition: Then and Now.' Stay tuned."

The door, he thought. The door.

Budgie ran through the crowd, thinking he glimpsed Harmony's neon wig. But no. Just the play of light across a scalp. He pushed and ran faster. Bumped into people. Yanked out his gizmo and tried to get her latitude. Masked. Stopped, spun, ran again.

He squeezed through the clogged up rude boys at the door. Got into the corridor. Looked up and down. "Where would she fucking go?"

This was the part of the movie when Budgie should frown and look thoughtful. This was the part where he would say: 'Oh, the old playground' and go there. And there, he would find her. Swinging slow on a swing. He'd approach. After some tense moments they'd start talking about old times and figure out what they always liked about each other. They'd work it out. That's what was supposed to happen now.

Budgie frowned.

He still had no idea.

They had no old times. Not together, at least. If there was a place she went when she was sad, he sure didn't know anything about it.

He walked. Where? He had nowhere to go. Just away from that party. Beneath the advert ceiling, which should be all romantic stars and rain clouds, he walked. Instead of a climatic soundtrack, kitsch jingles blared. When he should have something clever to say, some sort of insight, he just swore and pounded his fists together.

His head swam. Sweaty and cold. Budgie wiped his forehead with the back of his hand. He pulled it away. His arm moved but his hand stuck to his forehead. His wrist was a stump that became a mouth. The mouth vomited all over him.

His hand dropped off his head to the floor and crawled away. Budgie reached for it with his other hand—the one still attached to his arm—and it, too, fell off. It chased, then mounted the other one. His stumps both vomited rainbows. He stepped toward his humping hands and slipped in the bright puddle. Colors smeared all over him. His head tottered on his neck and he tried to steady it. It fell off. He watched his headless body twitching. Scrambled voices screamed out of his neck.

He knew he should think something about all this but all he could think was; "Stay calm, Budgie. Don't lose your head. Stay calm Budgie. I'm right here."

He sat straight up, shrieking.

Something cold and damp against his forehead. And his feet. He still had his feet? Thank Santa. But where were his boots? What was he trapped in?

"Stay calm, Budgie."

The ceiling had turned off. No adverts played. It was just egg white. He looked around. The corridor was gone.

"Don't lose your head."

"I'm right here."

"I know, I know. Just stay calm."

He grabbed his face. His hands were back on his wrists. He scratched his arms. A shadow pulled them down. This, he tried to bite. It hit him in the face.

"Hello Budgie, who's a pretty boy?"

He opened his eyes and sat straight up.

The room was dark but he recognized the smell. "Harmony." His croaking voice hurt his throat. "What the..."

"Just stay calm. I'm right here."

"Okay, okay."

"Don't lose your head."

"I won't."

He closed his eyes and took deep breaths. Something cold was strapped to his feet. Something like air con wafted across his skin and he thought he'd never felt anything so good as that chill. He rubbed his hands together. Still there. "What happened?"

"Can you take the light now?"

"I think so."

Harmony turned on the light. Budgie cringed and sneezed against it. "Too much?"

"No, it's fine. Just makes my head..."

Huge black bags hung below Harmony's eyes. She lit a cigarette with a shaking hand.

"I don feel good," he said.

"You look a lot better."

"You look like shit."

"Oh."

"No, I don't mean like that," Budgie said. "You okay?"

"I'm fucking fine," Harmony said. "I'm just tired. How are you is the question."

"I'm... I dunno. What happened?"

"Want a smoke?"

"Not really, but yeah, I'll take one."

Harmony lit a cigarette and passed it to Budgie. She sat on the bed beside him and felt his forehead. "Your fever broke."

"I had a fever?"

"You had worse than that," she said. "You just kicked."

"What?"

"What's the last thing you remember?"

"Leaving the wake." He was chasing her. Didn't want to mention that. "What day is it? How long have I been..."

"Don't worry," she said. "Not long. You've been out a day. It's night. Day after the wake. Late."

"Okay." Budgie looked at the cigarette. It tasted weird. Thought about putting it out but that'd be a waste. "Did I overdose or something? Never o-deed before."

"You still haven't."

"Then what the fuck... Last thing I remember you were gone."

"I don't even know where to start."

"How about at the beginning?"

"I left you at the wake," Harmony said.

"I remember."

Harmony had not been this venom angry in a long time. To be really enraged, you have to be betrayed. To be betrayed, you have to expect something. She had not expected anything from anyone in ages. And now, like an idiot, she'd let herself expect something from Budgie.

And what had he done?

"Pressed that fucking murder button with every other asshole in the room." She smacked the corridor wall.

"FUCK!"

Her own heart humiliated her.

Without meaning to, she'd let herself fantasize. About getting out, about getting upstairs, about finally having someone to be with her. She'd sat on her couch, daydreaming a new life, thinking Budgie was different, imagining love and romance and all that fucking shit.

Then what?

He'd just gone along with what had to be about the dumbest rude boy, macho crap in existence. Just hit that button like every and any other asshole. Smiling while he did it. Killed that kid. And there was no reason for it. None. Jingles or whatever his name was meant Budgie no harm. There was no angle there. Just a bullshit superstition about ghosts no one even believed in.

She fumed through the corridors. In her pocket, her gizmo vibrated. "Oh, fuck that." She yanked it out. If it was Budgie, she was going to block him. They were done. Squeezing the device so hard she thought it might crack, she looked at the screen.

It came from Budgie but was not a call.

A distress signal.

The screen showed Budgie's name and his two powerbars. One for the drugs and one for the health. The health one was shrinking fast, dipping into the yellows.

"What the fuck?"

The screen changed to map and gave a location. Then back to the power bars. Shrinking.

"When I found you, you were laying in the corridor. There was blood coming out of your nose and it looked like..."

"Like what?"

"I can't be sure cause maybe the blood was smeared around but it looked like your eyes were bleeding too. Out of the corners."

"So what did you do?"

"Your powerbar had stabilized. In deep yellow."

"Shit."

"But it didn't look like you were getting any worse. You were hot though. Burning up. I should've left you."

"You didn't."

"No, I got a shopping cart and dragged you back here."

"Santa."

"I didn't even notice. You didn't feel heavy. Just hot and wet."

"Adrenaline." Budgie thought of carrying Sputnik through the hall.

"I guess that's one thing to call it: *The power of adrenaline.*" She shrugged and lit another cigarette. Budgie didn't ask for one. "Called a doctor."

"And he said?"

"Withdrawal. Said you were kicking drugs."

"That don make no sense. I'd just taken a lot of drugs. And that takes about a week. You said it was like what? A night and day?"

"You're body was expelling them. He said he'd never seen anything like it. Neither have I. You were sweating like... I had to force water down your throat and you kept throwing it up. Still cold. Like it hadn't even warmed up in your gut. That's your third blanket."

"Shit," said Budgie.

"Yeah. The doc wanted to stick around to watch like you were some sort of medical curiosity. He even offered to pay me. You believe that? I told him to fuck off."

Budgie smiled.

"Should've seen his face."

"I bet."

"Speaking of water..."

Harmony brought him a bottle from the fridge. Budgie drank it fast. Always heard that'd give you cramps but it tasted good. He had another.

"I don't know how you managed to call me."

"I didn't," Budgie said. Then he paused. His head worked a bit better now and he remembered TeeVee making some comment about how he was going to be less dependent on drugs. He hadn't thought to ask what that meant. "At least I don't think so."

"Then who..."

"I need some rest," Budgie said. "I'm sorry, I'm just exhausted. You mind if I sleep here?"

"You've puked, bled, sweat and shit here," she said. "Might as well sleep too."

"Sorry," Budgie said.

"I've had worse guests."

"Yeah, me too."

＊＊＊

Budgie twitched his hand. All night he'd lain paralyzed with ads and movies beaming through his head.

"What's the matter?" Harmony said. "You stink again."

It was true. He smelled like drugs. Sweat soaked his body. He wanted a drink of water but felt no hangover. Just tired and worn out. "I dunno," he said. "Feel fine."

"You look like shit."

He stroked her face. It was nice to wake up next to her warm flesh. His memories straightened but there were still blank spaces. "Thanks," he said. "I feel better." He could separate the real from the fake now. Except for one thing. Had that been real when the whole crowd had stopped moving and just turned this and that direction as the music cables ordered? It seemed too bizarre to be true but the image was vivid.

Harmony sat up. "What time is it?" she asked and then answered herself. "Noon." She touched the wet sheet. "Seriously. You okay?"

"Bad dreams," Budgie said, not sure if he was lying.

"Speed always does that to me," she said. "Even if I flush it, it still screws up my sleep."

"Yeah, like that," Budgie said even though it was nothing like that. He'd endured his share of pill-fucked dreams but those were different. These must be the side-effect TeeVee was talking about. The brain dreaming the mod into itself or whatever he'd said. Just naming the thing made Budgie feel better. Apparently, it would fade. "Damn, I'm hungry."

"I don't have anything here." She burrowed back under the covers.

"We can order in. I have some cash."

"You should save your money." She flung the covers back and slipped from the bed.

"Don't worry about it." Budgie wanted to trust her. He watched her dress. How much of his thinking was fogged by her looks? Harmony didn't look like a killer, not even with that shaved head. Her eyes were too gentle, her skin too soft. "I can pay," he said. "It's not a problem."

"Your decision." She stepped into some pants.

Budgie crawled from bed and dressed. What threw him about Harmony, he decided, was that she was not typical. Most girls were just interested in your wallet. But he brought nothing to the table. Why would she bother with him? There must be an ulterior motive somewhere but he couldn't figure it. Then again, maybe she really was diff. How many rude girls did you see around? Not many.

Even that scared him. It went beyond the comfortable levels of nonconformity and became something he couldn't quite define. Reminded him of the monster under his bed that had so scared him when he was kid, until he had saved enough stolen pennies to buy a toy. Good ol' Sergeant Motherfucker's Monster Killing Laser Gun.

Budgie smiled as he buttoned his tunic. It'd been a long time since he thought of his Sergeant Motherfucker toys. All of them were meant to ward off childhood hallucinations. The commercials had terrified him but they were supposed to.

They all started with some horrible situation. Like the closet monster was about to rape your Mom. You didn't even know what rape was but it was hinted at. Some awful and dark thing. The kid, who always looked like you, would cower and then, when the suspense had reached a crescendo, would find the Sergeant Motherfucker toy.

Armed and angry, the kid stormed into the room. If you changed the focus of your eyes you'd see the kid morphing into Sgt. Motherfucker. The kid wouldn't kill the monster but he'd drive it back into the night where you could hear it crying. Mom would be so happy and grateful that the kid got a big piece of chocolate cake in a brightly lit kitchen, while the product shot came up.

"What are you smiling at?" Harmony asked.

"Just thinking about kids' toys. You ever have Sergeant Motherfucker?"

"No," Harmony said. "I had Sally Spreadlegs."

"Same company I think."

"You might be right," Harmony said. "They kinda looked alike."

Budgie could tell from her tone that she was already sick of this convo but he pressed on. "I had his monster killing gun and his boogieman-proof blanket. Bought them with money I'd pocket-lift from the drunks who passed out near my hutch. Man, there was this one guy—"

"Stupid," Harmony said. "Those toys are stupid. I don't wanna talk about them."

"You're always so touchy about this shit."

"You wanna order the food or what?"

Budgie joined her on the couch. "Yeah, sure." He tried to log into his gizmo but it failed to load then crashed. He tried again.

"What's taking so long?" asked Harmony.

"I dunno, my gizmo is running slow."

Harmony sighed and pulled hers out. "Mine is fine," she said. "You should get a new one."

"Mine was good before."

"Whatev, looks luddite to me." Harmony shared her screen with the television, found some nearby restaurants and, after a brief discussion, ordered a couple of All Day Breakfasts. "Why are you so defensive about that toy?"

"My gizmo?"

"No. Sergeant Motherfucker."

Budgie didn't know how to explain. He just assumed that childhood toys filled people with happy nostalgia. Sergeant Motherfucker had been like a father to him, his protector and best friend. "I dunno," he said. "Why you always got sharp words about shit like that?"

She shrugged.

He knew he had to pursue the convo until he got some results, until he hit the nerve in her that she had hit in him. "So what's your problem with Sally Spreadlegs?"

"It's just a stupid fucking toy," she said.

Budgie searched her voice for some doubt but found none. Harmony was sure of herself.

"Really stupid."

"A lot of kids like it," Budgie said.

She shrugged.

Budgie's chest tightened. "But I guess you're too hardcore for me."

"No shit."

Budgie laughed.

"What's so funny?"

"Nothing, it's just…" He couldn't believe how easily she could puff him up and take him down. And she didn't even seem to care. "Just nothing. You make me happy." He tried to put his arm around her.

She held back.

"What?"

"What do you mean 'what'?"

"I mean, you pissed at me?"

She looked at him like he was an idiot. "Yeah."

"But, I don get it."

"What? You think that because I played nurse maid we're all good?"

"Yeah, something like that."

She shook her head.

"I want things to be good," Budgie said.

"Uh-huh." After a long moment. "Me too."

"Then what's the problem?"

"The problem is, they're not good. I grabbed you out of that hall because I'm a decent fucking person. But I can't—" She swallowed something. "I can't."

"No," Budgie said. "Fuck this."

She looked at him.

He heated. "You're fucking right, Harmony, shit ain't good. Shit ain't never gon be good. Ever. None of it. And that don matter. So fuck that." He took a deep breath and tried to calm down. "I fucked up, aight? I shouldn't have pressed that button. But I was off my head and it was the normal thing to do. I mean what the fuck? I ain't like you. I don always know what's right."

"I don't—"

"But I do fuckin' know what's wrong. And this shit here—this mopey weeping bout 'I can't.' That's just wrong. That's just fuckin' wrong." He shook his head and ground his jaw. "Look, it's all fuckin' wrong. That don' mean we can't. That don mean we can't try."

He stood up. Wanted to choke and kill something. "I don know how to say it!"

Harmony reached up and grabbed his hand. She said nothing, just squeezed it. Pulled him back to the couch.

The door rang and they both jumped.

Harmony answered the door.

The deliveryman was a short guy whose eyes lingered too long on her body. When he saw Budgie, his gaze snapped into focus and he named the price.

Budgie moved his hand slowly, keeping his eyes fixed on the delivery guy's face. *Wrong time to fuck with me.* "How you doin'?" Budgie passed the man his card.

"All right, busy today." He smiled and swiped the card under his collar. "A lot of hung over people ordering food."

"Sunday morning." Budgie pocketed his card.

"Yeah, it's always the same. All right, see ya."

"Yup." Budgie closed the door. "Motherfucker," he whispered and returned to Harmony. She already had her box open and was eating.

"This is good. I love bacon. Thanks." She gestured towards the coffee table. "I got the cutlery."

Budgie wanted to say something. Like 'we good' or 'so things are okay' but the moment felt too fragile. His words might break it. He sat down and ripped open his box.

The smell of cooked meat and eggs twisted his stomach. He ate heaping forkfuls of salty hash-browns. Harmony flicked on a movie channel. They watched, only speaking when she muted the advertisements.

He pulled his gizmo out of his pocket and opened up the file he had sarcastically marked, "Sell Out Fucker."

"Hello," the text read. "We are happy to hear that you've decided to make a change for the better by joining the—" Budgie skimmed through the words until he got to the meat.

Harmony glanced at his gizmo. "What're you doing?"

"Recruiter sent me a file. Info about the job and what-not." He glanced over the text. "Directions, what I need, time, that sort of thing. A lot of thanks yous and congratulations. Too many."

"Are you going to live up there?"

"I can't afford it," Budgie said. "I'm gon getta place down here."

"That's dangerous."

He wanted to tell her he'd be safe but couldn't mention Teevee. She'd know soon enough. Once TeeVee put the protect word out, everyone would know. Budgie would have to face some questions from her then. Whatever line of bullshit TeeVee spun, she wouldn't believe it. "I can look after myself," he finally said.

"Can you?"

"Well, fuck, gon find out one way or another." He shoved hash browns into his mouth. Budgie told her about the recruiter rolling him for his money and his trophy from Wolfe. "So, like, hard to save."

"A recruiter rolled you?"

"The basic bribery."

"A fucking recruiter?"

"Mr. Commisong."

"And you can look after yourself?"

"Got Griff, didn't I?"

"Nah, you need a proper partner." She scratched her chin. "You wanna stay here? Semi-perma like?"

Budgie glanced around the room, trying to pretend the idea hadn't occurred to him. It made him feel low, hoping she'd say that. Like he was scheming on her. Made him feel a bit better to start the haggling. "Seems like a good place," he said. "How much?"

He expected Harmony to drive a hard bargain. Instead she smiled. Was she worried he'd say no? Was she broke? He might get a pretty good deal here. Hated himself for thinking that. For wanting to exploit her.

"For free."

"What?" Budgie had never been offered anything for free. Even his Mom had presented him with bills for goods and services rendered. Giving things away was bad form, implied that you couldn't pull your weight or that the product was shoddy or that the person wanted some other, unnamed, payment. But looking at Harmony he felt sure that she meant something else. "Free?"

"Yeah. I'm already carrying this place. I'd need you to kick in on food and whatnot. Like what you consume. But I already got the rent and you gotta buy food anyway. As far as the walls go, I may as well share."

"That's a strange attitude," Budgie said, more to himself than to her. "Were you breastfed or something?"

"Mom couldn't afford it—so no." She grinned.

Budgie thought she was enjoying his discomfort but something about her eyes, some hard worried look, made him think she was uncomfortable too. She wanted him to say yes. Why? What was she after anyway? Maybe he should be asking to get paid to stay here. Was free a lowball? "I, uhhh... Free? That's quite an offer."

"You're pretty fucking dumb." She slapped her food on the table.

"What? Why?"

"Thing that comes to the top of my head is that you don't know how to act right."

Budgie wanted to say something clever. Instead his face burned.

"I can't believe you're haggling. Trying to get a better deal than free? If you don't wanna stay with me then fine. Fuck off. Door is that way."

"Wait." Budgie tried to process all this. "Lines got crossed somewhere."

"Yeah, well, don't they always?"

"I don mean it like all that, I just... No one ever gave me anything before and this is a big thing to give. And I don want you to rip yourself off. I like you." Budgie marveled at the words. He swallowed and felt his face getting even hotter. He reached up and touched her arm.

She resisted but not too hard.

"You're important to me. I don know why but I don think someone could pay me to hurt you."

"I know they couldn't and you wouldn't," she said. "It's written all over your face."

She reached into her pocket and passed him a cigarette. Didn't even ask for money.

Budgie wondered how much was written on his face. Too much and it'd get erased.

"But do me a favor, Budgie..."

"What's that?"

"Try not to be so fucking dumb. It makes me feel stupid for liking you. And it scares me."

"I'll try," he said and smiled. "No promises."

"Except that you'll try."

"See," Budgie said and exhaled a cloud of free blue smoke. "I knew it cost something."

PRODUCT PLACEMENT

Are you on the EDGE?

SITCOM killed it last night.

Are there any bootlegs of the SITCOM show?

@SITCOM @SITCOM @SITCOM @SITCOM @SITCOM

Where can we find SITCOM?

When does SITCOM play next?

Who the fuck is SITCOM?

@SITCOM @SITCOM @SITCOM @SITCOM @SITCOM

You can get old SITCOM bootlegs HERE

You can get a new SITCOM mix HERE

Is this a real SITCOM account?

@SITCOM @SITCOM @SITCOM @SITCOM @SITCOM

"Just hold your arm still," said Sitcom. "You always been so afraid of needles."

"Not afraid just…"

Sitcom slid the hypodermic into Slug's arm and pressed the plunger.

"OUCH!"

"Quit whimpering. Wouldn't even have to do this if you just stayed sober like I asked."

"At a wake?"

"Yeah, at a wake." Sitcom pulled the needle out. "How you feel now?"

"I'm straight." He rubbed his arm then pulled his tunic down. "I'm not in trouble am I?"

"Nah but you owe me for the sobriety." He shook his head. "I get why you'd be fucked up at the wake but do you really got to keep dosing the next day?"

Slug shrugged.

"Like you know we're going to have appointments and that I need you sharp." Ever since Sitcom stopped getting high at his parties, he preferred to hold his meetings the next day. Being crisp and clean guaranteed him an advantage over some drug sodden rude boy. But he needed Slug to be in the same condition. And he never was.

"Sorry boss."

"Whatever." Sitcom looked around this greasy washroom. "So you ready? Cause time is ticking."

Slug nodded.

"You're late."

Griff saluted.

"Sit down." Sitcom flicked through his gizmo. Not even looking at anything. He knew the file. "You want to tell me why?"

"I got gutted at the wake."

"I heard."

"By Budgie."

"I know." Sitcom glanced around. Budgie was supposed to be here too. "Do you know where he is?"

"He didn't show up?"

"That's a question, not an answer."

"I don't know then."

"Maybe he didn't get your message," Slug said. "Been something wrong with the gizmos all day. Mine is real slow. Not the only one either."

"What the fuck?" Sitcom looked over his shoulder. "Is anyone talking to you?"

"No, I just thought, cause he's not here."

"Why the fuck I even bother to sober you up? You got better sense when you're stoned."

"That's what I keep saying."

"Just be quiet." Sitcom looked back at Griff. "You keep smirking like that and I'll cut those upturned lips into your cheeks."

Griff's face straightened.

"That's better. So yes, Budgie was supposed to be here too but he's a no show. That's fine. Might even be for the best. I'm breaking you two up."

"No tears here."

"Your tears are not my fucking concern, prospect."

"Yes Sir."

"You two had beef. Looks like it got straightened out and you came out the worse for it." He tapped his gizmo on the table. "Didn't even land a blow from what I hear. Just got gutted."

Griff blushed.

"From what I hear, you had it coming too. Talking shit in the forum about a century rude boy. You. A prospect. Talking shit. About a superior."

"But he…" Griff cleared his throat.

"Go on."

"You know what happened and the rulebook says—"

"Rulebook?" asked Sitcom. He thought about saying to Slug, you ever hear of any rulebook but the guy would either still be holding to his quiet order or say yes. "I don't know about any fucking book that says you bitch around with your partner in the forum. What rule is that?"

Griff turned all sorts of red.

"So I've terminated your partnership. You're lucky that I don't just do the same to you. You know why you're lucky, you know who you can thank for that?"

"No Sir."

"You can thank Budgie. If he hadn't notched Wolfe, if we didn't need the extra bodies in the new sectors, I would cut your throat behind this shit. We clear?"

"Yes Sir."

"As it is, you're on thin ice. Very thin. I'm hearing too much about you. Too much bragging about mugging slummers and molesting their kids. Too much talking. And too much getting gutted when it comes to blows."

"I—but that guy hit me."

"I don't care about that guy. That girl you were touching up though? Loyal fan of mine. Put money into my pocket. You think she comes to any shows now?"

"No, I guess not. Sir."

"You cop a feel and it takes money out of my pocket. It takes money out of the Vidicon coffers. It makes you unprofitable. A losing venture. Then you got the balls to sow discord?" Sitcom spat on the floor. "You're going to hear about this sooner rather than later but I have special orders regarding Budgie. You're not to touch him, talk shit about him or pull any more nonsense about him. If that gutting did not already teach you the virtues of silence, let my words do it for you: Your beef with him is over or my beef with you begins."

"Yes Sir."

"And because I don't trust your 'yes sirs,' not when your face is pink hate, I'm assigning you a new partner. One that you can learn some respect for the real rules from. You'd be well advised to listen to him."

"Who?"

"Slug," said Sitcom. "Tomorrow, you're going back out on patrols. Meet your new comrade."

"Ah, shit," said Slug. "This about me getting too fucked up last night?"

Sitcom smiled.

‖‖ ‖‖‖‖‖‖‖‖ ‖‖‖‖‖‖‖‖‖ ‖‖‖‖‖ ‖‖‖‖‖ ‖‖‖‖‖ ‖‖‖ ‖‖‖ ‖‖‖‖ ‖‖‖ ‖‖‖ ‖‖‖

"You get this?" Sitcom showed his gizmo to Slug. Griff had gone. Good riddance.

"Everyone got that."

About as subtle as a hammer to the teeth, an all points message to the Vidicons from TeeVee blinked on the screen. He'd found the cure to their slow gizmos. When you downloaded the patch, there was a series of orders regarding Budgie. Not to be touched or trifled with. Sitcom shook his head.

"Patch works," said Slug. "Gizmos are back up."

Of course it worked. TeeVee was only curing a virus he'd invented. This whole thing worried Sitcom. It was bad enough that the guillotine lottery had been fixed but to use the connection to infect Vidicon gizmos then turn them zombie was insane. Not only did it compromise the sanctity of the lottery, it left the gang without effective communication for a day. If word had got out, they could've been attacked. They could have lost.

When he pointed that out, TeeVee said the risk was worth it; their security was improved. TeeVee would have the address books of the Vidicons, and any questionable loyalty would be revealed. Even said that Sitcom should thank him.

IIII III II IIII II I IIII IIIII IIII IIIII IIIII IIII IIIII IIII IIII IIIII IIII I III

"Why?"

"Because I'm doing this for you."

"I don't know what you mean."

"You will when those execs come calling."

"Execs?"

"Those zombies are all going to be talking about you, Sitcom. Spreading you through the information network. When EDGE crowdsources that, they're going to sign you."

"They won't know it's spam?"

"Hype is hype. They won't care."

IIII III II IIII II I IIII IIIII IIII IIIII IIIII IIII IIIII IIII IIII IIIII IIII I III

"What's up with this Budgie shit?" asked Slug.

"I can't discuss that," Sitcom said. He didn't say it was because he had no idea and TeeVee wouldn't tell him. "And you shouldn't question it. Even if..."

"I won't question it, you know that boss."

"I know." Sitcom sighed.

"You worried?"

"Are we on a fucking date? Why are you inquiring after my fucking emotional state as if it's some business of yours?" Sitcom smacked his palm against the table. "Sit down."

"Yes Sir." Slug squeezed into the seat across from him. "Sorry, I didn't mean to—"

Sitcom waved his hand. "You want to know the first rule of leadership?"

"Sure."

"Never give an order that won't be obeyed."

"You think Vidicons'll fuck with Budgie?" Slug held up his gizmo and frowned. "But this is a direct order."

"Most will obey, no doubt. But even if some don't, even if one don't, it looks bad." Sitcom ran his finger across some spilled coffee. "As usual, it falls square on us to stop that from happening. You getting my bandwidth here?"

"You mean, Griff?"

"Yeah."

"You want me to notch him?"

"Santa no. You do that it's gonna make things worse. That's the sort of shit that forces people to take sides. Just keep him close. He starts acting up, you report to me. Even if he looks like he's starting to act up."

"Be easier to kill him."

"If it comes to that, it's gotta be handled right. Needs to be a public display. An example set. A party."

"Yeah."

"But if it comes to that..."

"You'll let me do the wet work?" Slug leaned across the table and licked his lips.

"Who else?"

"Thanks boss. I don't like him."

"Would it matter if you did?" Sitcom's gizmo rang. He looked at the screen. "That was quick."

"Problem?"

"No," Sitcom said. "We got another meeting."

░▒▓ ▒▓▒▒▓▒▓▒▒ ▓▒▓▒▓▓▒▓▓▓ ▓▒▒▓▓▓ ▓▒▒▓▓▓ ▓▓▒▓▓▓ ▓▓▓▒▓▓▓ ▓▓▓▓▒▒▓▓ ▓▓▒▒ ▓▓▓▒ ▒▓▒▒ ▓▓▓

"So what do you want?" Sitcom knew who these two were and what they wanted, but he didn't like their nice suits and smarmy smiles. Didn't like being approached by strangers offering handshakes while he stood at the bar. They should've waited at the table.

"You don't look like security," Sitcom said while Slug circled behind them. The big guy cracked his knuckles and smiled over their shoulders. The whores in the waiting room, who weren't busy with customers, took shelter behind the bar. "You look like execs. You bring security?"

"I can tell you what we don't want." The one who seemed to be in charge glanced over his shoulder at Slug and then back at Sitcom, his upper lip covered in sweat. "We don't want any trouble."

"Who does?" Just what sort of people did EDGE send into the red levels to negotiate with gangs? Sitcom would've expected harder folk, but these two lacked any sort of killing dispo. Sitcom could spot a murderer—a real murderer, not just a brawler—easy enough, but these two were neither. That made him nervous.

"Well, yes, be that as it may, we came down here with an offer." The guy swallowed hard. "Some people told us where to find you—"

"What sort of offer?"

The guy glanced back at Slug.

Sitcom got pissed off. "You're talking to me."

The guy's head snapped back and he stared at Sitcom like a scared rabbit.

Sitcom took the edge of his voice. "What sort of offer?"

"We're from Edge ReOrbs—"

"Got that."

"—and we heard that you were pretty popular in the reds—"

Sitcom cut him off when a hand gesture. "Go get us a few pints Slug," he said. When the big guy was gone, Sitcom smiled. "Gotta keep a certain rep up in front of the underlings. Don't take it personal."

"Ah yes. Of course."

"Let's have a seat then." He led them to a booth and sat across from them. The two looked like brothers, all squished up together with their matching suits. "So tell me what you've been hearing."

"Just that you throw the best parties down here. That your mixes are really wet."

"The slang is fucking condescending. I'm a business man and an adult. Talk to me like one."

"Okay." The guy instantly seemed more comfortable. "We want to capitalize on your name, which is huge at the moment. That, usually, would be one thing—an important thing—but you also have considerable credibility with the mall rats, the kids we call the cool makers, and credibility sells like a son of a bitch. We want you to put together a few songs to distribute on the green levels. As you know, our distribution is unmatched."

"So I hear," Sitcom said, thinking of all the times he'd heard TeeVee harp on that.

Slug returned with the drinks and put them on the table.

"Go sit at the bar for a while," Sitcom said.

Slug smiled at the bousgies, who tried their best to look friendly, and retreated to the bar. He cackled with a hooker.

"Brass tacks. How much money are we talking about?"

The guy sipped his beer and scrunched up his face. Must be used to weaker brews. "Two thousand globals as an advance against future profits. If you have a hit we'll talk about more globals when your next song comes out. You also get royalties from the downloads."

"If I don't have a hit?"

"Then you owe us a couple grand."

"I have to think about it." Sitcom briefly considered selling the music then and there, without asking TeeVee about the terms. If it had been anyone else, he would have. But not TeeVee. Sitcom was not about to sell a product that TeeVee owned without making sure the price was right. And if TeeVee said no, then that was it. "Give me a week."

"Right, sounds good," the guy said. "Let me—" He reached into his jacket.

Sitcom pulled a dagger and aimed it directly at the man's heart.
The guy paled, his hand still in his jacket.

"Easy," Sitcom said. "Pull your hand out slow."

"I just wanted to give you my card."

"Fine. Pull it out slow."

"Okay, it's just a card." The guy held a tiny rectangular piece of
paper. His fingers shook so hard he dropped it on the table.

Sitcom slipped the dagger back into its sheath. "You have to excuse
my reflexes. But here's a piece of advice: It's considered pretty impolite
to reach into your pocket during a meeting in the reds. Best to keep
your hands where everyone can see them."

"Thanks." The man pushed the card across the table.

"Surprised you don't have that in a manual."

"I'll make sure to suggest it." The businessman had another swig of
his beer. This time he kept his face straight. He looked to his partner.
"What did I tell you? Credibility."

The lackey nodded, his mouth wide.

"That sort of credibility you can't buy cheap." He turned his attention
back to Sitcom. "At least not this week. Next week? Who knows? Don't
think too long."

"I never do."

INFO DUMP

"Today charges were brought Against Uncle Joe's Anti Meme Meme by other corporations under the anti competition laws. They claim that Uncle Joe's old-fashioned remedy makes some memes owned by Monsanto hyper effective, while destroying the ability of competing memes to attach. The product has been temporarily pulled from shelves. We go to corporate law expert on the spot, Biggles Tomfoot, for commentary. Take it away Biggles."

The door opened and bright light stung Budgie's eyes. He stood alone and blinking in the elevator. Wiped his sweaty palms on his pants and stepped into the green levels.

The illumination was meant to mimic the sun, but having never seen the sun, Budgie couldn't say if it was accurate. Just seemed bright. While his eyes adjusted, he listened to the muzak and convos of people on their way to work. The sting left his vision and he checked the directions on his gizmo before turning left and walking toward the huge Salem billboard. Metal shutters covered in adverts clattered from the ground, revealing the guts of the stores they protected.

Most of the crowd was older than Budgie and on their way to work. Later in the day the house-spouses would emerge to go shopping. Budgie felt like an alien here but, when he glimpsed his reflection in a store window and hardly recognized himself, he realized that he fit right in. Just a young go-getter on the way up. Except for his cheap haircut. He wished he had a cap to hide it.

Still, whenever someone glanced at him, he felt like he had a big glowing sign on him saying: "DOESN'T BELONG, BEWARE." But no one looked at him very long or hard. Their eyes were distant, a fog between them and the world. Total self-involvement. Expensive oblivion.

Must be nice to be able to walk around all locked up in your thoughts. You couldn't do that on the red levels. If you didn't pay attention you'd get hurt—perhaps not by a thug, maybe just by tripping or walking into a jutting wall. There was always something. It was a sharp world.

Funny how easily you could recognize a tourist on the reds. It didn't even matter how they dressed; their slumming costumes usually looked authentic enough. But if you shared an elevator they didn't speak or look at you. Like they thought ignoring their surroundings made them safe. Budgie was used to talking to strangers, to sussing them when they were close, and holding hostile stares. Sticking your head up your ass didn't make you invisible; it made you easy prey.

He wondered if he had any tells like that—if these people knew he wasn't one of them. If they saw through him, they sure weren't showing it. And what would they do anyway? Nothing. He could handle himself. But he should probably fog his eyes and stop looking up.

The ceilings were so high and the corridors so wide. He was used to having about three meters of clearance above him, but up here he must have a solid fifteen. The width had increased by the same proportion. There were windows and condos above all but the biggest stores. All the open air made him feel crushed and small. The space never bothered him when he was running a scheme. But he supposed he had other things on his mind then.

Budgie took turned at the Salem billboard and kept his eyes open for the office door. He found it crushed between two shops. No sign, just an address. He stepped inside and immediately felt more at home. A cramped staircase led down to another door, which opened to a waiting room.

A few people sat on hard plastic chairs, eyeballing Budgie. He scanned them. No one he recognized.

A woman watched him from behind a pane of bulletproof glass. "Budgerigar Saltmarsh," she said through the speaker before Budgie could speak.

"Yeah," he said and nodded.

"You're early."

"I didn't want to be late."

"Don't worry, that's good." She said something that Budgie couldn't hear. Must have turned the mike off. He watched her mouth moving and then she said to him: "Just grab a seat. Someone will be right with you."

Budgie slouched against the wall and the others went back to their magazines and gizmos. He was just another rude boy looking for a job. This was one of the only places in the mall where that wouldn't raise interest.

He wondered what gangs these guys were in and why they had left. But. All that had to be left downstairs. Gang clothing, odors or mention of gangs meant instant dismissal. The rule made sense to Budgie but he wondered why someone would come to the greens if they loved their street family enough to fight bout it up here.

A door at the other side of the room opened and a man in an open-collared dress shirt and corduroy pants poked his head out. "Budgerigar Saltmarsh."

He wished they'd call him by the short form.

"Come in."

The waiting floaters shot Budgie dirty looks as he crossed the room. He recognized the scheme. They all did. The man was messing with their heads. Letting the guy who just arrived in before them even though they'd prolly been waiting for ages. From school onward, he'd been the victim of similar psyops, from teachers and dealers and whatnot. Never benefited from it before. Felt a bit guilty as he stepped through the door. The guy in the dress shirt closed it and shook his hand.

"Hello Budgerigar. I'm Mr. Jones. Nice to meet you."

"Likewise." Budgie wondered if the man noticed how sweaty his palm was. "You can just call me Budgie," he said. "Everyone does."

"Okay. Just come this way." Mr. Jones took him down an empty beige hall to an office. "Take a seat."

Budgie sat down.

Mr. Jones consulted a tablet and turned the office camera on. "You were recruited by Mr. Commisong?"

Budgie nodded.

Mr. Jones raised his eyebrows. "How was that?"

"It was fine."

The guy was fishing for info. But, even if people liked the snitching, they never liked the snitch.

"Why do you ask?"

"We get some complaints about his methods."

"I have no complaints."

They looked at each other.

"At any rate, I think you'll find that things work a bit differently up here." Mr. Jones pulled a clear plastic package out of his desk drawer. "This is your work uniform. This uniform is mandatory. It costs ten globals. If you don't have the money now, it can be docked against your salary. Which would you prefer?"

Things are different up here. The robbery happened under bright lights and on camera. Official. "I don't have ten globals so, I guess dock it."

"Very good." He tapped his tablet and passed it to Budgie. "Place your thumb there."

Budgie did as he was told.

"The uniform cleans every stain except for blood, alcohol or anything drug related. We don't particularly care what you get up in your personal life but, when getting up to it, you will not be wearing one of our uniforms. We do care about that. If that uniform is stained, you will be either be terminated or required to buy another without the first purchase incentive discount."

"What's the regular price?"

"Fifteen globals."

"I'll take good care of it."

"I don't blame you." Mr. Jones tapped his tablet and the door opened. A man dressed in the same fitted, white unitard that Budgie just bought entered. "This is Mr. Dowsin. He's your trainer."

Budgie shook hands with Mr. Dowsin.

"You listen to what he says and you won't go far wrong." He checked his watch. "Time for my break."

"First off," Mr. Dowsin said when they got into the hall and started walking. "Call me Rick."

"Okay."

"Second—how badly did they roll you?"

Budgie just shrugged.

"That bad huh?"

"Yeah."

"It gets better."

"Where we going?"

"To the tube. It delivers us to the border regions of the mall, where you can put on that expensive new suit of yours. They'll give you a pass card after a couple of weeks, if things work out. Then you can go by yourself. For now, just keep coming in this way and meeting me."

"Sounds good," Budgie said. It was all he could think of to say. "Sounds great."

"Don't be nervous." Rick opened a door and they walked to another flight of stairs. "The job is easy and the people are pretty decent. You'll handle it." Another door. More stairs. "I was nervous my first day too. It's a big change."

"Yeah, it is."

They came out on a platform. A half circle was carved into the wall across from where they stood. A smooth path scooped out of the floor.

"Do you smoke?"

"Yeah," Budgie said.

"Well, you should have one now. This will be your last chance for a while."

Budgie lit a cigarette. This place reminded him of the alleys. No ads, just exposed chrome, where wires snaked out of metal boxes. He finished his smoke while Rick talked about what a long commute it was. "At least we'll have the pod to ourselves."

"That's good." Budgie wanted to say everything was good. He suspected that's what the job info meant by 'having a positive, upbeat attitude.' "I've never been on a train before."

"It's not a train. Train has tracks. This runs on a bedrock of sound. It's a sonic pod." Rick punched something into the control panel on the wall. A sleek but battered train with chipped blue paint moved silently into the station. "And you can drop that chipper 'everything is great' nonsense.

"I uh…"

"I've read the pamphlet too, you know. But the guys who wrote it never did the job, so fuck em."

"Okay," Budgie said. "Just trying to make a good impress."

"Yeah, I get it, but it gets old." Rick gestured at the train. "These pods go to border stations in the industrial sector, picking up workers on the way." Rick stepped back from the wall and kicked at the floor with his boot. "This old mall is still expanding. The core is getting bigger and there's a lot of work in construction."

"Constructing what?"

"More mall. Converting the factories to stores and living units and building other factories still further out. More walls between us and the outside. I want to get into construction. It's booming. That's where most of the rent money is going. Give The T-Dot Center a few years and it'll be competitive with New York or London."

The train doors opened. The zombie air came alive and Budgie instinctively stepped back. A buzzing sound shook the station and the air in the entrance blurred.

"Don't be scared." Rick walked to the side of the blurred air and rapped it with his hand. There was no sound but Budgie saw that he hit something. "This is the decontamination. It's made out of compressed noise, contained shockwaves. Same thing the pod rides on. And it moves fast."

"Is it safe?"

"Safe as a train. A very dangerous train. Uses less energy too. Unless it explodes." Rick smiled. "You going to tell me how great that is?"

"I guess not."

"Don't worry, it's not all that bad." Rick stepped through the blur. Poking his suddenly clear head out, he said: "What're you waiting for?"

Budgie joined him in the cylinder. The floor vibrated below his feet, giving him pins and needles up to the knees.

"No seats," Rick said. The foggy wall behind him shifted and the door shut. They were in transit.

"No ads either," Budgie said.

"No no profit in 'em here," Rick said. "The bosses rob us so throughly, that no other company can skin any money from us." He smiled and Budgie noticed that he still had his natural teeth, though one was missing. "They tried hanging posters but people kept tearing them down. You can take a rude boy outta the reds but you can't take the reds outta a rude boy. So they say."

Budgie could picture it—a long boring ride, nothing to do except fuck some shit up. "They took the cameras out of the red levels too," Budgie said, thinking Rick might be interested in the gossip.

"Really?"

"Yeah, same reason. People kept breaking or stealing them. Or they'd put a porn lens on them so all those security guys were busy jacking off instead of working. So they just gave up. Still have them in some elevators but you can't see 'em or get at them. Thing was, on the reds, everyone saw the workers putting them up."

Rick laughed. "Guess not much has changed."

"Yeah," Budgie said. "Kid stuff."

"But FYI, you shouldn't say things like that. At least not to the hypervisors. I don't care but they can get touchy." Rick shrugged. "Trying to clean up the image of us drones I guess. For them, keep the chipper thing."

"Oh, okay," Budgie said. "Sorry."

"Like I say, I'm wet. I know what it's like. But the bosses aren't from the reds."

"Are you?" Budgie said. "If you don't mind me asking."

Rick shook his head. "I used to party down there but I never lived there. My parents did, but they worked their way out. If they caught me getting into trouble they would have beat me senseless."

"How'd you end up doing this?"

"I like being outside," Rick said. "I really like it. I mean, it's not for every one. Some people can't take the open spaces. It freaks them out. But the people who like it, love it. I'm one of those. You like to read?"

"Not really," Budgie said.

"You should check out Lenny Niedenberger," Rick said, undeterred. "He wrote, 'Superstition: Then and Now.' It's in the Info Dump, like .04 globals or something to download. I don't like to read much either but I liked that. It's a sort of history of the mall and about, you know, why we're so nuts."

Budgie grunted and looked at the blank wall. He wasn't interested in books. Couldn't even really be bothered with the forum. The only text he read was adverts. Who cared about history? And who said they were all nuts? Must be some sort of green level bullshit. But maybe Harmony would know about the guy. "What's that name again?"

"Lenny Neidenberger."

"I'll check it out."

"You won't regret it."

<hr>

Whispers and weirdness: Harmony was familiar with both, and if she couldn't handle either she wouldn't be standing at the bar, waiting for a cup of coffee and a bag of drugs. So when the Vidicons—who'd been standing beside her, hard-mugging—grabbed their drinks and moved to the back of the room, she paid little mind. When she saw that same one whispering to the others in the bar mirror, she just tapped the counter. When they all started grinning and laughing, she turned around.

Whispers and weirdness. That was one thing. Laughter was another. She did not handle laughter.

She kept her quiet. What was there to talk about? Adjusting her neon pink bob wig, she walked across the barroom floor. Those smiles shrank with every step she took. The laughter stopped.

The Vidicons leaned back, eyes wide and lips tight. She smiled. Big and fake and corny. Sat down.

The bartender placed her coffee on the table. The Vidicon who started the whispering, opened his mouth to speak. Harmony brought her fingers to her lips. "Shhhhhhhh." She stirred some sugar into her coffee and had a sip. It was garbage but it was hot.

She smiled at that Vidicon.

Then she threw her coffee into his face.

He yowled.

The others stumbled away from the table and tooled. Harmony stayed in her seat.

The guy yodeled and grabbed his face. Harmony gestured to the bartender for another cup. He put his gizmo down and nodded. Picked up the pot and walked.

"Scuse me," he said as he navigated through the tooled Vidicons. Poured a cup.

"Could you leave the pot?"

He hesitated and Harmony handed him a quarter global. "Keep the change," she said.

He collected the money, put down the steaming pot and left. Behind her, in the quiet, she heard his gizmo beep back to life.

She poured more sugar into her coffee and waited. If these Vidicons were going to do anything, it'd be done by now.

The one with the face full of coffee wiped the remainder off with his sleeve. His skin was lobster but it wasn't a serious burn. He'd stopped making that terrible noise and stared at the pot, doubtless thinking about it shattering across his face.

"At least you didn't have to drink it," said Harmony. When he just stared, she shrugged. "Thought you liked a good laugh. Figured from your giggles that you were a bit of a comedian. Slapstick not sophisticated enough for you?"

He ground his jaw. Prolly wanted to tell her to go fuck herself. What rumor prevented him? Was he thinking about his balls chopped off and shoved in his mouth? Her powerful friends? It must've been something good to keep him seated so sweet and placid. She tilted her head.

"Maybe if you told me what you found so funny before, I could better tailor my humor to you." She lifted the pot and topped up her coffee. "Because that's what I wanna do, you know: Tailor myself to your advanced fucking tastes."

He swallowed and his eyes darted around. With math all over his face, he calculated how much rep he was losing. A lot. Every moment he lost more. If he didn't tell her the joke, he'd lose just about all of it. Funny thing was he probably started cracking wise to gain rep.

"I wuz jus sayin' that I'd turn floater too if it got me into your pants." He winked.

Harmony turned her face blank by reflex. Even this blankness said something and she disliked what it said. A face should be quiet. Hers spoke too much and too loud. It said guilt. Her mouth said something different. "What the fuck you talking about?"

"Talkin' bout your man."

"Who's that?"

"Budgie."

"What the fuck you know about him?"

"Just what I hear bout him being in certain areas, doin' certain things. Areas he got no business being. Things he got not business doin'." He held his left hand up to show it was empty. The fingers signed that he was moving slow and not for a weapon, before he reached into his inner pocket. "Then today, moments before you show, I get this. He pulled out his gizmo and flicked through it. Passed it across the table and leaned back. Smug-like.

Harmony picked up the gizmo. It was a bright red, alpha level message from TeeVee. But she hadn't got one. Must have been attached to a patch. She's stopped downloading Vidicon code when she heard rumors they were selling psychographic info to EDGE. Now the alphas included messages and orders to encourage downloads.

Not that it mattered. If the info was important, you heard about it soon enough

As she read it, he repeated it from memory, *"Any harming of Vidicon gamma, Budgie, will meet with my ire."* He smiled. "Had to look that up. *Ire.* Means wrath, anger. Means don touch Budgie. What's that mean?"

Budgie made some kind of deal.

"Means mind your own fucking business," she said, betrayal curdling her words.

"Since when is Vidicon turning topside not our business? Since when is that something we don mind?"

Harmony spun his gizmo back across the table. "Means a scheme, Shit-for-brains," she said. "Obviously."

She didn't want to sit here looking at his smug face any longer. Her dispo was an ember and every time this guy spoke, he blew on it. Soon flames would erupt.

She wiped a suddenly sweaty palm on her pantleg. Right now, she wanted to choke Budgie. She'd run risks for him and he'd been maneuvering behind her back. Never told her that an alpha was involved or that some mass message about him was about to go out. She'd been wanting to help him keep all this on the down low. And for what?

There was scheme all right. It was on her.

"You got the obvious answer, huh?" the Vidicon said. "A scheme? Must be sucking some alpha cock to get in on a scheme like that. Or am I being too sophisticated for ya?"

"You," Harmony said, leaning forward, "talk too fucking much."

"How bout you try to shut me up?"

About to try just that, she reached forward to grab the coffee pot.

Hands gripped her shoulders and yanked her back into her seat. A rude boy wrapped his forearm around her neck.

Adrenaline pumped. She wanted to thrash her way out. It'd be futile. Instead, she took a deep breath and went limp. Stared across the table and into their boss's eye. "Heh," she said. "Got me."

"Got you," he agreed. Then a long, grinning silence.

Shit. He was more scared than her. Cause now he had to do something. But there was that note from an alpha saying that Budgie was not to be harmed in any way. Would this be harming Budgie?

Aside from that, there was her reputation, which had doubtless preceded her. If he pissed her off and failed to finish the job, he knew she'd be coming for him and, moron he might be, didn't like his chances.

But if he did nothing, just let her go, he'd look weak in front of his boys. He had not restrained her as much as he had restrained himself. And his brains weren't sharp enough to cut a way out.

His fear made her nervous. Frightened people are capable of very special sorts of stupidities. She should put him at his ease, tell him that if he stopped, she'd call it a draw between them.

Except that'd sound like begging. And she wasn't going to do that. Not only did it offend her pride, it was bad tactics. Right now, he was scared of her. If she begged, she'd look weak. Then her only protection would be his charity and good sense. She didn't have a lot of faith in either.

She stared at his face, hard, even as his eyes scanned his cohorts, trying to search out some guidance in their expressions. Finally, he looked back at her.

"Flirt," she said.

He snarled and reached across the table and towards her face. In spite of herself, Harmony blinked.

He grabbed the pink wig off her head. She'd been expecting a blow. This was somehow worse.

Grinning, he put the wig on and vogued. "I look pretty boys?" he asked. They chuckled.

Harmony's face burned.

"I look sweet?"

She bit her lower lip.

He tossed the wig on the table. Looked at it and the coffee pot. Laboring towards his conclusion, he picked up the pot and poured coffee on the wig. When he realized that the coffee was spilling off the table and onto his lap, he swore, grabbed the wig and shoved it into the pot. Soaked it. Yanked it back out. Then, sopping and hot, slapped it onto Harmony's head.

He put his fingers on his chin, as if assessing his work. "Looked better on me," he decided.

Squinting against the coffee running down her face, grinding her jaw against the bile in her throat, Harmony glared at him as hard as she could muster. She fantasized revenge. She wanted to curse and threaten. She did neither. Just stared. Not fear that held her tongue. Not cowardice that prevented her violence. Not that.

But the thought of knots within knots. Just as this rudie had restrained himself even as he'd restrained her, she'd been tied deeper to Budgie. What could she do now? Leave him and look the coward? She was stuck. Making a threat that she'd have to follow up would just tighten those knots.

"What?" he said. "You don like slapstick?"

"Flirt," she said. "You tease."

The Vidicon with his arm around her neck, wrenched backwards. Harmony spilled out of her chair. The back of her head smacked against the floor. A dizzy red blotch coagulated in her vision. Through this, she looked up at them looking down at her. Waited for the boots.

One of the Vidicons leaned forward and spat into her face. Their boss slapped him upside the head. "Where's your manners?" he asked. "Don spit on a lady when she's down. Wait for her to get up."

They laughed.

"You gon get up?"

Harmony shook her head.

"That's what I thought." Backslapping and laughing, the Vidicons left.

Harmony stayed on the ground a moment longer, staring at the ceiling. She wiped the spit off her face with her sleeve, then slowly, got up. She pulled her wig off, threw it on the table where it lay like a dead, pink rat.

The bartender appeared with a cloth and wiped down the table, not looking at her. Business as usual, she supposed.

She asked him for the bathroom key. As she paid and he handed it over, their eyes met. He briefly looked like he wanted to say something.

"Thanks," she whispered.

He shrugged.

In the bathroom, she locked the door behind her and took a deep, hitching breath. Then she vomited into the sink.

Brown. Coffee. Slapstick.

Budgie stepped out of the vacuum chamber wearing a bright orange Remploy/Dupont decontamination suit, which fit tightly over his expensive white unitard. He looked out on the world through a clear mask. Rick, who wore the same inhuman outfit, nodded at Budgie. "How am I?" Budgie asked into the micro-phone beside his mouth.

"You're secure," Rick said, his voice clear in the speaker system built into Budgie's helmet. "These suits are tough as hell and they almost never get punctured—I've never seen it, don't know anyone who has—but almost perfect isn't good enough."

"The pollution is that bad?"

Rick didn't answer. Apparently the question was too stupid to bother with. "Locker," he said and pointed.

Budgie opened it and put his bousgie clothes in, closed it and set his code. He'd broken into enough to know how to work one. He followed Rick to the truck.

Each wheel was twice his height and a ladder led up to the cab. As Budgie understood it, this two-kilometer long machine traveled to the dumps where robots loaded it with plastic, metal and glass (which could be broken down and built into new things) and the organic matter that would be cleaned and used as soil in the mall's farms. Budgie's job was to stand over a hole, where this raw material was being dumped, and watch for clogs. When something got stuck he'd poke and lever at it until he worked it loose. For some reason, this took training.

"C'mon," Rick said. "We're running late."

Budgie matched his pace. He'd taken a long time to get into his suit, though Rick said he'd done all right for his first day and assured him that getting clothed and unclothed was the hardest part of the job. 'Rest of it's hurry up and wait, mainly,' he said. Budgie hoped he wouldn't be too bored.

"Watch your step." They climbed the steel ladder and entered the cab, which was bigger than his old hutch. Budgie instantly felt more at home. The huge domed dock had gotten under his skin. The helmet made it feel a bit better by closing him in. He wondered how he'd feel outside. He'd heard that it was completely unbounded by walls but found that hard to picture. Not even the images of outside did it—they were, after all, locked in a one-meter teleprison.

He felt more nervous and excited than he had in long time. It was even better because he was sober. Looking across the cab at Rick, he understood how someone could love this job. A couple of people sat on either side of them. Rick had introduced them but Budgie couldn't remember their names. Even if he did, everyone looked alike in these suits and masks.

For now he'd just play it quiet. Although Rick had told him that no question was stupid, he'd feel stupid asking for names again. One of the men locked the cab door. It clanged shut and the machine lurched. Budgie tumbled into the man beside him, who roughly shoved him back. "Watch it," the mike said in his ear.

"Okay, sorry," Budgie said.

"My fault," Rick said. "Should've warned you."

"How long a trip is this?"

"Few hours."

"Did anyone bring any cards?" Budgie smiled. No one laughed.

One of the men looked at him for a long moment. "Stop being so fucking chatty."

Budgie heard mumbled agreement. Just what was this fucker's problem anyhow?

"Turn your ears off if you don't like it," Rick said and glared at the man. "Or tune in some radio."

The guy grunted and turned a dial on his chest. "Dunhill Morris is no longer in communication," a robotic voice said. All the others did the same. Except for Rick.

"Did I do something wrong?" Budgie asked. He didn't want to piss off everyone on his first day.

"No."

"Then—"

"It's just a long commute. You'd be surprised how quick people run out of things to say to each other. We don't talk much. Just leads to problems. Sooner or later people get under your skin and it makes it hard to sit in this little room with them for hours. We usually just listen to the radio or sit and think. Some people sleep. I listen to audio books."

"So, no cards?"

"Nah. They used to play games but that created more problems than talking. Some people always lose. What's the point of coming to work if you just gamble your wages away before you get home—or even worse, before you even get on site?"

"Guess that makes sense," Budgie said. "How do I work the radio?"

"That dial on your chest puts you out of communication and then you just say what station you want or what show. Most of these guys like Bob Anger but I can't stomach him. He makes me wanna puke."

Budgie flipped the dial. He didn't know what station he'd like so after a few moments he just said "Bob Anger." Rick must've been able to read lips because he looked at Budgie and shook his head.

INFO DUMP

"Hello Friends. Today I have a special guest with me. Mall Security Chief, Rock Cockett."

"Hi, Bob."

"Hello Rock. Let me get right to it. The rude boys."

"The rude boys?"

"What's the plan?"

"Well, they're mainly a red level problem. I think we've done an excellent job of keeping the problem contained."

"Are you crazy or just lying?"

"Neither Bob, I'm just saying that—"

"We are in the midst of an incredible, an abso-fucking-lutely incredible, crime wave. You can't turn on the news with hearing about more robberies, more muggings, more rapes. And you're saying that the threat is contained?"

"It has been the policy of this force, long before I took the helm I might add, that people who go to the red levels—adults, that is—go there knowing the risks. We advise against it but we cannot investigate every incident that occurs down there. The whole point of the red levels is to isolate the antisocial elements in the populace."

"But it's failed. People can pass between levels with no problem. Rude boys can come up here as they please—"

"That's not strictly true—"

"—Can come up here as they please. And the perverts amongst us can go down there. Has any thought been given to a sort of universal chip? A tracking device? So we know who these people are."

"You've put a great deal of thought towards it."

"But how about you guys? Huh? Have you put any thought to it?"

"Not really, Bob. I think most reasonable people understand that a universal chip is an extreme solution and not even much of a solution. Besides, the Citizens' Privacy Council owns quite a few shares in the mall and—"

"Oh, so now I'm unreasonable? Parents who want to keep track of their kids are unreasonable? But the whoring bastards who want their privacy so they can go down there are reasonable? They're veritable pillars of logic, I suppose."

"Look, we don't recommend that anyone goes down there. But if an adult wants to go into the reds then that's their business. We don't legislate everything."

"You don't legislate anything."

"And you do?"

"I would. I'd ship the whole red levels outside. That would solve it."

"That's a ridiculous position. You're talking about a death sentence for petty criminals."

"Petty? Chief Cockett, you crazy lying bastard, these people are not petty criminals. They're murderers and thugs. Rapists and junkies."

"Some of them were just born down there. You'd kill them, too?"

"They're the worst ones. The ones born down there. Like that guarantees virtue. You just have to be born in the reds and all of a sudden you're a pillar of the community? Don't make me laugh. And to call it killing or a death sentence is just hysterical. It's an exodus. It's a real punishment. Sure, some of them would die, but they'd be out of our hair."

"I don't think you've—"

"Now don't get upset, Rock. I'll give you a few minutes to cool down. But when we get back from this special message from Universal Chip Tracking Solutions, there'll be more hot talk with me, your host, your voice, Bob Anger, and my special guest, Security Chief Rock Cockett on 'You're a Crazy Lying Bastard with Bob Anger.' Stay tuned."

"Now watch what I do," Rick said.

"Okay." Budgie twisted his neck to peek outside, but it was no good. Rick's body blocked the exit.

Rick hung out the door and grabbed the ladder on the outside, put his foot on it and climbed up. "You see that?"

Budgie didn't answer. He just stared out the door at the empty space. His eyes felt like they were being sucked out his head. He had never seen so far.

"Budgie?"

"Yeah, I saw."

"What're you waiting for?"

Budgie turned his body like Rick had done, grabbed the ladder and put his foot on a rung. Gusts of muscular wind shoved his body. He climbed, then crawled onto the roof. The moving air scared him and he gripped the truck.

"It's just wind." Rick grabbed his arm and pulled him to his feet. "Don't be afraid to stand. Get a look around, get your bearings."

Budgie braced himself but couldn't focus. The scene was just too big to take in. His vision was no longer locked up by adverts or walls and he saw further than he'd ever known possible. His eyes ached and he felt dizzy. Looked up at pure blue. A huge light burned up there, like a paused flash bulb. "The sun?"

"Don't look right at it."

Scared, Budgie looked down. The ground was naked, cracked dirt, hard as concrete. And it just went on and on. Out of this sun-fried earth grew the mall.

"Holy fucking Santa." It was not how he'd pictured it. He'd always just kinda assumed the mall was a smooth dome, but it looked jagged and boxy, a confusion of angles, a broken puzzle of black and white. Sharp and improbable.

Budgie tried to remember his schooling. Reciting old lessons gave his brain something to cling to. Those black parts were the Jansen Panels that gave the mall solar power. Huge white fans ringed the mall and chopped up the sky with every rotation. But that didn't help. Every word was a tiny cage and outside would not be caught.

Even the T-Dot Center, which contained everything and everyone he had ever known, looked small. It might hog a whole horizon but it still looked puny against the endless blue canvass. Just a pathetic island in the middle of nothingness. "This is…"

"You like it out here?"

"Yeah. Wow." Budgie's breathing slowed.

"Good. Most people who can't handle it, can't handle it immediately. But turn around."

"I can't even describe it." Budgie whispered.

He turned. In front of him, reaching into the sky was a wall of trash, crawling with massive robots, each one dwarfed by its habitat. The dumpster-shaped bots had thick tentacles ending in hooks, which grabbed garbage, tore it up and loaded it into their backs.

It reminded Budgie of an old nature show he'd seen a few years ago, where hard-shelled beasts crawled over a coral reef. He looked up at the air, expecting a massive shark to come floating by. But nothing happened.

"I wish I could see this again for the first time," Rick said. Even through the speakers he sounded nostalgic. "You get used to it after a while. But sometimes, you can still sort of see it."

"Is he ready yet?" one of the other men asked.

"Grab a pole," Rick said and bent over. Several three-meter long, thin metal rods were strapped to the roof of the road train. Budgie took one and followed. "Watch your step."

They walked for about twenty minutes. Budgie tried to watch his footing but spent more time gawking. His thoughts skipped and stuttered. *Oh shit, oh shit, oh shit,* in an endless loop.

"This is your hole," Rick said. "We're starting you off on organics until you get the swing of the thing. Softer stuff and fewer clogs."

"Okay," Budgie said.

"Everyone ready?" a voice asked in his ear.

A chorus of 'yes'. Budgie didn't say anything but felt his insides agree. *Yes.* That was the only way to describe out here. Not *Oh Shit,* but *Yes.*

"Doors open, access code, 4132 X-Bobby-E K."

A circular hole opened beside Budgie and he stared down into a gaping metal mouth. Sections of roof shot out from the truck and stabbed into the side of the dump like giant, blunt knives, forming bridges. The roof rocked beneath his feet then settled.

A robot scuttled across the plank and towards Budgie. He stepped back from the fast moving and unwieldy machine. Its garbage filled back tilted up and opened, dumping a load of trash into the hole before bolting away. Another followed right behind and did the same. The hole chewed.

"It keeps going like that," Rick said. "You saw how they dumped that in?"

"Yeah."

"Now, what sometimes happens is they make a mistake and pick up something too big for it to fit. So it clogs up the hole or doesn't get out of the robot's back. You've got to loosen it and knock it in. Understand?"

"Yeah," Budgie said.

"Always use the pole. Always. That clear?"

"Yeah."

"Good. I don't want to see you lose a hand or get knocked in. If you start to get pulled towards the hole release the pole. They'll charge you for it but not too much. Anyway, we have plenty of those and you only have one of you." Rick looked around. "I'm sticking with you today. I'll do the first clog, so you can see what I do and then I'll let you do the next. Takes a few weeks of training. But after that you'll be an expert."

Budgie laughed. He felt giddy out here. Stoned but without that chemical feeling in the flesh. The robots continued in their line up, never more than four at a time, each one dumping a full load without incident. "About how many clogs happen a day?"

"Three or four. Used to be more but the machines have better techs now." Rick shrugged. "It gets boring."

Looking around, Budgie doubted it. "Did it always look like this?"

"Whisper to Budgie from Rick," the computerized voice said. "Do you consent to private conversation?"

"Yes."

"Sorry, the guys don't like too much chit-chat," Rick said. "No it didn't always look like this. You've seen old movies right?"

"Yeah. But movies, they just don't do it."

"Yeah. Used to be trees and plants all over the place. Well before we were born though."

"What happened to it all?"

"You really should read Lenny Niedenberger."

"Why?" Budgie suddenly remembered that TeeVee could be watching, almost sensed him right behind his eyes, and felt guilty. This information seemed too important for that psycho to have. It felt profane to transmit this back into the mall. He wished there was a way he could turn his percepts off. "What does he say?"

"The pollution was mainly genetic. Not all of it but mainly. Companies created plants that dominated the natural versions. They couldn't keep it contained and they spread through nature, killing off the other plants."

"I've heard about that."

"Yeah. Just good old agriculture. Until viruses hit everything. Guess you can't totally tame nature without killing it."

"It's just all gone." Budgie tried to picture what it looked like out here before.

"Yeah," Rick said. "But there's still something here, don't ya think?"

Budgie nodded. He didn't know what, but it was definitely something.

"Mister Socks must die." Prada sucked at the scratch on her hand. "I'm sick of that bloody cat."

"C'mon," Sindy said. "He's a good little kitty."

Prada grabbed her drink off the bar. The bordello had closed a few hours ago and all the johns and most of the working girls had gone home. Sindy and Prada, being possessed of the least seniority, stayed behind to clean up. They'd finished an hour ago and were now enjoying a few drinks. Both had tomorrow off.

"He's not a nice little kitty. He's a filthy alley cat and a menace." She held up her hand. It still bled. "You see what he did to me?"

"You were trying to throw him out."

"Blame the victim, that's typical. But I wasn't trying to throw him out. I did that after he scratched me." She swigged the warmed liquid cocaine. "He was meowing at me and I thought he wanted me to pet him."

"You know he doesn't like to be petted."

"Sometimes he does."

"Not near his stomach. Did you try to rub his belly?"

"That's beside the point."

"I bet you did, I bet you—"

"I don't care," Prada said. "That cat has got to go."

"I have a pest problem in T-Dot Center, red level zone 416." Prada spoke slowly so her old fashioned television could collect the words. As they appeared on Craiglist's Red Light Flea Market, she continued. "Need this pest taken care of with maximum prejudice. Contact me. We'll meet and talk shop."

She flipped off, lit a cigarette and waited.

The secrecy felt silly but Madame Hazel loved Mister Socks. If she learned of this plot, Prada would be out of a job or worse. It was the worse that scared her. Hazel didn't have the sway of a bigger Madame like Jane, so Prada could always find another job. But Hazel had a nasty habit of removing body parts.

The Tickle House was a funny bordello.

Hilarious.

No brutality was tolerated from the johns. It was the exclusive province of Madame Hazel or that scruffy old tomcat. If a john had cut her hand, he'd find himself without a finger. That was Hazel's idea of justice, an eye for eye. Most of the customers were kind. Weird but kind. Liked to tickle or be tickled but that wasn't illegal. Then again, on the red levels, what was?

Prada squashed out her cigarette. She had never liked Mister Socks. He was hideous and looked out of place in a nice bordello. His ears were torn off, most of his teeth were missing and cataracts fogged his eyes. He should be skinny but the scraps the working girls fed him kept him plump and muscular. His short orange hair was spotted with white patches and these were often spotted with blood. Yup, Mister Socks was one ugly bastard.

Prada liked the luxurious fur of a Persian or the exotic insanity of a Siamese. Cats like those would fit the ambiance of her bordello. Mister Socks looked like he had just wandered out of some grungy panel house after a catnip binge. He acted the same.

Her television pinged. A message. She logged back into her account with her remote control. "I can take care of your problem." The message in the inbox read. "When and where do you want to meet?"

"Reply," Prada said. "Tonight. 7 o'clock. The Joyce."

"Fine by me," the reply came. "I'll be wearing a red flower. See you then."

In the next ten minutes there were sixty more replies. All of them cock shots. She deleted most of these and took her message down from Craigslist.

Clapper watched the woman. She glanced around the bar, saw the plastic rose pinned to his chest, and smiled florescent. She sashayed over, her tight clothes and exposed cleavage oozing sex.

"Hello," he said. "I'm Clapper."

"Can we talk here?" She sat at his table. "I've never done this before and this place looks busy."

"The busier the better," he said. The half pint of wine he was drinking made him feel suave. "Data smog. No one will be listening. Would you like a drink?"

"Sure." She flipped the table switch and tapped the screen. "Liquid cocaine," she said. "The job I have is—"

He held up his hand. "Not yet. Wait until your drink arrives. We don't want to be interrupted now, do we?"

"No of course not." Her face turned red. It was probably a blood cell mod. People liked it when their hookers blushed, maybe because they so rarely did.

The waiter scanned her card and Clapper glimpsed the name on it. Prada. Memorized the number. He liked to know who he was doing business with.

"Okay," Clapper said. "Now what were you about to say?"

She leaned forward and Clapper got a whiff of delicate perfume. "This job I have for you, it's kinda weird."

"They all are," he said. "Who do you want dead?"

"A cat," she said. "Mister Socks."

Clapper thought he'd heard it all. He really had. "Why in Santa's name would you hire me to kill a cat? They sell poison. To anyone."

"Well, d'uh. I know that." Prada sat back. "But no one can know I did it. Mister Socks—he just has to disappear."

Clapper looked into the girl's pretty face. "I suppose you have about thirty seconds to convince me that you're not some crazy sending me on a psychotic wild goose chase."

"I'm not crazy."

"Crazy people are the only people who ever need to say that." He checked his watch. "The clock is ticking."

"Okay. Mister Socks is this cat where I work and I hate him." She pointed at a small cut across the back of her hand. "He did this to me. But the Madame loves him. So I want him dead but I don't want her to know a thing about it. I'll get fired."

"Too bad," Clapper said.

"What? You can't do it?"

"No, it's not that. I'd hoped you were a nut. Then I could at least charge you for hours while I pretended to take care of this pest of yours. But that explanation, well it's just so incredibly banal." He liked the sound of that word. He'd have to use it more often. "I suppose the oddest things are the most banal."

"So can you do it?"

"Yes, but it will cost you, let's see, five globals."

"Five globals!" She shook her head. "You know how many offers to that post I had?"

"And do you know how many of them figured you were talking about a person and would have notched you just for offering such a degrading task?"

She frowned. The idea hadn't occurred to her.

"This job is an insult. I'm not a damn exterminator. I am a notch artist. And I happen to like animals." He took a short, sharp swig of wine. "A lot." He slammed the glass down. "Five globals isn't even negotiable. And if you don't pay I'm gonna find out where you work, Prada, and tell your Madame all about this. It's not cricket but people would understand. This whole situation is not cricket. I shouldn't even agree to it."

"I'll pay," she said, blushing hard. She looked shook. Clapper had forgotten that his anger had that effect on people. He was so rarely angry.

"I need pictures and I need to know everything you know about this cat. What's his name—Mister Whiskers?"

"Mister Socks."

"Notching a cat." He shook his head. "Makes me sick."

"Could you make it look like an accident?" Prada asked.

Clapper took another drink and restrained himself.

⬛⬛ ⬛⬛ ⬛⬛ ⬛ ⬛ ⬛⬛⬛ ⬛ ⬛ ⬛ ⬛ ⬛⬛ ⬛⬛ ⬛ ⬛⬛ ⬛⬛ ⬛⬛⬛ ⬛ ⬛⬛⬛ ⬛ ⬛⬛⬛ ⬛ ⬛⬛ ⬛ ⬛ ⬛⬛ ⬛⬛ ⬛ ⬛⬛ ⬛ ⬛ ⬛⬛⬛

But five globals was five globals.

At least that's what Clapper told himself as he followed the cat through the streets. He'd cased the beast for two days and two nights. It was only a cat, but Clapper was a professional. He knew where the cat was going, and ducked into an alley to intercept it.

He hated these thin, back corridors. The alleys were a labyrinth that led deeper and deeper into itself, outside of his or any gang's jurisdiction. This was the territory of the Alley Gnomes. They usually stayed deep within the network of fissures that connected the different streets in the mall. But if you intruded...

Clapper peeked onto the street. Mister Socks sauntered toward him, his head held high and jaunty. Clapper pulled a tin of tuna from his pocket and tapped it with a can opener. Prada said the cat could not resist that sound.

She was right. Mister Socks strutted into the alley and stared at Clapper. "Here kitty-kitty-kitty." Damn, he felt like a fool. The cat came closer and sniffed at the can, which Clapper opened.

"Meow?"

"Yes," Clapper said. "That's right. Meow."

He pried the lid off the the tin and setting it down, reached for his boot knife. Mister Socks tilted his head and looked at Clapper for a long moment. *He's on to me*, Clapper thought. *Nah*. It was just a stupid damn cat.

Mister Socks took a few cautious steps forward, lowered his head to the tin and ate. Clapper pulled the knife from his sheath and gripped it ice-pick style. One good jab should do the job. He should slash but hated the idea of the cat making noise. Clapper didn't think he could handle yowling.

He raised the knife. Took a deep breath.

The cat pounced at him, a fury of claws. Bright lines of pain shocked Clapper's face and he dropped his knife. He grabbed blindly at Mister Socks. The cat greeted his naked hands with sharp claws and bit Clapper's eyebrow, its single tooth digging deep before tearing the flesh.

"Fuck!" Clapper yelled and the cat dragged a claw across his tongue. Then it jumped off.

Tentatively, Clapper opened his eyes.

Mister Socks stood about a meter away from him. Growling. Back up and fur hackled.

Clapper picked up his knife and swore, birthing fresh pain in his mouth. He could let it go—should let it go—but the damn animal looked so fucking cocky.

He scrambled to his feet and sprinted at it, the knife in his fist.

The cat bounded away. He chased, stumbling in a blood blind fog. The cat dodged down some stairs that ended in pitch-blackness. Clapper skidded after him.

He was three steps in when he realized what a bad—what an unbelievably bad—idea this was.

You didn't go into the deep alleys. Never. Not if you wanted to come out in one piece. Before Clapper could slow his pace and reverse course, his foot caught on something soft and furry.

He was in mid air, legs and arms flailing, reaching for a grip and finding none. He heard an indignant meow and hit concrete. His head whipped forward and bright red light bloomed in front of him. It turned blue. Then red again.

He tried to move and couldn't. Felt like puking. Maybe he did. Had he had knocked himself out? Couldn't be sure. What time was it? Was Prada here?

Something meowed and soft feet pitter-pattered across the back of his head. His face rested against concrete. Couldn't make any sense out of it. It was so dark and confusing...

His stomach hurt. He was stabbed, but by who?

His hand on the hilt, squashed beneath his body.

"Here, kitty kitty kitty," a wheezing voice said in the darkness. Another meow. "You brought me a present," the voice said. "Let's see what it is."

▌▐▐ ▐▐ ▐▐▐▌▐▐ ▐ ▐▐▐ ▐▐▐ ▐▐▐ ▐▐▐ ▐▐▐ ▐▐▐ ▐▐▐▐ ▐▐▐ ▐▐▐ ▐▐ ▐▐▐ ▐▐ ▐ ▐ ▐▐

It'd been a few days since Prada had heard from Clapper or seen Mister Socks. She was wondering what had happened when the cat strutted into the Tickle House. He looked even more insolent than usual and, as he trotted past, regarded her with surly green eyes.

Hazel came out from behind the bar. "Oh, Mister Socks," she cooed. "Where have you been?"

He meowed and rubbed his head into her leg.

"You have such a pretty collar," Hazel said. "Now who gave you that?"

"A collar?" Prada walked toward Hazel and the cat. This must be part of the plan. But it made her nervous all the same. What was Clapper playing at? This should've been simple. Her stomach clenched and she silently swore that she would never trust another murderer.

"Yes and it's such a pretty collar." Hazel scratched the cat's forehead. "It has a capsule attached." She unscrewed it and removed a slip of paper. "We're going to see who Mister Socks belongs to, yes we are, oh yes we are."

Her fingers were quick and deft from a lifetime of tickling Johns. She unfolded the note and read it with a smile that turned into a frown.

Prada backed away. She'd seen that look in Madame Hazel's eyes before.

Venom spiked Hazel's whisper. "Did you try to have Mister Socks killed?"

Prada's back touched the wall.

Hazel flipped the note around. There was a photo of Clapper above some handwriting. His head was bruised and his face covered in blood. "You hired this man?"

"No Madame, of course not." Prada rubbed the hand where Mister Socks had scratched her.

Hazel noticed.

Prada tried to speak. Her throat clogged.

"Do you believe her, Mister Socks?" Hazel purred, rubbing the cat's ears.

The cat hissed.

"Me neither." Hazel reached into her flowing skirt and pulled out a dagger. "You know that I believe in justice, Prada. Always have, always will."

A booth blocked Prada's path to the exit and the bar was a dead end.

"If some drunken prick hits one my girls in the eye I take his eye. Just one. It's only fair." She stepped forward. "Now you, Prada—you tired to take my pussy away from me. What do you think I should take away from you?"

The cat meowed.

"Harmony?" Budgie slipped into her hutch, nervous to see what mood she was in today.

"In the bedroom. Be right out."

He sat on the couch, resting the shopping bag beside him and pulling out the clothes he'd bought. It was all bousgie shit but he needed it. After a week at his job his one set of green clothes were frayed. And he couldn't wear his rude boy uniform anymore. Word was out. Wearing his uniform or taking his scent pills would be like waving a flag in front of a bull. TeeVee's order was good for now but there was no sense being stupid.

As he folded the clothes into a pile he felt a hand in his short hair and a kiss on his cheek. Harmony, in pajamas. She looked good. More important, she looked content. These days, that was rare.

He smiled, stood up and swung his arms back and forth in front of his bent body. "Bo, bo, ba, bo," he sang in an exaggerated husky voice. It sounded warm and gentle to his ears but he had no way of knowing what it sounded like to Harmony. "My girl is so pretty, Bo, bo, ba bo."

"I take it back," she said, punching him in the shoulder, a little too hard. "You should be serious again. It's so disturbing when you do that."

"Bo, bo, ba bo, Harmony gets disturbed, ba bo bo bo." He tapped his feet beneath his swaying body for the grand finale and spread his arms wide. "Ba-BOOOE!!"

"You're in a good mood." Was she? He couldn't read her.

"Always am when I see you." Budgie hugged her and sat back down. Wished she felt the same.

"Always are since you started working." She looked at his clothes. "You went shopping?"

"Had to," he said. "Needed some clothes."

"Spend more than you make." She sat beside him and rifled through the pile. "They're nice." Her voice had a serrated edge.

"Not too bad I guess." Since Budgie took the job, Harmony had been up and down. Sometimes she got stormy, other times, too giddy. Wouldn't say why. "What's up with you?" he asked. Not for the first time.

Her eyes read murder. "You're not telling me the truth."

He flinched.

"I wanted to give you a few days to see if you would but you haven't. It doesn't even bug you. Look how fucking happy you are."

"What're you talking about?"

"TeeVee."

"Oh."

"You didn't think I'd notice?"

She had him in a corner. What was he supposed to say?

"You know the Vidicons stopped using me in schemes? I can't even go out without people..." She paused. "Without people pointing at me."

"Pointing?"

"Yeah."

"I didn't know it was that bad."

"What the fuck that's supposed to mean?"

"Nothing, but like... Pointing?"

She ground her jaw. Gave him that look like he was stupid. Been getting that look a lot lately.

"I'm sorry," he said. "We should get out of here. Move upstairs." Things'd be better then.

"Yeah." She shook her head. "But first you're gonna tell me what's going on. Like why the fuck is TeeVee protecting you?"

"Sorry," Budgie said. A blush bruised his cheeks. "I wasn't tryin' to keep it from ya. Figured you knew. Was kinda wonderin' why you didn't say anything."

"I never got the fucking bulletin."

"That was all points."

"All points on the patch. I don't download that shit."

Which wasn't his fault. "That don make no sense. Why not?"

"We're not talking about that. Why didn't *you* say anything?"

"Worried you'd be pissed off. Worried how pissed you'd be." He'd been dreading this moment, hoping it wouldn't come. Past few days, he'd even convinced himself that it might not. "I don want to lose you."

"You think you'll lose me over this?" She crossed her arms. "You better come the fuck out with it then." Before Budgie could react, her mood switched gears. She kissed him on the face, sat on his lap and wrapped an arm around his neck. Rested her head against his. "I can't leave you, idiot."

Can't leave you, Budgie thought. *Not won't.* What's that supposed to mean? He stroked her head. She seemed to need it. Sometimes, she seemed fragile, only held together by hugs. Other times, he was afraid to touch her.

"We're stuck together," she said.

"That a problem?"

"It might be. You better tell me what's going on. Cause I need to figure out just how pissed off I am."

"I'll save you some time," Budgie said. "Very."

"I'm used to that."

He pulled a pack of cigarettes out of his pocket and lit one. Tobacco was the hardest drug he'd done since starting work, and he was not eager to get high again. Not after that kick. Nightmares about it still kept him up. "TeeVee is renting my percepts." Budgie looked at the blank television, too afraid to look at Harmony. "I'm gathering info about upstairs for him. Or outside. I dunno."

"Why?"

"I need the cash. And he promised to protect me."

"Not that—why does he want the info?"

"He likes info."

"No." She took Budgie's chin and forced him to look at her, like she was investigating his expression. It made Budgie feel self-conscious and he smiled before realizing how wrong that gesture was. "TeeVee wants to do something with that info. You don't know what?"

"No." Budgie watched her forehead. Old trick. Made it look like you were meeting someone's eyes when you couldn't. "I thought you'd be angrier."

"I'm worried." She took one of Budgie's cigarettes and lit it. They'd stopped paying each other long ago. "It's too fucking pathetic to be angry about." Harmony smiled, all wide and fake, and waved into Budgie's face. "Hi TeeVee!"

Budgie waved back. "Hi Harmony," he said.

She frowned and furrowed her brow. "Was that a joke?"

"Yeah, of course."

"You sure?"

He had the sick feeling of a debt unpaid. Deserved whatever he got from her "I think I'd prefer it if you were angry."

"Me too." She rested her hand on his and gave it a squeeze. Budgie squeezed back. "He's just looking out for you because you're his property."

"I know." Budgie exhaled smoke.

"That doesn't bother you?"

"What's diff?" he said. "I mean things didn't turn out how I thought. I kinda hoped people would be cool with me down here—once they knew that I had an alpha on my side—but they all hate me. Shoulda guessed. And I don even like being inside anymore. I just want to move upstairs and get out of here, but if I get audited then I get chipped and I'm stuck down here. For good. Nothin' to do then 'cept die or turn gnome."

"And TeeVee won't protect you if you aren't getting him the info he wants."

"There's that too, yeah. But…"

"But what?" She tilted her head. "Don't tell me there's more."

"There's more."

"!"

"He converted me into a DNA computer to help him crunch."

Harmony's mouth dropped. "You're a computer?"

"Yeah."

"We just went out of my league. The fuck does that even mean?"

"I don't know. I haven't changed. Had some bad dreams and I ummm…"

"You what?"

"I don know if it was real or what but I saw something really fucked at Sputnik's wake." He looked back at her, squashed out his smoke and lit another. Suddenly craved some drugs or booze or something. His head was an ugly place to be and he wanted out. Maybe later. Right now he just had to push right through. "Remember I asked you if you saw those fucked up lines?"

She shook her head.

"Well I did. Everyone was dancing and everything right, and then they all stopped. These big pink cables came out of the ceiling and hit the top of everyone's head cept mine. The music told them to turn this way and that and they just did as they were told. Then they all started dancing again. No one noticed."

"You saw this?"

"Yeah. Like I say, thought I was hallucinating but I saw it. Know I did. Keep dreaming about it too. And then there was the withdrawal thing. I don think I can take drugs, even if I wanted. And I don even want to."

Harmony pulled her mouth tight and stared at her lap, thinking. "It sounds like memetic engineering," she said after a long moment.

"What's that?"

"Purposely infecting people with thought viruses."

"Never heard of it," Budgie said. Just the mention of viruses made him feel funny after seeing the naked earth. Those things were serious business. "Like, I've heard of people getting sick in their memes but—"

"You should read more," Harmony interrupted. "It's been around for years. Adverts use it. But I've never heard of anything being so, umm, direct. Closest I know is cults."

"What are those?"

"It's when a group of people think whatever their leader wants. But to do that you've got to control diet, sleep, everything about them. Ads are kinda like demographic cults. Like you can meme bomb any small group but the more people you try to infect, the weaker it gets. Music is a really good wrapper for it cause it already makes most people do stuff, like dance. Makes them suggestible to begin with and rewires the brain."

"How do you know all this?" Budgie was impressed and doubtful. "Like, you see them?"

"Just read a book every so often. The Anarcho Cookbook has a huge section on meme bombs. Not about building them. Just about wrecking them. Like jamming their signals and whatever, but the theories are—" She gave him a peculiar look. "What would TeeVee want with that?"

"I don't know," Budgie said. "Like he's weird and all but he seems kinda decent in his way."

"I love you Budgie but you need to shut up and let me think." She frowned and scratched her cheek.

Budgie grinned. The expression felt idiotic. Maybe he really was a moron. He knew he should be angry that she told him to shut up but he glowed instead. She loved him? That was great. As screwed up as this situation was, he didn't care. He just wanted to go dancing through the corridors. Boe, ba boe.

"Fucking weird that I didn't even get the bulletin," she said. "About the patch."

"Yeah."

"Was there anything else in that message?"

"Just the patch for whatever was wrong with the gizmos. Fixed it right up."

"I bet." Harmony nodded. "That makes sense."

"Why?"

"He's datamining that party. Through the gizmos and through you. He must want to sell it."

"Sell what?"

"The meme tech. He must want to sell it. He could get a huge amount of money for something like that. We're talking billions." She lit another cigarette. "We *are* gonna have to move upstairs," she said. "And soon. After he unloads that tech he won't need you anymore. And he could sell it at any time. He's made sure of that."

In electro ghost market, grocery phantoms wandered, flickered and shouted while yellow light crackled on the tips of their limbs. Branches of ring tone lightning thundered in TeeVee's brain and hawked gum scrub. Scoured curtains of logo shimmered like heat mirages. Illusion of a thought tentacle reached out, touched the veil, singed its suction cups and stank like calamari. Squid laugh tracks howled backwards distortion. TeeVee ducked these sound shards. Fragments of another sonic explosion. Detonation of strobing danger. TeeVee congealed into flesh.

Cold wetness startled him into flinching upward. Hurt struck his temple. He'd banged his head on the tap. Red pain stars poured from the faucet. He blinked them away.

His lungs felt full of liquid and he coughed again, this time vomiting a rainbow into the water-filled sink. "Santa," he whispered as he realized what he'd done.

Instead of having his usual, Riki-Tiki tongue bath, he'd come in here to infect himself with germ killing bacteria in his shower. He'd done that. He remembered that much. But when he got out to wipe his face over the sink he accidentally clicked back into his brain, and boom, he was hit with all the mall's television broadcasts. Right in his electro-soul. Must have dropped his head into the water and inhaled some.

He straightened and coughed again. He pulled the plug and returned to his couch. Took a hit of opium and turned inside out.

*I slip my dick in slits with a quickness, I get more pussy and props than Jehovah's got witness—Sez, is what, is the Hypochronic D—*And flip off this nostalgic shit. Fecal processions occupied habits in an abyss. Chasm of sparkling chardonnay with smart liquid ring tones so you knew when to drink. Gulping, the flavored portal opened flashing green for GO. TeeVee focused it until the door blistered and popped. TeeVee saw his room. Sitcom sat down. Black bag at his side. Talking.

"I brought you tribute. Garter snakes for Riki-Tiki."

TeeVee let chatbot respond to that. Key word hypertext TRIBUTE, EMO, context wound in. "Thank you."

He dove into the Vidicon forum where Griff's words hung like bright red paintings. The boy had danger in him. A game-show host screamed obscenities. His words turned to porn and shot back through TeeVee's head on jism lightning bolts. Something in there got knocked up.

TeeVee interfaced with reality via his body. "Just let the snakes go and she'll catch them."

Sitcom reached into his bag and dropped the snakes on the floor. They slithered away. "May I smoke? Tobacco?"

Chatbot auto response: "Yes."

Sitcom lit a cigarette. Cross reference. Searching. Winston: Leave the Bull Behind. Budgie eye-view. Boot watching, click, click. Parakeet, click the door open.

Teevee hated returning to the meat. Have beef tonight. His palms tingled. So cold and numb. When was Sitcom leaving? TeeVee switched into his gizmo. Back into forum.

"I have something to talk to you about," Sitcom says. "Budgie?"

PILLAR: No. You don't owe me an explanation. You don't owe anyone. But, I've gotta say, the dissent is getting under my skin. Some of those little punks have big fucking mouths."

GRIFF: I don't give a fuck what you say. These guys are not allowed to fuck with the rulebook. We're all below that. You guys are just too pussy to do anything.

Fucking. Mouths. Pussy. Force fed beef. Shook head, lost that image. Red Griff text.

A snarling actor's face screams. *Top of the world ma.* TeeVee snapped back out of the forum and paid close attention to Sitcom. He disabled his chatbot and spoke: "Don't worry about it." He moved words to his mouth one at a time to avoid vocal blurring. "I'm not."

Aches in the flesh stimulated activity. TeeVee watched his body grab his hookah and take a hit. The home crowd cheered. Riki-Tiki darted across the floor and nabbed a garter snake by the skull. Crunch. Some cold blood. She'll lick that up later. Fire in bowl, bubbles. Laugh track.

"So why are you here?" *And when are you leaving?* TeeVee stimulated dopamine to enhance pattern recog.

"Some guys from Edge approached me the other day. They'd heard I was big down here."

Edge logo. Small e in glowing circle. *Guess I'm on the edge.* "Word always gets out." It's supposed to. *Start phase two, record viral input on blank reOrb.* Old hijacking drama plays on speed reel to reel. "This was expected. What's your point?"

"They want to distribute me on the lawn. But I figured I should come to you first with their terms. You should know, they'll have some actor boy playing me—and they're gonna soften the music so no one down here would recognize it, but they want my name and some tunes."

Files. Payments. Contracts. A hostage held a gun to the kidnapper's temple. Trigger pulled and brains froze midair. ReOrb sounded harsh. Needed to erode frequencies while maintaining memetic content. *Slip it in with a quickness. Get more diamond props than—*"How much?"

"Two thousand globals." Sitcom butted out his smoke and lit another. "As an advance against future earnings. Then a five percent cut of those. I don't know how you want to split it."

"Seventy thirty is standard." Words were a skinny data flow. Compressed nonlinear mind juice squirted through a mouth gun. His tongue was a cocked hammer, pounding out thought bullets. "Bump them to six for the advance and don't take less than five. They'll pay it. They paid three for Jet Screamer and he was awful." He shouldn't have said that. Now that song is there. Eep Op Ork. Fucking meme.

It's take hours to get rid of that one. "But you, I, we do have a more important condition."

"What's that?"

"Locations."

INFO DUMP

"Today roughly 1000 small parrots were released, each one squawking a simple message—"Buy Jane's Book! Only 6 tokens! It's great! Buy Jane's book!" Shortly after the stunt, book sales of "Fucking Like a Pro: How to Keep your Man" by Jane Jane skyrocketed. Although this is one of the most successful word of mouth campaigns in recent memory, the publishing house has vigorously denied any involvement. Much to the chagrin of their impressed stockholders, the publisher attributed the unusual event to overzealous supporters of Jane Jane from the red levels.

"Pet Stores, however, are not amused and filed a complaint with the MTO. They claim that the stunt amounts to an anticompetitive parrot giveaway. They are demanding to be paid for 1000 parrots by the publishing house and want a share in any profits the stunt has caused. The MTO Board of Directors was unavailable for comment."

A hand on his arm shook Budgie awake. Then a kiss on his forehead. He opened his eyes. Harmony knelt on the bed beside him, her loose top revealing small breasts. "What time is it?"

"Don't worry, it's Saturday. No work."

"Yeah. I know. Thought I'd sleep in."

"You can go back to bed after," Harmony said. "I just had an idea."

"Don wake me up every time you have an idea" Budgie rolled over and closed his eyes.

"This is important." She shook his arm again.

"What!" It'd taken Budgie a long time to get to sleep last night, but once he did, it had been his first deep sleep since TeeVee had converted him. His brain was getting used to the noise and filtering it out.

Having fought so hard for sleep he loathed to leave it. But Harmony gave him no peace. "I'm tired."

"You're so grumpy in the mornings. Even worse than normal."

"What do you want?" He strained to sound reasonable. "I'm really tired, serious."

"I can get the music from Sputnik's wake."

What could Harmony want with that?

—the people turning left and right. "Where?" He pulled the blankets up to his chin.

"In the forum's music section. They post copies of every show. That's where I get my Sitcom orbs. Get up." She bounced off the bed and left. He was just too comfortable: Warm blankets and a soft mattress. But he heard her talking out there, and then heard her shout, "Got it!"

"Like I care." Budgie threw the blankets off and sat on the edge of the bed, trying to shake the exhaustion. The clock informed him it was just before six. With a growl he stood and walked into the next room with his pajama pants swishing around his legs. It was too early. "This better be good." He sat on the couch.

Harmony told the television to play the file. Text appeared on the screen. "FILE NOT FOUND."

"What the…" She tried again. Then different sources. Same thing. "It's not there. Not even a gizmo bootleg."

"I need a coffee and a smoke." Budgie shuffled to the kitchen and poured an instant from the wall tap, grabbed his cigarettes from the counter. Lit one and coughed. "What's this supposed to prove anyway?"

"I just wanted to analyze the file. Check out what you saw at the wake. See if anything was there." She shook her head. "I've never had this happen before. If anything, Sitcom is way overexposed. No one has even uploaded anything or if they have, it's been scrubbed."

"But so what? I mean, what the fuck we going to do anyway? TeeVee could have made that part self-erasing like one of those disposable movies they used to sell." He sipped at his coffee. "Sorry Harmony but this is bullshit."

"I hate not knowing something." She took one of his cigarettes. "If this shit is going to be sold I want to know how to jam it so they can't turn me into another zombie asshole."

"But TeeVee will be watching this so..."

"Arrogant." Harmony shook her head. "I bet he's asleep. And anyway, he wants to watch you on the greens and outside. He knows you're not working today so why would he bother? You think he had nothing better to than watch you? You're not that interesting, Budge."

"Thanks."

"It's true."

"I hope." Budgie wasn't sure that TeeVee ever slept but he knew that the guy probably did have more important things to do than watch him eat breakfast. He wasn't going to win the argument with Harmony. But something about what she'd said about being a 'zombie asshole' bothered him. "You ever read any Lenny Niedenberger?"

"Yeah." Harmony tilted her head. "Surprised you've heard of him."

"What's that supposed to mean?"

"I've just never seen you read."

"Cause it's fucking boring. But a guy at work was telling me about him and I thought of you. What's he like?"

"Niedenberger? He's all right"

"Rick thinks he's great."

"A lot of people do." Harmony shrugged. "But, if you ask me, he's your typical liberal shithead. Thinks everything can be solved by more recruiting offices down here and better jobs. Bigger cages, longer chains. And he thinks we should move outside again, but I don't think anyone wants to do that."

"Only because they don't know," Budgie said.

"Don't know what?"

"About outside."

"You like it out there, huh?"

He nodded.

"But that's beside the point. People don't know and they don't want to. Most people never even think about outside. Too busy doing other things."

"Like shopping?"

"Or robbing. Niedenberger has too much faith in people. Keeps thinking someone convinced them to be like this, but I think they want it. I mean, if I can see what a con this place is, why the fuck can't they? Answer is, they can. They know the mall's bullshit but they just don't care. He does some interesting history, I'll give him that."

"I've been listening to a lot of Bob Anger." Budgie butted out his smoke. "When I work."

"What? Why?"

"He makes me laugh. Besides, I know if I'm listening to him TeeVee's prolly not in my head. I bet he can't stand the guy."

"I'm always surprised anyone can. He's such a prick."

"He hates us, that's for sure. Figures we should be bumped off."

Bob Anger was like the condensed version of everything that was wrong with the mall. He was a loudmouth who liked to talk tough but would last about five minutes in the reds. Let's see him walk up to someone down here and call them a crazy lying bastard. But Budgie liked to listen to him before going outside. The show reminded him of all the crap he was getting away from.

Funny thing was, Bob Anger probably didn't even believe any of what he said. It was just another line of shit that sold. All of those listeners believed it, of course, not understanding that they were being lied to. Or not caring. Or, like Budgie, just enjoying the lie.

The show was about the most crass and cynical thing he'd ever heard. And that was saying something. Promoting the murder of a whole class to sell advertising time? That took a lot of balls. The Vidicons could learn from Anger. It beat the hell out of protection rackets.

Maybe TeeVee realized that.

Budgie felt like he was staring into a precipice, the wind gusting at his back. Something big was going to change.

He could feel it, but he couldn't see what.

He clicked open his pack of cigarettes, hoping they'd dull the sting of his sudden craving for synapacide. He lit one and looked at Harmony through a cloud of blue smoke. She coughed.

"You're just pissed because he stabbed you." Slug pushed though the corridor, grinning. *"Oh Budgie, I'm so sorry. Oh Budgie."*

Griff clenched his jaw. It was bad getting stabbed in front of everyone, but getting stabbed by some asshole who'd turned toppy was worse.

"It's not like that." He followed in Slug's wake. "I was right. He's turned floater."

"And he broke your nose too." Slug laughed. A low yucking noise. "Splat."

"Who the fuck is TeeVee anyway?" This partnership was going even worse than his first. "I've never even heard of him."

"I met him," Slug said. "Working with Sitcom—I met him."

"And?"

"He's not someone to fuck with." Slug rubbed his chin. "I didn't like him. He was spooky."

"Did he seem like a good rude boy?"

"Didn't seem like a rude boy at all. But it's not my business." Slug poked Griff in the shoulder. "Or yours. Forget about the whole thing. We're not paid enough to think."

"Fuck that," Griff shrugged away from Slug. "I'm not forgetting a damn thing. It's no fucking good and it won't stand. I won't let it."

"You'll do what you're told."

"What side are you on anyway?" Griff asked.

The big guy stopped walking and looked down at him. "Who the fuck do you think you are?"

He shoved Griff's shoulder hard enough to spin him. Griff's face got hot and all he could think about was the tattoo on his bicep. *Who Dares Wins*. The first rule. "What?"

"You don't question me, you little fuck," Slug grabbed Griff by the tunic. "I'll make what Budgie did to you look like a fucking day at the bordello. You listening?"

"Okay." Griff held his hands up. "Okay. Easy."

"Bitch." Slug let go. Shook his head. "Don't forget."

Griff's dispo turned murder. He kept stride beside Slug. This wasn't going to happen again. He wasn't going to be humiliated again. Just ask his dad how many times you could humiliate Griff. Not one too many.

There was an alley up ahead. "I know a shortcut."

"Where?"

"Cut through there." Griff pointed at the dark opening. "We'll come out on the next street."

"No alleys," Slug said. "They're swarming with gnomes."

"Who's the pussy now?" Griff hoped it was the right button to push.

"Have it your way." Slug said. He turned into the slim corridor, leading the way. "Fuckin' call me a pussy," he grumbled. "Not afraid of nuthin.' You're the one that should be afraid, with all that big fuckin' talk of yours."

The alley was too narrow and Slug too tall to allow Griff a good windup, but the machete was sharp. He slashed downward at the neck.

Slug made a wet noise and stumbled forward. Griff brought up his foot and kicked him in his big ass, knocking him down. Slug twisted his body and landed, facing Griff. He held the side of his neck, blood squirting between his fingers. His eyes were wide and stupid.

"Thou shall not snitch." Griff glanced over his shoulder. Alley Gnomes could be surrounding him even now.

No one there. He raised his machete and looked down at Slug. "And everyone is big," he said. "Until you hit them from behind."

INFO DUMP

"You're acting like such a man, Mr. Anger."

"What's that supposed to mean?"

"Men see everything in terms of power. Everything! And nothing more than sex."

"And that's important—why?"

"Well the ladies should know that if you castrate your man over the dinner table he will not want to make love to you. Tell me, does your wife do that?"

"I'm not married."

"Can't imagine why."

"Now look, I'm—"

"You see how angry he gets, girls? It's important to be submissive. Don't dominate. If you have opinions, keep them to yourself. Act like everything he says is interesting or funny. It might feel forced and fake at first but in time you'll grow used to it."

"I resent that. I can respect a woman who—"

"Yes, Mr. Anger. You're very smart."

"All right. What you're saying is..."

"Tell your husband to take control in the bedroom. Then let him. Put his happiness first. See how his female co-workers (his sub-ordinates and maybe his boss) dress and surprise him in the bedroom by wearing that uniform! Role-play and every role you play should be one that makes him feel powerful and in control."

"It's a bunch of crap ladies, if you ask me, but we'll be right back with our guest Jane Jane, who's selling her book, 'Fucking Like a Pro; How to Keep Your Man' on You're a Crazy Lying Bastard with me, your host, your voice Bob Anger. Stay tuned."

PRODUCT PLACEMENT

Life & Happiness. IT'S ALL ABOUT YOU—YOUR WANTS, YOUR NEEDS, YOUR MOODS, YOUR DREAMS.

Baby soft skin for grown-ups. Johnson's can regrow your skin without any messy surgery. You choose the age. We provide the lotion. JOHNSON'S."

100% Guilt Free. Nicorette Fresh Mints Chewing Gum. Gives you the kick you need.

Dreams are without limits. MAIDENFORM BRAS.

I believe that mascara is the savior of woman kind.

3 big fat life lies we tell ourselves
I didn't have a moment to catch my breath.
I have a problem
Things aren't going my way.

Only a woman could think of this!
Three Genius female innovations.
Comfy, vibro-thong.
The Preggers Safety Case.
Robo-Vac with the happy hubby attachment.

When you're strong don't hold back.
Secret #19—I snort when I laugh.
Secret, strong enough for a woman.

Budgie yanked the pole. It resisted and he put all of his weight against it. The huge chunk of triangular plastic that was wedged in the robot snapped in half and tumbled into the truck's gaping hole. Budgie regained his balance, stepped back and looked around.

It was a nice day. Clear blue sky with a bright sun. When he first started doing this he had asked if the sun was always full—not realizing that he was confusing it with the moon. He still hadn't lived that down and his co-workers now called him Sunny. All these names got confusing.

A silver cigar shape rocketed overhead toward the mall. "What's that?" Probably another dumb question.

"Airship." Rick squinted at the splinter of silver. "Some bigwig from the WTO is probably flying in to meet with some bigwig from the T-Dot MTO. Must be a Russian. They like to meet in person. Don't trust Avatars. Not since Stalin 2."

The sound of heavy breathing in Budgie's ears. Rick must be working on something. Budgie watched the ship.

"Rumor is, they want to get more trade going between the different malls. Actual goods, not just info and copyrights. But first they gotta find a way to make some money off air flight. It's probably impossible."

Budgie didn't say anything. He didn't know anything about it and wasn't interesting in learning. The cloggers called Rick 'The Professor' cause he was always lecturing about something or other. Whenever he started up, someone would say: "The prof is teaching another lesson. Listen up, Sunny." This time was no different.

Who'd said that? Even though Budgie had worked here for over a week, the cloggers were as quiet as movie monks and it was hard to figure out who was who, just from the voices. It didn't matter anyway.

He watched the cigar circle the top of the mall and disappear. His eyes suddenly ached. He closed them for a moment. The airship must have landed.

The cigar shape played in a loop. TeeVee adjusted the contrast to make the ship stands out against blue sky. Magnified it. Budgie's vision broke up a bit here, but it was all right. TeeVee jumped up visual centers in Riki-Tiki, transferring processing from scent. She squealed and scrambled across the room. He stimulated dopamine to increase pattern recog.

Got it.

He cross referenced the new information with maps of T-Dot center. So many maps. They all locked together to form fakes and defeat logic and they were all wrong. Except one. But which one was that? The Budgie satellite lens cut a big hole in the data smog. Every map had different locations for the airbases, but there was only one contender left now. One map. It lined up with all the other data TeeVee has collected. It had to be right. He built a 3-D image of the mall.

Three colors. Red. Green. Blue.

TeeVee balanced it all in his head and sent Sitcom the updated locations.

ⅢⅢⅢⅢ

"Hi." Harmony leaned across the table to kiss Budgie as he sat in the booth.

Budgie presented his cheek, embarrassed by the public affection. He looked around the restaurant, wondering if anyone knew who they were or where they were from. Like Budgie, Harmony, wore bousgie clothes. Unlike him, she also wore a black, bobbed wig.

This was his first time in a green level restaurant. To muzak, acrobats contorted on a rotating stage in the center of the circular room. Across the walls, a fuzzy collage of pastel pictures moved like vinegar in oil.

One time, when Budgie was a kid, he saw a puddle catching light and reflecting a swirling rainbow. He'd thought he discovered some incredible new magic, a bit of fantasy that had somehow slipped under everyone's vision. Santa knew, he'd never heard anyone talk about this amazing phenomenon. He showed it to Sputnik, believing his friend would marvel at it. But Sputnik had just shrugged and said, "It's only oil. A litterbug must have leaked." Budgie'd felt like a total ass.

He looked around the restaurant, at the acrobats and the wall art. Everything in the mall glittered but nothing was gold. A greasy residue clung to his feelings.

"You're quiet." Harmony adjusted her wig. "I look okay?"

"You look great." An acrobat bent her leg behind her head. She wasn't even human. Just some animatronic thing. "I'm kinda tired is all." Budgie tapped the table to see the menu. The steak was priced free. The sizzle cost a quarter globe. Budgie swore.

"Bad day at work?"

"No." He wanted to order a half pint of Colgate Irish Whiskey. Instead, he got some Canada Dry Tonic Water. There was no ashtray on the table. "Is this a smoking section?"

"Duh," Harmony said.

He lit a cigarette and felt a small gush of wind as a silent hood came to life beside him, pulling the smoke into the porous wall. He expected an ashtray to appear but it did not.

A uniformed waitress put a pint of clear soda on his table. Garnished with a plastic lime. "How old are you kids?"

"Old nuff," Budgie said.

She shrugged, pulled a tin ashtray out of her apron and set it beside the glass. "No booze," she warned and left.

"Bitch," Harmony muttered.

"What?"

"Flirting with you like that. Right in front of me."

"What?" Budgie asked again. "She just smiled."

"You know how long it took her to bring me my coke?" Harmony grinned but it looked forced. "But you get an ashtray? You're too damn cute in that little outfit."

"You think I have a chance?" Budgie leaned out of the booth to watch the waitress. Nice ass. He looked back at Harmony. "Would you mind if I got her number?"

"Fuck you."

"Please." They both laughed. "You check out apartments today?"

"Why don't you get your girlfriend to do that?"

"Seriously."

"See for yourself." Harmony slid her gizmo across the table. "I like number three."

He looked at the pictures and the prices, periodically dragging on his cigarette. "It's the most expensive."

"But it's the nicest."

"Yeah, it is."

"Best security too."

He slid the gizmo back. "If their security is any good, no way they rent to us."

"I didn't think about that."

"It's not cheap," Budgie said. "None of them are. Even saving, I dunno. Did you look at the hostels?"

"Yeah."

"They any better?"

"Good place to get your throat cut. Think about the red levels without the moderating influence of gangs. No rulebook in play that I could see."

"Nice." He tapped the table.

"What?" she asked.

"Well, it's your money so, I dunno."

"It's your money too."

"Not once I launder it into your name." He stubbed out his cigarette. "Then it's yours."

"And fuck you too."

"I'm just sayin'—"

"You're just sayin' that I'm scheming on you."

"I'm not saying that at all. I'm just sayin' that I gotta take your word for it. It's diff, you know, from having collateral. Funny to depend on someone and have no way to secure their co-op."

"You can trust me."

"*Can* don come into it. I *have* to."

"So forget about it then." She leaned back in her seat and looked at the acrobats. "They're all too expensive."

"Yeah." Budgie rubbed his temple. "Prolly won't work anyway. Why would anyone rent to us?"

She glared at him. "Because we can pay."

"Can we?"

"Sort of." She sipped her beer. "Way I see it, I'm cut out of schemes right now."

"Yeah."

"But that ain't gonna hold." She leaned forward. "You've gone toppy but I'm still deep Vidicon. I'm not going to let them forget that. I'm two gen red. They think they're gonna toss me out like some newbie? Not fucking likely. No offense."

"None taken."

"If I sublet my place and pay someone to watch it, I figure I can still turn a profit. Not much but a few globals in reality and a lot more on paper. In case of audits."

"Okay."

"Then, on top of that, I'm gonna go to the betas, let them know what's up. They know I'm a good solider. I'll be back in rackets within a couple months. Once we get you outta everyone's sight, people'll forget. They're like that. So we gotta cover, what—first and last?"

"And a security deposit."

"And that."

"And after all that," Budgie said. "We still fall short. Besides, how you think anyone gon take to you working Vidicon while living on the greens?"

"You figure they like me living on the reds?"

"Don avoid the query."

"They won't mind. Not if I make myself useful."

"Don sound realistic." Budgie shook his head. "Like I can't see them cutting you in."

"It just makes sense."

"In a way but sense? Serious? *Sense?* Better make dollars too and it ain't gon to."

"You got a better idea?"

"Better than what?" Budgie took a deep breath. "How useful you gon be if—no *when*—you get chipped? How dead am I gon be when I can't carry a place up here by myself cause you got stranded and I end up back at square one." He shook his head. "You call doin' all that an idea?"

"It was a thought."

"Barely." Budgie shook his head. "We gotta do this clean."

"That's bit fucking rich. Coming from you and all."

"Yeah well…" She was right. He'd sold his percepts and was worried about her pulling schemes? "Clean as can be."

"And how clean is that? You see a way to do this without running chip-worthy risks and you let me know."

"I gotta think on that." Budgie put his palms on the table. "But before all that, I gotta take a shit."

"Thanks for sharing."

"No prob."

Budgie made his way among the tables. He caught the waitress looking at him. She averted her gaze then sneaked another peak, but Budgie didn't feel much like flirting. He shoved the Men's Room door, his boots clicking in the pale florescent room.

He entered the stall and swiped his card across the top of the toilet so that the seat—advertising Colgate Whiskey—would open. Having bought 3 minutes he dropped his pants and sat down.

The motion detectors in the stall caused the door to play adverts. Big-breasted women threw themselves at men who used the right cologne—the same one for sale next to the sink—and drank the right beer—the same one for sale at the bar. He paid a token for a few sheets of advert covered toilet paper and wiped off with a minute to spare.

It seemed like a waste to just get up so he sat there thinking about Harmony and work. He had a dialogue with himself, playing the role of Sunny, hard-nosed clogger in love with a good girl from the wrong side of town. Could he trust her or would he lose everything? Tune in tonight at eight to find out.

"Twenty seconds!" The screen started a countdown. Playing above that were glowing red instructions on how to buy more time. Budgie waited, determined to get his money's worth.

He washed his hands with a little packet of powdered soap he always kept on him—cheaper that way—and glanced at the cologne machine. He reached for his card before thinking better of it and leaving the washroom.

Harmony smiled when he sat down. "See your girlfriend?"

"Yeah," Budgie said. "Sorry I took a while but I had to buy her a drink before I took her to the toilets." He shrugged. "Can't skimp on romance."

Harmony checked her watch. "Five minutes? Yeah, for you that is a while." She smiled. "A fucking eternity."

"She seemed happy."

"Let's not." Harmony frowned. "I don't want to joke about this."

"You really think I'd—"

She held her hands up. "I don't want to think about it."

"So you understand what has to be done?" Brice Steel asked.

"I think so, yes Sir, but…" Mall Security Chief Rock Cockett fidgeted in his seat and looked at his lap.

"But what?" Brice rested his elbows on his desk. "Don't tell me you're having an attack of scruples."

"No Sir. It's not that."

"Then what?"

"Well, I'm a fan, Sir. Most of us on the force are. I don't think the boys are gonna like this."

"The boys aren't going to hear about this. Except for the ones you pick."

"I don't know who'd want to kill him."

"What?" Brice said. "Kill him? Who said anything about killing him?"

"Well Sir, maybe I misunderstood but I thought you just said that you wanted Bob Anger 'taken out of circulation.'"

"I did *not* say 'taken out of circulation with extreme prejudice.'" Brice cursed under his breath. He'd have to explain this whole operation. Maybe, like the Russians and Americans, Brice should have set up a separate bureau to deal with this sort of thing. But secret agencies cost a lot of money and undermined the power of the MTO. Besides, there was no telling when they would turn on their masters. Only that they would.

As it was, The T-Dot Center was hovering on the edge of acceptable profitability for a top five mall. He couldn't afford a whole division of spooks. The CEOs would get paranoid about trade secrets being stolen and leveraged into a state monopoly. Some would probably leave for friendlier malls, taking their stores and money with them. No. Intelligence services undermined the security they were supposed to create. Rock would have to do. Even if he was bit thick. "I just need him to be discredited."

"But why, Sir? The man is an ally. He doesn't bad mouth anyone important, not really. Just the rude boys and, Santa knows, we could do without them."

"He's too popular." Brice leaned back in his seat and looked at the ceiling. It played a moving image of blue sky with the sun and moon both shown. Fluffy clouds formed suggestive shapes.

"How can you be—"

"Popularity is a good thing." Brice's gaze wandered around the opulent office. Zen fung shui. He didn't believe any of that superstitious nonsense but it made a good impression with the right honorable corporate heads. Even if they didn't believe it either. "A very good thing, for a media personality. It makes a lot of money for the company that owns him. But Mr. Anger is a special case. Men like him have always existed, of course, and they have led the world into a great deal of trouble. That's why we tamed them—gave them television and radio shows." He tapped his fingers on his desk and thought of his meeting with the Russian representative from the World Trade Organization. "You remember that file I gave you last week? The girl I had you bring in from Fatman?"

"That teenage crackpot?" Rock frowned. "Thought she could jump into new bodies. Called herself Ken? Yeah, I remember."

"Well, turns out she, um, he, isn't a crackpot. The tech is legit. We're going to have to release it."

Rock whistled through his teeth.

"Eternal youth. Moscow had a similar thing appear in their mall. We can only assume that the thing is showing up elsewhere. Techs have a habit of emerging in more than one location at the same time. There's no way to cap this and why should we? The profits will be enormous and we must ensure that T-Dot gets its share. We're working out the copyrights right now. But you're going to be busy."

"Yeah," said Rock.

"So you see, then?"

"See what?"

"About Mr. Anger."

"I, uh. No."

"We're going to have to implement some of Mr. Anger's suggestions. This is a good tech but it requires living young bodies to work. Only place to get those is the red levels."

"I don't see why we can't buy them."

"Because not enough people will sell them. And that'll drive prices through the roof. The reds are poor but they're not poor enough. Yet. But, if we move them outside, then they'll do what they have to. They'll be starving. We'll trade meat for meat."

"Why not just farm them?"

"Because that's inhumane."

"Well, Sir, I'd just like to say that I hope you choose me to lead this fascinating new initiative." Rock stood at attention. "I have extensive experience with—"

"First things first. Bob Anger."

"What about him?"

"If we start shipping reds outside—starting with the criminal element—while he's on the air, both he and his listeners will see that as a win. They'll think that we caved into their letter writing campaigns. His power will grow and he'll look legitimate. Success does not make people shy. It makes them more aggressive. He'll want more and his fans will be mobilized. When he demands something people will expect it to happen and expectation has a nasty habit of becoming reality."

"So he's dangerous?"

"Not yet," Brice said. "As it is, Bob Anger serves a purpose. Aside from the profits his demagoguery generates, it helps people to blow off steam. They watch him complain, they call in to complain and they feel as if they've accomplished something. Even the people who hate him. It keeps all these people from actually organizing and becoming… Unrestful. But Santa help us all if they think all that steam they blew off actually scalded something."

"So, he's not dangerous yet…"

"But he will be. His listeners more so than him. And the reds, well, they're unpredictable. More so when we start sending the worst amongst them outside. We're going to have enough problems with that without throwing the greens into the mix. You remember the chip riots?"

"Yes Sir."

"This is a very similar situation. We do not want to add an unrestful and empowered green level to our problems." Brice smiled and tilted his head, a gesture meant to put Rock at ease. "Your loyalty to him surprises me. You were on his show the other day."

"Yes Sir. I had permission—"

"I know you did. But did he treat you with respect?"

Rock blushed. "No Sir."

"And yet…"

"He has some good ideas sir. Nothing I could agree with in public but I understand why he's frustrated. I think we should at least sterilize the people we chip. It would be easy." Rock looked at his hands then back at Brice. "Still, he made me look like a real asshole."

"I heard that. Everyone did."

"I did my best, Sir."

"And that's all I ask. I just hope that you, my chief, understands that we aren't in a struggle with the red levels. We need them. We're about to need them even more. And he keeps saying that we should act, that we should do this or do that. It's simply not his business."

"But Sir, the crime wave is—"

"A small price to pay. And greatly overrated by the media to begin with. We need the reds much more than we need Mr. Anger. Why, without them, you'd be out of a job."

Rock's lips hardened and his head jerked a nod. "What exactly do you want me to do?"

Wearing nothing but silk briefs, Bob Anger put his whiskey on his table and flexed in front of the mirror. His workout program was going well. Just a few months ago, he'd been too skinny to be the big booming voice of a generation. But now his muscles looked ready to burst through his skin. He wasn't too big or bulky, just solid.

"I am THE BEAST!" He slapped and kissed his bicep before picking up his whiskey protein shake. He had to get to bed soon. The morning show came early.

But, hey. A couple more drinks and his evening smoke would relax him. "The nighttime ritual of gentlemen." He selected a cigar from his humidor. "Of real gentlemen."

He ran it under his nose and thought about calling his agent to see why they hadn't been able to crack the big American, Asian or European Markets. It'd be nice to get out of The T-Dot Center and make some real money.

He sank into his black leather couch from Chesterfields and picked the book of wooden matches off the coffee table by David Lloyd Thompson. Striking one, he let the sulfur burn off before touching the flame to the cigar tip. Blue clouds of smoke formed around his head.

Something odd about the taste. Smacking his lips, he glanced at the ashtray. There were cigarette ashes in there. He was sure of it. He took another long drag of his cigar. "What in Santa's name?"

The room turned black and white like an old movie. His limbs felt full of sand. He dropped the cigar. Too tired to pick it up, he watched it burn a hole into his rug.

His door opened.

A man wearing a gas mask entered.

▌██ ██▌█▌██▌▌ ▌█▌▌██▌▌█ ▌█▌▌█ ▌█▌██ ▌█▌█▌ ▌▌██ ▌█▌ ▌██▌▌ █▌▌ █▌▌ ▌▌█

"Got him?"

"Yeah, I'm just getting him dressed," Lieutenant Edwards buttoned up Bob Anger's shirt, fastened the tie and slipped the inert arms into a suit jacket. "He's ready."

"Okay." Rock's voice was clear in Edwards' ear-piece. "Take him. Be quick."

Edwards dragged Bob across the floor and opened the door. A metal laundry cart stood ready, its lid open. No one was in the hall. "He's a heavy fucker." Edwards dumped the radio host into the machine. He shut the lid and opened the control panel. "Give me that code again."

"Four One, BOB, six six seven, anti-ten. Trent."

"Hitting go." Edwards tapped the enter key.

He removed his gas mask as the laundry cart lurched forward. It was none of his business where it went. All he knew was that he was getting a big fat paycheck for what amounted to an hour's worth of work and a lifetime of keeping his mouth shut. That was fine. He didn't like a lot of talking anyway.

▌██ ██▌█▌██▌▌ ▌█▌▌██▌▌█ ▌█▌▌█ ▌█▌██ ▌█▌█▌ ▌▌██ ▌█▌ ▌██▌▌ █▌▌ █▌▌ ▌▌█

Bob Anger awoke from a nightmare in someone else's bed. He sat up, feeling sick and strange. Where was he? He remembered sitting down to smoke his cigar—a gas mask—

Something had happened, but what? And this room? It was a gaudy and horrible place. The sheets were red and—

"Oh Santa." He'd been set up.

He had to get out. Now.

He wobbled to the door. There was something wrong with his motor functions. He managed to push the door open and, click-boom, lights.

The media.

A few feet away, some little whore gave an interview. She had two black eyes and wept. Said something about how hard Mr. Bob Anger had hit her—

The reporters shoved octopuses of microphones into his face, yelling questions. He gestured for silence.

"Oh-kay," he said when everyone went quiet. "Look, just look here, I don't know what all this is about." He slurred his words. They were crystal clear in his mind but he couldn't get them out right. *I sound drunk.*

"Mr. Anger! Mr. Anger!"

He held up his hands. "Now look, I'm not all drunken and, you know, I'm really drugged up, so let me just say, that I don't know what all of you guys are doing here, but I..." It was no good. His face leaked tears.

The chaos resumed. "Mr. Anger!"

"Mr. Anger! Do you come here often?"

"Mr. Anger! Were you too busy having hot red level sex to do your show this morning?"

"Mr. Anger! Do you consider it hypocritical—"

"Mr. Anger! Is it true about your Dirty Sanchez?"

"MR. ANGER! MR. ANGER! MR. ANGER!"

He threw his hands up again. "Now, what, who says that I'm not, doing this, what time is it anyway bub, get that outta my face and let me tell you something, you crazy lying bastards."

Laughter drowned out his words.

"You did good," Brice flicked off the television and smiled at Rock Cockett. "You'll get a substantial bonus for this."

"Thank you Sir."

"But now onto other business. How are our security recruitment numbers doing?"

"They're up since we started paying more."

"Good. Brice sat back in his plush chair. "Something tells me, we're going to need all the people we can get."

"Should I come with you?" Harmony asked.

"No," Budgie said. "TeeVee is funny about company."

"Okay, just remember about the brain worm."

"How could I forget?" They'd decided that the best way to make money was for Harmony to sell drugs on the greens. Then just cross their fingers. Because, if she got caught, it was over for the pair of them.

"Doesn't need to be very high quality—better if it's not. Those kids on the lawn will eat anything. You think he can get crap like that?"

"There's no one else I can go to." Budgie crossed his arms. "Snort Donkey stopped taking my calls."

"So this is what I'm selling to those execs?" Sitcom looked at the selection of orbs. One was pink. He rubbed his thumb over its rubbery surface. "Never seen one like this before."

"That's your first single," TeeVee said.

"They get to decide that."

"Sure they do. And they'll decide that *that's* your first single." TeeVee sucked on his hookah. "It won't even be dried. Even if they think they've toweled it off. That one right there, is your first single."

"Thanks for taking an interest," said Sitcom. "But that'd invalidate the contract and leave us in the hole for a couple thousand globes. You can sneeze at that?"

"I'm not sneezing at anything. They won't even want to dry it off." TeeVee exhaled smoke. "I understand your appeal and I know what's best. You're my product after all."

Product? Sitcom frowned. "You sure?"

"They won't mind," TeeVee continued. "That song is pop gold. I dried it out good. It'll be a hit. Besides, it's in your contract."

"And is that a deal breaker?"

"Everything in that contract is a deal breaker."

"Worry is in my nature," Sitcom said. "I worried when you said we needed to take down the Dog Goblins. Warring over music control sounded crazy and I guess it was. But it was a good move. I don't think we would have got this deal if we hadn't done that." He looked at the floor. "I worried and I was wrong."

"You're getting at something."

"Yeah, suppose I am." Sitcom lit a cigarette. "Lately, I get the feeling that there's a scheme going on and I haven't been cut in. Not saying I mind. I don't. Nor to I expect to be cut in on everything. But I'd like to know what's going on for the good of the Vidicons. People are talking and I'm trying to defend you, but I don't even know what I'm defending."

"You're talking about Budgie."

"Partly, but yeah."

TeeVee went very still. Sitcom fidgeted. There was a long silence.

Sitcom pulled on his cigarette and cleared his throat. "How long have I known you, TeeVee?"

"Since we were children."

Sitcom nodded. "Long enough to know you pretty damn well. Long enough to know that when things seem coincidental around you, they aren't. You remember 3-Kard?"

"Sure I do."

"Same here. And I remember that he fucked you over once and I asked you if you wanted me to notch him and you said no. Then you smiled. Then 3-Kard's life just kinda crumbled around him. Drugs started hitting him wrong and he went nuts—"

"I remember what happened."

"—and then he killed himself. Cut his own dick off and bled to death. They found him on top of his fridge."

"Yes."

Sitcom took a deep breath. "I remember how you looked when that happened. You got the same look when you told me about this orb." Sitcom held it up and examined it. "I know you pretty well, TeeVee, and I know you're up to something. Something to do with the green levels. Something heavy." He dropped the orb back into the case. He was playing a dangerous hand. "You've never steered me wrong yet and I trust your judgment better than my own—even when it seems crazy—but I've gotta say I'm getting a bit curious. A bit worried. Do you want to tell me what this orb is and why the fuck you're sticking your rep out for a little fuck like Budgie?"

"No," TeeVee said. And then he smiled.

"Okay." Sitcom had pushed the issue far enough, further than he had ever pushed anything with TeeVee and further than he ever wanted to go again. "It's none of my business anyway."

"Wait a moment," TeeVee said, still smiling.

Sitcom froze. It had been so long since he'd felt mortal fear that he almost didn't recognize it. He expected to see a dagger flying at him but TeeVee just stayed very still, looking serene and stroking his mongoose. "Yeah?" Sitcom said. "What is it?"

"You shouldn't worry so much."

"Why's that?"

"I am inevitable."

Sitcom nodded. He did not want to think too hard on what that might mean.

⊪⊪ ⊪⊪⊪⊪ ⊪⊪ ⊪⊪⊪⊪⊪⊪⊪ ⊪⊪⊪⊪⊪ ⊪⊪⊪⊪ ⊪⊪⊪⊪ ⊪⊪⊪⊪ ⊪⊪ ⊪⊪ ⊪⊪⊪ ⊪⊪⊪⊪ ⊪⊪ ⊪⊪ ⊪ ⊪⊪

Budgie ran into Sitcom in the Bistro below TeeVee's hutch.

The beta squinted. "You visiting TeeVee?"

"Yeah," Budgie said, nervous. He didn't know how Sitcom felt about him going topside.

"I wouldn't if I were you. Not today." Sitcom looked over his shoulder then back at Budgie. "He's in a funny mood. Anything I can help you with?"

"Just after some brainworm."

"You're going to TeeVee with that?" Sitcom raised his eyebrows. "What about Snort Donkey?"

"He ain't talkin' to me."

"You don't go to an alpha with petty shit like that."

"No where else to go."

"You never even tried me."

"Sorry Sir."

"Brain worm? Pushing on the greens?"

Budgie nodded.

"I can hook you up. You need anything else?"

"No." Budgie followed him across the Bistro. What did he mean when he said that TeeVee was in a funny mood? He didn't want to ask. Shit, he didn't even want to know.

"You're out of uniform." Sitcom sniffed the air. "And you're not scented. Why?"

"I, well Sir, I don think people would like it if I wore the uni." Budgie strained to hold Sitcom's eyes. "Lotta people are pissed at me. Just sort of figured I was out of the Vidicons."

"You are not out of the Vidicons. I know TeeVee is using you for something and that sounds like scheme to me. So wear your bousgie clothes upstairs but down here you wear your uniform and odor. Cologne if you're having trouble turning the pills off." Sitcom tilted his head like a curious dog. "Dressing like that doesn't make you safe, Budgie. It makes you look weak. If you're wearing the uniform, the boys'll be less inclined to fuck with you."

"Yes Sir."

"You're a rude boy and a Vidicon. Dress the part, act the part. Hold your head high. You're working directly under TeeVee now. Trust him?"

"Yes Sir."

"I don't believe you. But you should. I've never known him to betray an honorable Vidicon. Or to forgive a fuck up. Which do you want to be?"

"I'll try, Sir."

Sitcom pushed the door open and they stepped into the corridor. "Where are you living at?"

Budgie gave him Harmony's address.

"I'll swing by tomorrow with your dope. What time will you be there?"

"I get home bout six thirty."

"Hope you don't mind if I step on it, considering it's for the lawn." Sitcom pulled out his gizmo. He gave Budgie another once over and shook his head. "I can't be seen with you looking like that. Get a uni." Without a handshake or waiting for Budgie's reply, he strode away.

Budgie lit a cigarette. It was a long walk home.

Griff flinched back into the doorway when Sitcom and Budgie stepped onto the stoop. Budgie was dressed up like some pampered, slumming bousgie. Griff had trailed him to this place, trying to figure out what the fuck the greasy little topper was up to.

So.

Sitcom was part of this too. That meant that Griff had better be careful. Even more careful than he had been. And he'd already gone total incog. Just until he was done.

Then he would go very public.

PRODUCT PLACEMENT

EMPIRE OF FUCK. From Atlas Studios. The award winning game that allows you to travel deep into the red levels and build a porn and prostitution ring that starts in the reds but eventually reaches up into the blues. Choose from 14 major malls. In each choose from 5 players, ranging from the sneakiness of the CEO to the blood and thunder of the lowliest rude boy. **EMPIRE OF FUCK. Available now.**

"Tonight at 11. The Bob Anger scandal continues. Has the kingpin of talk succumbed to the pleasures of the flesh? We have network celebrity astrologer, Fruity Zodiac, to tell us about the stars, who they've married and who's doing what movies, and how they may have influenced Bob Anger's behavior. Join us at 11."

DAYS OF NATIONS, POLITICS AND EMPIRE. Travel back in time to the days of nations. Master the forces of propaganda, war and economics. Play as Hitler, Stalin, Bush 2, Churchill, Trudeau and many more as you bring your nation to greatness or ruin. Available now from ATLAS STUDIOS.

Budgie saw the rude boys up ahead, and they saw him.

He forced awkward steps, thinking too much about walking, trying too hard to look casual. He watched his feet, avoiding eye contact. Sitcom told him to hold his head high but Sitcom didn't have to live in enemy territory.

Stares crawled over his skin. Refusing to look didn't make him invisible. Best to just get through this as fast as possible.

He picked up his pace. The Vidicons were silent and watching, scenting each other. The power of the gang.

He was gonna make it. They weren't gonna do shit. Something exploded in front of him and he flinched.

A bottle. He looked at it for a long moment, his body very still. *What am I gonna do? What the fuck can I do?*

If he turned to face them there was no talking. It would be past words. It already was.

He knew. He'd stomped his fair share of toppys. If he faced them, he'd have to fight. Could TeeVee's orders defend him then?

Doubted it. These guys were drunk and alcohol knew no obedience. He was on his own. No gang to back him up.

Just keep walking, he told himself, his pride stinging. He wanted to get one of these guys alone. How many toppys had said that to him? 'You're pretty tough with your gang but lets see how good you are by yourself.' They always wanted a fair fight and they never got one. Only other Vidicons deserved that. Sitcom was right about wearing the uniform. If he was dressed and scented he could better claim his privilege.

His hands clenched into fists, his knuckles white and his breath hard. A killing dispo. But he'd lose a battle. That never used to matter but now—what about Harmony?

Shit, if he could survive. Just a few weeks. Get his money good and hidden, he'd be living on the lawn and wouldn't have to worry about this. He'd never have to come down to this shithole again.

He forced his hands open and walked.

"Fuckin' PUSS-AYE," someone shouted. Loud laughter. Budgie's face heated. He walked faster. If he did not leave now, he'd fight. And lose.

He wanted to go home, get his uniform and come back out looking for these fucks. He'd take them down one at a time, not giving any of them the soft-ass gut wound he'd given Griff. No, he'd fucking kill them. Stab them in the necks until they were dead, dead, dead.

He walked. Checked over his shoulder to see if they followed. They didn't.

His imagination flared, getting more and more violent. He reached Harmony's complex, ascended the stairs and entered the hutch. Slammed the door behind him.

"What's wrong?" she asked.

He sat down on the couch beside her and gave her a kiss on the forehead. "Nothing," he said. "Sitcom is gonna come by with your brain worm tomorrow."

"Sitcom? No shit?"

"Yeah. I told you he is close to TeeVee."

"I know you told me but... coming here?"

"You thought I was talking outta my ass." His words were too harsh. He didn't mean to bark at her.

"Kinda," she said, her voice soft.

"I gotta work tomorrow." Budgie lit a cigarette. It helped. "So you'll have to wait around here to meet Sitcom. But day after, get a place on the greens. Don matter what. Put the money down. On anything. I don care what."

"Yeah," she said. "I want to get out of the situation."

"The situation is very bad," Budgie said. Some Vidicon had called him a fucking pussy and he couldn't even tell her. It hurt to think of it. He'd been punked.

He knew that she couldn't get a place to live by tomorrow, and maybe never. But, just for right now, he needed to believe it was possible.

"I'll look," she said.

Grateful that Harmony had let the phony dream linger, Budgie ground out his smoke pulled her onto his lap.

"Budgie!" She didn't resist.

"What?" He put on his 'who me?—I'm innocent' face. Felt good to have her close, to feel her heat radiate into him. She was so soft, little and lovely. "One day, we be free."

"You're an ass."

"Then you're steady fucking an ass and what does that make you?"

"An ass fucker." She tapped his forehead with her index finger. "Just like you."

She kissed him. Her lips held against his for a moment and the kissing became deeper and warmer. Budgie explored her tongue with his own, just lightly tapping and stroking. She pulled her shirt over her head and thrust one of her small breasts into his face. He licked and nibbled at the nipple, gently scraping his teeth against its hardening tip. He cupped her buttocks.

Harmony stared at nothing, her eyes distant and content. Budgie liked that look. He'd done that to her. It wasn't the sordid pride of fucking a whore, bringing someone low, making her crawl to worship his cock.

No, he was proud that she liked him, proud that he made her happy.

He pulled his mouth away from her nipples and said: "I'll go get the orgasms."

"No." She stroked the side of his head. Her fingertips tickled his ear. "I want to do this for real." She smiled and leaned forward to bite his earlobe. Budgie trembled. "You aren't going anywhere," she said, the words shivering into his head. "Not for a while."

He hugged her tight then forced her away so that he could kiss her breast. She rubbed her crotch against his and Budgie got hard. He tried to undo her pants, fumbled with the buttons and got distracted by the kissing. She finally reached down and flicked the button open. Then, as if to mock his clumsiness, undid his pants as well.

Harmony stood and dropped her slacks. They gathered in a bundle around her feet. She stepped out of them one foot at a time, while Budgie quickly undid his boots and yanked his pants off. When he was naked, she straddled him.

Budgie gripped his cock by the base and impaled her. She grunted then bounced, Budgie grabbed her ass, trying to control the pace. He stared at her nipples then at her face, then back at her nipples before leaning forward and kissing her neck. She tilted her head so that he could kiss more of it. He nibbled.

"Ouch," she said. "Not so hard."

"Oh. K. Sorry."

This was the first time Budgie had fucked someone without popping an orgasm. His penis felt numb but there was something good about doing it like this. It felt out of his control. Mysterious. Would he come? Would she? He didn't know. There was no written guarantee. She moved faster and breathed hard, making little grunting noises.

Budgie squeezed her. Their sweaty cheeks pressed together and slipped. She wrapped her arms around his neck. Harmony slowed down and looked at Budgie.

"My legs hurt," she said. "And I'm starting to dry out. Are you going to come?"

"I don think so." His left leg was asleep. "Do you want to give it a pass?"

"Yeah." She pulled herself off and sat for a minute, looking puzzled.

"What?" Budgie asked.

"It's weird. I like fucking you and not coming more than fucking anyone else and coming."

"Let's not brag bout that in public."

She smiled. "Those other boys were just masturbation." She kissed him. "I *liked* not using the orgasms."

"Me too, but..."

"But what?"

"I wonder if I'll ever come again without them."

"We have a long time to find out," Harmony said.

The exec listened to the song on his headphones. Eyes closed, he bobbed his head, ostensibly to the music, but not to any rhythm that Sitcom knew.

He took the headset off and placed it on the table. "You have a deal. We'll release that uncut and it'll be a fucking number one." He held up his hand for a high five. Sitcom just stared at it. The man lowered his palm.

"I need that in writing," Sitcom said.

"Of course."

The man reached into his briefcase for his tablet and Sitcom produced the paper that TeeVee had given him. "This is my contract," he said and laid it upon the table.

The exec looked at him for a long moment and said, "We have a standard—"

"This is my contract."

"Let me see it." He pulled it toward him.

He read carefully, flipping through the agreement, occasionally looking back at another page. "This is actually acceptable," the exec said. "It's similar to our standard contract except it guarantees you that song will get its airplay, which we plan to do anyway. And the places you want to debut..." He frowned.

"What?"

"How'd you come up with these locations?"

Sitcom pokerfaced.

"Just give me a moment." The exec pulled out his tablet and typed. Looked at it. Typed again. Talking with someone. He took a picture of the addresses with the tablet and waited. Sweat broke out on his forehead. "Holy shit."

Sitcom coughed.

The man put down the tablet and signed the contract. Sitcom did the same. They exchanged copies. "I see why you have that on paper."

"Oh?"

"Those locations. How did you get a proper mall map? Let alone figure out the best locations to launch songs from? We have teams working on that sort of thing and, they've come close but—" he slipped his tablet into the case, looked around the room with paro eyes and whispered— "But it looks like you have the exact right map."

Sitcom shrugged.

"Nevermind. I can't blame you for keeping that quiet." He squinted at Sitcom. "You know, I'm pretty sure something like this could land you a good job in our marketing department. Where the real money is."

"I'd like that."

"You're very proactive, you know that?" The exec smiled and Sitcom wondered how much money he'd just made. "It's a good thing."

"I told you, I'm a businessman." Sitcom hadn't even read the document. There'd been no time.

"You sure are," the exec said. "Just give it a few days and you'll be a star."

"When does all this start?"

"You should know that, considering it's in your contract." The exec smiled and stood. "You'll be in rotation all night on Edge and its affiliates. Broadcast first in the locales you specified. We're gonna make a fortune."

Tonight? Sitcom's life was about to change and he better take care of his unfinished business. He had to call Snort Donkey for the brain worm and he had to find Griff. Slug hadn't reported anything in too long and that worried Sitcom. No news was bad news and loose ends tied nooses. They weren't going to tie his.

PRODUCT PLACEMENT

TAKE FRESHNESS TO THE MAX. Colgate Whiskey.

(Photo of pop star dressed like porno nurse, brandishing a dildo in one hand. Stares at camera, ass and tits pushed out. Same popstar sits beside her nurse doppelganger on hospital bed. Legs spread, holding an icepack to head, looking nervous and maybe a little curious. Has a super sexy black eye.) SKETCHERS FOOTWEAR

Everybody talks. Real friends listen. CAROLAN'S LIQUER. This time it's for you.

The only additive is the fire you light them with. Winston cigarettes are made with a blend of 100% tobacco—for a naturally smooth taste created by the earth, water and sun. A flavor unmatched by any additive. [No additives in our tobacco does NOT mean a safer cigarette. WARNING from competitors: Smoking causes Lung Cancer, Heart Disease, Emphysema and May Complicate Pregnancy.] WINSTON. LEAVE THE BULL BEHIND.

Budgie slipped his arm from beneath Harmony's sleeping head, not wanting to wake her. He'd woken up a few minutes before his alarm. Work beckoned and that blaring alarm was a bad way to start your day. He switched it off. "Fuck you, machine. I win."

He dressed, kissed Harmony on the cheek and left the bedroom. He put a token in the coffee machine and turned the news to low volume. Budgie tuned out the voices as he fixed himself a sandwich for lunch. A picture of Bob Anger flashed on the screen.

"Holy shit." Budgie sipped his coffee. "He looks like that?" And he'd been caught at a bordello?

Budgie barked a laugh. It wouldn't be news if it was anyone else, but that sanctimonious bastard had started a media feeding frenzy. The press loved a hypocrite. They camped outside his home, waiting for him to answer their accusations. Again and again the footage rolled of Bob Anger stumbling out of the whorehouse, his face red and sweaty. The prostitute's interview played.

"He likes the rough stuff," she said. One of her teeth was on the blink, apparently knocked loose from the kinetic energy system. "Real rough."

Budgie checked the time. He had to get going. He slung his knapsack over one shoulder. Last night he'd packed his Vidicon uniform and tools. He'd stow them in a locker somewhere away from work and change into it on the elevator coming down. Weekday mornings, going to work, there wasn't much point. Coming home was another story.

The corridors were quiet. Always were at this time. A few old drunks lolled around while a few shatter-faced kids looked for another party but most people slept. A deep silence in the red levels. The blaring, flickering ads were attached to motion sensors so they didn't waste energy playing to empty halls.

But the litter bugs were out in force, their metal feet clattering against the floors, swarming the corridors, eating garbage and breaking it down into chemical slush, which they deposited into receptacles. Budgie guessed that it was recycled and maybe used as paint. Or something.

He liked the little guys. They were good for something other than kicking and exploding. They kept the halls neat. Without them and the air purifiers it'd be like living in a sewer. Someone, he couldn't remember who, had told him that the litterbugs weren't a corporate invention. Apparently some old guy, sick of the filth, had created and released them. But the corporations knew a good idea when they saw it and modified the bugs so that they could harvest the litter. Broke them so they couldn't reproduce and sold them. Budgie doubted that the old guy had ever seen any money.

There was a case like that just a couple of years ago, when some rude boy drug pusher had invented a chemical that broke down sewage. The MTO took the invention, saying that they had the authority to seize patents they deemed necessary to the survival of the mall. Budgie didn't know if they had the law behind them or not but, seeing how they could afford any law they wanted, it didn't seem to matter.

If the MTO seized a patent from a company lab the business would be reimbursed for R&D and would get an innovation bonus from the rental slush funds. Because the rude boy was trying to invent a new hallucinogen and had only discovered the other use when flushing it during an unrelated security raid, he was not entitled to a single global. Something to do with breaching anti-competition by-laws with unlicensed research. If Budgie remembered right, the drug dealer had actually been sued. He wondered what had happened to him. They couldn't send him to the red levels and they probably couldn't get any money out him. Probably hired him in a lab where he'd slave off his legal bills.

Budgie dropped his token into the elevator. A few minutes later he stepped into the brightly lit greens. It was so much busier up here. The start of another workday. The reds and greens operated on opposite sides of time, locked together in a ying-yang logo, colliding and merging and linked by the weekends, where lives got ground up between the two.

Soon enough. Budgie would be outside and he could stop thinking about this sort of thing. He could just relax and be quiet and worry about the simple shit, like pushing a clog out. Out there, he was Sunny, not Budgie.

IIII IIIIIIII II IIIIIIIIIII IIIIIIIIIIIIIII IIIIIIIIIIIIIIIIIIIIIIIIIII

"Trojan Protocol 23 is trying to contact you from a remote machine. Allow? Deny?"

"Allow." TeeVee auto-botted his body.

The song played. Again and again. His vision was a tightly packed network of blue lines, some turning bright pink as his virus seized them. The audio network was scale free and his trojan hijacked nodal points.

Get that bitch open like a junkie's vein, stick my dope dick in the fallopian tube, slick as shit dipped in lube, and go insane as I bust a nut, rough and tough, through the membrane.

He put his pieces into position so that checkmate—a chess board popped up and TeeVee got rid of it—

That's all. Just checkmate.

Patience is a virtue.

Act now and lose everything.

ACT NOW!! PAY LATER!!

No. That virus had to infect *everything*, turn your blue lines pink. Then TeeVee could access Edge's distribution network and load any song he wanted into audio. *My sperm carries guns and hijacks the egg, like frat boys on a beer keg.* Crank it full tilt electro-boogaloo through the mall. And he knew exactly what tango he'd have these fucks dancing (LESSONS FOR ONLY TEN GLOBALS) to. He shook his head and cut that off. If he ACTED NOW and PAID LATER he'd only get what?—consult map—a few food courts, a plaza and a ski hill. Not good enough. Needed the whole thing.

Need it? Want it? Got it?

"Riki-Tiki, about how long before I have total access?"

"Ten hours."

He hit the opium pipe.

▓▓▓ ▓▓▓▓▓▓▓▓ ▓▓▓▓▓▓▓▓▓ ▓▓▓▓▓ ▓▓▓▓▓ ▓▓▓▓▓ ▓▓▓▓▓ ▓▓▓ ▓▓▓ ▓▓▓▓▓ ▓▓▓ ▓▓ ▓ ▓▓▓

"Asshole." Griff watched Budgie leave his complex from behind a pane of mirrored glass. After a bit of persuasion, a waitress had let him hang out in this bar after it closed. She moaned through the tape covering her mouth. "Shut up."

She squirmed on the ground.

"I told you—this is not about you. This is about the system. The code. You got that?"

She made another noise and Griff thought about kicking her in the ribs.

She went silent. Stared at him with wet eyes.

Griff pulled a vial of green powder from his tunic, tapped some onto the back of his hand and snorted.

"Nah," he said after a moment. "I'm not going to kill you or hurt you. Just be nice, okay?"

She nodded.

"Good girl." Griff looked back into the street.

Budgie seemed gone but he sometimes returned. Griff checked his arsenal. Throwing knives rimmed his belt. Between these hung two big blades. One sharp and thin—a stabber—the other wide and long—a hacker. He'd also lined his sleeves with razors, just in case that little bitch tried to grab him. She'd get a surprise then.

He lit a cigarette and snorted another bump. The woman sobbed behind him.

Slug's gizmo buzzed in his pocket. He pulled it out and plugged his own into it. Looked at the message.

SITCOM: Haven't heard from you.

SITCOM: Anything to report about Griff?

Griff smiled. Typed.

SLUG: Nothing. He seems fine.

SITCOM: Good to hear. Bit of a fucking ponce.

Griff ground his teeth.

SLUG: He's okay. I like him.

SITCOM: No accounting for taste.

SLUG: I gotta go. Need to wack off and take a shit.

SITCOM: What?

SLUG: bb

Griff turned the gizmos off. He looked at Slug's for a moment then smashed it against the floor. This was his moment. He didn't want it to get all fucked up by calls.

It was too important. He was holding up the rule of law. Shit, if people stopped paying attention to the rulebook, where did that leave them? They'd just be animals. And no one was above it. Not TeeVee, not Sitcom, not Budgie and definitely not his little piece of pussy. No one.

If he did this right, he'd get the message across. They'd move against him for sure, just out of revenge, but he could schism into another gang. One that paid attention to the rulebook. Then, when the gamma Vidicons followed him, those betas and alphas would see what sort of support they really had for this toppy-protecting bullshit.

Not much.

Griff tried to think of names for the new gang. All the good ones were already taken. The Blud Logic, the Dog Goblins, Vidicons. Shit, there was even the Etceteras. But no problem. He wasn't much of a thinker; he knew this. Someone who joined him would think of something. And then he'd have an army, marching through the corridors. First thing he'd do was raise the protection rates. They weren't getting enough and every time he mentioned his idea, the Vidicons would look at him funny and ask if he was catching the greed.

Hey, that was it.

"The Greed." Griff dropped his cigarette on the floor and ground it beneath his boots, each one strapped with a basic, single-piece knife

"Fuck," Harmony said when the doorbell woke her. The clock read just before seven. She rolled out of bed and got dressed. It must be Sitcom with the brain worm. Or maybe Budgie had forgotten something and was running late. Not bothering to check her surveillance she hit the open door button. "That you, Budgie? Forget your card?"

"No bitch. I sure ain't fucking Budgie."

Harmony stopped in the bedroom door. In her living room, beside the couch was a skinny white guy in full Vidicon war gear. The powerbar that marked how fucked up he was said that he was plenty stoned. He was wet with sweat and his bloodshot eyes looked like holes bored into his head. They flicked back and forth.

"Griff." Her best knives were behind him.

She kept a butterfly in her bedside table. She'd have to get it. Fast. "What are you—"

"Nice place you've got here." He cracked his knuckles. "Amazing what some green globals can buy you."

"What is this?" Harmony took a step back. "Social call?"

"Don't you fucking move." Griff stepped forward. "Not one inch."

Yeah, fuck that. Harmony spun and ran. Slammed the door shut behind her. It bounced back open.

She reached the beside table and yanked the drawer.

Too hard. She pulled it right out and scattered its contents onto the ground. Her butterfly knife bounced away. She scrambled after it.

She saw legs out of the corner of her eye. A boot flying up. Something big and hard hit her. A red light flashed and the world turned gray.

Griff stood over Harmony, panting and gripping his hacking knife. He hadn't needed to use it. One good kick to the face had brought this bitch down to size.

The butterfly knife she'd been reaching for lay against the wall. A cheap blade. It couldn't be the one she used on Wolfe's brothers. Would it even penetrate his fabric armor? He picked it up and poked at his chest. Not even a dent. He stuck it into his pocket, grabbed Harmony up by the armpits and heaved her onto the bed.

He pulled a roll of steel-weave tape from his pocket and looked at the clock. Seven A.M. "I've got all day to play with you."

Griff fastened her limbs to the bedpost. He wanted her to be awake for this. Or she would never learn. No one would.

You don't fuck with the rulebook.

The rulebook fucks with you.

PRODUCT PLACEMENT

SOLITUDE BAGS. Put one of our comfortable lightweight, white noise generating sacks over your head and relax. Block out the outside world. 1.6 globals.

Tired? Coffee just not getting you going in the morning? Can't handle the blaring noise of your alarm? Use the stimulant alarm clock. Just hook it up to you arm before bed and it will wake you up with a jolt of adrenaline, followed by enough slow release caffeine micro capsules to keep you perked through the day. Easy. Soundless. Alert. 6.4 globals.

Do you have drugs in your pocket? Do you know what to do with them? Buy this year's CONSUMER REPORT SPECIAL. We tell what drugs to mix, what drugs to take alone and how to take them for a sudden impact or a slow, extended buzz. 0.3 globals.

SUICIDE GIRL dolls for grown ups. Not everyone can afford a real life **SUICIDE GIRL**. But now you have a choice. Buy your life-size doll with moving, animatronic, gyrating waists, licking mouth and bobbing head. Now with insta-clench asshole and moisture generating vagina. You can dress them up and you don't need to take them out. **SUICIDE GIRLS.**

Ebony, shemales, Japanese, schoolgirls, bukkake, blondes, redheads, babes, chubby chix, hairy chix, desperate housewives, legs, machines, nipples, panties, pee, scat, grannies, security, mall rats, bestiality, sub and dom, bikini, anal, Asian, cartoon, natural tits, smoking, feet, drunk, sleeping, screamers, moaners, and fetish. Hunting for porn in the info dump? **Look no further.** PORN HUNTER. We get you off. 0.2 globals per month subscription. The only download limit is your imagination.

Harmony awoke on her stomach with her face buried in a blood-soaked pillow. She tried to move her hands and found she was bound hard and fast. Memory hit like a hammer. She held her head up, gasping for stinging air through a razor blade mouth. Her tongue darted over her teeth. A few were missing. Others were loose. She grunted.

"Shhhhh."

Griff sat beside her on the bed. He dabbed her face with a wet towel, his touch sickeningly gentle. She flinched, and pain fishhooked her checks.

"Just be quiet for now." Griff smiled, a low and lecherous expression. "You'll have plenty of time to scream later."

The white towel was red.

"What do you want?"

"I want your boy toy to get the hint. I want him and his elite buddies to leave the rules alone." He snorted, and wiped at his nose. "I know it's old fashioned, but it's just the way I am." He reached down her back, his fingertips tickling her skin. His hand slipped beneath her panties and squeezed her crotch. "You sure got a nice tight pussy."

Harmony tried to wriggle away but the tape held her fast.

Griff's breath dragged through his nose. "You like that, eh baby? You little fucking slut. You like that, huh?" He forced two fingers into her. Harmony shoved her face into her pillow. Crying. Frustration. But she couldn't let him see that. She bit the pillow. It hurt.

She held her body still and felt Griff stand up. Felt him pull his fingers out.

He circled the bed, his boots dead thuds against the floor. There was another noise that she couldn't recognize, that she didn't want to think about. A moment later a needle pricked one of her ass cheeks.

An injection.

"There's enough orgasm in there to keep you randy all day," Griff said. She heard his belt buckle snap open. Pants dropping to the floor. "And if a little slut like you needs more, then I brought more."

Clothes thumped against the ground. Sweaty meat pressed against her back.

Harmony clamped her jaw. Pain scalded her broken teeth and swollen, bleeding lips. It distracted her. But not for long.

"You hear about Bob Anger?" Rick asked.

"Yeah." Budgie and Rick sat together on the pod, coming to the end of the commute. "I can't believe that shit."

"Me neither." Rick looked at Budgie for a long moment. "I don't know what everyone is gonna listen to today. I'm fine, but everyone else likes him."

"Wouldn't say I liked him," Budgie said. "Just entertaining. He was fucking nuts though."

"I'm happy he's gone," Rick said. "And I make no bones about it. You see how fast his fans turned against him?"

"People turn fast." Budgie said. "I wonder what they'll have on instead of him."

"You haven't heard?"

"No. Wait, let me guess. Lenny Niedenberger."

"I wish," Rick said. "Old Bob and his Total Truth Hour."

"What?"

"Yeah, Old Bob." Rick grinned. "So much for having his ideas suppressed eh?"

"Who's he?"

"Man, you are outta touch. No television in the reds?"

"Nah, I just don't watch much talk stuff or news or anything. Just movies. I like nature shows. Especially the ocean stuff." He shrugged. "My girl don like any of it. So who's Old Bob?"

"He's a conspiracy theorist. Thinks that there was a UFO invasion, that outside is still livable. Says there's still Arabs in the middle east and cloned dinosaurs in the jungle. Ghosts, aliens. That sort of thing. You know. Crackpot." Rick grinned. "But I'm gonna tune in today. It'll be good for a laugh."

"Guess I will too," Budgie said.

"The funny thing is that I went to his sites on the info dump. A bunch of his hardcore fanboys are saying that Old Bob and Bob Anger are the same guy. Bunch of others are saying that there's a conspiracy afoot, that Bob Anger was set up by Old Bob. The rest are telling all of them to shut up."

"Why?"

"Figure this is their big chance to get some credibility. They don't want the other crazy assholes to fuck it up." He shook his head. "No one seems to realize that the whole thing is a sideshow." Rick glanced at Budgie. "You all right?"

"Yeah," Budgie said. He'd had a funny feeling for a moment but it passed. "Goose over my grave."

"Come here bitch." Griff yanked Harmony's head up to face his cock. It was hard to get a grip on her cause the little whore didn't have any hair, but he held her tight by the ear. "Ugh," he said and spurted cum onto her forehead. He wanted to rub it in with his dick but he wasn't stupid. She'd try to bite him. He released her head and slapped her across the face. She glared at him, her eyes burning and wet, semen dribbling into them.

"That the fucking best you could do?" she said, her voice fuzzy and swollen. "Pump me full of orgasms and still can't get me off?" She smiled, showing her broken teeth. "Worst fuck I've ever had. And you hit like a pussy. You come like a—"

"Shut up, you, you... slut!" Griff raised his fist.

"Or what? Fuck you."

He threw his fist down at her and she shoved her forehead into the blow. Griff heard a wet crack but felt nothing. He looked at his hand. He'd broken it.

She laughed.

He grabbed her pinky finger and bent it back. It snapped. She gasped.

Griff pulled his fist back up to take another swing and she smiled. Why couldn't he stop her from smiling? He grabbed her jaw with his broken hand and pulled back to punch her. Harmony twisted her head. His hand slipped in the blood and cum. She bit down on his index finger.

Hard. So hard.

He yowled and pulled his hand free, tearing flesh against her teeth. He hit her with a right hook, whipping her head sideways and onto the pillow. That shut her up. That put out her lights.

"Fuck!" Blood gushed from Griff's finger and poured down his arm. Bone grinned at him. He'd have to wash that. No telling what a whore like this was carrying. But first he punched her. Hard. In the ribs.

"Fucking bitch." His eyes wet with frustration and anger. He hit her again. "You fucking bitch."

He wanted to break her. He had all day to make Harmony beg. He promised himself. He'd find a way.

Griff bent down to her ear, keeping a safe distance. His voice shook in his throat. "I hope you can hear me, you bitch. I'm gonna love you with a knife and I want you to know it's all Budgie's fault. You're gonna hate that fuck by the time I'm done with you."

INFO DUMP

"So it is with great regret and a heavy heart that I am stepping down from the helm of my show. I thank you all and only hope that you'll forgive me."

    —From Bob Anger Press release.

"Rumor has it that Bob Anger has just signed a contract with a new publisher to write his memoirs. We hear it's going to be called "I'm a Crazy Lying Bastard." The weepy tale of how he fell into sin will show a total turnaround in his thinking. Now we'll have a kinder, gentler Bob Anger. It'll be huge. Even bigger than his other stuff. You heard it here first."

    —From THE RUMOR MILL.

"I think this whole incident just shows how good my girls are. The brothel he was caught at was one of my franchises. If even Bob Anger can't resist my time-tested and male approved techniques can you imagine how your hubby will react? Remember to pick up my best selling book, 'Fucking like a Pro,' and see what all the fuss is about."

    —From Jane Jane interview

"The Bob Anger incident is more or less meaningless except that it underscores our obsession with celebrity. And our hypocrisy about their—and our—behavior. And their hypocrisy too. I'm actually working on a book on this theme and it should be out sometime next year."

    —From Lenny Niedenberger interview

"So before I start, I'd like you to know that I am not Bob Anger. But to keep things interesting I'm offering a 500,000 global reward for anyone who can prove that I am. You hear that guys? You can enter this contest by paying 20 globals to the Old Bob Total Truth Show, sponsored by Total Vodka. And I look forward to hearing your entries. Anyone with a really good case that might fall short of truth, will be invited on the show. And I'm hoping that Bob Anger might even give it a shot. Word is, he needs a job."

    —From the Old Bob Total Truth Show.

"Time," said the voice within Budgie's helmet.

The robot dumped its last load of the day and scuttled back into the dump where its red lights dimmed. Budgie stretched his aching back and returned to the truck's carry cab. His lights dimmed too.

Purple clouds bruised the sky and the stars were skin glitter sprinkled across the wound. The moon, a bent bone. Budgie wished he could work out here at night, but no jobs were available. Rick said that people who worked at night loved it too much. Budgie could see why.

It was a different world. The days were stark and clear but the nights were mysterious. You could almost imagine teeming forests and dinosaurs, aliens and ghosts. But maybe that was just a mental echo of the Old Bob Total Truth Hour. Still, looking up at the stars, Budgie felt small in a way that the day did not make him feel. Night was like being outside all over again.

During the day you couldn't see through the sky but at night you could see forever. It was the next step. He wondered what total darkness would be like. He'd never seen it. Indoors, there was always a bulb burning somewhere. Light even leaked into Harmony's bedroom.

Budgie waited for his turn to climb down the ladder. The T-Dot Center was a shadow on the horizon. That was all. No windows blinked lights. It was a world that only stared at its own insides, and it looked very small from out here. He could almost hear the buzz of activity, like a cello thrum at the edge of his senses. But it might be an illusion. Just as no light escaped the mall, perhaps no sound did either. He looked away from that dark spot against the indifferent sky and climbed down the ladder.

Griff stuck the pliers into Harmony's mouth and clamped on her final tooth. An incisor. Her head was bound back by tape wrapped around her feet. The tendons on her neck stood out like metal cables about to burst through her pale, sweaty skin. Her bloodshot eyes rolled back. She gurgled and gasped, bloody foam leaking and spraying from between quivering lips.

Griff pulled. Hard. Then twisted.

The tooth snapped in half and Harmony yowled like a burned cat. She spat blood onto Griff's already wet hand. He examined the half-tooth in the pliers, tilting it this way and that in the light. He dropped it into the pile on the bedside table. "What a lovely smile you have."

Harmony's eyelids flipped back down.

He grinned. He hadn't broken her in the way he wanted, hadn't gotten her to say the things he wanted her to say and now she was beyond all of that. But she was broken. She vomited onto the pillow and Griff smiled wider. He tapped her tape-bound forehead with the pliers. She wasn't even an animal anymore. Just dry-heaving, sweaty flesh.

He was happy he'd raped her earlier and then again a bit later on. She was too repulsive to fuck right now. Rather, she was so repulsive he didn't even need to fuck her. Seeing her like this was enough.

"It's almost time." He sat on the bed and looked at the clock. "Wonder what Budgie will think about all this. Think he'll come for me?"

She groaned.

"Cause I'll be waiting." He bent towards her. "Lovely smile," he repeated. "But it could be wider." He picked up a knife from the bedside table, changed his mind and grabbed Harmony's butterfly knife. "Recognize this?" He passed it back and forth in front of her eyes. They didn't respond, just stared straight ahead.

Griff flipped it open and rested the dull blade against the corner of her mouth. He sliced through the cheek with long, buttery strokes. The blade hit the hinge of her jaw. The lower flap of cheek flopped down, pouring blood. Harmony clamped her gums together. He pulled them open with his free hand and put the blade to work on her other cheek, cutting through the slightly resistant lip and then getting into the soft fat, which split so nice and easy. He pulled the knife out, drawing it across her tongue.

A pretty smile.

Griff bent down and kissed her once on her salty forehead. A very pretty smile.

"Your boy is gonna be home soon. Wonder if he'll want a turn? If not, I might make him take one anyway."

Harmony blinked.

"This ain't the movies," Griff whispered. "There's no last minute rescue coming for you. No 'save the world, get the girl, champagne on ice' for you. Not even any devastating one liner before death. It just ain't like that. 'And the one who stabbed me is...'"

He plunged the knife into her throat, his face close to hers, watching her eyes, while he twisted the blade this way and then that, digging out cartilage.

Harmony's eyes were stained glass balls that reminded Griff of one of those kid's toys that you shook up to get the ticker-tape parade going. Except, instead of a triumphant scene, there was nothing but hate and anger. These vanished inside a blizzard. Then even the blizzard was gone. Those eyes still stared.

He released his grip on the knife, not bothering to pull it out. The bed was red and wet. A snake of blood oozed out of Harmony's asshole, mixed with cum and shit. Disgusting, Griff thought.

Just wasn't the same now she was dead. Alive she had been a victim. Dead she was just a mess.

Griff checked the time. Still had plenty.

He knelt on the bed to carve his tag into her ass cheek.

And heard something behind him.

"You're early," he said.

Sitcom flipped his skeleton card key across the scanner without bothering to ring the bell. He never announced his presence when visiting underlings, liking them to know that their house was his house. It kept them from getting any fancy ideas. Quite often, just to drive the point home, he'd walk straight to the fridge and help himself to a beer. Sometimes, if they were eating, he'd grab a handful of food off their plate.

The door opened and Sitcom caught the iron stink of blood. A lot of it. Sniffing, he reached for his knife and slipped into the hutch.

Was anyone even home? A voice came from the next room, mumbled words.

He ghost stepped toward it. The voice stopped. A shuffle and a click. He peered around the corner.

Griff.

On his knees, he wore no shirt and faced away from Sitcom. He dangled a thin blade.

On the bed, a mangled chunk of flesh, leaking blood from every natural hole and some manmade ones. Griff dug into this body with his knife. Carving.

Sitcom hissed.

Griff tilted his head. "You're early," he said.

"I usually am."

Griff sprang to his naked feet and spun to face Sitcom. His face dropped. "What're you?"

"I'm not interrupting anything am I?"

"You bastards," Griff sputtered. "You think you can just ignore the rules but you can't." He swallowed hard and brought his knife up, in a fighting pose.

Sitcom kept his body loose.

"I thought I'd take care of you later but this is like a two for one sale."

"Put the knife down, Griff."

"Fuck you."

"Fuck me?"

"That's what your fat friend said too."

"You mean Slug?" Sitcom grinned. "My friend? *Friend?* Oh, but boyo, I am a much colder thing than that."

"I killed him."

"Congrats." Sitcom wagged his knife at his side. "From behind, most likely. What's your rulebook say about that?"

"Fuck you."

"All this foreplay betrays your cowardice." Sitcom stared hard into Griff's eyes. Nothing there except sadism and greed. He'd caught it bad. "If you're gonna make a move, then fucking make it."

Griff opened his mouth to say something.

Sitcom pistoned his elbow. He flicked his wrist and his knife spun through the air, halving the distance between the two men, then halving that too. It plunged into Griff's solar plexus. No noise. The blade buried deep. The hilt stuck out like a tombstone.

Griff waved a hand in front of his chest to block it.

Too late, Sitcom thought. Much too late. "You are one slow fuck."

Griff sat on the corner of the bed. His ass slipped off and he tumbled to the floor, dropping his knife. Sitcom grabbed another blade from his belt. He sauntered forward. "And you're clumsy. And you're fucking stupid. And you're a fucking problem. My problem. And you will be solved."

Griff gawked at the knife in his chest. A liquid, red worm slithered out of his mouth. He looked up at Sitcom and grabbed the hilt of the blade with both hands. Yanked it out. Blood squirted. Griff waved the blade and tried to stand. "You fuck." He burbled purple. "I'll fucking—"

Sitcom kicked him square in the face with the treads of his boot. A puff of blood from Griff's nose.

"You really fucked up my day." Sitcom glanced at Harmony. Griff had mutilated her face. Sitcom shook his head. "She was nice product and decent Vidicon. And she was a customer. What the fuck is the matter with you?"

Griff was beyond hearing. He lay on the floor gasping, each breath forming a red bubble over his mouth that popped and spilled down his cheeks.

Sitcom crouched beside him. The prospect heaved and twitched. Not wanting to get his hands dirty, Sitcom cut the artery on the far side of Griff's throat, directing the surge of blood away from him. It painted the wall then weakened. Griff's expression ran out of batteries.

Sitcom wiped the blade on his pantleg and stood. This was a bad situation. And bad situations did not get better. They got worse. He checked the time, saw that Budgie was running late. Lit a cigarette.

"Always on me," he said looking at the corpse. "Probably because I'm always on time." He sighed. "And I liked Slug too, you prick."

PRODUCT PLACEMENT

YE OLDE KNIFFE SHOPPE. We buy and sell knives of all kinds. From antique items such as cane swords and Special Forces knives to newer designs such as The Elite Ultra Thin Dagger. Krises to machetes, throwing to boot knives, knuckle-dusters, serrated blade to dull edged stabbers, used and new. And we're now carrying a wide selection of rude boy tunics in all colors, made in standard tight fabric armor weave and in the impenetrable, yet still reasonably priced, spider web weave. We cut our prices so you can cut your enemies. YE OLDE KNIFFE SHOPPE.

SAAB: Individuality starts at 38.9 globals a month.

In the elevator, Budgie slipped out of his bousgie clothes and into his stinking Vidicon uniform.

He slapped his knife and knucks onto his belt. That'll make any motherfucker think twice, he thought, and smiled. Funny how these clothes and that smell made him feel. Like he was back in his body. The last few weeks were a strange diversion. This was the real Budgie.

Just another rudie.

And if anyone tried to fuck with him they'd learn a quick lesson. His fingers tap-danced over the hilt of his knife. He almost hoped someone would try. He was ready. Coming back indoors made him a bit crazy. Sometimes he felt like a zoo animal pacing back and forth across his cage floor. But when adrenaline cranked he could almost see a crack, could almost break out. Even if he lost a fight and got cut, it still felt right. Like brushing up against elemental forces. In a way it was like being outside. In another way it was its exact opposite.

Soon he'd be out of the Vidicons and on the greens. He leaned against the elevator wall. It was good to move up in the world, he knew that, but it felt like betrayal. Sure, he had to look out for number one but his whole life had been about the tribe. Budgie was a pack animal.

At least there was Harmony. They could start a family. That'd be his new pack. Good thing too. He needed one.

A drunk staggered into the elevator. Seeing a rude boy, he mumbled an apology and stumbled back out. He didn't know Budgie was a floater and didn't want to. Just afraid of that uniform. The doors closed again and Budgie bit down on his smile. It wasn't right.

He wished he was more like Harmony. She used the Vidicons, she wasn't a Vidicon. There was a difference. Budgie didn't just wear the clothes, he was the clothes. He was what they represented with all the responsibilities and privileges. The book and the bosses told him what to do. Without all that, he didn't know who he was or who he was supposed to be. It had never mattered. He was Vidicon, a foot soldier in an underground army that fought for survival and expansion. Beyond that, he just didn't know.

Until meeting Harmony he hadn't cared. He'd walked around with a head full of celebrities and adverts, and that was that. Maybe he'd gone television. How could you even tell if you were nuts? How did you know what other people thought? Maybe everyone was a bit television.

Budgie reached his floor and stepped out of the elevator. He walked fast and swung the bag of work clothes at his side. Looked straight ahead. People moved out of his way, most trying to avoid eye contact. A man in a blue suit that advertised Colgate Whiskey pushed a shopping cart full of speakers blasting distortion with a heartbeat bass. That guy reminded Budgie of something.

He had been there, in the corridor—

The night that Sputnik was notched.

Budgie's fingers went numb. He suddenly had a danger feeling and braced. Nothing happened.

Must be memories.

But something else yanked on his gut. He couldn't say what. Must be nerves.

Budgie strode past the Colgate mascot, refusing to look. He wanted to forget him. He invited bad luck. And bad luck always accepted the invitation.

A couple of Vidicons cruised through the crowd toward him. Pillar and Nightcap. Budgie tensed but tried not to show it. Nightcap's head jerked. Must have eye-deed me, Budgie thought. Or nose-deed. Nightcap said something to Pillar. They both stopped, hands on their hips, close to their weapons.

Looking. Sniffing.

Budgie tried to look confident. Even if bravery couldn't make things better, fear could only made them worse. His insides shrank. The bad omen of Colgate Man. Trying to breathe some looseness into his muscles, he approached the two Vidicons.

"Budgie." Pillar nodded.

"Pillar." Budgie glanced at Nightcap. He had to keep both these guys in front of him until he knew what was up. "Wasabi?"

"Should be asking you that." Pillar looked Budgie's uniform up and down. He sniffed the air. Budgie quietly thanked Sitcom for his advice. This had confused them. Whatever your average Vidicon might think with their head, their gut had a loyalty to the uniform and scent. They were not so quick to attack. "Word is you're toppy."

"Fact is," Nightcap corrected. "Fact."

"I answer to you?" Budgie puffed out his chest.

Nightcap made a pfffft noise like the air escaping from a tire.

"If you're gonna do something," Budgie said, "get to it before I do."

"We've got orders." Pillar glanced around, clearly not wanting anyone to see him talking to Budgie. But someone would see, someone always did, and there'd be gossip. "And orders are orders are orders."

"We got orders?" Nightcap could only smell Budgie and the cologne would not smell right or cover the odor of the greens. The combo provoked him. "I didn't hear no orders. What fucking orders we got?"

"Hands off, are our orders," said Pillar. "So you just fuckin' heard 'em, right?"

"Think I must be going deaf too."

Budgie held quiet, ready to pounce.

But, in Pillar's face, was something that Budgie recognized from his own. He didn't want to do anything. Not really. But his partner did.

Maybe Pillar was thinking about turning toppy too.

The thought turned Budgie cold. Cause, if Pillar was thinking about it, others would be thinking it about him. And if Pillar wanted to keep his life together, to avoid this bad fate, he had to make sure people didn't think those things. He might do anything to keep them from questioning his hardness.

"We all got our fucking orders," Budgie said. "You think I like mine?"

"Why I give a fuck bout what you like?"

"How about you give a fuck about me not having any orders vis a vis chopping your throat?" Budgie grinned. "How about you give a fuck about doing what you're told to do? Or you in the habit of making your own rules?" He paused and looked at Pillar. "No offense but your partner is none too bright."

Pillar shrugged.

"Fancies himself as a bit of a maverick." Budgie leaned into Nightcap's face and sniffed. "Funny, I don smell alpha ranking on him. But here he is, full of fucking questions. Full of thoughts. Ideas. You a bit of an intellectual, eh Nightcap? A thinking man?"

"I just—"

"Cause you should think bout this," Budgie pressed and paused. "What happens to a Vidicon who disobeys a direct order from an alpha? You should think bout that meeting, where you walk in and say, 'I din know we had no fucking orders. So I went and interfered in that which did not concern me. Yeah, I attacked a superior. Why? Well, Boss, I had a personal problem.' Think bout that meeting."

"So it's a scheme then?" Pillar asked.

Budgie ignored the question. Pillar needed an exit and Budgie gave it to him. He'd put all this on Nightcap, who was doing the math. Unable to solve the problem, he sniffed Pillar for guidance.

"Don you smell him," Budgie said. "You're the thinkin' man, how bout you figure this out by yourself."

"What?"

"Ya got what to gain from attacking me? A bar story? A bit o rep? A bit o blood on the knucks. And ya got what to lose from doin' the same? Your head. Maybe they go soft and just chop your hands off.

That is, if I don. Either way, you ain't gonna enjoy that newfound rep when they strip that uni and leave you out here alone and you find yourself dealing with people like you. Cept you'll have no orders to protect you. You might even have a diff set governing conduct towards your person. Something like, make his life long and make it painful."

Nightcap looked at his boots.

"Touch me," Budgie whispered. "Touch me, you little blind fuck and see what happens."

"Easy," Pillar said. "Easy."

"Yeah," said Budgie. "It's easy."

Nightcap sulked.

"Yeah. I'll take it easy," said Budgie. "Your boy gon to do the same? Gon respect the fuckin' rules?"

"Nightcap?"

"Fuck this." Nightcap looked up from the floor and straight at Budgie with those black goggles. "Bet you think you punked me. Huh? But you ain't gon be protected forever. You barely even protected now. You just need to wait for it. That's all: Just wait. And if you think I fall down easy? Pfffft."

"I'm waiting now, motherfucker."

"And you keep waitin'. It's comin'." Nightcap slapped Pillar's back. "Fuck this noise. We gon get drinks in a Vidicon bar. You fly home now or wherever, lil Budgie. We'll chat later. Bank on that."

Budgie watched them go. His eyes met Pillar and, for a moment, thought he glimpsed gratitude. Knew he should feel some kinship with that but, even now, geared up with aggression, Budgie was too much the rude boy. All he could think was: *You bitches just got punked by a floater? Vidicons must be going soft. I'd have cut me.*

He spat.

██ ██ ██ ██ ██ ██ ██ ██ ██ ██ ██ ██ ██ ██ ██ ██ ██ ██ ██ ██

"Checkmate: Ken Lexus has checkmated you."

TeeVee opened his eyes and looked around his hutch. Riki-Tiki sat on his lap, licking his chest. TeeVee took a hit of opium. Holding the thick smoke in his lungs he wondered when he was last in his body. It seemed like a long time ago but his brain was a touch bent. Even his fingers felt too long. Oh, they were. He'd spent a day stimulating his pituitary gland.

He stood and stretched. It felt good. He was a couple centimeters taller. From up here, he could really see that his apartment was a mess. The style was all wrong. You can't be triumphant in a cramped hovel.

TeeVee sat back down and re-lit his bowl. He sucked in cold smoke. Bubbles in the bottle. He should call that prostitute to clean this place up before he went to work. That way, everything would look just right.

He closed his eyes and pinged her. She picked up. "Bubbles. I need you to come here." Tits and ass. Personal profile. She likes romantic dinners and doggy style, hates stinky feet and cheap watches.

"No. Not fucking. Just to clean. Maybe make me some scrambled eggs. Right now. I'm hungry."

It had been a long time since Sitcom had to deal with a mess of this scale. Usually, when someone got notched, you wanted them to be found in all of the gory glory. Not this time. This time, it'd be better for the problem to just vanish. If not done in public, let it be done in private. Griff who?

Sitcom rubbed paper towels against the blood, but it just streaked around the floor.

"Where the fuck is Budgie?" He dropped the dripping red towelettes into the toilet. "I could use some help here."

He yanked the lever. Nothing happened. He'd already used up the day's prepaid flush allowance. And he had no more toilet tokens. "How the fuck am I supposed to fucking clean this the fuck up?" He kicked the wall.

He lit a cigarette and studied the red toilet water. He'd have to bag it. He searched the drawers beneath the kitchen sink until he found a box full of neatly folded plastic bags. Grabbing another fistful of paper towels, he returned to the bedroom, stepping over Griff's corpse. He still hadn't untied Harmony. Better to let her leak onto the bed than onto the floor.

This was a nice hutch. He wondered if Budgie could carry it by himself. If not, maybe Sitcom could put in a bid. If he could get this fucking blood out. If not, he could probably get a deal. No one liked stains.

What I need, he thought as he got back on all fours, *is a good towel. These paper things are a scam. I need something with some nanoids. One of those jobbies that suck up the mess and break it into chemicals, maybe even reform it into part of the towel. Next time I do a job I'll definitely have one of those. That'll just be part of my arsenal. I'll bring a towel.*

He scrubbed a big circular streak and swore below his breath. Maybe he should check the info dump for some hints about how to do this properly. But there wasn't enough time to research. He should know anyway. Having to look up something like that mid-job was a bit too gamma for him. It stank of rank amateurism. He'd have Budgie do it.

"Harmony," Budgie shouted as he walked through the door and hung his bag on the peg. "I'm home."

Sitcom stood in the bedroom doorway.

"What the fuck?" Budgie said. Sitcom's hands were bright red and he held a fistful of blood soaked paper towels. "What the..."

"You're late."

"Harmony?" Budgie's stomach froze. "Where's Harmony?"

"Look, I've got some bad news—"

Budgie strode towards him, his brain flickering like a damaged florescent. Griff's body lay on the ground, but Budgie couldn't make any sense out of that.

Sitcom tried to block him at the door. Budgie shoved him aside. Stepped into the bedroom.

"Harmony?" Just a jumble of images; a macabre hallucination of blood and torn flesh. "Harmony?" Everything disjointed. Why were Harmony's legs at that angle? What was the red stuff around her neck? If Sitcom was here then why was she naked? Was she okay? "Harmony?"

Sitcom put his hand on Budgie's shoulder.

Budgie heard breathing behind him. Sounded like a snake hissing. "Harmony?"

Budgie tried to step forward. His feet ignored him and remained plastered to the floor.

Then Budgie saw the tape around her hands. All the disjointed images slapped together and become a clattering mess of hatred and grief. "Harmony!"

His breath got hot. Felt like air was being torn out of his lungs. Everything turned black and white. Except for the blood. It stayed red. It stayed bright.

"It's a fucking mess," Sitcom said from behind him. Budgie only half heard the words over the screaming in his head. "When I got here—"

"My fault," Budgie said. He stumbled back into the doorway. *If I had been stronger, had forgotten about Sputnik*

This was cause of me.

He turned to face Sitcom but couldn't feel his body. He was just eyes and ears tethered to a ghost mind. "My fault."

Sitcom wiped his forehead, leaving a red stain across his gray face. "I don't know that fault matters all that fucking much." He dabbed at the blood with the paper towel. It didn't wipe off. "Just a mess. I got here and—"

The words were just chattering noise. A profane racket in the corpse silence of the room. This was just business to the beta. It was messy and unseemly but, at the end of the day, nothing more than an operation gone a bit off. Nothing that would matter in a week.

Budgie had to make this matter. Any meaning that came from this came from him.

Harmony wasn't just a commodity. *A shame to lose but oh well, what the hell, you could always get another.* No, it wasn't like that.

She was a human. Not a product. Her death was important. She was Harmony. *Was.*

None of these guys gave a fuck. None of them had cared about Sputnik, none of them would give a shit about Harmony. He could picture the leering mouths as they gossiped about what had been done here. Some would go to bordellos, their imaginations inflamed, and role-play this with whores. It would be turned into another fucking spectacle, another kink fantasy. Another snuff movie.

Everything in Budgie and about Budgie meant fuck-all now. He wasn't going to play this shitty survival game anymore. Unhinged from the rules, unbound by money and fuck personal gain. He took a deep breath.

That old murder switch flipped.

Nothing but cold.

He looked long and hard at Sitcom, waiting for the man's noisy mouth to turn quiet. The beta had no glamor now. Small. Pathetic. A global grubbing bastard dressed up like a clown. Black and white, covered in red smears. He was nothing.

"This is a nice hutch," Sitcom said. "Are you going to put a bid in on it? Cause once we get this cleaned up…"

"You want the hutch?"

"Depends on the cleaning. I mean, after we get the bulk of this out, we can call in some pros."

"We gonna cover this up?"

"Griff, at least," Sitcom said. "He's just gonna vanish. But Slug should get a wake. Maybe Harmony too. That'd be a pretty good launch for my—Hey did you hear? I got signed."

"That's good news." Budgie wanted to cringe at all this but he just couldn't. He forgot how. How the fuck do you cringe? At anything? "Do I get a cut?"

"That's not strictly cricket."

"And this is?"

"Yeah, well, good point. We'll talk on it." Sitcom patted his pockets. "You got any toilet tokens? I'm out."

"Sure." Budgie found a couple tokens in his pocket and passed them to Sitcom, who took them, thanked Budgie and turned around. He started walking away, jingling them in his cupped hand.

That jingle was very loud.

Budgie flipped his blade out, stepped forward and swung. His arm was mechanical. His blade dug into the base of Sitcom's skull and sank up to the hilt. Sitcom's body went stiff and he gasped, inflating his chest. The air wheezed out of him and the weight of his flesh pulled the knife down. There was no will left in the man and no muscle control to hold him up. Just meat and gravity.

We're the same now, Budgie thought. *Just meat. Just gravity.*

He released the hilt. Sitcom's knees buckled and he fell, his face a wet splat against the floor. His right arm twitched a Morse code rhythm. His left leg responded with the same jerky movements. He shat himself.

Budgie took one deep breath then another. He bent down, pressed his boot against Sitcom's back and yanked his knife out. Wiped it clean on his pant leg.

He walked to the bed and cut the tape that bound Harmony's hands. His stomach floated into his throat and choked him. He cut her legs down. He touched her shoulders. Her beautiful shoulders.

She was so cold.

He gingerly eased her onto her back and sat down beside her. After a long moment of staring into her eyes, nothing in those eyes, he grabbed her hand and squeezed. Everything got blurry. He grunted and gasped, drawing hot air into hysterical lungs.

Budgie pulled his tunic sleeve across his eyes and wiped at his face. The fabric scratched but felt better than the quaking grief. He wiped until his face was raw. He dropped Harmony's hand, hugged her body and stared at the wall. A cockroach stared back.

PRODUCT PLACEMENT

SHOP. EAT. REPEAT.

Café Noir. See what the hub-bub is about. Be served by Humphrey Bogart-bot in our Black and White restaurant. Café Noir. Let us steal your night away.

ASPIRIN! It cures everything!

Oh Hungry? Oh Heroin.

COLGATE WHISKEY. Freshens your breath while you drink.

In today's hurly burly world, sometimes you need a break. Sometimes you need a KIT KAT.

Smarties Matrix. Eat the red ones. If you dare.

All he could do was tuck her in.

Budgie pulled the blanket up to Harmony's chin and wrapped it tight beneath her shoulders. Not wanting to look at her shattered teeth he forced her mouth closed. It popped back open.

"Shit."

Her face was mutilated beyond recognition. He wondered if it would be that way, even if she wasn't cut up. Would death alone vandalize her features? With the life drained out her, she was nothing. Not the girl he had loved. Just a hundred pounds of flesh and bone. Pet food on the ghoul market.

"Harmony." He stroked her cheek. There'd been a time, not so long ago, when he would have sold this body. A lot of people wanted human corpses and, if you had the right connections, you could usually get more for a dead person than you could pull from their pockets. Now, selling a body seemed obscene. Some things should not be for sale.

But *should* didn't count for a lot. Truth was, they were for sale. Everyday people pimped corpses and everyday people bought some. It didn't matter what they *should* do. They did what they did and they made good money doing it.

"A pocket full of globals and a head full of schemes," Budgie sang in a low voice. It was the chorus to some song. He couldn't remember its name. Some song that Sitcom liked to play.

He lit a cigarette. This apartment stank of blood and death. He breathed it in.

He had to strike back. But at what? Who? He didn't know.

"No," he said. "That's not true."

TeeVee must be behind this. Maybe he didn't want Budgie to move upstairs or maybe he didn't like Harmony knowing about his song that made people move. But, like *should, why* didn't matter.

Neither did *how.* They'd obviously wanted to set up Griff, prolly to keep Budgie's loyalty, but it had backfired. Sometimes schemes did that.

Harmony must have put up a good fight, struggling long enough to put Sitcom off schedule. Or maybe Sitcom just had a bit too much fun with her. She was beautiful. Used to be, at least. Sitcom prolly couldn't resist.

Maybe he saw the hutch and wanted it.

It could just be that.

"Fuck." Budgie punched the mattress. He dropped the cigarette on the floor and spat on it. "Fuck!" His fist shook. Squeezed it as hard as he could. Budgie yelled and punched himself in the face. Not hard enough. He tried again. Needed to knock the thoughts out his head.

But they kept coming.

Nothing was free down here. Smack. TeeVee would pay for killing Harmony in the only currency that mattered now. Smack. All pay. Smack. Fuck them all. Smack.

Budgie stopped hitting himself. Something dripped down the side of his face. Might be blood, sweat or tears. He wiped his hand across his cheek. It came away red but diluted. Must've been all three.

Budgie tore off his jacket. Tossed it onto the floor. Bent beside Sitcom. He maneuvered the man's stiffening arms out of his tunic and looked at it. The tag read, 'spider-web weave.' Nothing but the best.

He kicked Sitcom in the ribs. Hard. Again and again. They cracked like popcorn. All Budgie could think was maybe, if Sitcom had been wearing regulation fabric, maybe Harmony could've got her blade between his ribs.

His boot hovered over Sitcom's face. He thrust it down on the skull. Threw all his weight behind the stomp.

The head shattered easy as a watermelon. Grey chunks spilled on the floor. Thick, dark blood oozed out.

Something about it reminded Budgie of outside. Of the cracked, bald ground that somehow hinted at gooey life beneath its surface.

He stripped his clothes off and put on his white work unitard. Let it hold the blood. He rolled in the blood.

He got up and pulled his pants over it. Grabbed Sitcom's tunic and shoved his arms into Sitcom's sleeves. Unclipped Sitcom's belt and yanked it off, replacing it with his own. Then he patted the pockets down for some drugs. Found the brain worm and chucked it. Found a few caps of OxyContin and popped those. In an inside pocket, he found a steel vial in the shape of a robot head.

Robo. You only click one once.

He'd save that for later. For now, he needed some alcohol to wash it all down. Maybe that'd bleach his brain clean. The punches hadn't done it, maybe some designer head fuckers would.

Budgie pulled his knife from his belt and faced Sitcom's smashed remains. He held the blade in the foreground. Looked at his reflection in the steel. TeeVee could be watching this. He hoped he was.

"You see that TeeVee?" he said. "You see this you fuck? This blade'll be in you before this night is done. Just try to stop me you fuck." The knife shook. "So help me Santa, you're a walking dead man.

And after I chop your filthy fucking meat, I'm coming into the next world to chop your filthy fucking ghost."

But TeeVee wasn't watching Budgie.

He was in pristine, ultra light madness. Thoughts twitched like shock therapy fingers. Digits in the last section of blue lines morphed into a hot pink glow. Illuminated from inside, he washed the excess grime off his head. Skull cleaning. Scrubbed out adverts and fuckwits, big mouths and toothpaste. He wanted to be alone.

"Now let's open this up."

A wooden horse appeared. TeeVee smashed it with an instant hammer. Then he stepped through a door and into marble opulence. A golden lever marked 'sound file number one.' Pulled it.

It played deep bass. So deep, it'd turn the mall into a squark Box. Pitches at 16 and 16.002khz, combined, turning bodies into tuning forks. And no one would even hear it. Just feel the symptoms.

This was the warm up. Eyeballs shook in sockets to cause hallucinations. Brains rattled against skulls. Headaches, aggression and, best of all, diarrhea. Because these fuckers didn't just deserve pain. They deserved humiliation. TeeVee had the remote and he could make you shit yourself.

He grinned and laughed. *Top of the world ma.* Die as you have lived. In your shit.

"What you saying in there?" a female voice hollered from the next room.

The maid. TeeVee looked around his hutch. Cleaner than before, but imperfect. At least the dirty dishes were put away. That would have to do. "Come in here for a second."

"Sure." Bubbles sashayed through the door, dressed like an old French maid. Skinny gartered legs stuck out from beneath a short skirt. Her fat ankles were squeezed into black high heels. Just visible, her lace bra thrust her tits together. They were sprinkled with glitter and heaved every time she took a breath. Big round eyes batted above a sharp little nose. She held a mop in one hand and licked the top of the handle. "You finally decide you want something more than a clean floor? You—"

"No, thank you."

"What then?" Her body stiffened. She suddenly looked bored and surly. "I'm busy."

"This is good enough. You can go now."

"I haven't even mopped yet."

"That's fine. I'll pay you for five hours work." He fished out a credit card. "Zero point zero two globals," he said into the tiny microphone.

Flicking his wrist, he tossed the card at her like a throwing star. It smacked into her shoulder, leaving a bright red mark.

"Ow." She rubbed the spot before bending down to pick up the card. Kept her eyes on TeeVee.

"Sorry," he said.

"It's fine." She spread her legs, pulled up her skirt and squatted. No underwear. The pubic hair shaved into a corporate logo. With one expert move she swiped the card through the lips of her vagina and made an exaggerated cooing noise. She handed the card back to TeeVee. "Guess I can take the rest of the day off. This was my last job."

TeeVee took the card between his fingers and passed it beneath his nose. Smelled like warm pumpkin pie. He felt a sudden convulsion of pity. Pumpkin pie always reminded him of being a kid. But knowing the cause did not lessen the effect. He stared at her chubby ankles. In a better world she might have been doing something better. She squeezed into this one. An uncomfortable fit.

"Look," TeeVee said. "I can't tell you why, but I have something to inject you with."

"I already got paid and I'm off the clock so—tough luck."

"No, a needle."

"No thanks." She stepped back from him. "Last time I took a hypo from a customer I woke up in a new bordello."

"I'm not a pimp," TeeVee said. "I'm trying to—"

"Help me?" She grinned. Her teeth were bright and cruel. "Help yourself, that's what I always say. Look, if you want to knock me out before you fuck me you have to do it at the bordello and I get checked for health before you leave. Them's the rules. Sorry. I didn't make them."

"Never mind then," TeeVee said. His mercy evaporated. It was just another advert playing in the depths of his mind. Be good, it said. Be kind. Rewind.

"What is that animal anyway?"

"It's a mongoose."

"A mon-what?"

TeeVee felt foolish and embarrassed for trying to help this woman. She probably thought he was a moron. "Just get out of here," he said. "My dispo is taking a hard turn towards murder."

"Okay." All of the stupid cruelty and sexed up cunning vanished from her face, replaced with pragmatic fear. "I'll leave the mop by the door."

"Thank you."

She strode out of his sight and the outside door clanged behind her. "Idiotic bitch."

He retreated into the marble and called up the display of the T-Dot Center. "Open audio conversion into memetic code."

"Opened."

This was his baby. Anything he said would be converted into infectious rhythms and harmonies that burrowed into the deepest algorithms of human consciousness. Once loaded into those fundamental logics, the brain would pass them up into the mind where they masqueraded as divine commands from some inner deity.

And I'm not feeling very benevolent today.

███ ██ ▌▌██ ▌▌ ▌██ ▌▌██ ▌▌█ ▌██ ▌▌▌█ ▌██ ▌▌█ ▌██ ▌ ██ ▌▌ █▌ ▌ ▌▌█

Budgie downloaded the last of his whiskey, slapped the glass against the table and leaned against the wall. Two young Vidicons sat at the bar. He didn't recognize them but they knew who he was. He could tell because they kept glancing over their shoulders and whispering.

Budgie rested a hand on his blade and stared hard at the back of the bigger one's head. The smaller one saw him looking and nudged his friend who turned around.

"What!" Budgie's voice was loud and electric. "What! You looking at something you fuck? What?"

The guy flinched. Budgie felt like he had a window into his head. This Vidicon thought Budgie should be ashamed, that he should be hidden away, afraid. But he wasn't. Instead he sat alone and blood-caked in a bar, getting pissed, wearing a tunic with beta trim and looking like he was in an all together murderous dispo. That did not make sense. And things that did not make sense made rude boys nervous. Right now, every cell in this Vidicon's body sounded an alarm and he had to choose: Fight or flight.

He stood.

Budgie remained seated and glaring. He wanted this guy to try. He imagined knife fucking his sick little heart. In and out. It played like a movie fight scene. For the briefest of moments he actually thought he'd killed the two guys. Then he came back to reality.

The Vidicon held up his hands and slapped his partner on the arm. "No trouble," he said. "No armshouse here." He avoided Budgie's stare and said to his comrade: "Let's get out." They scurried toward the front door. One clutched his stomach and moved faster.

Budgie thought about throwing one of little chucking knives he had taken from Sitcom's body. But no. He had more important things to get to.

First another drink.

The bartender saw him coming and quickly poured another whiskey, set it down and hid his hands beneath the counter.

Budgie hardly looked at him. The liquid burned.

The bartender suddenly grabbed his guts and bent over.

Groaned. "Damn." He beat a hasty path around the bar and into the washroom.

Budgie felt his own stomach go liquid. The constipating effect of the OxyContin eased the sensation. He could deal. "Fucking stress."

He reached for his card to pay and decided against it. What did his good name matter now? He checked over his shoulder and saw the washroom door close. He left the bar.

"Open file three," TeeVee thought. "Nuremberg protocol."

PRODUCT PLACEMENT

Turn up the Heat. Super slick, pumpkin pie scented perma-lube guarantees NUREMBERG PROTOCOL

Did your ex do you wrong? Want revenge? The VD shop has the answer. If you just spread a thin layer of our herpes cream on their toilet seat you'll find that **NUREMBERG PROTOCOL**

One way. My Way. Offering lifestyle solutions for modern living NUREMBERG PROTOCOL

Never worry about leaving your lipstick on his dipstick again NUREMBERG PROTOCOL

Moving faster and further than our competition. We bring you NUREMBERG PROTOCOL

Be a one man party. Drink Bacardi. Now in **NUREMBERG PROTOCOL**

Do you smell? Down there? Poonfume has the solution NUREMBERG PROTOCOL

With new Yo Yo diet and steroid pills we can safely fluctuate your weight up and down within a forty-pound range. For the unpredictable woman, looking to increase her wardrobe. **NUREMBERG PROTOCOL**

Do you want total war? Play Warring Nations the game that brings you NUREMBERG PROTOCOL

The bar door swished shut behind Budgie. He hoped to vanish into the crowd before the bartender returned. But after traveling no more than three storefronts, spooky déjà vu crept up his arms, leaving goose pimple footprints.

A woman in a trench-coat and black stockings stopped directly his path. Budgie paused. Everyone had stopped. The whole teeming mass of jostling bodies in the corridor held still. Budgie's head floated above his neck. Every speaker played the same song. Green level muzak.

He grabbed his head by the ears and yanked it back onto his neck.

His thoughts layered into a double negative. One part of his brain heard beats and rhythms. Another built these into a meaning that he couldn't quite explain. The muzak told people to hold still, stand at attention and form into single file. The people obeyed. Empty stretches formed between them. Budgie looked into the eyes of the woman in front of him. They were blinking glass orbs, no more realistic than a sex doll. Possessed of no more humanity than a plastic parody of a person.

"The fuck?"

Budgie spun around. Everyone had done the same thing. He turned back to the woman and snapped his fingers in front of her face. Nothing. Budgie threw a mock punch at her nose. She didn't even flinch.

His thoughts solidified into a cohesive whole. He still heard two versions of the muzak but he had adapted.

It was like rude boy sign language. He heard the beats like he saw the hand movements. He translated them. He changed the nonverbal orders into words while the others changed them into obedience.

The pink lines at the party. His brain had changed those orders into visuals. But why?

"TeeVee."

He must want Budgie to react like this. Maybe to watch his work. Maybe to power it. Budgie felt like the only living battery in a dead machine. There must a reason why he kept running.

The people around him lurched then marched like ants. In the synced up steps, Budgie glimpsed some awful truth and lost it. Is this is how it felt to be a ghost looking at the living? Did they too feel such contempt and hatred?

"Fuck it." Budgie was about other business.

TeeVee pulled down screen after screen, each one showing percepts. Now they were television and he was audience. Backwards looking glass.

Only two globals. Cut that. Ads shouldn't be sneaking in. He wanted to do this right. He conjured up a lazy boy and a fake beer. Sat down. Pretended to drink.

Disappointing. A green level satellite held still, looking at a wall. And where was Sitcom? Off-line. Gone. There were only two possible causes for that. Either he was malfunctioning or he was dead.

And Budgie. Something odd about him too. He was in the corridors, a good camera angle, but something nagged at TeeVee. He blew the screen up to full size and recognized the street. Cross referenced the flash map and plotted course. Coming here? Why?

TeeVee returned to Sitcom's still blank television. He wanted to see into his old friend, to be intimate with him, but he was gone. TeeVee called up the last five minutes of transmission from Sitcom's gizmo and found his latitude.

He pulled down another screen.

Budgie gripped Sitcom's key between his thumb and forefinger. He didn't know if it would work on TeeVee's door but had no other choice. If it failed, he'd be stuck in this hall. He glanced at the little dancing skeleton imprinted on its smooth surface.

Before he swiped, the door creaked open.

He thrust his body aside and panted with his back against the wall, waiting to see a knife slice the air.

Nothing happened.

But something would.

The moment he stepped into that room, a dagger would greet his throat. This was how people died. In corridors. Guided by other plans. Killed by rude boys with knives.

He slipped his left hand into his brass knuckles and dropped the skeleton key to grasp his blade.

I'm gonna fucking die here, he thought. *That's all that's gonna happen. No one will hear about it, no one will know. I'm just gonna fucking die.*

His breath hissed and something slithered out of the room. A snake. Budgie's foot flinched then stomped on its head. He held his breath. Harmony.

He didn't care if he died. Shit, he wanted to die. Let TeeVee stab him. As long as he could get a good, killing blow in, he wouldn't mind. As long as carried TeeVee to the afterwards on the tip of his knife.

He covered the lower part of his face with his left forearm, hoping the spider-web weave was as impenetrable as the adverts said, and stepped into the doorway.

No one was there. He looked around, ready to pull his arm over his eyes. Still nothing.

Budgie took a cautious step towards the next door. Then another. The outer door clanged closed. Budgie jumped.

Budgie kicked the other door open. TeeVee sat on his couch, watching him. Budgie darted in.

TeeVee remained still as a statue. Too casual.

Budgie charged, shrieking volcanic anger. But someone had turned the sound off. Drained the color.

He slashed at TeeVee's throat and missed. He stabbed and hit the couch beside TeeVee's head. He threw a punch and his fist bounced off a cushion.

More rage. His tooled hands pistoned back and forth. None touched TeeVee, each empty blow sending Budgie into deeper fits of impotent anger. Chunks of fabric and stuffing flew. TeeVee just stared.

Budgie threw his weapons to the ground and tried to wrap his hands around TeeVee's throat. He could not clench them together. Every time he brought them close, every time he thought he might be able to do it, his hands slipped on the air and dodged away from his target.

TeeVee stroked his glaring mongoose. "I'm looking at you looking at me, looking at you, looking at me." He flicked his head, as if the thought was a bug buzzing around his ears.

"Fuck!" Budgie strode to the chair and kicked it. It sprang through the air, hit the wall and landed on its feet. "Fuck!" Budgie yelled again and threw his body into another kick. The chair hit the reOrbs and sent them bouncing to the ground. He glared at TeeVee.

"You didn't seriously think that my own property could damage me did you?"

"—what?"

TeeVee slipped his fingers into the mongoose's mouth. It chewed around them. Not even a scratch.

What the fuck was Budgie going to do? Maybe stab himself in the face. His knife lay on the floor.

He wouldn't be able to do it. Not like this.

He yanked out the vial of Robo. Brought it to his mouth and gasped at it like a fish in air. He could not get if lips around it, but if he could just get it into his mouth, if he could just...

TeeVee stood up, walked across the room and plucked it from his fingers. Sat back down.

Budgie screamed.

"It looks like you killed my couch." TeeVee picked up a piece of stuffing between two fingers. He held it in front of his face and sniffed it before flicking it to the ground. "If it makes you feel any better I loved this couch. It's hard to get a decent one."

TeeVee blinked and the invisible grip released Budgie's hand. Budgie smacked himself in the mouth, hard enough to draw blood and send him spinning to the floor. He landed on his ass.

"Hey Budgie," TeeVee said. "Stop hitting yourself."

Trembling from exhaustion, Budgie laid on his back. He stared at the ceiling. It had nothing to tell him.

"Robo?" TeeVee examined the vial. He put it into his pocket and sighed. "Always the robo."

"You mu-mu-mu-mu—"

TeeVee stroked his chin and the stutter released.

"You murdering fuck," Budgie croaked.

"You're upset about Harmony?"

"Fucking right." Budgie spat and sat up.

"Fascinating. I've seen this sort of thing in old melodramas but I never thought I'd see it real life."

"Happy to amuse you." With shaking hands, Budgie tried to light a cigarette and broke it. He tried again. Success.

"I am not amused." TeeVee said quietly. "I watched you kill Sitcom. And I believe you've made a mistake. I had nothing to do with that murder and neither did Sitcom. It was Griff. And Sitcom killed Griff."

"Really?"

"Yes."

"Not 'really' like that, you fuck." Budgie blew out a cloud of blue smoke. "'Really' as in, if you *really* fucking believe that's why I killed Sitcom, then you don't know the first fucking thing about it. Or anything."

"Care to enlighten me?"

"No."

TeeVee rubbed the mongoose's ear between his fingers

"Her life isn't free," Budgie said.

"It never was."

TeeVee had misinterpreted the comment but what the fuck was the point of correcting him now? Of talking?

"I cannot understand why you would ever think I'd want Harmony dead." TeeVee leaned forward.

"Cause she knew."

"Knew what?"

"About your plan."

TeeVee laughed. It sounded like scraping metal. "Of course she didn't know about my plan." TeeVee's voice carried no trace of the laughter. "No one but me knew. I'm the only one who knows what I'm up to. The rest of you, you couldn't even begin to conceive of me."

"Oh yeah?"

"You think you killed Sitcom to prove some point. You thought to avenge yourself on me for some point. Whatever you tell yourself, you've missed the point."

"Care to fucking enlighten me?"

"You came to kill me because it's easier than killing yourself. That's all. Cowardice. Confusion. The usual."

The words slapped Budgie across the heart. It was his plan to move upstairs that had pissed Griff off. Publicly humiliating the prospect at the wake had made things worse.

TeeVee had wanted to protect Budgie. But why? Soggy guilt rotted his insides. He chewed his cheeks. "Maybe you're right."

"Maybe?" TeeVee shrugged. "Do you realize who you are talking to? Can you fathom how much money I'm costing the mall and the whole world right now?" He leaned forward. "No one is shopping or working in the entire T-Dot. No one."

Budgie squinted.

"This is one of the five largest economic centers in the world. And everyone is just standing still. Do you think Harmony could have understood that? Do you think you can? Even seeing it, do you understand it?"

"No."

"I didn't think so."

The tenor of TeeVee's voice betrayed him. Budgie saw something he had never even suspected. This guy was an alpha, one of the very top dogs in the reds, but he was a lonely, bitter man. Pathetic.

TeeVee wanted an audience. Needed one. Whatever he planned, he wanted a witness to bask in his genius. To be impressed. To tell him that he was worth something.

Him. Budgie.

If the world didn't respect TeeVee as friend, then he'd make it respect him as enemy. He'd chosen fear over love but he wanted both. Maybe he thought they were the same. Maybe they were.

Budgie pulled on his cigarette. The whole thing made him sick. TeeVee radiated a disgusting vibe. Something old, weak and sleazy. He had a clingy stink.

"You puny little shits," TeeVee said. "You all think you understand something. But you don't. You're insects. Fucking ants."

"What are you then? The five-year-old that stomps the anthill? My hero."

"You'll see what I am." TeeVee turned bright red like some irate octopus. "I'll show you." His eyes filled with pitch black ink. It streamed down his face like tears. "Upload percepts into satellite unit Budgie. Firewall protect Budgie. Unleash rapture protocol and un-pause file number 2, Audio conversion into memetic code."

Budgie's brain turned inside out. He looked down and his hands fell off. The stumps vomited a rainbow.

The colors swirled.

PRODUCT PLACEMENT

NUREMBERG PROTOCOL ———— APOCALYPSE PROTOCOL
NUREMBERG PROTOCOL ———— APOCALYPSE PROTOCOL
NUREMBERG PROTOCOL ———— APOCALYPSE PROTOCOL
NUREMBERG PROTOCOL —'——— APOCALYPSE PROTOCOL
NUREMBERG PROTOCOL ———— APOCALYPSE PROTOCOL
NUREMBERG PROTOCOL ———— APOCALYPSE PROTOCOL
NUREMBERG PROTOCOL ———— APOCALYPSE PROTOCOL
NUREMBERG PROTOCOL ———— APOCALYPSE PROTOCOL
NUREMBERG PROTOCOL ———— APOCALYPSE PROTOCOL
NUREMBERG PROTOCOL ———— APOCALYPSE PROTOCOL
NUREMBERG PROTOCOL ———— APOCALYPSE PROTOCOL
NUREMBERG PROTOCOL ———— APOCALYPSE PROTOCOL
NUREMBERG PROTOCOL ———— APOCALYPSE PROTOCOL
NUREMBERG PROTOCOL ———— APOCALYPSE PROTOCOL
NUREMBERG PROTOCOL ———— APOCALYPSE PROTOCOL
NUREMBERG PROTOCOL ———— APOCALYPSE PROTOCOL
NUREMBERG PROTOCOL ———— APOCALYPSE PROTOCOL
NUREMBERG PROTOCOL ———— APOCALYPSE PROTOCOL
NUREMBERG PROTOCOL ———— APOCALYPSE PROTOCOL
NUREMBERG PROTOCOL ———— APOCALYPSE PROTOCOL
NUREMBERG PROTOCOL ———— APOCALYPSE PROTOCOL
NUREMBERG PROTOCOL ———— APOCALYPSE PROTOCOL

Vivian Shuckhart grabbed her chest. Heart attack. She was having a damn heart attack. No wonder, when she considered the stress she'd been through.

Her daughter was a cunning little bitch. To think the girl would blackmail her after all the hard earned money she'd spent on her as a baby. Just so she could hire someone to breastfeed. After all the globals she'd poured down the kid's greedy little throat, after all the times she'd waived the IOUs.

But Vivian's heart didn't actually hurt, nor was her left arm numb. She sat up and looked around, trying to make sense out of her surroundings. She was out in the main section of the mall. But how? Last she remembered she was inside watching television. And then...

Nothing. Now she was out here. So was everyone else. It was so quiet. Just the muzak.

Then a few people started talking, their voices high and cackling. Vivian picked herself up. "Does anyone know what's going on?" she yelled. The people nearby stared at her. Some shrugged.

"No," a man said.

"Mom!"

Vivian turned around.

There was her spoiled little brat of a daughter, dressed up in all her sordid mall rat glory. Was that the same outfit she'd been wearing the night that little punk had groped her? It was. Or at least it looked like it. But—

"They're saying it's aliens, Mom." Excitement contorted the girl's face. "They've come to fix up the planet for us. They're saying it's gonna be fine, they're saying—" Her mouth pulled back and she pointed over Vivian's shoulder, her eyes all wide and fiery. "There's one Mom, there it is. You see it, LOOK! You see it? It's so beautiful it's—"

Vivian smacked Lexus across the face, snapping her head to the side. The girl's knees buckled and she fell to the ground where she crouched on all fours. Vivian couldn't believe what she'd done. In public no less.

A man, shrieking, ran at her. "Give me my FUCKING PINEAPPLE."

His pink face blurred into a fleshy blob. The blob formed paisley wallpaper, a room lit by dim red lights. Some naked boy whimpered and stared up at Vivian from a bed, teary eyed and in pain. Just how she liked them.

"Why are you doing this, mommy?" he cried.

"Don't call me that!" She kicked him in the ribs. "I told you to never call me that!"

Vivian got wet.

████ ███ ███ ██ ██ ███ ███ ███ ███ ███ ███ ████ ███ ███ ███ ████ ███ ███ ███ ██ ████ ███ ███ ███

Fatman slammed the door. Locked it. Huffing and puffing, he backed away. They were after him. Everyone. His casino had lost on every bet.

Fists pounded on the door.

He shook a bump of white powder onto his hand. They were gonna take his debts out of his flesh. Pound after pound.

He had no weapons. He was a legitimate businessman for Santa's sake, not some street thug.

—Bach.

It wasn't quite a weapon but—

Fatman snorted the coke and pocketed the vial. He dragged the machine out of the closet and positioned it against the door. He unscrewed the back panel and hit the big red button for manual firing.

A harpoon shot out, rocking the Bach's body as it crashed through the door.

There was a shriek. Fatman grinned and hit the pull-back button. Something wet thunked against the door. The harpoon dislodged and returned, covered in gore. Fatman hit the red button again.

"You want blood?" he shouted. "Have some blood!"

████ ███ ███ ██ ██ ███ ███ ███ ███ ███ ███ ████ ███ ███ ███ ████ ███ ███ ███ ██ ████ ███ ███ ███

"Thank you," Dino said to the adoring crowd. "Thank you."

"Great job," someone yelled.

"You did it!"

"Thank you, thank you." All the important people were here. Brice Steel and the whole MTO, reps from the WTO. All of the greatest minds in advertising and fishing. He grinned and waved.

This was Dino's big speech, about how he'd revolutionized advertising, about how he caught The Widow Maker and about what they should all do to improve their own lives. He had the answers. He was Mr. Dino Mondo.

In the crowd, he saw a familiar face. Jundi, the girl he'd been passionately in love with during school. She hadn't aged a day. Perfect and seventeen, still dressed the same as the first time he had seen her. And the last time. When she'd broken his heart.

I love you, she mouthed, and Dino wondered at his ability to read lips. *I've always loved you.*

"Me too," he yelled. The crowd parted. He held his arms wide and she ran toward him. Everyone applauded. Then he felt something cold in his stomach.

He looked down. His shirt turned red. A man's fist was inside him. It yanked back out. Held a silver pen of all things. The fist thrust back into Dino's chest. He looked up. Where was Jundi? This was a stranger.

The howling and cheers all changed into a cacophony of torture. "Give ME BACK MY FUCKING PINEAPPLE," the man screamed into Dino's face. His breath was fetid. "I know you HAVE it and GIVE IT BACK!!"

Dino fell to his knees. This must be a dream. Some sort of nightmare. *I'll wake up soon.* He looked up and saw Jundi. She smiled and reached towards his eyes.

▪▪▪ ▪▪▪▪▪▪ ▪▪ ▪ ▪▪▪▪▪▪▪▪▪ ▪▪▪▪▪▪ ▪▪▪▪▪▪ ▪▪▪▪▪ ▪▪▪ ▪▪▪ ▪▪▪▪ ▪▪ ▪▪▪ ▪▪ ▪ ▪▪▪

If cats thought in words, which they didn't, Mister Socks was thinking, *Fuck this and fuck these crazy-ass people. I'm getting the hell outta here.* He darted through kicking legs, hopped over a man being raped with a pool-cue and dodged into the alley.

Safety. He trotted into the darkness. He felt hungry and confident. There was a lot of meat.

▪▪▪ ▪▪▪▪▪▪ ▪▪ ▪ ▪▪▪▪▪▪▪▪▪ ▪▪▪▪▪▪ ▪▪▪▪▪▪ ▪▪▪▪▪ ▪▪▪ ▪▪▪ ▪▪▪▪ ▪▪ ▪▪▪ ▪▪ ▪ ▪▪▪

Bob Anger smashed his radio but it just kept playing. Through broken speakers, Lenny Neidenberger mocked him. That greasy little egghead sat in judgment like he was so good and pure. Like they hadn't gone to college together. But, oh Lenny was perfect. Just so precious and good. But Bob knew better. He knew who was behind all of this.

It was Lenny.

He stomped the radio. Everyone was after him. The media used the bloody claws and fangs he had given them, the CEO expressed regret about Bob's "lifestyle decisions." Every asshole had an opinion.

It made Bob sick.

But why wouldn't this damn radio shut up? "When things are repressed long enough," Lenny said, "they have a way of bursting to the surface. Anyone who thought about what Mr. Anger was saying could have told you that he'd end up like this. In every fanatic beats the heart of a hypocrite."

"Oh you're so fucking smart," Bob Anger said. "A fucking genius aren't you? Calling me Mr. Anger, trying to fake respect, you dirty damn phony."

He knew what he had to do. Kill Lenny Niedenberger.

Bob grabbed a kitchen knife. He glanced at the big portrait of himself on the wall then turned his attention to the even bigger mirror.

Lenny stood there.

"You fuck!" Bob shrieked. He punched the mirror. Lenny threw a punch at the same time. Their fists met and the mirror smashed. Shards of broken glass clattered to the ground.

High-pitched voices, like squealing mice, yammered from the shards. Each one held a tiny Lenny. Each one talked and talked. Bob dropped to his knees, let go of his knife, and pummeled the fragments with his fists. Blood splattered over the floor. A sharp edged chunk of glass bounced up after a blow and pierced his wrist.

Bob yanked it out, snapped it in half, slicing his finger tips. He had to grind Lenny back into sand. But he just kept making more and more Lennys. Blood leaked from his wrists and hands. He cut himself again and blood started to spurt. His blows slowed and he fell face first into a puddle of his blood, broken mirror and chattering Lennys.

⬛⬛ ⬛⬛ ⬛⬛⬛ ⬛⬛ ⬛ ⬛⬛⬛⬛⬛ ⬛⬛⬛ ⬛⬛⬛ ⬛⬛ ⬛ ⬛⬛ ⬛⬛⬛ ⬛⬛ ⬛⬛ ⬛⬛

"What the fuck?" Lexus looked around the massive office. The expensive radio played muzak.

"Pardon?" said the man behind the desk.

Last thing she remembered that creepy old man—what was his name, Ken?—had injected her. Now she sat here? In a lab coat?

And was that Brice Steel, the mall CEO, across the desk from her? She rubbed her eyes.

"You drive a hard bargain, Ken, but I think—"

KEN KEN KEN

Lexus stood up. He looked across the barroom table at Ken. She remembered his future.

"Oh no you don't," she said.

"You're not my MOTHER!" yelled Ken.

She grabbed a pen off the table. She jumped across the desk and stabbed him in the neck.

"MOMMY!" shouted Ken.

She stabbed him again and again.

⬛⬛ ⬛⬛ ⬛⬛⬛ ⬛⬛ ⬛ ⬛⬛⬛⬛⬛ ⬛⬛⬛ ⬛⬛⬛ ⬛⬛ ⬛ ⬛⬛ ⬛⬛⬛ ⬛⬛ ⬛⬛ ⬛⬛

"Fuck." Budgie opened his eyes. He wished he'd never closed them. Breath swelled in his lungs. "Fuck."

TeeVee reclined, deep into his couch. "How'd you like that?"

"You're trying to... You're killing everyone."

"Everyone in the T-Dot Center at least." He sighed with disappointment. "Unlike currency, I failed to go global. At a certain point, the odds of getting caught outweighed the benefits. Just getting the right map of this particular mall was difficult enough. I needed an outside source for that and, even then, I needed to see that ship landing on that pad."

"I saw that," Budgie said. "I."

"Edge has a wonderful distribution system but I needed that map. I had to know the right points to release this virus for maximum infection and the right places to move the people for maximum impact. There'd be nothing more frustrating than getting quarantined." TeeVee sucked on his hookah. "So thank you. Your eyes helped a great deal. My only eyes on the outside."

"I did this?" Budgie kept his eyes wide. In a terror of blinking. "I helped?"

"Don't feel too guilty. I am inevitable."

"What the fuck is that—"

"From all this, I must emerge. Whether it be New York, London or Moscow. I must emerge. I am only the first. I am the blueprint. To prevent I, the malls would have to change everything about themselves. And that too is destruction. But as things stand: I am inevitable. Even if I am not I. Even if you are not you. You could just as easily be me. I could just as easily be you. You and I are we. I is legion. Either or any and every way, I, you, we, this, all of it, I am inevitable."

"But why?" Budgie cringed away from all of this death. He tried to focus on Harmony, but couldn't. By deluging him with blood, this bastard had even stolen her from him. She was just another face in a murder collage. TeeVee had made her meaningless. "Why?"

"This *is* the why, Budgie. This. There is no why beyond this." TeeVee laid his pipe aside. "This is why. Why is this? Everything else is the lie that leads to this why. Why to this? Because this is apocalypse." He rolled his eyes back into his head and another set of pupils stared at Budgie. "An old word: Apocalypse. From Greek. Means the lifting of the veil. A revealing. A revelation. It creates nothing. It just shows that which already there. Their souls are unveiled."

There's no sense here, Budgie realized. To understand this you'd have to share a frame of reference with TeeVee. No one did. They saw fragments of his mind in the shows they watched, heard little bits in the radio they listened to. But TeeVee was that world. His soul was made of electronic messages passed between millions. It wasn't human. TeeVee looked like a man but that was all.

"You're a fucking monster," Budgie said.

"And monsters rule this world."

Budgie wiped his face and left bloody tears on his fingers. Must have been crying when he was under. Must have sobbed when he watched the progression of gore that TeeVee had unleashed. Well, his rep didn't matter anymore. Could cry all he liked. No one would care.

Budgie realized that he was sober. He felt very calm, but beneath that calm was solid anger. It couldn't move, couldn't even be expressed, it just filled him up like cement. Unrevealed. Veiled by his poker face. "I don get it," he said. "I just don understand this. How could you…"

"You are ants," TeeVee said. "You are the walls that the echo bounces off but I am the voice. You looked into the abyss. It looked back. And you all heard me and you thought that I loved you the same way that you loved me. Well I don't love you and I never have. Why would I? Our objectives are different."

He leaned forward.

"When all of this is over, I will infect the future. I'll be the new measure of infamy. Before this was the Nazis, 10 million dead. The Soviets, a hundred million dead under Stalin. The African genocides, hundreds of millions. The American slaughterhouse. And now this. Millions dead in days. Killed by each other, all because of me. And me because of you. There'll be movies about this, there'll be endless talk and I'll be immortal. My voice screams the future."

TeeVee held up his hand. "This flesh would have rotted on my bones, only fit for fish food. But what I've done here will shake the ages. It will echo." He lifted a beatific face. "And you'll be in those movies too. The man known as Budgie. Who was he? What did he do? You'll be a bit actor in this drama that builds the next world around the blueprint of my voice. How do you want your final moments to be portrayed? Right now we're living in a million movies, analyzed by a million professors, watched by a million students. What do you want them to say about you?"

Budgie felt years weighing on him, forces of history and futurity coming to rest on his back, his spine bending beneath it. But it could not—could not—touch his rage. He'd been used as a pawn by a psycho. "I'd like to be the hero that kills you and stops this."

"Well, that's not going to happen." TeeVee picked up a piece of couch that Budgie had cut loose. "Though no one can say that you didn't try. I wonder what they'll think about that, on balance—considering it was you who gave me the final tools I needed to pull this off. And for what? I can't even remember how much I paid you. Less than Judas, I know that. If it's any consolation, I think you're gonna look less like

a villain and more like history's biggest sucker. You'll be a sort of
life lesson, the moral being: 'Don't sell your brains kids, unless you
know who's buying.' Maybe something else. I don't know. The next
world is not my business. Only the end of this one."

"I know what I want," Budgie said.

TeeVee stroked his mongoose.

"And I know what I don't." Everything had been stolen from him.
He had nothing else to lose, nothing left to care about. There was
only one thing left. "But I don know if you can do it."

"Try me."

Budgie stood straight and rubbed the back of his neck. "I want out."

░▒▓ ▒▓ ▒▓▓▒ ▓▒ ▓ ▒▓▓▒▓ ▒▓▓ ▓▒ ▓▓▓ ▓▒ ▓▒▓▓ ▓▒▓▓▒ ▓▓▓ ▓▒▓ ▒▓▒ ▓▒ ▓▒▓ ▓▒ ▓ ▓▒▓

Budgie's brain chewed everything he'd seen and spat it back up in a
moving picture show. Mangled bodies laying in their own blood and
shit. Babies used as clubs against their own mothers. Men hanging
themselves while others applauded. Gang rapes, and the gangs turning
on each other with broken glass.

And that last image of TeeVee. Loading a new reOrb into his mix,
whispering code and sucking smoke. He'd touched Budgie's shoulder
and called him son. Told him that he'd parted the sea for him, so
that Budgie might carry him into the future. Then he wished him
good fucking luck and cut his mongoose's throat.

If Budgie put the journey into particulars, if he thought of the look
in that woman's eyes, of the streak of blood against that old man's
face, he would not continue. He'd just sit down and die. Inside. He
had to forget it all. He did not know how.

Leave it indoors. There was a whole other world out there. And
it was poisonous.

Would the door even work? For what it was worth, TeeVee promised
Budgie that he'd hit no obstacles and, so far, he hadn't. The people
had ignored Budgie as he ran up the levels. The door would work.
It must.

Feet blistered, legs aching, Budgie hit the big blue button and
stepped back.

He couldn't even blame TeeVee for this. He'd only pulled the veil
aside. He was built in their image just as they were built in his. He
was inevitable.

"I am inevitable."

The door creaked and shifted upwards. It was huge, built to allow
the passage of the trucks.

The first gust of air hit Budgie and he held his breath. It would
poison him. By the time the door was half open and all of outside

laid ahead, he gave up and pulled in a deep, cold lungful of air. Then another.

How long it had been since a human had done such a thing? And how long it would be before they did it again?

He breathed and stared. But he did not die. He didn't even feel dizzy.

He stepped through the door, his boot hitting hard packed dirt. Sky.

The sun rose while the moon stared down like a silver eye. Beyond that, stars. None of it cared.

The door clanged shut behind him. He didn't even turn to look. He'd seen enough of the mall.

The outside would kill him, too, but it didn't matter. He knew what he didn't want. To die in that fucking mall.

All it had was greed for the blood and blood for the greed. The future had the unknown. Maybe there'd be a tribe out here. Maybe starvation.

Budgie took another small step.

Fuck it, he thought. Nothing is inevitable.

INFO DUMP

"This is Issac Knowalot reporting from New York. We have breaking news from the T-Dot Center where one survivor of what's being called the T-Dot Disaster, has been found.

"According to early reports he is in a trance of some kind. Investigators say that his brain was modified and that they'll soon have more details. It appears that he was near what our Accu-Disaster-Tracker simulation tells us is ground zero. Perhaps even right there.

"Investigators aren't the only ones who are hopeful that he'll shed some light on this recent calamity. The movie rights to the T-Dot Disaster have been secured by an undisclosed company and anonymous sources tell us that they are eager to get some facts before they go into production on a made-for-television movie.

"For more reaction at the scene we join our on the spot reporter Burburry Jack. Take it away Burburry..."